P9-BYU-871

"A fast-paced, accomplished novel."
—*Library Journal*

\*

"An irresistible page turner."
—*Booklist*

\*

"The action never lets up."
—*Houston Post*

\*

"I wish I had written it . . . the kind of fast, gripping hunter and hunted book that makes authors jealous."
—**John Gardner,**
**author of James Bond novels**

\*

"A heart-stopper . . . a powerful thriller."
—*Cleveland Plain Dealer*

\*

"Wonderfully written and completely thrilling."
—**Susan Isaacs,**
**author of SHINING THROUGH**

\*

"The original and imaginative plot races along like a furious rollercoaster . . ."
—*United Press International*

# CAMPBELL ARMSTRONG

# BRAINFIRE

**Harper Paperbacks**

Harper & Row, Publishers, New York
Grand Rapids, Philadelphia, St. Louis, San Francisco
London, Singapore, Sydney, Tokyo, Toronto

This is a work of fiction. The characters, incidents, and
dialogues are products of the author's imagination and are
not to be construed as real. Any resemblance to actual
events or persons, living or dead, is entirely coincidental.

**Harper Paperbacks** a division of Harper & Row, Publishers, Inc.
10 East 53rd Street, New York, N.Y. 10022

This book is published by arrangement with the author.

Cover illustration by Neil Shigley

First Harper Paperbacks printing: October 1990

Printed in the United States of America

HARPER PAPERBACKS and colophon are trademarks
of Harper & Row, Publishers, Inc.

10 9 8 7 6 5 4 3 2 1

For John Sterling
and for the late Peter Watts,
with great gratitude

And for Jeffrey von Durstewitz,
*Freund, Ratgeber, und Flüchtling aus Oswego*

It is not possible to define.
Nothing has ever been finally found out.
Because there is nothing final to find out.

CHARLES FORT,
*The Book of the Damned*

# BRAINFIRE

# PART I

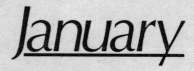

All would be well.
All would be heavenly—
If only the damned would stay damned.

—CHARLES FORT, *The Book of the Damned*

# 1

It was snowing. Winds had blown great drifts, surreal sculptings that lay, pockmarked and powdery, along the bank. The early-evening sky was already black, the moon a vague configuration of silver broken by heavy cloud. Starless, cold: a landscape of colorless disenchantment. Beneath the heavy artillery, under fortifications where infantrymen moved back and forth, several figures stood knee-deep in snow. Pale lamps had been rigged below the guns, throwing weak lights in the dark.

The Scientist, Andreyev, a small man in a greatcoat so copious that it might have been wrapped several times around his body, raised one hand in the direction of the Ussuri. Faintly, by what little moon broke the cloud cover, ice slicks could be seen.

"He'll come from that direction," Andreyev said. He looked at his three companions. The Politician, a squat figure shaped like some heavy bookend, wiped a layer of snow from his moustache and blinked down toward the river. The Colonel was smiling in a chilly way, the expression apparently frozen to his face. Only the KGB man appeared to have any un-skeptical interest in the sequence of events—but that, after all, was his job: watching, listening, like someone forever scrutinizing the hand movements of an internal clock.

"If he ever fucking comes." The Politician was a Georgian and liked to think of himself as a realist, a man with a private connection to the core of truth.

Andreyev looked quickly at him, conscious from the corner of his eye of the Colonel stamping his feet for warmth. There was a silence interrupted only by the wind pushing through snow. The Politician spat and beat his gloved hands together. Andreyev turned his face back toward the river, sensing the massed Chinese presence on the far bank. He was cold, cold to the bone. The wind came again and he thought of it blowing from the Sea of Japan, scouring the streets of Vlad, diffusing itself in its interminable journey somewhere in the Dzhugdzhur.

"I think this is a fucking sideshow," the Politician said, and spat once again, rather deliberately, as if he imagined specific targets in the snow. "A carnival. A freak show. That's all."

In the background the KGB man coughed quietly. He had a face of almost irritating anonymity: he was the person you meet at a party and escape from on the pretext of finding another drink. Andreyev watched him a moment, then looked away; he was afraid of being caught in a conspicuous stare.

The Politician had taken a small metal flask of imported malt liquor from his greatcoat and was swigging from it—his personal defense against the ravaging virus of climate. Andreyev saw the metal glint in the reflection of the lamps. A freak show, he thought. What else? There could not be a place for

uncomfortable shadows in a world of strict material-
ism. Strip the mysteries away one by one and you are
left holding a hard kernel that is the ordinary, the
known. A carnival, a freak show. He was sorry for the
Politician's limits, the lines he had inscribed about
himself. Even the way he stood in the snow with the
flask tilted to his mouth seemed to Andreyev a form
of definition; and what was definition but a trap, a cir-
cumscription in which you found yourself well and
truly caged?

"Colonel," the Politician was saying, his voice
rising through the wind, "what do you make of all
this? Don't you feel idiotic standing out here? Eh?"

The Politician nudged the Colonel, who turned
his frozen smile to the man: "I retain a certain open
mind about this," the Colonel said.

"An open mind!" The Politician began to laugh,
shaking his face from one side to another. "An open
mind! When a man talks of having an open mind, my
friend, I know he's scared shitless about something!"

The Colonel smiled, this time with obvious uncertainty. From behind, the KGB man cleared his
throat as if he were about to say something; but he
was silent. The Politician stopped laughing and
corked the metal flask, shoving it back into his coat.

"Where is the wonderwoman?" he asked of Andreyev.

"She isn't far away," Andreyev answered.

"I bet she's fucking warm, eh? She's not standing
around freezing her ass off, is she? I don't see her
standing out here suffering—"

Andreyev was embarrassed suddenly for the
man. He had been shaped, molded, by the dictates of
the official line, the Party pamphlets, the behavioral
manuals, the strange etiquette of power that distilled
itself in an ignorance of personal conflicts, permitting

you to think one thing while you uttered another, as if what it came down to was a series of secrets you kept from yourself: the paradox of orthodoxy, Andreyev thought. He shivered now: the wind was a serrated blade of ice rushing through him. He turned once more to the river, seeing how slicks of ice, buffeted into phantasmagorical shape by the force of the wind, gleamed like white metal in the pale moon.

And then he thought of Mrs. Blum and of how the Physician was always reminding him of her fragility, always, a constant litany of possibilities. *Too old, too damned old. You'll kill her yet.* Monitoring pulse and heart, listening to the faint life meters of the old woman as if they were poetry of an ancient kind, ready at all times with the capsules of amyl nitrate, the phials of epinephrine, the Physician reminded Andreyev of some solicitous nephew with an expectancy of an inheritance.

Mrs. Blum—how very easy it would be to lose her, to see her slip over that precipice she always seemed on the edge of; he thought of how her skin appeared to have been walked upon by a hundred small birds, the thinning of her white hair, the cloudy dark eyes. *You'll kill her yet.* No, he thought.

He watched the Colonel, who was staring through field glasses in the direction of the river. Was it happening? he wondered. He looked toward the river. He thought he saw something move. A wind flurry? What was it?

He started forward a couple of feet. Yes: he is coming, he is coming. Dark, indistinct now against the black frozen trees, something was moving. Andreyev felt a sense of triumph that he knew was less than objective; but just the same he could not resist turning to the Politician and smiling, as if to say, Well then? Well then?

*    *    *

Below, from the riverbank, the figure was moving haphazardly through the drifts, moving with no particular sense of direction or purpose—save, like that of some mindless moth compelled by the chemistry of its own perceptions, the attractive warmth of the lamps.

## 2.

The Chinese soldier was taken by Jeep to a room in the base hospital, a windowless cell containing tables, chairs, a filing cabinet. He did not respond to the questions of Andreyev's assistant, who spoke to him quietly in both Cantonese and the official Mandarin—languages, Andreyev realized, that might have meant nothing to the soldier anyhow. He was a small man with a broad Mongol face, hair so black as to be almost navy blue; he simply sat and stared at the Grundig tape recorder as if with astonishment. But you could not tell from the face what was going on inside. The ID papers, taken without protest from his tunic, established him as one Hua Tse-Ling, a low-ranking soldier of the Chinese regular army. Andreyev handed the papers to the Colonel, who perused them slowly and then passed them to the Politician. The latter, who had no knowledge of Chinese and whose personal alliances within the Politburo were hawkish in matters pertaining to China, gave them quickly to the KGB man, who placed them inside a manila folder.

"Why did you come here? What brought you here?" Andreyev's assistant was a woman of forty with cold eyes and a heartless quality in her voice. It was hard to imagine her in any intimate way, even in such a forsaken place as this outpost where eligible women had the rarity of tropical fruit. In her curiously sexless clothes, a heavy coat worn over long colorless boots, she had the appearance of an androgyne.

Hua Tse-Ling did not look at her, did not answer her questions, gave no impression of understanding where he was or what was happening to him. The reel of the old Grundig recorder turned stiffly, squeaking.

"What good are these questions?" the Politician asked. He was nibbling on his flask again; which, given the KGB presence, was perhaps a reckless thing. Andreyev could imagine the report, something turning up one day in the Politician's file—*drinks too much*. The KGB man stared momentarily at Andreyev and there was something of impatience, even a slow-fused temper in the look.

"He doesn't understand," said the Politician. "Anybody can see that. Shit!" He spoke in a brusque way, someone accustomed to barking questions and getting immediate answers; but there was a defensiveness too, as if he were accustomed to having his own blood drawn in the pecking order of things.

Andreyev turned back to the Chinese soldier: what lay inside that dark-blue head? If he could lay bare the scalp and probe the brain, what ruptures and crevices might he find? What disturbances?

There was a silence in the room now.

Abruptly the KGB man came to a personal decision. In a move so quick that nobody in the room could quite follow, he whipped the back of his hand, a pallid but forceful blur, across Hua Tse-Ling's face. The soldier slumped sideways. A line of blood, the color of a dark rose, broke the surface of his lip.

"Was that necessary?" Andreyev asked. He felt disgust: in his world of research papers, graphs, laboratory techniques, electroencephalograms, alpha and beta waves, in this controlled world of hieroglyphic and symbol, each loaded with a precise significance of its own, he did not encounter the randomly violent. And now it appalled him. He looked at the figure of the soldier with pity.

"He doesn't fucking talk," the Politician said. "Why doesn't he talk?"

Andreyev said nothing. Kneeling, he took a piece of tissue paper and dabbed the blood on the soldier's upper lip; he noticed the glazed reflection in Hua's eyes. *The mind has gone,* he thought. *Just like a match blown out.*

"Now he's the fucking Red Cross," the Politician said, searching the room for some support of his bluster. But the KGB man was turned away and the Colonel was moving restlessly around the walls of the room in the manner of one who expects to discover the beauty of a hidden window, a view, a fine sunset taking him unawares. Outside, the wind was high again, shaking the silences, creating new drifts of snow and delightful aesthetic accidents.

The room, Andreyev realized, was filled with eddies of tension, little currents of vested interest, rivalries: they had not expected the experiment to work—but now they were more interested, each for his own reason, than they wanted to be. Take your pick, Andreyev thought: the military, the intelligence community, or the Politburo itself: it was like a lottery, the suspense of waiting for the winning ticket to be drawn. He stood up, stepping back from Hua Tse-Ling.

"Hua Tse-Ling," he said.

The soldier showed no interest, no recognition.

"Hua Tse-Ling," he said again. Nothing, no response, zero. A little frustrated, Andreyev longed for them all to leave the room so that he could get on with his work.

The Politician was laughing. "Big deal," he said. "Big fucking deal."

The KGB man switched off the tape recorder: "Let's stop all the talk," he said, confident in his world of bizarre secrecies, hidden dossiers, codes, smug all at once with the knowledge of a darkness nobody else in the room could penetrate, not even the Georgian. "Stop all the talk and do your damn tests."

Andreyev looked at him: the broad face you would not remember from a crowd, the pendulous lower lip, the bottom jaw that jutted like a fleshy hook. Intelligence, he thought: how easily a word is misapplied. He was cold, suddenly colder than he had been in the snow.

"Do your tests, do your tests," the KGB man said, now smiling slightly, the fleshy hook wobbling; but it was a parody of mirth—for the smile concealed myriad sins of both the past and the future; it secreted inquisitions, interrogations, all the arcane terrors of an unfathomable craft—and Andreyev realized suddenly that he was afraid of the outcome, that whatever lay ahead would have the insignia of the man's smile, that mirthless terror, stamped upon it.

"Do your tests," he was saying again. "Then we can shoot the bastard and get a good night's sleep."

## 3.

The tests—Andreyev thought at once of how comfortable he was with his world of tests; it was a battery that recharged him, a tranquilizer that soothed him; it was a place without conflict and stress. That it was also stripped of human connotation, rendered manageable by figures on charts, graph paper, made it somehow complete for him: a world without love and envy, without passion and rage—the benumbing clinicality seemed to him a wonder. Muscular reflex and coordination; examination of gross motor responses; an EEG that revealed only a slight irregularity of pattern in the soldier's brain—all this had nothing to do with the grubbiness he had felt before; it wasn't connected with fear and loathing, or sullied by paranoia: even the needle that carried sodium pentothal to Hua Tse-Ling's circuitry shone with an awful cleanliness. Even the fact that the tests revealed nothing of any significance did not unduly worry Andreyev; and the failure of the SP to alter the soldier's condition in any remarkable way—it was a chemical fact, a gospel of the blood. Andreyev was happy in this small world of balances and measures and quotients.

Katya said, "There's hardly any muscular reflex."

Andreyev, who had been looking at Hua Tse-Ling and sipping hot tea from a plastic container, was abruptly pulled back by the sound of his assistant's voice. He watched her a moment, remembering with some small shame the only time he had achieved intimacy with her—too many glasses of vodka at some scientific dinner, the ride through the streets of Moscow, the tiny rooms of his small apartment (cluttered; he had been embarrassed by his discarded underwear lying by the unmade bed); the drunken fumbling with her clothing and how, with an eagerness that appalled him to recall, she had assisted him with the clips and snaps and hooks of herself until she was naked in the cold bedroom, her gaunt figure reminiscent of a pioneer photograph, sepias shading into mists, an obfuscation of imagery and clarity; and the lovemaking, if you could call it that, a fumbling of octopi unexpectedly swept up on a beach, her arms and legs creating more limbs than merely four in his memory now. And as he looked at her across the room he understood that she was ready for him again, that he had only to say the word; a comprehension that moved him to sorrow, an insight into the loneliness of her life.

"Did you hear me?" she asked. She was smiling. A quite unpredictable glow touched her face when she smiled.

"I heard you," he answered. He had an image of himself from a point outside, a flash: forty-three, a small man, his flesh chalky, an impression of somehow *crumbling,* of coming apart at the seams. He shut his eyes and when he opened them again he looked at Hua Tse-Ling; a part of the soldier was already dead; deep inside, some kind of congealing.

"They're going to kill him," Andreyev said quietly.

Katya looked at him, raising her head quickly from her notes. "Does it surprise you?"

Don't, he thought. Don't let that sense of pity come, prevent that simple extension of humanity. But what could you do? There were times when the protective veneer he was supposed to wear like a suit of armor simply cracked open; and when he looked at Hua Tse-Ling he saw more than a laboratory study, he saw a man whose death warrant had already been signed. He wished he could reach inside the skull, understand the lacerations of consciousness; but there was inaccessibility—the very nature of the thing you studied was elusive as your own shadow: a whole box of tricks you could not open.

"No," he said. "It doesn't surprise me."

"What does?" she asked. She put one hand up to her brown hair, an imaginary curl. "Doesn't the success of this surprise you?"

Andreyev thought of success: Hua Tse-Ling had crossed the river—and at what cost? Was it just a freak show? After all, was it just that? Then he was thinking, despite himself, of how power operated, the ways in which it would try to make use, for one vicious reason or another, of all this *success*—a concussion of forces, the military and the scientific in a lamentable collision. *It's the way of things,* he thought. A simple justification: the way of things. What could one do? You could not live your life in a preserve jar, could you? It was important to go on, to continue work and ignore that other world—let it all slide away from your mind, the Kremlin summonses, the quickened interest in the eyes of generals, the inquisitions of the KGB. Let it all slide, it was the way of things: what could you do?

He heard his name being paged on the intercom. It surprised him: *Professor Andreyev.* He remembered where he was, a building in the center of a wasteland, a snowy wilderness. He went to the nearest telephone.

It was the Physician.

"How is she?" Andreyev asked.

"What do you expect me to say?" The Physician's voice was harsh; for that reason Andreyev thought of his childhood and how the crying of rooks would awaken him on summer mornings—barking birds, he had thought then, winged dogs whose noises rolled and rolled through the trees around the house in Kaluga.

"You can't go on exhausting her," the Physician said. "I can't let you—"

Andreyev said, "It's not my decision, you know. Do you think I have a say in what happens to her? You're being naïve if you think I can stop all this with a wave of my hand—"

The Physician, calmer now, said, "She's seventy

years of age, Professor. Does that put you in the picture?''

And then the line was dead. Andreyev held the receiver a moment, and when he set it back he noticed the initials *PVS* carved into the white wall above the instrument. They had been cut deep and they looked to him like fresh wounds.

"I don't think we can do anything else," Katya said.

Andreyev looked once more at Hua Tse-Ling, then at the window of the room they were in—at the black glass against which, with increasing violence, the wind drove crystals of snow.

**4.**

Hua Tse-Ling—thirty-six years of age, according to his ID papers—was taken from the hospital and had his hands tied behind his back by his executioners— six infantrymen and a sergeant. The Colonel, the KGB man, and the Politician watched the proceedings in a neutral way. What did the death of one miserable Chinaman matter, the latter had asked, laughing, when you had more than eight hundred million of the bastards to worry about?

Hua was led to the wire fence around the compound—pushed rather than led, his limbs stiff, his head held at a forward angle.

The KGB man said, "What do you make of this experiment, Colonel?"

The Colonel drew up the collar of his coat and shivered. "Interesting."

"Interesting?" The KGB man lifted one hand and, in a gesture that was in part intimate, in part intimidating, prodded the Colonel's chest. "You're sitting on a fence, friend."

The Colonel shrugged, a gesture of uncertainty. "I'm only a soldier. An observer. I'm not qualified to say."

The Politician, who had no interest in this conversation, watched the condemned man move to the fence. He dropped his flask, which sank into the soft new snow. He went down on his hands and knees to dig for it. When he found it he had difficulty getting to his feet, perpetrating a comedy of errors in the snow—fumbling, slipping, sinking. The KGB man gripped him by the elbow and helped him to stand.

Hua Tse-Ling was being roped to the wire fence; his face, from a distance of several hundred yards, suggested the smooth surface of a balloon, totally without feature. He had not been blindfolded, a generosity, an etiquette of assassination that in the circumstances would have been absurd.

The guns popped like last year's fireworks and what might have been a noise of reverberating viciousness was muffled by the falling snow; and the echoes, such as there were, were sucked away beyond the wire fence and the clump of trees in the distance. Hua Tse-Ling hung against the wire, his face tilted to one side in that unlikely loose way of death.

"Well," said the KGB man. "End of experiment."

"Or the beginning," said the Colonel.

Pale smoke from the rifles was beginning to disintegrate in the wind and the snow as if nature, in one of her many conspiracies, were secretly erasing the traces of death.

# 2

She could hear the Physician's voice coming to her through the drift of consciousness, meaningless clusters of words: *soon warm everything well warm don't worry don't.* And she was aware of motion, of the wheels of a locomotive running over rails. *Clackclacketyclack.* But wherever was she going? And what was the Physician, Domareski, trying to tell her? Her eyelids were heavy, half-moons of some dense metal. She couldn't look, she couldn't get her eyes open. Aaron, she thought—where is Aaron? He had to be in the garden, walking between the pines, the baby held in his strong arms. She wanted to call his name but knew there wouldn't be an answer. Why wouldn't he answer her? Aaron, beloved Aaron. *Soon the pain will be gone be gone gone—* Something sharp entered her arm and, even with her eyes closed, she could see the glint of Domareski's needle. A slight incision: *no more pain.*

She was a young girl, eyes clear, hair gold. She was a young girl and Aaron was her husband—but why was she panicked, thinking about him now?

There were shadows, shadows within shadows, as if whatever feeble light fell was made to pass through barricade after barricade, obstacles. It was the panic, thinking of her husband, wondering where she was moving and why: it came down to fear. And even Domareski's voice—*relax I'm with you nothing bad can happen to you now*—even that soothing voice she so trusted did not diminish her feelings. Why would a young girl be traveling on a railroad? And why was Domareski afraid too?

Something in his voice. Something she *caught*. It was a thing he was trying to conceal in the deeps of his mind: a darkly moving fish sliding through murk and silt. But she caught it. *Relax relax relax no more fear no pain.* She could hear him sigh, she could hear the clasp of his bag close: click. The sound of his feet on the floor. Then he touched her, his fingers cold upon the back of her hand. Don't leave me alone, she thought. Don't leave me. She felt the tips of his fingers between her knuckles. Then the pain was gone and when she opened her eyes, conscious at first of some blistering white light in the compartment, she gazed down at her hands—claws, knuckles distorted by arthritis, flesh tight and polished with age: the hands suggested pebbles misshapen by tides, smoothed by the comings and goings of oceans. No. They aren't my hands. How could they be? She was a young girl. Sixteen, seventeen. How old? How old? These could not be her hands.

She turned her face away from Domareski. There was a white window, windblown snow. The train— but she couldn't remember stepping onto the train, or being carried; visions, dreams, remembered fragments of motion. Who could ever be sure?

"Relax," Domareski said. He was standing over

her. He held his black bag under his arm, clutched to his side.

"I want to see Aaron," she said. It was not her own voice, it hadn't come out the way she had wanted it; it was deeper, old, infirm.

Aaron. She saw a hand rise in the air and watched it flutter slightly—a bulbous hand, gnarled—and then it fell to her side again, as if she were ashamed of it. The young girl, the old love: they were things trapped in photographs, ancient daguerreotypes, deceits. None of it had ever happened. There hadn't ever been an Aaron, a child.

She turned her head to look at the Physician. I'm sorry. I'm very sorry. He was trying to tell her that. She could hear the words.

"Did you ask about my visa?" she said.

"Yes—"

She looked toward the window. Dark smoke, blown from the front of the train, whipped through the swirling snow. The visa, he was trying to tell her: I'm sorry. I'm really sorry.

"Please," he said. "Don't try to sit up. Later. Not now."

"What about the visa?" she said.

"I promise," he said. "It's a matter of clarifying things with Comrade Sememko, that's all."

She shut her eyes, thinking it strange that Domareski's medication caused her to feel an absence of herself—as if the physical body no longer existed and you became a creature composed entirely of mind and nothing else. *It's a matter of clarifying things with Comrade Sememko.* But the Physician was lying to her again. She opened her eyes, thinking of how the snowy light hurt her, and looked at him. But he was busy, pretending to be busy, with the clasp of his bag.

"People don't always need to do what they're

told," she said. "Don't you understand that? There's a point you reach when . . ."

"Yes." He opened the bag, looked inside, snapped it shut. "You should sleep now. Please."

Sleep? What good to her was sleep? It was a kind of dying, losing your hold on things, slipping and sliding down a slope at the foot of which there lay darkness. She didn't want that dark; she wanted light, remembrance, rooms filled with sun and warmth, a memory of seeing Aaron walk through the pines with the baby in his arms. But why now did these seem like the memories of another person?

She could feel her eyelids close. She could hear Domareski turn from the bed toward the door, the slight noise made as he slid the door open, then shut it behind him. Alone. *Clackclacketyclack.* A white wilderness. She pressed her hands together, appalled by the way they felt to her. She thought: Don't. Don't feel them. They aren't a part of you.

She turned on her side, face toward the wall.

Aaron—but Aaron was dead. She remembered—when? dear God, when had this happened?—she remembered taking a pair of scissors and cutting a wedge of material from a garment, the insignia of widowhood. A tiny triangular space, an absence. Yes. Dead. And you are not a young girl, you are not sixteen, seventeen, whatever, married, married to Aaron, you are an old woman, an old woman twisted by pain and racked by remembrances and scared of—

*hua tse-ling*

*a soldier, a young man, hua tse-ling, he had come across the ice in his heavy overcoat*

I made him do it. It was me, she thought. I brought him.

*please please don't there's such pain such a blinding pain all that pressure in the skull*

He had been on sentry duty. Bored. Checking his rifle. His feet were cold. She had felt that terrible chill soak through him. Remembering something: thinking of his wife, a pretty young woman in Tapanshang, he had been thinking: the freezing weather, the terrible duty, the warmth of his wife—her name? what was her name? And then—

*I dropped the rifle in the snow and I*

She raised her hands, making slack fists of them, to her eyes. I made him do it. I made him do it. People don't always need to do what they're told. But you— you're a scared old woman with a worthless gift, something that was built into you in your mother's belly, nothing you can alter or eradicate or even forget.

Hua.

She had felt the bullets. That was the worst of it. How she had felt him being bound to the fence and then the guns had gone off and he had died, hanging to the fence like a broken icicle—beyond knowing what was happening to him, beyond caring, beyond any memory of a pretty young woman in Tapanshang. A grief. I brought him, broke his mind, took his mind as if it were nothing more than a stick of frail wood and snapped it and made him cross a river, cross the ice slicks, cross—

Why couldn't she cry? She had cried only once over it, only once in all her life. And that was with Aaron. Dear dead Aaron. Some loves—don't they say some loves are forged in the stars, made in the crucible of the skies? Some loves are fated and impossible to resist? Loving Aaron, and once—why had she told him?—playing a silly game. A silly lover's game. Making him do something, *willing* him to do something: and he had no control, none. A deck of playing cards. Aaron sitting at the kitchen table, counting them, separating them into suits, laughing as he did so because he had no understanding of why he was doing it or why he wanted to do it or what any of it meant—except, for her, a silly lover's game.

*You can make people do things? You can do that?*

What had she seen in his eyes then? Deep down, down in a dark place, what had she seen? Fear? Puzzlement?

*You can make people do things they don't have any control over?*

Yes. Hua crossing the frozen slicks. Dying against the fence. Yes. Yes.

*What are you? What exactly are you?*

Suspicion. That was what she had seen in his eyes. It isn't like that, Aaron. It isn't what you think. Please, my love. It isn't that way, it's a game, a game, I was pretending with you, make-believe—

Clear eyes and gold hair and sixteen and newly married. She stared at her hands. The pain was gone. She was drifting, floating downward, borne on whatever Domareski had injected into her veins. *You might even have made me marry you.* No. Forget it. It didn't happen. Don't you see, Aaron? A trick? A simple little trick? *What exactly are you? What exactly?*

**2.**

Standing alone in the corridor, watching the endless white waste stretch to an indistinguishable point where earth and horizon met in a seamless juncture, Domareski spent match after match in a futile attempt to light his pipe. He was aware, without turning, of Andreyev emerging from his compartment, approaching him slowly, swaying from side to side with the movement of the train. He had come to hate Andreyev in a way that was curiously impersonal, as if the object of his hatred were a symbol, not a person; and sometimes this intense sense of dislike had a quality to it that was almost tangible. It might have been a stone concealed in the corner of a pocket, a thing he could take out and touch whenever he needed to.

The train came slowly to a halt.

"She's sleeping?" Andreyev asked. Domareski said nothing. Andreyev, sighing, pressed his forehead to the window. "Your animosity is understandable. I just wish it weren't directed so forcibly at me personally—"

"Are you going to give me some bullshit about science and progress and the great new frontiers of human understanding, Andreyev?" Domareski turned his face away; he had the uncomfortable feeling that he might yield to the temptation to smother Andreyev in his greatcoat.

The Scientist smiled. "What do you expect?"

Domareski said, "A little compassion—"

"Compassion?"

The Physician stuffed the useless pipe in his pocket. For a while he said nothing. He was thinking of Mrs. Blum. What else had he thought of lately anyhow? Mrs. Blum—he was watching the needle go into her vein—the delivery of morphine, the brief transportation into dreams, places beyond pain. "You have made me a party to her addiction, Andreyev," he said. "You understand that?"

Andreyev looked out at the white fields. "I've done that alone? I'm *solely* responsible for that?"

Domareski shivered: a column of cold air shifted along the corridor, a touch of ice. "You could have kept this to yourself, Andreyev. You didn't have to make your damned research available to every inquisitive ass—"

"I was supposed to keep it *secret?* Is that what you're telling me? You live in another world if that's what you think. I had no choice!"

Domareski did not speak now; he simply wished for Andreyev to fade away, disintegrate. But the Scientist was holding the sleeve of his overcoat, the knuckles of his hands white and bleached. Dead man's hands, Domareski thought.

"Every damn bit of work I do is read by them. Don't you know that? I can't breathe without them knowing it! I can't make a telephone call without them knowing who I'm talking to and what the conversation's all about! Don't talk to me about secrecy, Domareski."

They were silent. The train had begun to move again, slowly gathering speed. Domareski stared from the window: he hated the landscape, its wretched secrets and silences, its forlornness.

Andreyev was whispering again. "They control me like they control you, Domareski. Did you ask to be her physician? Did you go out of your way to get the position? The hell you did. They told you, didn't they? They *ordered* you."

"They," Domareski said. It was as if his contempt was limitless, unfathomable; a rage he could not encompass in any manageable way. And he was tired besides: he was as drained as Mrs. Blum. He leaned against the cold window and looked at Andreyev, wondering at the forces that could reduce men to spineless coelenterates, to jellyfish.

"Yes. They," Andreyev said. "They give us no choices."

The Physician could feel the rhythms of the train vibrate beneath his feet; a racketing journey into nowhere through a landscape, a huge white void, that had not been created for habitation.

"How will *they* use her?" he asked.

Andreyev said nothing. He looked down at the floor, almost as if he were attempting to hide an expression of futility, of shame, from Domareski.

"They'll find a way," Domareski said. "I know those bastards will find a way."

Andreyev raised his face, looked quickly at the Physician, then averted his eyes and pretended to be interested in the door at the end of the corridor.

"She's not an old woman anymore," Domareski said. "She's not an old woman who suffers from arthralgia and whose heart happens to be weak. She's a weapon, Andreyev. She's a damned weapon."

Something to be used, he thought. To be deployed. A force. A force he had himself felt. How to describe it? It was as if the palm of a warm hand had been inserted under his skull and laid upon his cerebrum—yes, it was something like that. And he had heard her say, in a voice that was not a voice, *Please don't leave me, don't leave*— There had been a weird sense of violation, an invasion of his innermost self— a warmth, a light, something that cut through the protection of the cartilaginous case with the proficiency of a laser. There had been astonishment, fear, misunderstanding—this old woman, the shell of whose body had been weakened by age, had reached out to touch him in a way he had never been touched before. And he could not fit this realization into the classifications of chemistry, the definitions of physics, the simple comprehensions of psychology.

He looked at Andreyev. "Have you ever thought what would happen if she . . . turned on you? If she turned on us?"

Andreyev frowned. "I haven't considered it."

"You think she can be kept in control by a diet

of morphine and the promise of an exit visa? You think that's enough?"

"Yes," Andreyev said. "I hope so."

"You hope so." Domareski felt a wild despair, the cul-de-sac of some hopelessness. "You make me sick, Andreyev. This whole business makes me sick. How can you lend yourself to this . . ."

Andreyev was watching him and there was, Domareski thought, a warning in the expression, as if the tightening of the brow, the sudden lines across the forehead, were a means of saying: *Be quiet. Be still.* Something in the look made him afraid.

"I understand as well as anybody what she's capable of," Andreyev said. "To me it's a matter of research."

"Research," Domareski said. "You cover a multitude of your sins that way, Andreyev. The holy grail of research—"

"What would you do, then? What would *you* do?"

Domareski was silent for a while. He imagined Mrs. Blum's face, her lumpen hands, and what he felt was a sense of his own purpose sinking like a weight in water. It would not take much, he had thought before. It would take only an increased dosage. She trusts me. Trusts. He looked at Andreyev and saw an expression now of desperation in the Scientist's face; fatigue, weariness, the soldier who has been ordered to too many impossible fronts. And, despite himself, despite his own inherent controls, he said quietly, "I would kill her."

## 3.

The locomotive stopped somewhere between Irkutsk and Cheremkhovo; workmen, muffled in protective clothing, bent against a sudden blizzard, were clearing the line. She could see them alongside the train: they looked strangely anonymous, their faces masked, hats pulled down over their ears, scarves wrapped around their necks. They dug with huge spades. An oxyacetylene torch flashed, burning the collected ice on the rail. Instead of speaking to one another they made quick gestures, raising their hands, waving, flapping. She pulled her blanket over her shoulders, then sipped the hot tea that Domareski had brought to her.

"You look rested," he said.

She regarded him a moment, sensing that behind his smile, beyond the light in his gray eyes, there was some kind of discomfort. He's afraid of me, she thought. Afraid—as Aaron had been afraid.

He pushed his fingers through his long gray hair. Flecks of dandruff settled on the collar of his dark coat. "How is the pain?" he asked.

She sipped the tea, then said, "A little better."

"Medical science has its shortcomings," he said, and smiled. "Don't breathe a word of it to a soul—but arthritis happens to be one of them."

She set the cup down on the small table beside her bunk, conscious of the sight of her own bulky fingers and how they irritated her. She wanted to hide them under her blanket. She licked her dry lips and looked at Domareski. How could she talk of her mental pictures? How could she tell him what she had seen? That moment of excruciation, the searing of flesh, the rupture of bone, the outrage of a man's dying? Hua, she thought. And for what?

"I spoke with Comrade Sememko," he said. "Again. You have to say everything at least twenty-five times to a politician before he begins to understand what you're talking about."

He's lying, she thought. *I am old, I am being lied to and patronized—and yet he knows, he knows I can see, that he is like a sheet of thin glass to me.*

"He said the formalities will be taken care of when we get to Moscow."

"Moscow?"

"Didn't you know? That's where they keep all the rubber stamps." He was trying to make a joke, she saw that. But his smile was thin and his gray eyes uncharacteristically opaque—as if a vital part of him were elsewhere, not on this train, not in this compartment, but removed to some great distance. She pressed her hands together: there was a faint spark of pain.

"Anyway," he said, "why in the name of heaven do you want to go to Israel so badly? It doesn't snow in Israel, you know. What will you do all day? The sun will burn you to death."

He had risen, walked to the window; he was looking out at the workmen laboring miserably in the drifts. He shook his head back and forth.

"Ah. I promise you. You'll miss all this gorgeous snow, Mrs. Blum."

She closed her eyes once more: it was odd how sleep came back on her, rather like a tide. No matter how rested she felt, regardless of how long she had slept, there was always a drowsiness on the margins of her mind—like clouds, she thought, clouds rolling in from hills. A small comfort, a small death. When she stared into the clouds she surrendered her hold on the things around her, as if they were beads breaking apart on a string, scattering, rolling this way and that—

*An increased dosage*

Startled, opening her eyes, she looked at Domareski. But he hadn't said anything. He wasn't even looking at her. She struggled into a sitting position. An increased dosage? What did that mean? Why had she picked up on that? Now Domareski turned to look at her and there was a slight expression of sadness on his face. An increased dosage of what? She watched him a moment as he came back from the window. He sat on the edge of the bunk and picked up a leather wallet from the table. He opened it, flicking through the snapshots in the plastic covers.

"I think I know your family almost as well as you," he said. She watched the snapshots move as he flipped them past her—and the colors jumped at her, faces transformed by sunlight, photographs incandescent with captured light: they were not still, stiff, posed; they rippled, they were animated, figures coming off the surface at her. She took the wallet from him and she thought: My life. My whole life. Without this there is nothing else. The boy, Stanislav—no, he wasn't a boy anymore, he wasn't the child Aaron had held in his arms, he was forty now—but he would always be the boy. The slim girl he had married, the girl with the dark liquid eyes and the captivating name of Yael, the sound as of some soft bird skimming the surface of tranquil water—Yael; and the grandchildren—a sturdy boy who looked as Aaron had once looked, a girl as slim as her mother. The longing to touch them was painful to her. She had imagined and rehearsed it an infinity of times, seeing them run toward her, seeing all that shyness and strangeness break down in loving; she had felt her face pressed against them, their hair, their hands, how they would feel to touch. She knew them: in all their mannerisms, their delights, in all their moods and concerns and daydreams and ambitions, she knew them. And the long-ing, in its intensity, was worse than ever. It was a weight in her heart.

"You understand," she said to Domareski.

He said nothing. He nodded his head. He laid his hand upon the back of her wrist.

"I'm a prisoner in this country," she said. "I'm a prisoner."

He stared at her now and she caught it again: *An increased dosage, that's all.* And for a moment she was afraid of him, afraid of the man she had come to think of as her only ally—because she could not trust Andreyev, who was weak, who was even more of a prisoner than she, or his frigid assistant. There was only Domareski and she could not afford to be afraid of him. She gripped his fingers and looked directly into his eyes. Where did this fear come from?

"I've got to go to them," she said. "Do you un-derstand what it means to long for something so badly that each time you feel the longing you bleed? Do you understand that?"

"Yes," he said.

"No. No, you don't understand." She took her hand from his arm: her pain was bad, spreading, now a sensation no longer confined to hands and wrists but carried deep into her center. And she found herself weighing the death of the Chinese soldier, weighing that grief, against her own terrifying desire for these people in the collection of snapshots. Trapped: how could you live a life in such a trap? Trapped by a coun-try, imprisoned by your own wretched gift? But it wasn't a gift, was it? It was a part of being doomed, of belonging amongst the damned.

She watched Domareski rise and go to the door. He turned once and smiled, a smile pale to the point of nonexistence, a mere distension of lip.

"An increased dosage of what?" she asked. "Of what?"

He looked puzzled. "I don't follow you."

She lay back down, watched him a moment, saw the door slide open and then close; and he was gone.

## 4.

"He said he would kill her."

Andreyev heard his own sentence, his own thick voice. He watched the snow fall against the window of Katya's compartment, aware of an aroma trapped in the enclosed space, a scent he could not quite place.

Katya was silent. Watching her, he was reminded of Domareski's attitude in the corridor, and he felt the same old conflicts begin anew—it was reasonable and unreasonable, simultaneously logical and absurd. Domareski was both right and wrong at one and the same time. How did you deal with that?

Katya sat on the edge of her bunk, smoothed her skirt with a steady movement of her hand. "Do you think he will?"

Andreyev looked at her: he felt an unaccustomed sense of desire, a strange need to slide the bolt on the door and cross the room to her, throw her back across the bunk—a rape, not a communion; a violation in which he could dissolve conflicts.

He shook his head. "I don't think so."

"Why are you so sure?"

"He wouldn't have told me, would he?"

Katya clasped her hands on her knees. "He's a risk."

"A risk?"

"To all our work," she said.

She smoked a cigarette, fitting it into a holder. Andreyev watched the smoke drift to the cold window. The moon was up somewhere, smothered by cloud. A suggestion of silver, a hint of frosted metal. Domareski—he felt a sudden affection for the man, a sympathy with his disenchantment, attuned to his disillusion. He also resented the Physician's strength because it reflected, like a savage mirror, what he considered his own weaknesses.

Katya got to her feet, ejected the cigarette, stamped it into the floor. "You're prepared to ignore it?"

"Yes," Andreyev said. Why not? Why not indeed? "He's going through . . ." His voice trailed off; he watched Katya as she waited for him to finish.

"A phase?" she asked. "A stage? Some misgivings? There's no fool like a humanist fool, Victor."

An accusing edge to the voice: Andreyev could hear the slice of a razor blade slip through a thin substance. Who was the fool here? Himself or Domareski?

"You've worked very hard," Katya said. "Don't underestimate *how* hard, Victor. Don't misjudge anything. Do I make myself plain?"

He listened to the train, the roll of wheels over the slick tracks, and he thought of the years—years of labor, years of detection and painstaking investigation—and he felt the weight of accumulated disappointments. There had been scorn too; humiliation, embarrassment, a skeptical disregard of his work. *Do I make myself plain?*

"How often do you encounter a Mrs. Blum?" Katya asked.

"Never," he said.

"Well then?"

Andreyev went to the window, peered out into

the darkness, the rush of reflected light from the carriages that struck the snowbanks alongside the tracks. "I don't think Domareski would do anything to harm her," he said.

Katya was silent for a while. A restless hand went up to her hair; fingers patted the short, tight locks. How unattractive she is, Andreyev thought, glancing at her, glimpsing her half-open mouth, the small teeth. He was conscious of how close to her he stood; he stepped away from the window, turning his back to her.

"No," he said. "I think he wants to let off steam."

"And that's all?"

"That's all," he answered, struck by uncertainty now, remembering Domareski's strange assurance in the corridor—that strength, single-mindedness. An honorable man, Andreyev thought, in a world of deceit. An honorable man made to perform against his principles: was there a more dangerous creature than that?

## 5.

The Politician, Sememko, had a private car at the back of the train. It was guarded, more for reasons of paranoia than any fear of a breach in security, by two agents of the KGB; both were bored men who stood in the corridor and watched night fall through the snow. Neither looked remotely interested in the wilderness outside. They leaned against the walls, whistled, touched their automatic pistols, and sometimes exchanged quick phrases, jokes about the cold, prospects of Moscow, brief arguments over the merits of soccer teams—Moscow Dynamo compared to Lokomotiv, for example. They were men who had become accustomed to waiting, who had learned how to whittle their time away in tedious places. The red-haired one pressed his face to the dark glass and hummed a phrase from a tune he had recently heard on "The Voice of America" over a confiscated radio. The other, a lean man with thick spectacles, was walking around in small circles, observing the marks left by his shoes, trying to fit new footprints into old ones; he gave the impression of a novice tightrope artist who did not exactly trust his eyesight.

The red-haired one peered out into the blackness and asked, "Do you think they're screwing?"

Removing his spectacles, rubbing the lenses with a small rag, the other said, "I wouldn't touch her with your proverbial ten-foot pole. Would you?"

The red-haired man shrugged. "It would pass some of the time," he said. "You could always pull a bag over her head."

"You couldn't exactly pull a bag over her body, could you?"

Both were silent for a while, both thinking about the thin woman who had gone, not twenty minutes before, into Sememko's car. The lean man replaced his glasses and laughed, making a masturbatory gesture with his right hand. "It would be better than that," he said.

"I wouldn't bet on it," the red-haired one said.

Silence. Both men were still for a while, as if they were listening for the sound of sexual activity from behind the closed door of Sememko's car. But there was only the rhythmic ticking of the wheels on the track and sometimes the sound of the wind wailing around the train.

And then the door was opened; the woman stood

there in a square of bright yellow light. Both men stood attentively upright, looking at her.

She moved past them, stopped, and then turned to face them. She said, "I believe Comrade Sememko wants to see you."

## 6.

Domareski was alone in the empty dining car. It was late now and there was no longer any food or drink to be had. He sat at a table near the door; the white tablecloth, a piece of thin linen, reflected the pale light from a lamp. The overhead lights had been extinguished earlier and his lamp created the effect of a tiny oasis of illumination in the long car. Papers were spread in front of him; they pertained to matters he would have to attend to back in Moscow—as if, by the act of reading them, he could relegate Mrs. Blum to some substratum of consciousness, put her in a place where he would not have to deal with her. He was tired; he massaged his eyelids, blinked, stared at the papers on the linen cloth. A colleague—Glazkov— had recently found an enzyme in both thymus and bone marrow: it was called terminal deoxynucleotidyl transferase, or TdT, and Glazkov had been investigating its helpfulness in determining therapy protocols to which leukemia patients might respond. TdT, Domareski thought, and he had a sudden longing to get off this train, to assist Glazkov in any way he could, to put an end to this whole business of Mrs. Blum.

What was he anyhow?

A physician—yes.

He wasn't a hired thug, a technician with a needle. His business wasn't that of reducing old women to a state of wreckage from which there could be no return, no wholeness; it wasn't up to him to take a person and reduce that person to splinters. Damn them, he thought.

Damn them—

He turned his face away from the papers. Flecks of snow, maddened crystals, could be seen falling away from the window, disturbed by the wind and the motion of the train. He saw his own yellowy reflection in the glass. TdT, he thought. Leukemia. Therapy protocols.

*They.*

He remembered the face of Professor Yeremenko, his rather elaborate room at Moscow University, the man's contagious nervousness, the palm of one hand forever stroking a marble paperweight, a Bulgarian souvenir; he remembered Yeremenko's stumbling presentation, the stuttered proposition, the hooded reference to Mrs. Blum. There had been sunlight in the room, particles of dust shifting in an orange column of light, the room itself the color of a decaying tangerine.

*It will take you out of Moscow for a while, Domareski.*

Yes, Domareski thought.

Yes—

*Mrs. Blum has, hmmm, special talents.*

Domareski had heard himself refuse; he remembered the weight of his own negative response, how the refusal had somehow lain trapped in that orange room.

*I don't think I make myself plain, Domareski.*

How so?

*They have indicated that there are no choices. You have been selected for this, hmmm, special duty.*

Domareski recalled a fragment of ash in Yeremenko's beard; it had hung from a coiled hair like a small white flake. Why recall that now? A detail, banal, nothing. Special duty. He should have known that Yeremenko hadn't clambered to the top of the heap because of his humanitarian abilities; he should have understood that Yeremenko's summit had been reached only by circumnavigating the scientific dissidents and adhering, *clinging,* to the Party line. To that great nipple of the State. There was neither room nor space for rejection, for refusal. You did what you were told.

No choices. Special duty. Don't you understand? It is a simple case of administering morphine. It shouldn't upset you.

Domareski stared into the light bulb until his eyes hurt. *They. Them.* All his life he had been conscious of anonymous forces shaping the patterns of things. The creations of paradigms, matrices, obligations by which you lived. To stand up against them took a special bravery, didn't it? The courage of history, the simple courage of the fool: stand up and be counted—but the count was small, the lure of the labor camp, oblivion in the permafrost, overwhelming.

He saw the needle go into the old woman's arm. What did she think it was? A simple pain-killer? a tranquilizer? Something inoffensive? *An increased dosage.* That's all it would take, he thought. A mistake, he would say; an accident, a terrible accident. You don't have the courage to be a fool, he thought. You don't even have that, do you? You don't have the courage to kill her before . . . before whatever.

He tried to read Glazkov's paper again. The words streamed together in a sequence of nonsense. A sudden draft caused him to shiver, caused the papers to rise very slightly from the table.

A door had been opened behind him.

Quickly he turned his face to look.

There were shadows beyond the light, uncertainties. Was it Andreyev and his wretched assistant? They moved forward but still the reach of the table lamp did not define them.

"Andreyev?" he said.

It was, even if he did not know it at the time of asking, the last word he would speak in his life. One of the shadows moved in an abrupt, quirky fashion, a hand raised in the air. Domareski saw a simple flash in the darkened dining car, and as he felt a violent pain in his skull, as he experienced a remote awareness of bloodstains flying across Glazkov's papers, he lowered his face to the table linen, down and down and down—a sinking man whose last gesture was to overturn the table lamp, as if what he wanted most was to hurry the onset of his own darkness.

Like a flawed piece of apparatus in an experiment that has gone quite wrong, a cracked retort, a broken pipette, something no longer useful in laboratory terms, his body was thrown into the snowdrifts between Biysk and Slavgorod.

# 3

Rayner sometimes thought his wife made love with one eye fixed to some imaginary stopwatch, that she handled his flesh as if she were wearing surgical gloves. She seemed both intimidated by the physical act and aloof from it at the same time. He thought of someone performing an operation: open-thigh surgery. Her orgasms were quick, strangulated little things, a brief outcry and then a slide into a silence that suggested embarrassment. An atavism of sorts, he imagined: Isobel, Victorian wife, raised on a diet of conjugal manuals, wifely etiquette, how to behave with a lustful husband during "the bad time" of the month.

He rolled away from her and looked at his wristwatch on the bedside table. Seven-thirty: a sexual duration of seven minutes. Turning back, he glanced at her. She had the kind of beauty that suggested something rare preserved in formaldehyde; alabaster afloat in crystal liquid. She turns heads, he thought. When she strolls through a room—ah, how the heads do turn. But at the heart of this beauty there were chips of ice. Now, drawing the stiff linen sheet up over her small breasts, she lit a cigarette and blew a stream of smoke.

"These damned sheets are so cold," she said. "This entire hotel's such a drag."

Saying nothing, Rayner got out of bed and went to the window, wondering if the room were bugged, if perhaps somewhere a concealed camera had recorded the recent marital contrivance. He looked out into the sleet, a sky of slate, electrical conductors swaying on the tops of buildings; in the distance, rising like slabs, were apartment blocks. You could think of better cities to be in than Moscow, he thought. You could think of French food, Italian wine, the Aegean Sea; instead what faced you, from the confines of this monstrous hotel, was a city trapped in its own dreariness.

He turned to look at her, conscious of his own nakedness through her eyes: it was not a point of view that entirely pleased him. A little flab—less than some men his age, but that was a cold comfort; the pectoral muscles beginning to sag. Do I end up as one of those men with *boobs?* Bermuda shorts, Palm Springs, an electric golf cart, and tits, *tits* of all things? Isobel blew a perfect oval of smoke and Rayner had the odd desire to shove his middle finger through it.

Isobel sighed and, still clutching the white sheet to her breasts—as if Rayner were not her husband but some stranger who had improperly hauled her ashes—stepped out of bed and went in the direction of the bathroom. He listened to running water, pipes knocking. You fall in love at twenty-two, he thought. You think she is the most angelic thing ever to have been set down to grace the planet, her sweetness is almost *terrifying;* and somewhere down the length of fifteen years you lose it. How? Consider, Rayner. Does it sift through the old hands like your proverbial sand? Does it reach this state of affairs through the relentless accumulation of marital detritus? Or is it something even more simple, more sickening—like waking one day to find the fever forever gone?

Ah. God knows. He sat on the edge of the bed and looked once more at his watch. There was a meeting with Lindholm in half an hour; in the course of the meeting Lindholm would sit with the kind of expression of discomfort that suggests a man is seated on his hands. Let it be. Lindholm, even here in the Soviet Union, was still the Vice President; and somehow you had to overlook the fact that he was a Kansas hick who, Rayner imagined, would have been in his element staring at storage silos or calculating porcine percentages.

"The plumbing is shitty," Isobel said.

Rayner closed his eyes. Sometimes he sent himself back through time to a point when he had been a young man on the lower rungs of that seemingly endless ladder known as the State Department; this younger Rayner—darkly handsome, trim, desirable—had a gorgeous loving wife, fine prospects, a future that suggested the American Dream could, with the right kind of luck and labor, become a reality. He invented his own time-travel device, his capsule; and it made Isobel tolerable for a time. But it also brought regret, a sense of—ah, shit, things could have been different, Rayner. Things could have been somewhat better.

In a white bathrobe, she stepped back into the bedroom. She said, "It beats me why we worry so much about a country that doesn't even have a decent plumbing system." And she opened the closet, fingering various dresses that hung in a shimmering array.

A plumbing system, Rayner thought. It's all a

question of priorities, my love. They regard the transport of human effluence as being of less strategic merit than the megaton capacity of an ICBM. How do I explain that to you, darling?

She lit another cigarette and stared at her dresses. "What time is the dinner?" she asked.

"Nine," Rayner said.

"God." She touched the various garments. Rayner knew that she hated them all, that she was given to a kind of vicious dislike of dresses whose only crimes were that they had been worn once. At times, he perceived his life in terms of Isobel's charge accounts.

"The whole thing's preposterous anyway," she said. She was holding a black silk dress against her body, turning this way and that in front of the mirror. The black material was magnificent against her pale skin and Rayner, despite himself, felt the kind of desire that goes nowhere except into a painful knot.

"Dear old Lindholm, I mean—well, he's a nice old fuddy-duddy in his way, but this entire trip is useless. He knows it. We know it. Our friendly Soviet hosts know it. So why bother?"

"The Veep was promised a trip. He got his trip. It keeps him happy. It makes him feel he's a part of the great decision-making process we call democracy. He chats with the Russians and they chat back. Lindholm goes back to D.C., gets his pictures taken at the airport, reports to the Old Man, then he sinks back into his neat little box of obscurity again. Simple?"

"Stupid," Isobel said. "The black one, do you think?"

Don't ask me, Rayner thought. I only want your body. If there was some hope of response.

"Or the yellow?"

She went through the dresses, holding them

against her body, making faces at herself in the mirror, throwing them down on the bed: rainbows of silk and rayon and cotton, a heap of rainbows. Rayner thought of the discarded cocoons of weird exotic moths.

"Shouldn't you get ready for your meeting?" she asked.

He walked back to the window. Sleet whipped the night. Moscow, Moscow—why was he ensnared here, here in the most embalmed capital of Europe?

"I think the black," Isobel said. "Yes. Definitely. The black."

Rayner looked at her, remembering her insistence on accompanying him this trip. *I will not put up with the horrors of Washington in January,* she had said. *Stick that in your diplomatic passport and smoke it.* Now she did nothing, it seemed, except bitch: a whole lifestyle constructed out of verbal sniping.

"What do you think of the black?" she asked.

She looked so tantalizingly beautiful that he had to struggle to remember: she has a heart of crushed ice. And love seemed to him just then an appalling conundrum, a joke of God's—as if the human heart were a kind of whoopee cushion capable of creating not only humiliation but, worse, painful confusion.

## 2.

It was not exactly clear to Rayner why Maksymovich, the First Secretary of the Central Committee, found Kimball Lindholm so apparently fascinating; why Maksymovich, who stooped as if he carried a burden of lead between his shoulder blades, should continually watch Lindholm through half-moon spectacles in a manner that suggested intense interest. Nor was it clear why Maksymovich should make himself so available, so accessible, to the Vice President when it was well known that the First Secretary had little regard for the niceties of diplomatic protocol. When Kimball Lindholm made a joke—usually unfunny in its original English and presumably without any humor in the translation—Maksymovich would laugh, his thick body shaking; he would take off his tiny glasses, rub his eyes, wipe the lenses of the spectacles with a small rag, and blink at Lindholm as if to say: Stop, it's too painful for me to laugh anymore.

Rayner had the sense that a palm was being greased: a snow job taking place. It puzzled him—but then he was accustomed to the seemingly inexplicable changes in policy that frequently took place behind the closed doors of Kremlin rooms. After a time you simply stopped looking for a logic; tomorrow's policy might be the opposite of today's—and there would be no contradiction involved.

He found himself staring at Lindholm. The little man was huddled close to his interpreter, a look of some mild bewilderment on his face. Across the table, the First Secretary scribbled something on a note pad: a doodle created out of interlocking circles. Rayner sat back in his chair and looked quickly around the room. Save for a grainy portrait that depicted a group of rather indistinct figures, and a Soviet flag that hung loose from the ceiling, the walls were bare. Rayner gazed a moment at the pale hammer and sickle on the red background.

Besides Maksymovich and two nondescript men whose functions had not been made plain, besides Lindholm and the interpreter—a fragile man with flesh the color of an eggshell—the only other person present, apart from Rayner, was Haffner, the Assistant Secretary of State. Haffner was a creature of strict protocol; he sat in an oddly stiff manner, as if the national anthem were being played and he alone were capable of hearing it. He had all the slightly strange reality of a wax apple. And somehow Haffner's presence added to the general sense of futility that Rayner had felt from the very beginning. Lindholm had no power, no real power; but somewhere along the way—during the course of the campaign, during the final stages of the Convention, whenever—he had been promised a trip to Russia. And this was it. One could imagine the AP photographs in *The Wichita Eagle,* your very own Kimby Lindholm sitting at the nerve center of true power. It would, Rayner thought, give the farmers something to chew over. But why was Maksymovich putting on such a show?

Rayner looked back at Lindholm now. The Vice President, who had been asked to run on the ticket with Mallory because of his apparent appeal to that large section of the American populace who refused to admit that Eisenhower was *really* dead, was speaking to the interpreter; he spoke slowly, more slowly than usual, and Rayner found his attention drifting back, back to Isobel, back to the black dress and the pale skin and the vicissitudes of what, for want of any better word, you might call loving.

"It's my own personal feeling," Lindholm said, watching the interpreter, waiting, "my own personal feeling that the business of America is America."

Rayner felt Haffner become more stiff than was normal. Phrases such as "my own personal feeling" caused Haffner to have nightmares; Rayner was convinced of this. He heard the Assistant Secretary quietly clear his throat, a form of warning. But Lindholm was back home, stalking the wheat fields, scanning the prairies, chewing tobacco with his natural constituents. Rayner closed his eyes. He was amused. Lindholm did not have the good sense to know a blunder when he collided with one.

The interpreter spoke to Maksymovich, who smiled, nodded, raised a hand to his glasses. Lindholm apparently took this as a sign of encouragement to continue.

"I don't believe Americans have any business with foreign adventures, or interfering with some godforsaken hole in Africa, or sending troops halfway across the world just so some crackpot dictator can be kept in power."

Ah, sweet Christ, Rayner thought. Haffner leaned forward, suddenly animated; he took out a handkerchief and blew his nose. Rayner gazed at Lindholm, waiting for the next mistake. But Maksymovich was talking and the interpreter was listening, waiting. A comedy of errors, Rayner thought. Hilarity in high places. It was always possible that the little man from Kansas had imbibed too much vodka, of course.

Haffner said, "The Vice President is talking off the record, of course—"

But the interpreter ignored this. He was already beginning to translate for Lindholm the words of the First Secretary.

"The First Secretary finds it hard to understand your position, Vice President. . . . He wants to point out that your own views conflict somewhat with . . . the policy speeches of President Mallory . . . who does not seem to believe there are limits to American imperialism."

Rayner stared at Maksymovich. Lindholm, as if needing guidance, as if conscious of having overstepped a line of demarcation, turned to Haffner. American imperialism, Rayner thought. How would Lindholm wriggle out now?

The Vice President stared at his hands. Rayner

waited. From somewhere, doubtless, the little man from Emporia would find inspiration. Haffner continued to blow his nose.

Lindholm said, "Please make it clear to your First Secretary that I'm expressing, uh, my own personal views . . ." And here, oddly, Lindholm laughed. "In my country, a man is free to express his own views."

So that was it, Rayner thought. He had pulled the old freedom of expression out of his hat; the tired rabbit of democracy. Well, it was worth a shot—even if Rayner could barely keep from smiling. Maksymovich's expression did not change. He listened, was silent for a moment, then said, "President Mallory has been highly critical of Soviet activity . . . I refer you to his policy statements on Soviet activity in Africa, in Eastern Europe, and in Cuba. He apparently feels that Soviet help, that any aid we offer to those countries trying to establish a revolution—he feels strongly, I understand, that all this is quite immoral. Am I correct?"

Lindholm listened. He looked once again at Haffner, who, sitting with his eyes closed, appeared to have succumbed to a trance of embarrassment.

"President Mallory has made his position plain," Lindholm said.

"And yet you differ from him?"

Lindholm smiled, as if all at once he felt himself to be on safer ground: the quicksand was behind him now. "Hell, we don't always agree. We don't always agree."

There was a silence in the room now. Rayner watched the First Secretary—a strange inscrutability, a face of secrets, of knowing what nobody else knew. And for a moment, without quite knowing why, Rayner felt unnerved.

Then Maksymovich pushed his chair back and stood up and smiled. "I think it's time for us to eat."

**3.**

He woke, his throat dry, his head aching—the dehydration of vodka. The room was dark, he had no idea of time. He sat up, listening. He could hear sleet hammering on the window and the sound of Isobel breathing and he could see, by what little moonlight fell into the room, her pale outline, her dark hair spread on the pillow. *I think he fancied me. Your old Maksymovich or whatever he calls himself. I think he really took a shine to me.*

The dinner, Rayner thought. Something had happened at the dinner. He sat upright on the edge of the mattress. His muscles ached. He went into the bathroom and ran his head under the faucet, splashed his face, soaked his wrists.

*Asked me all kinds of questions, old Maksy did.*

Rayner raised his face from the basin, looking at himself in the mirror. A squandered look, a pallid expression: he had seen better days. What kinds of questions, Isobel? Did you give him your telephone number back in D.C.? Stuff like that?

He leaned in the bathroom doorway. She slept on her back, her head tilted slightly to one side. *Some were personal, some were impersonal.* You jealous fucker, Rayner thought. Grow up. Wise up. You're not a kid skulking around. Good old Maksy. He was just being palsy, no? A new chum, a pretty American lady. No more than that, right?

*He asked, Did we have any kids? What kind of house did we have? Things like that.*

No, Rayner thought. This wasn't the thing troubling him. Something else. Kimball Lindholm: but that was a darker area, he had mapped that territory already. Kimball getting downright drunk and trying to look dignified; but he had seemed more like a statue cut out of granite that way, something that would disgrace a public park in Emporia, a landing pad for pigeons. No, it wasn't Lindholm, it wasn't anything to do with how Lindholm had launched into another of his set speeches—how he would have stayed out of WW II, how he wouldn't have sent any of his boys off to fight any goddamn foreign war: your standard red-neck, cracker-barrel nonsense. Kimball's party piece, that was all.

Something else, Rayner.

*He asked me if I'd ever met Mallory.*

Did he now?

*He wondered what the American people thought of Kimball Lindholm.*

Rayner lay down. He placed his hand flat against Isobel's thigh. All at once he wanted her, cold or otherwise, he wanted her very badly. Drunk, the great alcoholic cancellation. Way too drunk. He remembered how, during the dinner, Maksymovich had caught his eye—something in the look, a quality of sudden hardness, a glint: like old Maksy was saying to him, *I am perhaps the most powerful man in the world, and if I choose to flirt with your wife—what can you do about it?* Drunk drunk drunk. He stared at the dark ceiling.

It came to him, as it always did in bad moments. She has a lover, he thought. Somewhere, tucked away, she has a man. It was a suspicion he had tracked down through the strata of his own jealousies. A man, a shadow, someone she loved. Grow up, he thought. Won't you ever grow up? That old green malignant deity again. She has the opportunities, doesn't she?

You're not always around to see what she's doing; even when you take her on trips like this, you can't be expected to watch her every moment of the day, goddam—a lover, someone she meets, someone she gives herself to, someone she *screws*. Dark rooms. Furtive little phone calls. Obscure restaurants. Inscrutable motel rooms—

Drunk. A drunken uneven sleep, a dream of his brother John, a vague dream that eluded him on waking—and yet he felt exhausted, as if at some point the dream had become nightmare, a nightmare he couldn't remember in the gray light of morning.

# 4

Prints and illustrations hung against the walls of the large office. They suggested a continuum of Soviet history, a line linking past with present, tradition with technology, the indomitable Russian spirit sanitized of its occasional blood-lettings. The Eve of Revolution Day gathering in the Mayakovsky subway station, November 6, 1941: Stalin had been strategically omitted and the photograph showed only Party dignitaries and Trade Union leaders; a group of antique Abkhasian peasants seated around a table, dipping pieces of *abusta* into various sauces; a gruesome picture, made the more awful by its grainy authenticity, of several dead German soldiers lying in the Moscow snow; Yuri Gagarin, smiling, dressed for his orbital trip in 1961.

Andreyev was depressed by the collection: it bludgeoned him with something he had no urge to feel. But time and again, irritated by the droning voices in the room, he found his attention drawn to the gallery of illustrations—Mother Russia. Was he supposed to *believe* that Domareski had somehow contrived to fall from a moving train? That the Physician had by chance opened a door and—given the treachery of ice—lost his footing? Andreyev shook his head, watching Sememko play with a bunch of papers. The ugly Politician, constantly patting his moustache or tugging at the lower extremities of his vest, was talking about the Ussuri experiment to a room filled with those members of the Presidium whose function it was to plan the future strategies of science and scientific discoveries. His voice droned, and Andreyev, looking up at the blurred grin of the cosmonaut Gagarin, caught only a few words and phrases: *naturally too early to say if there's any useful potential here . . . experiment seemed successful. . . .* There was a reference to acorns and oak trees, something clichéd and banal. Andreyev looked out of the window. Sleet lashed the city; the day was gray, the sky sullen with a sense of repressed violence.

Acorns and oak trees.

Andreyev clasped his hands together. He looked around the room, wondering at how the occupants managed to affect a physical resemblance to one another, as if there were some family relationship shared by each of them. Blunted faces, dark suits, white shirts, those thick necks that seemed to have been shaved as close into the skin as was humanly possible without bloodshed.

Sememko, looking self-satisfied, had stopped talking. He was sitting back in his chair, content with himself. Now Koprow had risen to his feet. Koprow the Hatchet, Andreyev thought—a thickset man, his head shaved bald and shaped like a bullet: you could imagine Koprow in other incarnations—a treacherous Renaissance monk, a strong-arm man in a circus, the assassin who emerged from a darkened doorway. It was Koprow who secretly liaised between the KGB and the Ministry of Science.

Andreyev realized that Koprow was looking directly at him. The stare was both cold and definitive; Andreyev could hear something buzz in his own head—the edge of some alarm, a quickened fear.

"I've read the reports, of course," Koprow said. The sudden fast smile that appeared on his face and then abruptly faded reminded Andreyev of a flawed neon.

"It's my understanding," said Koprow, pausing, gazing across the faces in the room in the fashion of one taking a roll call. "It's my understanding that to all intents and purposes the Chinese infantryman was dead on arrival. I refer, of course, to brain death. I also understand that certain tests were made and that these showed a total absence of reflex, coordination, an absence of any of the normal responses one associates with life."

Andreyev caught Koprow's eyes, then looked away, coughed, studied his papers.

"The question in my mind," Koprow said, smiling again, a leprous expression, "is simple. If the woman has such a destructive capacity, if her ability is such that she can, quite literally, *destroy* a mind, how are we to make use of this particular talent?"

Andreyev said nothing. He glanced at Sememko; the square fat hand was working the strands of the reddish moustache. Andreyev longed all at once to be out of this room: the trapped heat was suffocating him.

"Perhaps Professor Andreyev . . ." Koprow inclined his head toward Andreyev, then sat down.

There was a silence in the room; the awful silence of a clock suddenly stopped. Andreyev realized that he should stand, deliver his prepared speech, his explanation, but he felt oddly numb. I am paralyzed, he thought. Why had Domareski disappeared? Fool, he thought. You don't need the gift of clairvoyance for that one. He remembered Katya standing in her compartment, her reflection in the window; in his imagination he saw a coiled snake and heard the vicious rattle in the tail of the creature. Slowly, fumbling his papers, he stood up. The faces concentrated on him.

His own voice was flat, dry, his mouth opening and closing slowly. Someone was riffling papers. A fan blew warm air. Sleet rattled the window suddenly.

"I might begin with some background," he said. Why did his own voice fade in and out like the signal on a faulty piece of radio equipment? "Mrs. Blum was brought to my attention by a researcher in the town of Sokol, which happens to be her home. The researcher—all this, of course, is contained in my files—was pursuing the kind of work being done by Professor Sergeyev at the Uktomskii Physiological Laboratory in Leningrad . . . again, I refer you to my files."

He paused. The room was still, perfect as a photograph, nothing stirring: even the hot-air fan had thermostatically switched itself off. He hated it: the center of attention, everyone looking at him, everyone waiting. He hated this messianic sensation. He wanted to say: *I have answers to nothing, nothing.*

"The specific field I refer to is psychokinesis, or PK, which as you know"—he stared around at their faces: how blank they were, how insipid all at once, awaiting his definitions, his explanations—"is the ability to move objects by mental means. There has been considerable research done in this area. You are doubtless already familiar with Wolf Messing and with . . ." He dried up; his memory blanked, the roof of his mouth had become dry. ". . . Nelya Mikhailova. And you are no doubt acquainted with the research that has been done in that direction."

Andreyev took a sip of water. "You will see from the documents that have been prepared that what we have in Mrs. Blum far exceeds the capabilities of any of the subjects we have previously tested under laboratory conditions."

Koprow had begun to tap a finger impatiently upon the surface of the table. It was a hooklike finger, curled over, skinny. Andreyev was mesmerized by its movements: he had to wrench his eyes away and look back down at his papers.

"I am not going to say that we understand to any degree the nature of this woman's abilities. We've postulated, for the sake, frankly, of convenience, the existence of an $x$—call it what you like—an $x$ that represents psi-force. I'm not going to claim that this label is truly helpful, because it isn't. We don't know why she can do what she does, we don't know how she can do it. . . . Some form of mental wave, some kind of evolutionary throwback, some kind of energy that presently we have no means of measuring and therefore no way of comprehending . . . there have been any number of theories. You can pick and choose among them as you like. The fact remains that Mrs. Blum has the ability to interfere with the operations of other minds."

Koprow suddenly closed his folder and laid his hands flat on top of it; his skull gleamed beneath the overhead lights. Impatiently he said, "With respect, Professor Andreyev, we in this room are not exactly enthralled by theories. We are practical men. . . ." He looked at his various colleagues conspiratorially, searching for and finding a measure of assent. Practical men, Andreyev thought. They are all practical men. The euphemism was appalling. Koprow was smiling, as if he were attuned to Andreyev's discomfort. "As practical men, we are somewhat more interested in functions than in hypotheses. And what we have to ask ourselves is rather simple. What good is this woman to us?"

Andreyev turned his hands over, stared at the damp palms, at how sweat glistened in the lines; the collective tensions in the room unnerved him. He felt unsteady on his feet, weak, something vital draining out of him. He thought: A freak show, a sideshow, trickery. Why in the name of God couldn't it be as simple as that? Why couldn't it be mumbo-jumbo? The whole psychic bag of tricks? Palmistry, messages from the ether, the divine revelations of fake practitioners of trances, phony voices, bells ringing in pitch-black rooms, ectoplasmic materializations—why couldn't it be the simple lunacy of indulging in a conversation with a tomato plant? *Why did it have to be real?*

*What good is this woman to us?*

Koprow was still talking and Andreyev realized he hadn't been listening. ". . . There's the further matter of our control over this woman. Are we doing enough to ensure control? What guarantees do we have?"

Control, Andreyev thought. What control? She could turn on you and blow your mind into oblivion, into death.

Koprow said, "I understand that morphine has been administered to the point of dependency. And that she expects an exit visa for Israel in return for her cooperation. Is that correct?"

Andreyev nodded his head, feeling a tightness in the neck muscles, a dull pain beneath the scalp. Morphine, the perpetual daze of the dream, the languid glide into torpor, a freedom from pain—the promise of a way out, as if such a promise would ever be kept. He watched Koprow, seeing iron determination there, in the way the man held his head, clenched his hands, the firm set of the mouth.

"And all this is enough?" he asked.

Andreyev shrugged.

"Is it enough?" Koprow raised his voice and there was a faint echo in the room.

"I can't honestly answer that."

Koprow looked at his colleagues with mock exasperation. "Then what *would* you suggest, Professor?"

Andreyev stared at Koprow. "She's only interested in leaving the Soviet Union, Comrade Koprow. That's the only thing she lives for."

"Then why doesn't she simply spirit herself away?"

There was subdued laughter around the room, the tuning-up of instruments with Koprow as conductor. Andreyev understood: he was being challenged to say that the woman was under total control, that domination was complete.

Koprow was shaking his head. "The importance of control," he said. "I don't think we should leave any of that to mere chance, do you?"

Andreyev was suddenly meek, seeing himself small and redundant in the room, a nothing whose services might easily be dispensed with; initials on a piece of paper, the passing down of a judgment—how easy it would be for them to remove him. He wanted to say that she was very old, that her heart was tired and strained, that no more control was needed—but he fell into a silence.

"Her family in Israel," Koprow said. "It would be a simple matter, for instance, to have them . . . watched. Wouldn't it? Wouldn't it be simple, Professor?"

"Yes," Andreyev said. The shadow of the gun. Dear God. He had seen her beloved snapshots.

Koprow was silent for a time. He tapped his index finger upon the table and appeared to be gazing at the illustrations on the walls.

"I will recommend further control of the woman by means of her family," Koprow said. His words came now in short, stabbing sequences. "And I will also recommend—" and here he paused, letting his presence sink through the room, "—the possibility of a further experiment with Mrs. Blum."

Andreyev looked at Sememko. The Politician was picking his teeth absentmindedly, as if what was being discussed here were an agricultural plan, perhaps the introduction of a new rotation of crops, perhaps the feasibility of an increase in tractor production—but it was all one and the same thing, wasn't it? It was all a part of technology and its functions, material or immaterial; what did it matter in the long term?

He closed his folder, pressed his fingers to his eyes, and let the room dwindle to nothing in his brief self-imposed blindness.

**2.**

Rayner found something faintly enjoyable in listening to Haffner as he tried, in his circumspect way, to instill some sense of diplomatic etiquette into the Vice President. Lindholm, you could see, had his head inclined as if he were really listening, but some absence of light in his eyes suggested he was elsewhere—planning, calculating, thinking other things. The old prairie dog, Rayner thought. You can't teach him to jump through new hoops at this stage of the game.

They were sitting in the dining room of the hotel. Breakfast had just been eaten—rather tasteless eggs, dark bread, lukewarm coffee; Rayner surveyed the ruins of the meal. Four Secret Service men sat at the next table, eating with a kind of purposeful silence as if they suspected a Communist plot involving cyanide in the water pitcher. It was odd, he thought, how they never seemed to communicate with one another, how strangely introverted they were in their vigilance. Who could tell? Maybe they had developed a sophisticated means of communicating through head movements, gestures, a form of secretive freemasonry.

The dining room was otherwise empty. Lindholm's presence had obliged the management to feed its less illustrious guests elsewhere. There were at least sixty empty tables set for diners who would not show up. Spooky, Rayner thought—all that linen, all those napkins, knives and forks. A banquet for ghosts.

Lindholm was rubbing his jaw, squinting now at Haffner. Rayner knew the expression: *You can't teach your grandmother how to suck eggs, sonny.* Haffner droned somewhat, slipping at times into a kind of silence that suggested his uncertainty, how far he could go in offering a cram course in diplomacy to the Vice President.

"I don't want you to take this all the wrong way, sir," Haffner said. "I just don't think it advisable to sound off—"

"Sound off?" Lindholm looked at Rayner, half smiling. It was a political expression: he met his hecklers with that same quizzical look. "Was I sounding off, Ricky?"

Ricky, Rayner thought. He didn't much care for the folksy abbreviation. "I think Stewart's trying to tell you that it doesn't do much good to give the Soviets the impression that you and the President are in disagreement over certain policies."

Lindholm rubbed his eyelids. "You boys are pretty mad at me, huh?"

Rayner looked across the table at Haffner, who, squirming, raised a crumbling piece of dark bread to his mouth and chewed on it absently.

"I been kicking around politics a long time," Lindholm said. "Local politics. State Senate. The Congress of the United States. You boys know that. Hell. I never expected to be the Vice President."

What's coming? Rayner wondered. Was there going to be an edited version of the fable? Poor boy makes good? Land of opportunity and you don't need no silver spoon in your mouth?

"When I was offered the slot, hell, I took it." Lindholm stared at them in turn, as if he expected a response, as if this statement was an accusation: You'd have done the same, wouldn't you? "I kicked around long enough to know that it's a bunch of bull no matter what way you cut it. A Veep is a walking ceremony, that's all. He does nothing and he's expected to do nothing. But it doesn't mean that Mallory's got a goddamn dog collar around my throat and that when he says roll over, Rover, I goddam roll over."

Rayner listened to the small man's voice rise, surprised a little by the hint of passion in the tone. He saw Lindholm's hand settle momentarily on Haffner's wrist; he saw Haffner look as if he had never had human contact before.

"So you boys get a little hot under the collar. That's nothing. You really think the Russkis give a monkey's turd about what I say? They're being polite. They know I can say what I like and it doesn't change a goddam thing. Because *they* know something you don't seem to know. I'm only the Vice President—which makes me approximately nothing."

The Vice President, Rayner thought. A heartbeat away.

"I got one thing Mallory needs," Lindholm said. "I can turn out a couple of million voters for him. And that makes a difference—because these are people that would sooner vote the straight Republican ticket than put their John Hancocks to any Eastern liberal. Are you boys with me?"

Haffner swallowed his dry bread. "I appreciate the frankness, Mr. Vice President. But at the same time, I don't think—"

"At the same time crap," Lindholm said, and started to rise from the table. "I may have one of the most vacuous jobs in the goddam world, Haffner. But I don't need to bite my tongue when I feel I got something to say. And that's something. That's *really* something."

The Vice President dropped his napkin on the table and walked away, surrounded at once by the Secret Service men. Rayner watched them sweep out of the dining room, an incongruous vision: the orangutans crowding the small prairie animal.

Haffner sighed. "I tried," he said.

"I heard you," said Rayner. He looked at his watch. There was to be a tour of some new automobile plant later—strictly Intourist stuff—and a half-finished letter lay upstairs in his room, a letter to John. He stood up. There was still time to finish it before he had to run the gamut of spot welders and paint sprayers and inspectors—and listen to the standard speeches concerning Soviet greatness. And never a word about Siberia.

## 3.

Domareski. Something had happened to Domareski. She wasn't sure. A dream? Not a dream? She woke, panicked. A strange room, a hospital room, a slatted blind hanging at the window, flowers in a white china vase. The room was overheated; a dense warmth. Flowers. They would die in this heat, wilt and wither and shake their petals loose. . . . She sat up. Domareski. Why isn't he here? Why isn't he here with me now? But something had gone wrong, something she didn't want to think about now, an aspect of herself she wanted to relegate to a place where it wouldn't have to be dealt with. But it came back. *There was snow. He had fallen in the snow. No, not fallen.* But he was dead, dead. . . .

And then she noticed the man, Sememko, who was sitting in a chair at the foot of her bed. Sweating, mopping his forehead with a large handkerchief, Sememko. Then it seemed to her that she lost her hold on things, that all manner of perceptions collided as if there were some terrible accident of awareness, a short circuit of mind, a jumble of unclear images. Sememko mopping his brow, the Physician falling falling falling into the snowbank, Aaron speaking to her —*a witch? Is that what it feels like to be you? Is that what you are?* There was pain now too, coursing upward along the backs of her hands, rising into her arms; and her heart—an insane rhythm of heart as if it might explode in her chest, carry her away, carry her into death, into a place where the snapshots wouldn't matter, where nothing would exist, no family, nothing—

The man, Sememko, was saying something to her. Words, words—she couldn't get them straight. It was like the picture she had in her mind now of the

Physician, a cold picture, blurry. But worse—worse was the pain. Domareski knew. He knew how to stop the pain, didn't he? Where is he? Where?

What was this man saying to her?

Words. *The Israelis, well, of course*—

She looked at his face, at the fleshy tip of his nose and the enlarged pores. He is going to lie to me. I cannot believe anything he says to me.

Comrade Koprow himself, the man was saying.

No—she didn't want to hear about Koprow. Go back to what it was before, the Israelis. What was it about the Israelis? He was wiping his forehead again. Tell me, she thought. Tell me about my exit visa. Let me go. Let me leave. Put an end to this nightmare. Why had the Physician been killed?

Confused, she stared at the flowers. The man's voice went on, on and on; but he wasn't telling her what she needed to hear. Lies. Lies. When would they ever end?

Greatly impressed with your cooperation, he was telling her.

She wanted to cry now because of the pain she was feeling. A dryness clinging to the roof of her mouth, her swollen fingers covered with a cold sweat. The beat of her heart. Domareski. *Please!*

The man put his handkerchief away, smiled. Smiles. Expressions. Meaning nothing. Nothing at all. She closed her eyes. She tried to concentrate on what he was saying.

Your exit visa, of course—

She stared at him. As she did so, the door of the room opened. A woman came in. White uniform, dark hair held back severely. *Her.* It was her, the cold one, Andreyev's assistant, carrying a tray, a syringe, balls of cotton wool.

She watched the needle rise in the air, saw a faint

arching spray of colorless liquid, smelled disinfectant, something icy being applied to her arm—and then the needle. The needle sliced the skin, entered the vein. It hurt her. Domareski had never hurt her like this. Katya? Was that the name? The woman turned, saying nothing, left the room.

The bureaucracy affects us all, the man was saying. He laughed. He was its victim too. It affected him. Yes, paper work, more paper work, you know how these things are sometimes.

No, she thought. I don't know.

Comrade Koprow himself—*himself*—asked me to reassure you that it would be only a matter of a few days. A week at most.

A week?

Paper work, Mrs. Blum. Terrible. The Israelis are willing to have you, of course. It goes without saying. Paper work takes up so much time.

Lies, she thought. Lies. Why did she feel such a terrible exhaustion now? Why did she feel as if she were floating through some warm, viscous substance? It was hard, hard to concentrate, the man kept slipping in and out of her perceptions.

Please. Please. The visa. I ask for nothing else.

We understand. Family. We understand the importance of family. How much the reunion means to you. We understand all this.

He was smiling again, watching her, smiling, drifting in and out of her vision. She wanted suddenly to hurt him, to enter him and bring him pain. Paper work? Why should it be so much trouble? A rubber stamp? Why?

*Further cooperation.*

There. There it was. She caught it, slippery as it was. She caught it. There was more. She couldn't keep it straight, couldn't concentrate. Dear God, dear God, how much more could she give them?

Your family is well, I assure you, he was saying. No harm will come to them, I can promise you that.

She fought to keep her eyes open. What was he saying? What did he mean—no harm? Were they in some kind of danger? She wanted to sit upright, couldn't, kept feeling herself slip, the room darkening around her, the flowers dying by the bedside. What is he telling me about my family?

Comrade Koprow himself has guaranteed their safety, he was telling her. His word counts for a great deal. Believe me. No harm will come to them.

Silence. But not silence. She could hear faint sounds, nothing she could recognize, just faint indeterminate sounds traveling across dreadful distances to her. My family. My family, she thought. No harm will come to them.

Further cooperation, that's all.

No. No.

A small matter, nothing more.

She was caught in the drifts, she was floating—but it was through warm water now, it was easy, easy, a pleasant feeling.

We'll talk later, he said. When you're feeling strong.

Did she hear him go from the room? Something? Had he said, Here, this letter just arrived from your son in Tel Aviv? Read it when you feel more strong? Or was this another aspect of how the dream went? She didn't know. Had he laid an airmail envelope on the bedside table? Aaron. She tried to open her eyes to see. Further cooperation. A small matter. No harm will come to your family, you may be sure. The children, the grandchildren she had never seen, would run to her. And she would lose herself in the sweetness of it, she would surrender herself to loving, to what loving meant.

And now she was thinking of Stanislav, of the moment of his birth, feeling a storm within herself, a burning heat between her thighs and a sense that giving birth to this child might cause her to break apart, to splinter. And she was remembering Aaron, how proud Aaron had been; perfumes—broken pine cones, the feline scent of crushed juniper: Aaron walking in the woods with the small boy, hands held, that special link of love, that private thing between father and son that a mother could only watch from the outside. But there was joy, it was joy she remembered, it was joy she wanted all over again.

Aaron. Oh, God, not Aaron. *A witch? Are you some kind of freak? Is that what I'm married to?* Forget, forget, you are too old now to remember black things, too old to bring back the picture, the terrible terrible picture. But there it was and she saw it, there it was, locked behind her closed eyelids, penetrating even the sweet moment of dreaming love and joy, the picture—the barn behind the house. Aaron? Aaron? Where are you? The barn. No. But you shouldn't go in there where it's dark and smells of rotted hay and the excrement of horses you shouldn't go inside the barn because the picture lay there and you didn't need to see him you didn't need to see Aaron you didn't need to remember how Aaron had hung—up in the air—just hanging and limp and his body motionless and the shadow of a rope. . . . *A witch? A freak?* You saw the open eyes, the open lips, the dead limpness of the body as it hung from rope, how the rope had been tethered to some high dark beam, a chair kicked away; a man hanging there. Nonono.

A small matter. Was that what the man had said?

A small matter. There was no price you could fix to the value of love.

## 4.

It was falsely rumored of Comrade Koprow that he had single-handedly destroyed a German armored column during its advance on Kalinin—a rumor he did nothing to discourage but much to promote; courage, after all, was as much a weapon as terror. Now, close to midnight, he sat in the office of Maksymovich. They were allies of old, twins of the Revolution; between them they enjoyed the notion that they kept ancient fires burning. That neither entirely trusted the other was a fact both accepted; even between allies there had to be a certain caution, a certain circumspection.

Koprow, struggling with a nicotine habit, took a pack of imported English mints, Polos, from his pocket and broke open the green wrapper. He watched Maksymovich rise from behind his ornate desk and cross the rug—an elaborate fringed thing, the gift of some obscure sheik who had recently been assassinated in a bloody uprising supported by Soviet guns. He stood at the window, his back to Koprow, and for a moment he was silent.

"I'm too old to believe in fairy tales," he said after a time. "This Blum woman—she sounds almost too good to be true."

Koprow caught himself in the act of pushing the tip of his tongue through the hole in his white mint. It irritated him. He longed for a cigarette. He stuffed his hands in his pockets. "The woman's an aberration. A freak of nature. Those are facts. I admit it sounds farfetched but the point is—the only point is that she exists."

Maksymovich turned around. His little half-moon glasses slipped and he pushed them, rather delicately, back up his nose. "She exists. A natural Soviet resource. Like Siberian oil?"

"As you say."

Maksymovich returned to his desk and opened a folder that was marked *PRIORITY CONFIDENTIAL.* He had read it; he had read it so many times he knew it by heart. He didn't particularly want to believe it. But there it was. He closed the folder, laying the palm of his hand flat against it.

"She must never be allowed to leave for Israel," he said.

"Obviously," said Koprow.

"Naturally, too, I would like to see some further evidence of her abilities—"

"She has already been told that further cooperation will be needed." Koprow cracked the mint at the back of his mouth.

Maksymovich glanced at Koprow a moment. Then he sat down, gazing at the folder. He was thinking of Lindholm: there was no fool like an old fool. Mallory—well, Mallory was a different proposition. He sighed, trying to put the contents of the folder from his mind. Even from normally impeccable sources some things were not entirely believable.

"What about the people around her?" he asked.

"Andreyev is a coward," Koprow said, in a manner that suggested he had probed Andreyev's soul only to find, in its darkest recesses, a fatal structural weakness. "And his assistant—you don't need to have any worries over her." He inscribed a circle in the air with his hands, a circle of containment, of control.

Maksymovich nodded. He was beset by a sudden

restlessness, a need for action: sitting behind a desk, signing letters, looking over projects—all this was a bog of paper work and he loathed it. He removed his glasses and held them away from his face at arm's length—distastefully, as if they reminded him of infirmity and thus of his own mortality.

"In the matter of control—" he began to say.

But Koprow interrupted him. "I don't think that should concern us. She believes her son and his family might be in danger if she fails to cooperate."

"You're sure she believes that? You're positive?"

Koprow stood up, nodding his head, smiling a little. "I'm sure. She *wants* to believe it. That's the important thing."

Maksymovich looked doubtful a moment. "You're sure that nobody *around* her knows the truth?"

Koprow looked toward the window, mentally contrasting the size of this office with his own. He did not like the comparison at all. "I've taken every precaution. The letters are forged and mailed by an operative in Tel Aviv. A Jew, curiously. The most recent photographs were taken in a studio here in Moscow, using models. Naturally, they're not very *distinct* pictures, but they'll pass. How can I let this slip? We need every hold on her that we can get. How can I tell her that her family was killed by Arabs? Damned Arabs." He paused, thinking of the pictures he had seen of the bombed bus, the corpses. "How can I take away her *only* reason for living?"

Maksymovich smiled. "You sound quite humanitarian, Comrade. Now it's a question of deciding her next test?" He found himself gazing down at the folder again. All things were possible, he thought. If she were really good: *really* good. One small test could lead to something else. He looked at Koprow. "I think I know of something," he said. "Not altogether pleasant—but some things never really are."

**5.**

In the hospital room Andreyev thought: How frail she looks, how tired—and he wondered what life was left to her. She was sitting upright, her eyes glazed, her awareness shot. She seemed at times not to recognize him. He watched her, conscious of Katya standing at the foot of the bed—Katya in stark white clinical garb, her face drawn and severe, her mouth a single straight line that might have been created by stitching her two thin lips together.

Andreyev drew his chair closer to the bed. "Mrs. Blum?"

She looked at him. He thought: She sees through me, straight through me. He struggled with a terrible longing to get up, walk from the room, leave all this behind—but he didn't move: it was as if the presence of Katya, the whiteness of her clothing were meant to remind him of Domareski. Fear, he thought. You live with it. It becomes a daily staple. There are no days without fear. You do what you have to do. Other people define your existence in their terms. Identity, privacy, choice: all these become lost luxuries.

"Mrs. Blum—do you understand what I asked?"

Katya moved. Behind her, the door of the room opened. Turning, glancing, Andreyev saw the KGB man who had been at the Ussuri. And the fear heightened in him. Refuse, he thought. Find it in yourself to refuse. Then, despite himself, despite the wretchedness he felt, he heard himself say, "Your family, Mrs. Blum. Think about them."

Something flickered in her eyes. A brief light, then it was extinguished. Where is she? he wondered. What lies inside that head? Ashamed, he found he could no longer look at her. He glanced at the bedside table, at a pale blue airmail envelope. It had been torn open. *The kids are doing terrific. We can hardly wait to see you. The exit visa is sure to come through any day.* Get out, he thought. Walk away from this.

"Do you understand what I'm asking you to do?" he said.

She looked at him—and what he saw in her eyes was an expression of hatred, something so deep, so forceful, as to be impenetrable.

He was sweating, sweating and cold. "Do you understand, Mrs. Blum?"

She opened her mouth, whispered. He could barely hear her. "Yes," she said. "Yes. I understand."

The KGB man coughed in the background. Katya came around the side of the bed. Andreyev closed his eyes, as if this darkness might be enough for him to hide in. But you can't hide, he thought. There isn't a hiding place. There isn't a place left for you, Andreyev. If you ever had a soul, you long since bartered it away. And in return for what? Exactly what?

He opened his eyes. He saw her clenched hands. And it was clear to him that wherever she was, wherever she might be, she was no longer in this room.

*6.*

Rayner listened to Isobel, who, having kicked off her shoes in the manner of one both bored and exhausted, lay face down on the bed.

"If I have to tour another goddam factory," she said, "I swear I'll throw up."

Rayner stood in the open bathroom doorway and watched her. "They're very proud of their factories," he said. "You underestimate them. Some countries wouldn't have the simple decency to show you the latest in car manufacturing, would they?"

"Ha funny," she said. "But not funny at all. How much longer do we have to stay?"

"Dare I remind you—without it causing a war— that you *wanted* to make this trip?"

She didn't answer him. She turned her face away, sighing as if sighing were a last line of defense, a final argument. He stared at her. She had undone her blouse, unzipped her skirt. She doesn't know what she does to me, he thought. She doesn't quite appreciate how she contributes to my sexual fantasies. The dear lady. He crossed the room and sat on the edge of the bed, holding her hand. He knew her look: *I'm not in the mood. Tough shit.* Of course, he thought, another kind of person would not take that crap lying down. Another kind of man would, so to speak, grip the reins and give them something of a tug. He felt tired all at once and lay down beside her. She turned her face away from him. He looked at the curve of her hip, the undone zipper, the shape of buttock. This will be the death of me yet, he thought. In my sweetest, darkest dreams, she comes to me with insatiable lust—

He watched her blindly stub out her cigarette. A fragment of red ash floated to the floor, went out. He closed his eyes. He had something of a headache suddenly.

Isobel turned to him. "You didn't answer me. How much longer before we go home?"

Curious, he thought—he knew the answer to the question very well, he knew the itinerary by heart, he had even planned much of it, but it had slipped his mind. Sleep, he thought. Sleep and away—and wake refreshed. He sat up.

"Richard?" she said.

He moved toward the bathroom. "I need aspirin," he said.

"Look in the plastic bag," she said.

He turned halfway across the floor and stared at her; and he had the strangest feeling—it was as if he didn't recognize her, as if he had never seen her before in all his life.

She was sitting upright, watching him oddly. "Are you okay?" she said.

"What plastic bag?" he asked.

"Richard—"

"Did you say a plastic bag?"

She rose from the bed. "Look. You lie down. I'll get them for you. Okay? I think maybe you've got a bad case of the Red equivalent of Montezuma's Revenge."

He saw her come toward him. She was out of focus, like a picture badly taken. I need to sleep, he thought. More than anything. He felt drained, exhausted, his limbs seemingly incapable of supporting him.

"Go on. Lie down. I'll get the aspirin."

He saw himself move toward the bed—a strange view, a perspective of himself from a point overhead. *Do it. You know what you have to do.*

"What did you say?" he asked.

"I said I'd fetch the aspirin. Oh, for God's sake—is something wrong with you?"

"Wrong?"

He stared at the darkened window. The night was filled with lights, a city of lights. *You know. You know. Don't you know.* He sat on the bed. Now, he thought, concentrate on something, anything, the sound of Isobel in the bathroom, something like that, the sound of the plastic bag being opened, aspirin rattling in a bottle—*you can't hold off forever, you know it.* He closed his eyes. And something touched him—a sense of the most profound sadness he had ever felt in all his life. He was tense, his heart ached, he had the sudden belief that no matter what you did, no matter how hard you tried and struggled, life wasn't worth living.

"Richard? Richard? Tell me what it is."

A woman was walking across the floor toward him. She was carrying a glass of water in one hand. He had never seen her in his life. Who was she? Who was this stranger? He said something to her without knowing what. His language made no sense. Noises, nothing else.

"Richard, for Christ's sake!"

The woman was crying. Her mouth was slack and formless, tears welled up in her eyes—all this grief, and for what purpose? To what end? Concentrate, concentr—

The woman was holding him by the arm. He swung around, thrusting her aside, seeing the water spill, the glass break. Then he was moving across the room, moving and moving, barely conscious of where he was going or what he intended to do, just moving, his limbs weak, moving toward the darkened window. Isobel, he thought. *Isobel!*

There was an upward draft of cold air, the jagged

shards of broken glass, a nightmare of dropping and dropping and turning and twisting as he dropped. And from behind him, from somewhere behind him, even as he felt his heart sink like some heavy dead creature through black water, the sound of a woman's distant screaming.

## 7.

Even though he had not wanted to look at the folder again, even if he felt that he might simply go home, sleep, rise the following morning, and find solutions to all his problems, Maksymovich removed the sheets of paper and held them directly under the glow of his desk lamp. They had been examined. The signature had been scrutinized. And all the experts agreed: these were photocopies of genuine documents. He spread the sheets, rubbed his eyes, sat down. He looked at his watch, an expensive gift that had been brought to him by Lindholm. It was now just after three. When would he ever get to bed? And then there was this Blum woman to think about—and sometimes it seemed that his problems were endless.

He read the sheets. He walked around the room. He returned to his desk. He read them again.

## CONFIDENTIAL

In accordance with intelligence reports received over the past several months, it is now an established fact that in certain countries of the Eastern bloc—specifically in the territories formerly known as Latvia, Estonia, and Lithuania—there exist highly organized groups of anti-Soviet dissidents. Similar groups are known to exist in Bulgaria, Hungary, and Czechoslovakia.

Maksymovich closed his eyes. You grow old—in the old days you had the eyesight of a marksman. Now you can barely read for more than a few minutes at a time without pain in the sockets. He yawned. Groups of highly organized dissidents. That wasn't what troubled him. There would always be these malcontents, no matter how many of them you could round up.

It will be the continuing policy of this administration to assist the development and growth of these groups, specifically in the areas of communications and the dissemination of ideas. Accordingly, through the normal channels of the intelligence community, these groups will be given every possible means of technological assistance and cooperation. These will include electronic technology, training in the use of such equipment, the availability of literature, and any other such means that may be advisable in the propagation of anti-Soviet information.

The use of military assistance, the provision of weapons, is presently not under consideration until such times as the situation may warrant that form of cooperation.

Anti-Soviet information, Maksymovich thought. Meaning, of course, democratic propaganda. All the world's a battlefield of ideologies. The use of military assistance, the provision of weapons—well, naturally, all that would be quite without point. A crateful of M-16s to a group of Bulgar madmen would hardly make a dent. No, weapons did not worry Maksy-movich. What troubled him was something he always had problems in convincing other members of the Supreme Soviet to accept—that there were times when no amount of artillery could halt the movement of ideas; and by ideas Maksymovich meant dissidence. You had only to point to Soviet history itself to emphasize the fact: an idea strong enough can overcome any amount of weaponry.

His telephone was ringing. For a moment he hesitated to pick it up. The sheets of photocopies still held his attention. Could they really be genuine? He reached for the receiver. It was Koprow.

It had gone well. It had gone without a hitch. Maksymovich hung up the telephone. He picked up a pencil and began doodling his characteristic interlocking circles. Ideas, he thought. Was there anything more terrifying, more threatening, than an idea that flamed the imagination, that spread in a fashion suggestive of wildfire through human minds? that brought in its destructive path foolish notions of liberty, of freedom, of justice? His friends in the Supreme Soviet should be less afraid of ballistic missiles, warheads, nuclear submarines than of democratic notions.

He stood now, staring at a wall map of Eastern Europe. The problem with ideologies was how they proliferated: the more they promised, the quicker the proliferation. And what did all these Western ideals add up to? Dreams, dreams in which flashy objects glittered and beckoned, dreams of gadgets, of clothing, of art: and that was where the danger lay—in that illusion, so brilliantly fostered in the West, of freedom of choice. He looked at the map and thought of how only a month ago a group of so-called freedom fighters—riffraff—had been captured in the countryside around Vilna; radio transmitters, pamphlets, a handful of Czech guns. But the equipment had been American. Three weeks before that a renegade radio station, broadcasting out of Kuusamo, in Finland, had been seized and shut down. And during the past autumn no less than twenty different radical groups, ranging in size from a dozen to a hundred or more, had been arrested in places as far apart as Riga and Odessa and Brest. Ideas—a warfare of ideas.

He turned from the map, sat at his desk, picked up his pencil again. The absentmindedly drawn circles became tighter, denser. He thought of Kimball Lindholm: now there was one man with some very *safe* ideas.

Kimball Lindholm.

Mrs. Blum.

The circles grew smaller on the sheet of paper. He gazed at the photocopies in front of him. That signature—that strong, dark signature created by a hand of considerable force and willpower. *Patrick J. Mallory, President of the United States of America.*

So, Maksymovich thought. Patrick J. Mallory was supporting a guerrilla warfare of ideologies with all the technological assistance, all the avenues of intelligence operations he could muster. So. Maksymovich closed the folder, locked it in his desk, switched off the lamp, and stood for a moment in the darkened office. A guerrilla warfare designed to undermine the movement of revolution. So. But what Patrick J. Mallory did not have was Mrs. Blum.

# PART II

## February-March

All things cut an umbilical cord only to clutch a breast.

—CHARLES FORT, *The Book of the Damned*

# 1

It was raining in Grosvenor Square as John Rayner stepped out of the taxi and went up the Embassy steps, passing the uniformed Marine guard, passing the lines of people waiting to the left of the entrance for temporary visas, ignoring those who sat, with what seemed endless patience compounded out of hope and desperation, to the right, in that area where applications for permanent residency were processed. He undid the buttons of his wet raincoat and went inside the elevator, impatiently tapping his fingers against the wall, impatiently watching the numbers light and change. He got out on the third floor and went quickly along the corridor to Gull's office, barely glancing at the girl who sat behind the IBM. He went through to the inner office without waiting, without knocking.

Gull rose from behind his desk at once, his small white hand extended. Rayner took it, surprised by its warmth, for somehow he had expected the clasp to be cold. Gull watched him for a time with the kind of look reserved for convalescents. Concern, a mild anxiety, a wariness perhaps. Rayner took off his raincoat and dropped it across the back of a chair. The office was stuffy, overheated: those double-glazed windows trapped everything. After a moment, Gull sat down, took a pack of Players from his drawer, opened it, and then apparently changed his mind about smoking.

"Trying to kick it. Cold turkey," Gull said.

Making small talk, Rayner thought. Nobody knows how to deal with The Thing—like a plague, like something that might once quaintly have been called a social disease. It was present; but nobody wanted it around. Momentarily, Rayner stared at Gull. He had the face of a superannuated astronaut, all crisp bone and tight smooth skin, the hair cut close into the skull.

"It's tough," Gull said.

What was he referring to? Rayner wondered. Cigarettes or The Thing? The drawer was slammed, nervously opened, then slammed again. Christ, Rayner thought. Let him say he's sorry, sad, let him say, *If there's anything I can do,* and get it over with. Rayner looked at the window, at the rain, at how the wind blew the rain in zigzagging lines across the back streets of Mayfair: Little America. He shut his eyes a moment, remembering Isobel's face, remembering standing beside her in that awful chilling silence at Heathrow. For the first time in his life, Rayner had thought: She's human, she's burning up inside, she's being eaten away. They had talked. She had caught the Pan Am flight. Home to Washington, home to the empty house, the silences that would not be alleviated by a Government pension. Goddam—he was angry, an anger he didn't know how to spend, like having useless currency in a foreign country. Go home, he thought. Punch a hole through the wall or something.

"I could arrange leave, John," Gull said.

Rayner undid the stifling knot of his tie, opened the top button of his shirt. He would choke if he had to sit here for too long.

"No sweat," Gull said. "Just say the word and I'll push the old paper work through today. I know Himself will be only too glad to sign. Compassionate leave."

Compassionate? Himself, the Ambassador, what the fuck did he care? There was that anger again and it wasn't something he was accustomed to—because he liked to think he was fairly easygoing, didn't yield to stresses, that he wasn't one of your coronary eclipse types. Slow and nice and easy—but, Christ, this wasted sense of rage.

"Easy to do. Say the word." Gull picked up his pen, a fat and ridiculously expensive Meisterstuck, and tapped it on the surface of the empty blotter.

I make him uneasy, Rayner thought. I drag my dead brother around with me. I bring my anger and unhappiness into the lives of other people. Jesus, I should go home and swallow Mandrax and wake when all this grief and rage is gone and the system has found its own balance.

"I don't think I want any leave just yet," Rayner said. Why not? Work. Bury yourself in an avalanche of work. Let the whole goddam landslide cover you.

George Gull shrugged. "I understand, John."

"What do you understand?" Rayner heard himself ask. But it wasn't a question, it was a dog barking—and poor old Gull was put in a bad spot.

"I understand, well, you know, life goes on." Gull smiled in a funereal way. It was meant to be sympathetic, a way of saying, *Look, John, I've been there, I've been through this;* instead, it struck Rayner as ghoulish, the wax grin of the undertaker, the false solace of those entrepreneurs who, with their embalming fluids and mahogany caskets, profit from death. Poor Gull: there wasn't anything to say.

"What's your casework like right now?" Gull's voice, becoming suddenly brisk, seemed to reach Rayner from a far distance.

"Routine," Rayner said.

Gull got up. He stepped around the desk and laid his hand on Rayner's shoulder. "Look, John. What the fuck can I say?"

Rayner stared down at the floor, at the royal-blue rug that looked as if it had never been stepped upon. His eyes watered. Goddam. Sitting here in front of Gull and crying like a moron. What was this—this falling apart? He shut his eyes, fumbled around for a handkerchief in his jacket, blew his nose.

"Okay," Gull was saying. "It's okay."

Yeah, Rayner thought. It's okay, everything is okay. He reached for his damp raincoat and pulled it toward him.

"Go home, John. Come in tomorrow if it feels comfortable. But go home."

Rayner stood up—and what he was thinking of again was how Isobel had looked in the Departures Lounge at Heathrow, how that pale beauty, which had so besotted Richard and which Rayner had always thought of as being as lifeless as immaculate china, how that beauty had become a wasted thing, a ruin. And none of it, none of what she had said, made any goddam sense. It was gibberish, irrational. A man complains of a headache one moment, then the next—

He let George Gull help him into the raincoat. They shook hands again.

"Call me in the morning," Gull said. "If it feels right."

Outside, crossing Grosvenor Square, walking quickly toward Hill Street in the rain, Rayner thought:

If it feels right. If it feels right. He imagined Isobel in the clouds, jet streams across the Atlantic, her white face pressed to the window. Go home, he thought. But that was the last place he needed right at this moment in his life.

## 2.

By the time the early darkness had come he had found his way into Soho. The night was sodden, ripping apart all around him like wet paper. Being faintly drunk was no antidote. Along the black pavements lay the reflected lights of bars, strip joints, restaurants. He walked down Brewer Street, crossed Greek Street, moved in the direction of Soho Square. A drunk wandered in front of him, mumbled something unintelligible, then hurried on. Somewhere around here, Rayner thought—somewhere around here; and he found himself crossing Oxford Street against the traffic. Somewhere around here there was a bar where he might find Dubbs, if there was any point in finding Dubbs right now. He looked at his wrist and realized he must have left his watch someplace. Christ—how had he passed the afternoon? There was a memory of glistening tiles, a cistern flushing, some inebriated Scotsman trying to impress upon him the fact that there was some virtue in being a Celt—but it was disjointed, pointless. He had withdrawn into a vague alcoholic blur.

Now he wanted to see Dubbs, if only he could find the place. Tottenham Court Road. He walked until he came to the corner of Goodge Street, where he paused, imagining he could feel the reverberations of an underground train rolling beneath him. Goodge

Street, darkness. Dubbs would be fine consolation. He went inside the first bar he came to, passing unsteadily through the door, crossing the floor, conscious of men throwing darts, of two young guys dressed like rock stars slumming, of a clutch of secretaries laughing in a corner booth. He reached the bar and was about to order a drink, anything, when he felt Dubbs alongside him and he turned, turned a little too quickly, colliding with the Scotch that Dubbs held in his hand.

"My dear Rayner," Dubbs said. "I had an intuition, call it what you will, that I would be seeing you this very night. This very wet and miserable night."

Rayner had to work to bring Dubbs into focus. A rotund little man with the face of a red cherub. Black coat, astrakhan collar, three-piece suit—only the vest; the *waistcoat,* was a different color. Camel's hair. Black suit. There had been times when Dubbs reminded Rayner of something that had been ejected from heaven, a tiny angel evicted after an altercation with whoever manned the pearly gates. But Dubbs— Dubbs would not last long in heaven. There would be a clash of some egotistical kind between himself and God.

Dubbs put his hand on Rayner's sleeve. "You're terribly wet, John. I had a friend once who fell asleep on a park bench, slept through a rainstorm, and woke up with awful pneumonia. Have you been lying on park benches?"

Rayner turned to look at the barman, making a gesture with his hand that was either ignored or overlooked. And he was angry again, angry with everything: a feeling that focused on the manner of the barman.

"How the fuck do you get a drink round here?" he said.

Smiling, raising one eyebrow as if to scrutinize a specimen, Dubbs said, "Annoyance gets you nothing with a fellow like that. Uncouth type. Works better if you wave a fistful of money around. Here. Let me do it."

Dubbs pressed himself against the bar, ordered two Scotches, gathered up his change slowly. He looked around the room and nodded in the direction of an empty table. "Shall we?"

Something in the way Dubbs walked. How did you get to move like that? He appeared to glide, as if he were propelled forward on casters. Rayner followed him, conscious of his own clumsiness, his own awkward physical self. Drunk, he thought. And he tried to remember why, why he had needed to find Dubbs, what it was that had driven him through the rainy night. He sat down facing the other man, conscious of Dubbs waiting, waiting for something to be said. The silence all at once unnerved him; and it seemed to him that his memory, his recall, had gone off the rails somewhere along the way.

Dubbs lit a cigarette, a cocktail Sobranie. Pink with a gold tip, lit with great flourish from a Dunhill lighter. Dubbs, who seemed to find prolonged silences abhorrent vacuums, said, "Do Americans still say, Spill the beans, kid?"

Rayner closed his eyes, trying to concentrate.

"You've had too much, my dear," said Dubbs. "Methinks a further ingestion of usquebaugh would totally upset your already delicate mechanisms."

Isobel, Rayner thought. A whispered conversation in the Departures Lounge. But it makes no sense. It made no sense then, even less now. He squinted at Dubbs, who was flicking a flake of ash from his astrakhan collar.

"Well? Are there beans to be spilled, John?"

"Don't you know, Dubbs? Didn't you hear about it?"

The little man looked puzzled. "Crosswords and cryptograms and other such puzzles have always struck me as a profound waste of time, my dear. Speak to me."

"Richard—"

Dubbs inclined his head and momentarily Rayner had the feeling that all the superficial theatricality was laid back, that something menacing was barely visible beneath the surface. Richard. Yes, Richard.

"Your brother?" Dubbs said.

"Not a suicidal type, not Richard—"

"Straight, John. I need to hear things straight."

"Richard is dead."

Dubbs looked into his Scotch a moment, then raised his face and said, "How?"

"How?" Rayner turned, stared at the barman, watching him polish glasses with a grubby towel. Go home, he thought. Punch a hole through the wall, punch something out of that barman's face—an exercise in futility, that was the bottom line. How had Richard died? How?

Dubbs tugged at the sleeve of his raincoat. "Richard," he said. "You were telling me about Richard."

Rayner reached for his glass, spilled it, watched the whiskey soak through the paper napkin.

"John," Dubbs said. *"Please."*

"You don't expect to believe it, Dubbs. You *won't* believe it. He killed himself."

"How? How did he do that?"

"He jumped, Dubbs. Out of a fucking window."

What else was there to tell? What else was there to say? Moscow, Lindholm's delegation, suicide, a sadly beautiful widow—what for Christ's sake was there left to add to that? He looked at Dubbs as if he might find there, in that round red face, in those dark-blue eyes, a consolation, an explanation—but you chase reasons as prospectors become crazed in deserts, wild obsessions in dark places, and you go on digging regardless. That was the way madness lay; that was Whacko Avenue. Dubbs said nothing for a time, smoked another of his strange cigarettes, drained his drink, crumpled a strand of cellophane.

"You remember Richard, don't you?"

"Yes," said Dubbs. "I remember him well."

"Not the type, Dubbs. Not the type to kill himself. Right? *Right?*"

"I don't know the answer to that, John," Dubbs said.

"Career going along at your average pace. Marriage—tolerable, bearable, if not exactly a hothouse of sexual experiment. Now where, you tell me where, Dubbs, in the humdrum bits and pieces of his life is the reason for jumping, *jumping,* Jesus Christ, out of a fucking window!"

Dubbs did up the buttons of his coat, shivered as the door of the bar opened and a young couple came in. "John, I'm sorry about your brother. I'm really sorry. Let me drive you home."

Rayner felt a sudden weight descend on him, his head intolerably heavy, sleep coming on—sequences of shadows. He laid his face on the surface of the table. Dubbs shook him, helped him to stand, led him outside into the rain, where some strand of awareness came back. And he was remembering Isobel. *He looked as if he had never seen me before in his life. He just stared at me and said it wasn't worth going on. And then, then he went to the window, he opened it, then—* But this isn't Richard, he thought. Other men took their lives; not Richard. You could see Richard sink, slip into depressions, drop over the edge into despair, into the worst of times; and he would have gone to his physician because that was the kind of man he was. He would have gone to a doctor long before writing himself off. No, Rayner thought. None of this is Richard.

Dubbs was looking up and down the dark street. "Where did I leave my damned car?" he said. And then they were walking through the rain, Rayner's arm linked through Dubbs's. The car was a white Mini. Rayner slumped into the passenger seat, conscious of motion, of Dubbs changing gears.

Somewhere along the way, somewhere halfway up Baker Street, Dubbs said, "If he didn't take his own life, John, then you have to admit that something *very* curious is going on."

Curious? Rayner thought. Curiouser and curiouser: small lacquered Chinese boxes. What could be more curious than Richard falling?

Dubbs stopped at a red light and glanced at him. "His wife said he jumped, didn't she? Then either he really did take his own life or his wife is lying. And if you are quite unprepared to accept the former, what do you propose to do with the latter?"

No, Rayner thought. The brain couldn't cope. The terminals and the connections had been blitzed. He couldn't absorb Dubbs now, couldn't think his way clearly through Dubbs's logic. He blinked, staring out through the window. They had passed Lord's, heading for St. John's Wood. White houses in the rain. White houses and dark gardens.

Dubbs parked the Mini outside a Victorian house that had been butchered into a series of small apartments.

"Do you want me to come in with you, John? Would that help?"

"Tired," Rayner said. "Dead tired."

Dubbs patted the rim of the steering wheel. "Believe me when I say how sorry I am, John. Believe me." For a moment he was silent. Rayner could hear the rain on the roof of the small car. Dubbs appeared to rummage around for a cigarette, sighing when he failed to find one. "If you doubt this suicide, John, let me see what I can turn up tomorrow. Can I call you?"

Rayner looked toward the house, the dark windows. What could Dubbs turn up? What could Dubbs—grubbing around the undersides of groups of expatriate Poles, insane Latvians, Czech malcontents who cried into their beers—what could Dubbs turn up out of that collection of the disenchanted, the homeless, the betrayed?

Rayner fumbled with the handle, stepped out, then leaned back into the car and smiled at Dubbs. "Call me. Call me tomorrow. And thanks."

"Sleep, my dear," Dubbs said.

Rayner watched the white car drift down the street, then turned toward the house. He took his keys from his coat, dropped them in the shrubbery, padded around on hands and knees before he located them again. He opened the front door, stepped into the hallway. Goddam house, he thought. Dark little flats. Dreary cooking. He turned on the light switch and moved toward the stairs. He paused beside the table at the foot of the stairs. Mail. Letters, bills. He saw how the landlady had arranged them in tidy piles, one pile to each tenant. He picked up his own. Blearily, he flipped through it. Telephone company. Overdue library books. And a letter, in an airmail envelope, addressed to him in the handwriting of his dead brother.

**3.**

Ernest Dubbs, who lived in a basement flat in Fulham with a rather vicious parrot he had christened Rasputin, did not go immediately home after dropping Rayner off. Instead, he drove back by way of Lord's—thinking how glad he was that the wretched cricket season was months away, that one would not have to put up with the obnoxious English penchant for that slow and silly game in the meantime—and down Baker Street. He found a parking space in Manchester Square and sat for a moment in his silenced car, wondering if he should have put young Rayner to bed after all. Tucked him up tight, as it were: you could not predict the directions of grief with any accuracy. Sighing, he got out of his car and crossed the square, hurrying against the rain with his head slightly bent. Damnable weather. Ducks and drakes might find this to their liking, but not Dubbs, who was often beset by the notion that he had been born in quite the wrong country—that at heart he was a Mediterranean person: parasols on a white terrace, ice in the old Campari glass, a wedge of lemon, a slow sea falling on some stunning beach. So be it: he was stuck with a vengeant season and an accident of birth.

He took a key from his coat pocket and unlocked the door of a building, an old house stuck between a couple of the new plate-glass monstrosities. He stared absently at the brass plaque that bore the words THE MARLBOROUGH TITLE & TRUST COMPANY—all perfectly meaningless, of course. He entered, shut the door behind him, pretended he did not notice the smell of carbolic that hung in the air with the density of a heavy drapery. In the distance he could hear the rattle of metal—the janitor, Malcolm, mopping the tiled floors, dragging his old bucket behind him. Let us not have discussions with Malcolm this night, Dubbs thought. How are you? How's your cat? How's your parrot?

Dubbs moved to the stairs. He climbed, paused on the first landing, and saw Malcolm's shadow along the corridor. He went in the other direction, opening the door of his own office, turning on the lamp, seeing the giant shadows of his ferns loom suddenly upward against the pale-green walls. Dubbs did not care for this room. Too impersonal, too officious—but, God knows, you did what you could with what the Government gave you. He gazed at the ferns a moment. In good health, considering—and he went to his desk, unlocked it, removed a file, opened the file; no sooner had he begun to read than there was a light knock on his door and he thought: Malcolm, fucking Malcolm.

But when the door opened it was Evans who stood there.

"Burning the midnight oil?" Evans said.

What does it look like to you, my dear? Dubbs thought.

When they had been handing out cloaks and daggers, someone had quite forgotten to give Evans his cloak. He stood in the doorway, grinning stupidly. He gave Dubbs the odd feeling that he was not of this world, that he had simply dropped in from outer space to pass the time of day. What could you hope for anyway from somebody who *chose* to live in Esher? Dubbs shuddered: Evans had actually elected to buy a house out there. *There* was a good argument against free will.

"I'm on nights this month," said Evans, by way of explanation. "Manning the old wires."

"Ah," Dubbs said.

"Not much happening. Ha ha." Sometimes, as

if it were a form of punctuation, Evans would drop "Ha ha," quite without mirth, at the end of sentences.

Dubbs stared at the file in front of him.

"What's happening with you?" Evans asked.

Dubbs flapped a hand limply in the air, a gesture he knew would irritate Evans. Later, in his little house in Esher, Evans would say to his little wife, I'm sure he's queer, you know. Quite the poove.

"Oh," Evans said. "I just remembered."

"Remembered?" Dubbs stared at the other man. Those clothes—shapeless Burton suits that began to shine in the seat of the trousers before you could say Jack Straw. If Evans was an argument against freedom of the will, he was also a portable display of the banalities, the inadequacies, of English taste. Dubbs longed for sunlight all at once. Portofino. Sobranie cigarettes and a couple of fast Negronis. But here he was, stuck in a world of mild-and-bitters, chain-store clothing, little houses out in Esher.

Evans stepped farther into the room, his hands hanging at his sides as if he had forgotten them, left them behind in some other place. "I just remembered about Richard Rayner," he said. "It came over this afternoon."

Dubbs shut his eyes briefly.

"Isn't John Rayner your man over in Grosvenor Square?" Evans said.

Dubbs imagined he could hear glass breaking, things splintering, bulls rampant in china shops. He wished he had wings and could fly from the window out over Manchester Square; but where would you go in the rain?

"And Richard's the brother?" said Evans. He raised both eyebrows, waiting, still smiling.

Sometimes, Dubbs thought, bad news is the only pleasure in a person's life. Now Evans could say,

Sorry, I meant to say *was* the brother. Dead, don't you know? "I heard," Dubbs said.

"Oh."

"I heard he took his own life," Dubbs said. Took his own life. What an odd phrase that was. Took his own photograph. Took his own pulse. People were forever taking things that were their own.

"Ye-es," said Evans, fingering his necktie. It was Ardingly, Dubbs remembered. Those minor-public-school types still dreamed of Empire: it was something to do with education, he was sure. "Day before yesterday. Did you know that?"

"You know the time of death too?" Dubbs said, whistling in false surprise. He stared at the file in front of him, wishing Evans would disappear. The strange thing about Evans, though, was how he managed to linger without purpose—until eventually you forgot he was in the room. Dubbs flipped the pages of his file.

"Our man confirmed suicide," Evans said. "I daresay the Americans will ship the body out. They're awfully good at that kind of thing."

Sensitivity, Dubbs realized, was a gift. It was something you got at birth, something the Old Architect injected into your genes. Evans clearly had a severe *want* in that department. Ship the body back. What was it? Luggage? Bric-a-brac? Sign here, Mr. Customs Man: one dead item of flesh, formerly human? Irritated, Dubbs saw Evans prowl around the room.

Evans looked at the collar of the black coat. "I say, is that astrakhan?"

"And no mistake, my love," said Dubbs. "I use it when I haunt Shaftesbury Avenue. Draws attention to me, dear. You *know* how it is."

Evans smiled uncertainly. He lingered a few

more moments, apparently embarrassed. Then he turned and went back to the door. He made a little wave of his hand. "Back to the grind," he said.

Dubbs, stretching the palm of his hand out in front of him, blew a kiss across the room. "Sweet dreams, old chap," he said.

The door was closed quickly. Dubbs, sighing, gazed at his file, flicking the pages, wondering why they always seemed to have such impossible names—these people who somehow or other had contrived to find their way from the wilder shores of Europe to the sinking ship of Old Blighty. Bembenek. Bzoski. Dworakowski. Gaalaas. Four *a*'s, for God's sake. What did you do with four *a*'s? Hochhalter, Hrbhar. How did one pronounce that?

He felt weary, closing the file, closing his eyes. They came, and they continued to come, swimming rivers, zigzagging through minefields, ducking gun towers, crawling under barbed wire. Driven by some notion of freedom, of human dignity, they kept on coming. The driftwood of Eastern Europe, the dross of humanity, the poor suffering souls who saw the nature of the risk and were prepared to take the chance anyhow—and they became his responsibility. He was the one who had to keep track of them, who had to *listen* to them; and who had to find if, beneath their enraged stories, their insane relief, their bitterness, there lay anything of value to what, for want of any better expression, was called the intelligence community.

He opened the file. He skipped the Czechs, the Poles, the Hungarians. Begin with the Soviets, he thought. Where else? He lifted the receiver, dialed a number, waited. After a time he heard a dense European accent answer angrily.

"Paul? Paul, my dear fellow. This is Dubbs."

"Dubbs, you crazy? You know what is the time of day?"

"Better a polite little call, my dear fellow, than someone hammering your door down in the middle of the night, no?"

"Crazy. You're crazy, Dubbs."

"The day before yesterday a man, an American, died in Moscow," Dubbs said.

"So? What you want that I should know? American? I don't know no American. Let me sleep, you crazy bastard."

"It seems to have been a suicide."

"Hey. Moscow's a depressing town, Dubbs. It sometimes has that effect on a man's head."

Dubbs, sighing, reached out to stroke a fern. It was feathery, lovely; an amazing thing—something growing in this rotten little place. "I understand Moscow is not absolutely delightful, Paul. This I can comprehend. However, it's important—"

"Important? I know nothing. I know damn nothing."

"The American was called Richard Rayner," Dubbs said. Best to press on, ignore their interruptions. Best simply to *glide* over things. "Richard Rayner. You understand? Now I want you to mention the name amongst the members of your little group—"

"Group? What group? Dubbs, you sound like a dog that goes on barking up wrong trees. I don't know no group."

"My dear fellow, your little group that calls itself The Estonian Alliance, and which pretends to be a social club, and which, *incidentally,* meets every Thursday night at Number Eighty-five Roper Place in some sleazy part of Kilburn. I want you, Paul, to mention the name of this man—*Richard Rayner*—to the nice chums you have in this group. Savvy?"

"You're dreaming, Dubbs—"

"I am not dreaming, Paul. I am most certainly *not* dreaming about the fact that it is quite against the law of the United Kingdom to store hand grenades in a garage behind Number Eighty-five Roper Place, Kilburn. Am I coming through, my dear?"

There was a silence on the line. Dubbs could hear a woman's voice whining in the background, a Cockney accent. *'Ere, what time o' night's 'e call this?*

"How you spell Rayner?" the man asked finally.

Dubbs hung up. The Estonian Alliance. It was pathetic. The little groups, the so-called social clubs, the clandestine gatherings: as if it might ever amount to anything. They belonged in caves hidden high up in mountains, fighting a war that no longer existed. Dead and sorry men. The Estonian Alliance. How many more of them existed? How many more with those strangely innocuous names? He gazed at his papers, blinked. Weary again. The Friends of Tallinn. The Kalmuck Club. The Vilna Brigade Brotherhood. And the amusing ones—The Southwest London Polka and Dance Society. The Lovers of Accordion Music. The Hungarian Sunday Football League—madmen exorcising their patriotic rage with a leather football under dreary skies on Hackney Marshes. Pathetic, sad, Dubbs thought. The meetings in the back rooms of pubs, the front parlors of small suburban houses; here and there—like souvenirs, mementos of other incarnations—a handful of old guns, a rifle or two, a six-pack of grenades; perhaps some sporadic pamphleteering, or irregularly produced newspapers, perhaps some restless gathering at Speaker's Corner, where you could not separate the nuts from the zealots, the truth from the madness.

Why did you have to jump, Richard?

He picked up the telephone and dialed another number and waited for the irritated voice he knew would come, fresh from sleep, to answer.

**4.**

There was sunlight coming into the room and he woke, fully dressed, where he had fallen the night before—not making it to the bed, managing only to get his shoes off, to read Richard's letter, to crumple it with drunken annoyance between the palms of his hands, then to lie down on the sofa. His eyes hurt. The sunlight was bright, a February sun predominantly white, anemic, as if all color and warmth had been bleached out of it. He got up, staggered toward the kitchen, stared at the mess—empty beer bottles, the refrigerator door hanging open, something smelling spoiled, rancid. He picked up the coffeepot, lit the gas, not knowing how many days ago he had brewed the stuff. Hot and warm, something to get the heart started. Something to get things going. Today—today was when he would pull himself together, distance himself from grief, set it aside. Today was when you gritted your teeth and put a new shine to old platitudes: *Life goes on. Life is for the living. Let the dead rest.* It was going to be like that.

He waited until the coffee boiled, poured some, carried it into the front room. Tasteless and bitter. He went to the window. Sunlight in dead trees, burning on bare branches. He turned away from the light and went back to the sofa and picked up Richard's letter from the floor. He read it and thought: Study this if you will. Study this, show me the signs, the clues of self-destruction. Last night when he had stumbled in, when he had torn the letter open—what? Had he expected some kind of last will and testament? an apology? But goddammit, this wasn't a suicide note, this wasn't what the sad cases left behind when they locked themselves in garages and left the motor running or sat by their desks with a pistol to the brain. This was pure Richard, the whole letter was pure unadulterated Richard. The mild sarcasm, the flashes of political observation, the underlying iconoclasm. It was Richard.

Between you and me and the old gatepost, Kimby Lindholm is a sure candidate for his own Vegas show. Or maybe a guest spot on Bowling for Dollars. At worst, a quick tour of the Borscht Belt. And he doesn't even need a stooge.

The weather in Moscow, a mention of Maksymovich, a reference in passing to Isobel—"she can't make up her mind if she prefers Washington to Moscow, but then she can't make up her mind much about anything"—and that was it. That was the whole nine yards. The ball game. You'd better face it, he thought. What was the point in indulging further in sorrow or anger or whatever? It was a hard fact, forged out of ice.

He put the letter down, rose, walked to the window. He squinted into the harsh sun, remembering Dubbs now. Had Dubbs brought him home? Jigsaw pieces. Little splinters of yesterday. They didn't add up and he didn't even want to try.

Now his telephone was ringing. It was Sally. She said she had read about it in *The Times.* She said she was sorry. She wondered if there was anything she could do. He listened to the crisp, perfect English voice: it was as if she spoke with a fresh apple in her mouth. He speculated on whether sex might be a means of forgetting: orgasmic amnesia, say? The orgasm as a tiny form of temporary death? He could hear typewriters in the background somewhere and a voice saying, *Where's the bloody coffee then?* What was the name of that school Sally had gone to? Roedean? Now she did something in a publisher's office, something editorial which he didn't entirely understand: it had all seemed so vague when she had tried to explain once. But then Sally was a vague girl in her way, seeming to float through her life, as if even the simplest of things were indefinable.

"I'll come over if you like," she was saying. "I can get away. Do you want some company?"

"The sun's shining," he said.

"Funny. I noticed it too," she said.

"Super day for a spot of lunch?"

"You'll never get the accent right."

"Now you're being beastly," he said.

She laughed, but there was an edge to the sound, a cautious edge: it was how people laughed in cathedrals. Like walking on eggshells.

"Bertorelli's at one?" she said.

He felt a sudden indecision, some sense of purpose lacking; and he knew it came down to his own powerlessness, as if Richard's death had upon it some final imprimatur, an official seal, a solitary malign word: *suicide.* And that was how it was to be left.

"Bertorelli's," he said. "At one."

When he had hung up he knew she wouldn't be there on time; she was never anywhere on time. Unpunctuality was as natural to Sally as photosynthesis to a plant; and just as thoughtless too.

**5.**

It occurred to Zubro that of all London railroad stations Euston was the least pleasurable—something, of course, to do with the dirt, the grime, the droppings of pigeons; but more than that, as if he could feel pressing upon him a whole sense of district, of the miserable little streets that crisscrossed the area—the cheap hotels, the sleazy magazine shops, the drab warehouses. Sunlight, such as today's unseasonable brightness, bared the threads of the place even more so than usual. He paused in front of the Departures Board, looking at the strange names, the queer destinations. All around him people rushed to make connections and he thought: How oddly organized the English are—lives submitted to the dictates of timetables, of standing in orderly lines. The irony of this amused him: underlying the rush of these people, their apparent sense of purpose, there was something chaotic—buses that never arrived, trains that failed to come on time, cafeterias that served lukewarm milky tea. Even when they complained of their failing system, the English still maintained that odd sense of order: it was as if passion were alien to their nature. They made the most dignified drunks in the world.

He listened to the echo of an incomprehensible voice over the loudspeaker system. *The train now standing at Platform Two is the twelve-ten to Aberdeen, calling at Grantham, Doncaster, York, Darlington, Newcastle. . . .* The rest, mercifully, was lost to him—a babble of some distant thunder, the whistle of a train rolling down one of the local lines. He looked at his watch, then moved in the direction of the snack bar. He wore a black coat and carried a rolled umbrella. His suit was pinstriped, sedate, and he walked in a leisurely manner; and he considered the fact that one of the few things that distinguished him from the hustle around him was the measure of his pace. Otherwise, what else did he look like but some City type, some stockbroker, or solicitor, some chartered accountant whose weekends might be spent clipping rosebushes or trimming a privet hedge?

Outside the snack bar he paused. He saw Otto Kranz rushing toward him, the fat man reflected in the window. Zubro turned, began to walk back in the direction of the Departures Board. *The train now standing,* said the voice. A train with legs, Zubro thought: the peculiarities of the English language. *Edinburgh, Dundee, Arbroath, Montrose, Stonehaven, and Aberdeen.* He could sense Otto Kranz still hurrying, puffing, his fat cheeks exploding only to implode. Zubro liked this sense of the dance, of making it hard for Otto Kranz to catch up with him; it was some curious arrangement, a waltz they shared.

Zubro moved away from the board, went past the escalator that carried crowds into the underground system, and paused at a newsstand to buy a copy of *The Guardian.* Only then did Otto Kranz catch him. Out of breath, panting, his broad moon face blood-red, Kranz gave the impression of someone coming apart at every seam, of someone who has been put hastily, and temporarily, together. Buttons undone, coat flapping, necktie askew: why did Zubro allow Kranz to *disgust* him so?

They went out of the station together, crossing Euston Square. Kranz had his plump hand on Zubro's sleeve, drawing him toward a bench. The wood was covered with pigeon dirt. Rolling his *Guardian,* Zubro wiped the surface of the bench before finally sitting down. Kranz took a dirty handkerchief from his coat and mopped his forehead. It would be some time before he could find the wind to speak, Zubro thought. A flock of gray pigeons scattered overhead suddenly, startled by the outburst of a pneumatic drill nearby. Plump, heavy, they settled some distance away.

Kranz rolled the handkerchief into a ball in his fist. "I have some information for you," he said.

Waiting, waiting, Zubro saw a crazy old woman crawling around amongst the pigeons, scattering bread crumbs, speaking to the birds: *My darlings, my darlings.*

"I have an item," Kranz said. His massive face was dripping sweat.

"And?"

"I think it will maybe be of some interest."

"And?"

Kranz paused, blew his nose, perused his own effluence a moment, as if it were the most interesting thing in all the world. Zubro preferred to look at the mad old woman. He wondered why Kranz, after all his years in London, had never completely mastered the English language.

"A man committed suicide in Moscow," Kranz said.

"And?"

"It doesn't interest you, this fact?"

"Should it?" Zubro turned his face back to the fat man. The young American, of course. What next?

"You knew, naturally," said Kranz.

Zubro shrugged. One did not give fat Otto any insight into one's own knowledge; that would have been an altogether different game. The pneumatic drill started up again. A machine gun.

"I never know," Kranz said. "I tell you something. You look at me like I'm stupid or something."

Zubro stared at his watch. He had a meeting at

three. He tapped his rolled-up newspaper impatiently against his knee.

The fat man sat in a sullen silence a moment. The drill stopped. He licked his lips, which were wide and purple, reminding Zubro of two squashed grapes, and then he said, "Mr. Dubbs is very interested. Did you know that?"

Zubro said nothing but he felt a slight change in himself, a rise in temperature, the quickening of a pulse.

"Mr. Dubbs is putting out the word," the fat man said.

"And?"

"And what? This doesn't interest you? A young American kills himself in Moscow and Mr. Dubbs begins to dig like a crazy person? This doesn't interest you?"

Zubro rubbed the tip of his nose. He thought of Dubbs a moment, trying to see connections, threads. There had been a suicide, a tragedy—but why was Dubbs intrigued by this? He looked at Otto with a lack of interest.

"He has been calling every group," Kranz said, a note of some desperation in his voice. "All the night long, damn, calling here, calling there. And you tell me this doesn't interest you?"

"It doesn't interest me," Zubro said. He took out his wallet, removed three pound notes, gave them to the fat man.

"This is a damn insult," Kranz said.

"Think of it as charity," Zubro said, and rose from the bench.

"Stick your charity up your arse," Kranz said.

Zubro paused, looking down at the fat man. "I am glad to see that you are at last showing some mastery, however small, of colloquial English."

He walked away from the bench, listening to Kranz mutter. The crazy lady was still talking with her pigeons. Zubro watched her a moment, then moved toward the taxi ranks.

## 6.

The meeting Zubro had to attend at the Embassy of the Soviet Union was being chaired by the Assistant Minister for Soviet Sports, Stepanek—who had just arrived from Moscow—which made it somehow important, of course, but his mind was still with Dubbs. Why would that little queer be nosing around with his questions about Richard Rayner? Why was that so important? And something else, something else was troubling him too—the name Rayner, which lay at the back of his mind in the manner of a frail spark. Rayner. Familiar, yet not. So many names—how could one keep track of everybody? And what was the link between Dubbs and a dead American?

He gazed at the Minister, who was embarked on a course of rhetoric concerning the progress of Soviet sport. Such words as *prestige* and *achievement* drifted around the room. Stepanek had a nervous, agitated manner, as if he were being bothered by imaginary flies around his head. Dubbs, Zubro thought. He was able to keep abreast of Dubbs most of the time because of his informants within the expatriate groups— all of whom were, anyhow, harmless and crazy. But why was Dubbs intrigued by a dead American diplomat?

Stepanek had paused in his speech to drink a glass of water. His hand shook visibly. Zubro wondered about the pressures involved in the Ministry of Sports;

a matter of getting the best results, of course. At least it was tangible; at least there was a score at the end of the contest, an outcome, winners and losers. But there were other worlds wherein one might be less certain of the victors and the vanquished. My world, he thought. He looked at the faces around the table—the press attaché, the Second Secretary, a couple of clerks. How vacuously they hung on Stepanek's sentences! One would think sport the most important thing in the world.

"Our soccer team has made considerable progress in recent years," Stepanek said. Zubro noticed a slick of water on the man's chin. "And, it goes without saying, the forthcoming tour is intended to demonstrate how . . . how far along this progress has been pushed."

Soccer, Zubro thought. Nothing bored him more than the prospect of having to attend to the security arrangements surrounding a group of athletes. The hotel accommodations, the sexual escapades, the constant menace of defection. He was going to have headaches.

"And this soccer team is particularly special," said Stepanek. "It is expected to win its games. Again, it goes without saying."

Why say it? Zubro wondered.

"The first game will be here in England," Stepanek was saying now. He paused, stared around the room, his gaze momentarily meeting Zubro's. Fear, Zubro thought—fear in those pale eyes. This soccer team of Stepanek's simply had to win: there was no other course.

Now Stepanek looked down at his hands and Zubro noticed for the first time the absence of the right index finger. "And the second game," Stepanek said, "the second game will be the first encounter at international level between our country and the United States of America."

There was a curious smirk from the press attaché. "You mean we're sending our soccer team to *America?*"

Sacrilege and disbelief, Zubro thought. He looked at the press attaché, a cousin of one Sememko of the Politburo. Nepotism was an unreliable narcotic but presumably the attaché thought he might live in its sweet fumes forever. "I didn't think the Americans knew what to do with a soccer ball," he said.

"Their game has improved considerably," said Stepanek.

"By importing foreign players?"

"In this instance, their team will consist entirely of native-born players," Stepanek said.

But the press attaché, who was young, an upstart with dubious connections of blood, was not to be stalled. "I assume that we're not sending our *strongest* team over there?"

Stepanek reached for his water again. "At the express wish of Comrade Maksymovich, we are sending the strongest squad we can muster."

Stepanek stood up and looked at Zubro, and Zubro was all at once conscious of undercurrents in the room, as if this was a facade, as if all this talk of soccer was a masquerade, a game of shadows and charades. The meeting finished but Stepanek indicated with a gesture of his hand that he wanted to detain Zubro a moment—something of a private nature. As the others left the room, the press attaché laughing to himself, Zubro found himself looking out into the street, watching a black taxi cruise past in the white afternoon. Rayner, he thought. Rayner and Dubbs— there was an association, something that lay on the tip of his tongue.

Stepanek came around the table, carrying a clutch of papers. A scent of some kind came from the man, a pungent cologne.

"Security arrangements for the squad are to be as tight as they can be made," he said. "Again, this is the express wish of the First Secretary."

Zubro did not question this. He glanced at Stepanek. Fear again, fear came out to touch him, more tangible than the cologne.

"You will make the necessary arrangements for a party of thirty," Stepanek said. "Here. The list of the names."

Zubro took the paper but did not look at it.

"Twenty players," Stepanek said. "Two security agents. Four assistant trainers. The trainer himself. A doctor and a physiotherapist."

Zubro had it: it came quickly to him. There was a young man called Rayner who worked over in Grosvenor Square—James? John? A young man whose field of activity might lie aligned with that of the precious Dubbs. Then the dead diplomat was a relation? And Dubbs—what was Dubbs digging for?

He looked at Stepanek. "You said thirty. You mentioned only twenty-nine, I think."

"Ah, yes," Stepanek said, turning away, moving as if he had suddenly remembered some other urgent business. "I forgot to mention the trainer's wife. An elderly lady, by all accounts, and quite infirm."

In the doorway Stepanek stopped and looked across the room at Zubro. "Don't ask me why she's making this trip, Zubro. I don't know the answer anyhow."

And then Stepanek was gone and Zubro was alone in the large silent room.

# 2

*1.*

Andreyev shivered in the cold night wind that seared the tarmac at Heathrow. Ahead of him, Katya pushed the wheelchair in which Mrs. Blum sat. He noticed how the old woman's white hair gleamed in the reflected light of the terminal building. He paused, somewhat in the manner of one who has left something behind on the plane; then he was conscious again of Oblinski at his back—Oblinski, the KGB official who had been at the Ussuri. He watches me, Andreyev thought. He does nothing but watch me. He shoved his hands deep into the pockets of his overcoat, his right hand fingering the slip of crumpled paper he had carried all the way from Moscow. Why couldn't he stop himself from touching it? It was irresistible, like a cavity into which you keep pushing your tongue. He folded his fingers around it. He looked in the direction of the terminal, feeling the wind again, the way his overcoat flapped.

He moved forward. The athletes were going toward the terminal. They moved easily, with a confidence that was close to arrogance. Winners, Andreyev thought. Men who would be surprised at nothing. They talked and joked like kids treated to a special outing. Did they ever wonder about the woman in the wheelchair? Or had wonderment been processed out of them? From the shadow of the terminal a couple of flashbulbs popped. Now Oblinski was abreast of him. There was a faint smell of garlic about the man, garlic and tobacco and old sweat.

"London," Oblinski said. "Land of hope and glory."

Andreyev turned a moment to look at the broad face of Oblinski. His pervasive anonymity had changed to something akin to ugliness.

"Doesn't it stir you, Andreyev? Or should I say Dr. Domareski?"

The false name Andreyev had been given was a sick joke. He wondered who had come up with the idea that he should travel abroad under the name of the dead man. He looked away from Oblinski, who was smiling in a thin manner.

"London," Oblinski said again. "Does it give you ideas, Andreyev? Does it give you strange notions?"

"Should it?"

Oblinski shrugged. "People are free here, as I understand."

"Free?" Andreyev wondered why Oblinski should goad him this way. Did he know? Did he know about the piece of paper? Andreyev took his hands from his pockets and stared at the silver fuselages of planes that sat in the dark like sad grounded moths.

"Free," Oblinski said. He clapped his gloved hands together and whistled in a tuneless way a moment. "They don't understand, Andreyev, the only freedom is death."

There were more flashbulbs sizzling up ahead.

The only freedom, Andreyev thought: when you were accustomed to seeing reflections in broken mirrors, you didn't know which fragment was a true image, or if any of them were. Was Oblinski warning him? Was Oblinski saying: *Don't get any ideas, Andreyev. Remember Domareski, whose name you now have. Remember.* Andreyev watched Kazemayov, the team's striker, the star, raise his arms upright for the benefit of the press photographers. It was his characteristic gesture whenever he scored a goal. A simian face, the body like a barrel, massive thighs.

The door of the terminal was opened. The athletes streamed through, followed by Katya and Mrs. Blum. Again, Andreyev paused. Oblinski laid a hand on his shoulder and made a slight gesture with his head. Andreyev went inside the terminal building, hearing the automatic door slide shut behind him. It was stuffy and overheated. The only freedom, Andreyev thought. Did Oblinski know about the piece of paper? He wanted to touch it again, he wanted to take one more look at it and memorize the telephone number, the address—but when he had tried before he hadn't been able to commit it to memory. Fear, anxiety, whatever. Now he understood the stupidity of words on paper, of the tangibility of something physical, something detectable.

Please, he thought. There might be a chance. One slim chance.

Oblinski was pushing his way through toward Immigration, where he took a clutch of passports from his briefcase and laid them down on the official's desk. Behind a barricade there were photographers and reporters from the English sporting press. Kazemayov, in his element, was pretending to balance a ball on the tip of his shoe: a mute performance, a perfect mime, flicking the nonexistent ball up in the air and catching it with his forehead.

Andreyev stared at Mrs. Blum: her eyes, dark slits against a face made puffy and swollen by drugs, saw nothing. He was sweating now, wiping his brow with his sleeve, wondering how Mrs. Blum was to be used on this trip. He glanced at Katya, though not for long. Did she know? Had she been told? Did Oblinski understand the purpose behind it all? Or were they all waiting for the order that would come down, like some crazy babble, from a high place? He encountered a dark corridor of ignorance here and it made him uncomfortable.

The Immigration official was stamping the passports. Kazemayov, smiling, held three fingers up to the newspapermen, predicting the three goals he intended to score against the English team. Clowning, basking in the sharp, quick lights of flashbulbs, he balanced his canvas bag on the tip of his foot and circled around his laughing teammates. The trainer, Charek, a slightly crumpled man in his late fifties, chewed on the butt of an unlit cigarette and watched his star with quiet disapproval. The old school, Andreyev thought. The school of discipline and order. Charek would never ask why a sick old woman would be traveling with his party; Andreyev doubted that he even noticed her.

Now Oblinski was gathering up the passports and hustling his charges in the direction of customs. Andreyev followed slowly, pushing his hands back inside his coat pockets. The piece of paper, like some reminder of an appointment already past, was sticky against the sweat of his fingers. It might have been any old used bus ticket, an ancient receipt, a theater stub, something dog-eared and stuck away for no real reason. And then he caught Mrs. Blum's eyes again, thinking of how little she had responded to him in the three weeks since the young American's death, how withdrawn she had become—three weeks of silence, of an aloofness that suggested some inner vacuum. Dear God, what did I expect anyway? Friendship? Good cheer? He drew his hand away from his precious piece of paper and he wondered if, when it came down to it, he would have the courage to do what he felt he had to. Fragile, flammable—a piece of flimsy, sweaty paper.

He turned his face away from her, feeling some small shame, as if he were stripped and standing naked in a well-lit room. And he wondered if those about to be executed were ever able to look into the eyes of their executioners.

## 2.

The wind that sloughed through Mayfair, that carried scraps and shards and echoed down the entranceways to underground stations, slapped like a fist against the panes of George Gull's window. Rayner finished reading the sheets Gull had given him; he laid them on the desk, where, caught in the oblique angle of the reading lamp, they appeared blank and glossy. Tired, Rayner closed his eyes and lightly rubbed his eyelids.

The report was a piece of bureaucratic trash, compiled by some fastidious investigator at the U.S. Embassy in Moscow. The precise phrases, the cold little placebos of language, irritated Rayner enormously. *It is the conclusion of . . . We are of the opinion that . . .* What it came down to, if you could separate the shit from the blades of the fan, was an official verdict of suicide. But it was a flaky, whitewash job; and Rayner, who had contrived to relegate the memory of his dead brother to a nebulous zone of the mind, was angered. A dead man distilled in a series of impersonal platitudes.

Gull picked up the report and straightened the sheets. Without looking at Rayner he said, "It's official, John. It's sealed and signed and delivered."

Rayner said nothing. This pursuit of the dead was a chilling business. You tried to put the building blocks together but all you ever created was a jumbled alphabet. Even Dubbs, who had rummaged for days through what he called his "hapless little flock," had turned up nothing. Now it boiled down to a smug report, written up in Moscow by some Embassy flunky called Strachan.

Gull made a gesture with his hands, suggesting finality. He gazed at his broken cigarette in the ashtray with an expression that might have been one of deep regret. "The point is, John, you have to put it behind you. You have to."

He stared at Gull, who clearly had something else on his mind, if you were to deduce anything from the hesitancy of his manner. He got up rather awkwardly and walked to the window, the wind howling against the glass. With his back to Rayner he said, "I don't exactly like to bring this up, but your work's been suffering, John. What I'm getting at is—well, shit, there's a time when you have to quit farting around and get back down to it."

Gull turned. He appeared apologetic, his face slightly red. Rayner thought: He's *embarrassed.* Gull looked at the palms of his hands. Then he moved toward the desk and opened a folder, shuffling some sheets that lay inside.

"Like this stuff," Gull said. "It's been almost a

week since I asked you to process this Folweiler material. You haven't done it yet."

Rayner sighed, considering the limits of his official duties, the reason why he was in London in the first place. Folweiler, an East German refugee, had applied for permanent residency in the United States, and it was Rayner's task to run such applications from Eastern European fugitives through the intelligence screen: a matter of cables, telex inquiries, sifting the items from the various stations. The idea was that you might turn up a potential security threat to the USA; alternatively, the applicant might be useful for propagandist purposes—if he had been, say, a nuclear physicist, a great violinist, a sports star. What you usually got was small fry, sad and bitter little people who looked across the Atlantic with an unwarranted optimism. Folweiler was a stonemason from Dresden.

Gull tapped a finger on the surface of his desk. "I gather you've been spending time with Dubbs. Maybe that's what keeps you so goddam busy, huh?"

Rayner rose from his chair. How did Gull know about Dubbs? What was it? Raincoated shadows in Regent's Park, faint silhouettes on the platform of Holborn Underground Station? Watched, spied on, followed—had it come down to that kind of crap?

"I didn't know you had your goons on me, George," Rayner said.

"What the fuck do you expect from me? Days you don't show—how am I supposed to know where you are?"

Rayner gazed at the Moscow report. What did this character Strachan know, anyhow? "We can conclude that Richard Rayner might have been concerned with his career, depressed by his marriage, and that a combination of these factors contributed to his suicide." It was pure unadulterated bull. An amateur shrink in a cold gray city—somebody who hadn't even *met* Richard, presumably. No, Rayner thought. You had a mystery here, like a sunken ship lying in mud at some unfathomable depth. You had a mystery that couldn't be unraveled by a distant peasant called Strachan.

"Officially," Gull said, staring at Rayner, "officially, I have to warn you, John. Off the record, I just wish you'd get your ass in gear before everything cracks open and you find yourself drummed back to the States—"

"I hear you," Rayner said. "I hear you."

He reached for his raincoat and went toward the door. A grief, he thought: it subsides, yielding to some other feeling— like a consciousness of waste, of pointlessness. He opened the door and turned once to look at Gull, but he couldn't think of anything to say that would alleviate the leaden weight that lay between him and his superior. He stepped out into the corridor and walked to the elevator.

Outside, on the Embassy steps, he turned up the collar of his raincoat. The wind that sliced across Grosvenor Square was a thing of invisible ice. He went down the steps and moved across the square in the direction of Oxford Street.

### 3.

Rayner took a cab to Belsize Park, where Sally Macnamara lived in a three-room flat in a house that had seen better days: a white-fronted monstrosity, chipped and peeling and scavenged by the vicissitudes of British weather. The district, jammed alongside Hampstead like an impoverished relative seated beside a rich cousin at some unlikely wedding, had become run-down, but Sally took great pleasure in the ethnic mix of the neighborhood. She lived at the top of the house, and Rayner, as he climbed the stairs, was assailed by a curious assembly of smells and scents—curry, fried onions, the suggestion of a gas leak, a stick of incense burning somewhere. He was out of breath when he reached the uppermost landing, where he paused, listening, wondering if someone were climbing through the shadows beneath him, one of George Gull's gumshoes, perhaps; but the only noises were those of a muffled radio playing chamber music and the desultory sound of a sitar being plucked. He rang her doorbell and waited. The distant sound of the sitar grew more wild, a melancholy kind of abandon.

She came to the door with her hair wrapped in a moist towel, a housecoat thrown loosely around her shoulders and belted at her waist. Rayner stepped inside, trying to catch his breath. It was a strange room, a jumble of odd things purchased in secondhand stores, in thrift shops, in bargain basements. Rayner had a quick impression of peacock feathers, a tailor's dummy covered by an old fox fur, a poster of Lord Kitchener beckoning young men to early graves, Chinese paper lanterns, silks and linens spilling from a large sandalwood chest.

"What brings you out on a foul night like this?" Sally said. She took the towel from her head and began to rub the strands of her wet hair.

"Would you believe I was passing through the neighborhood?" Rayner asked.

"Nope." She threw the towel across a chair and looked at him. She wiped the palms of her hands on her housecoat. Then she stood motionless for a time, watching him, and it seemed to Rayner that in her disheveled state she was as much a part of the room as any of the inanimate objects it contained.

"You're right. I wasn't just passing through." He scratched his head. "I came from the Embassy. I thought: What the hell do I do on a night like this? Here I am."

"I've got a dish of cold won ton in the refrigerator if you fancy that," she said. "I think there's a single bottle of Heineken, if you want it."

He smiled at her. Culinary disorganization, he thought. He looked around the room. On a small cluttered desk there lay a thick manuscript whose pages were interspersed with rough strips of torn paper.

"What's the book?" he asked.

"You wouldn't believe me if I told you," she said. She was lighting a cigarette, a pastel-colored thing that reminded him of the cigarettes Dubbs smoked. She blew a stream of smoke, watched it spiral upward, then said, "It's a book we're going to publish called *I Was a Jew in the SS.*"

"You're putting me on," Rayner said.

"I wish I was." She went to the desk and looked at the typescript. "But it's serious."

Rayner was silent for a time, looking around the room, noticing nothing in particular, yet conscious of some uneasiness in himself—as if he were seeking a refuge in this crazy apartment but failing to find one. He replayed the scene with Gull, turning the Moscow report over and over in his mind: maybe if you repeated the official verdict often enough to yourself you could believe it. Maybe you could just swallow the shit and then go on with your life—

"I've never quite understood what you do at your Embassy," Sally said.

"I'm a serf," Rayner said. "Low on the ladder."

"For example?"

"Well, if you were to come in and apply for residence in the United States, your papers would pass across my desk."

"And what would you do with them?"

"Process them."

She watched him a moment. "What's your exact title?"

"Assistant Consul."

"You're a bad liar, Rayner. Something in your eyes."

A bad liar, he thought. "What do you think I do?"

"You're some kind of spook."

"Spook?"

"CIA or whatever it is. Central Idiots Agency," she said. "We did a book on them last year. All the spooks have friendly faces, little smiling masks."

Little smiling masks, he thought. He watched her close the pages of the typescript with a shudder. She sat down, the cigarette hanging from her mouth, her legs splayed apart—and he felt a rush of affection for her, a feeling he understood could easily grow to that point where love was supposed to begin: giddiness, folly, all the rest of it. The way she walks through her life, he thought—not giving a damn what other people think, that wonderful lack of self-consciousness, an independence he liked. He remembered how they had first met—at the opening of an art gallery that apparently specialized in sculptures created out of scraps of old locomotives. They had talked, then left together. "So bloody pretentious," she had said. "Have you ever seen anything like it?" Her past, he found out, was checkered with old lovers turned friends, men who would call her at the most irregular hours for consultation in matters of the heart. He wondered what kind of talent it took for a person to defuse a relationship in such a way that all the old lovers became close buddies—and sometimes, rather despairingly, he speculated on whether he would be similarly demoted in the near future. Still another voice on the telephone in the dead of night. Am I growing *jealous?* he wondered. Is that how it starts?

He watched her move cautiously around the cluttered room. She was looking for an ashtray; failing to find one, she dropped her cigarette end in a coffee cup. When she sat down again the housecoat hung open, her small breasts visible. She made no move to cover herself.

"Is there anything new on your brother?"

"Nothing," Rayner said. "An official suicide."

Sally closed her eyes. "You still don't buy it?"

"I don't buy it," Rayner said.

"Then your brother's wife is a liar?"

"No. I don't think so—"

Sally shrugged and looked at him. He turned his face upward to the ceiling, gazing at the expanse of yellowing plaster from which there hung odd, spidery mobiles—frail things that moved and shifted in the thinnest of drafts. Light, rising through a lampshade of stained glass, cast various tints. Trippy, Rayner thought. The rich girl from Roedean goes slumming through the detritus of the psychedelic age.

"Explain," Sally said.

"Look, I don't have the answers—"

"Philosophy. Introductory course. Are there unanswerable questions?"

I don't even have the questions, Rayner thought. Then what are you trusting? Disquieting feelings? Tiny jabs of uneasiness? Memories of Richard were snapshot albums in which you caught his face in a certain light: a boy with a fishing pole, grimacing in the sunlight one autumn day on Lake Oneida, the glories of some lost fall; a young man, filled with life and promise and hope, pictured climbing into his first automobile, a preposterous 1955 Packard that had once been a hearse; the university graduate heading for Washington. Even Dubbs, Rayner thought, even the little angelic Dubbs had urged him to accept the death as self-imposed. How could he?

"So what do you do in a situation like this, darling?" Sally asked.

*Dahling.* Rayner listened to the word. He wandered over to the manuscript and looked at it. Dahling. He flipped the pages and read: "When I first joined the SS, nobody suspected my Jewishness. It was a bitterly cold day in February 1936." He shut the typescript, smiling to himself.

"Don't mock it," Sally said, rising, approaching him, putting her arms loosely against his shoulders. "If we didn't publish those books, how could we ever afford to do anything with literary merit? The schlock pays for the books we pin medals on."

"Yes, dahling," he said.

"I keep saying, Rayner, you don't have the breeding to get it right. You have to drag it out. A long vowel."

He held her against him. She was skinny, long, provocative. He wondered if this was all he had come for—this sense of burying himself against her, of losing the rough edges of loss.

She drew her face back from him and smiled. "How did you get to be a spook?"

"I told you, Sally. Assistant Consul. That's me."

"Seriously. I was wondering if you simply enrolled or if you filled out a form, or if they came and sort of sought you out—"

He put his index finger against her lips. "Consular service runs in my family like a congenital disease. Didn't I ever tell you that? My grandfather was the American Consul in Venezuela. My late father served for years in the Embassy in Rome. Remind me to give you the whole family backdrop sometime."

The sudden sound of the telephone was shrill. She stepped away from him to answer it. The conversation was low, whispered, protracted. He moved around the room, touching things, looking into the manic eyes of Kitchener, staring at a British Rail platform sign that said DORCHESTER. He wondered if you could spend your life grinding East Germans through the security mill—a situation, an occupation, that was caught and fixed in some hopeless place between Immigration and the Central Intelligence Agency. Assistant Consul. But it wasn't quite that either. If the job had a name, nobody had ever told him what it was.

Sally put the telephone down, sighing as she did so. She turned to watch Rayner and he thought of her many lovers, faceless men and indeterminate couplings, as if he were viewing them through frosted glass.

"Assistant Consul," she said. "I'm disappointed, Rayner. I imagined you were one of those deeper sorts. Still waters and all that."

She put her cigarette out. He wanted to know who had been on the telephone, but he didn't ask; even if she had answered it would have been something impossibly vague. *An old friend, haven't seen him in ages, really. . . .* A dictionary of old friends, he thought. An encyclopedia of former partners. She came across the room toward him and, as if she had intuited some small jealousy in him, some vague resentment, put her arms around him. It was more a gesture of comfort and companionship than of desire.

"Are you going to stay?" she asked.

"If you want me to."

"It's what *you* want, Rayner."

He looked at her face, seeing not the thirty-year-old woman but the schoolgirl, dreaming of her as a child, of her school perched on the cliffs above the English Channel. She moved back from him and dimmed the lamp. Then she lit a candle, which she placed on the mantelpiece. He stared at the flame, a violent yellow flicker shivering in an imperceptible draft. She undid the belt of her housecoat.

He stepped toward her, conscious all at once of a slight sound, like that of a foot moving on wood, from beyond the door. He stopped, turned to the door, put his hand on the knob, hesitated.

"What is it?" Sally asked.

He pulled the door open and looked across the dark landing. Some way down the stairs there was a pale light. A shadow passed silently in front of it. Wood creaked. And then there was silence. Rayner went back inside the flat. He closed the door and drew the bolt, thinking of George Gull's goons, of how they came and went in the darkness like clandestine lovers on brief, illicit trysts.

"Was somebody out there?" she asked.

He shook his head. "I thought I heard a noise."

"The house is full of noise, John," she said.

He watched her slip the housecoat from her shoulders and toss it, with an amazingly casual gesture, to the floor. There are ways down, he thought, narrow avenues that could lead you to destinations beyond puzzlement and bewilderment—exit hatches out of darkness. He went toward her, his hands extended in front of him.

**4.**

Anatoly Zubro had no great regard for people like Oblinski. He considered such men—unimaginative, mere hacks, toilers in the field—to have no class, no *élan.* Just the same, as he sat facing Oblinski in the lounge of the Royal Kensington Hotel, where the soccer entourage was billeted, he had the irksome sensation that Oblinski knew more than he was able to tell. Something, maybe the smug little quirk in the expression, the muted mirth in the eyes, suggested to Zubro that Oblinski had a huge secret he would never share. It was a damned unsettling feeling, whatever prompted it, and Zubro felt an unaccustomed uneasiness.

Zubro looked across the lounge to the far corner, where there was a bar at which sat several elderly men—old colonial types, he thought, looking as if they had just had their rubber plantations repossessed. Sometimes, when he didn't want the hack to know he was paying attention, he would listen to snatches of the conversation from the bar. There was an amusing bitterness being bandied around: part regret part nostalgia. "It was in Lumpur, I remember it awfully well. . . ." "No, old man, you're barking up quite the wrong tree. Fella's name was Sayid, and it was Ceylon, bloody Ceylon. . . ." Zubro crossed his legs, conscious of the sharp crease in his pinstripe pants, aware of the shapelessness of Oblinski's heavy flannels.

Oblinski leaned forward, tapping Zubro lightly on the knee.

"Naturally, one does not anticipate any problems," Oblinski said. "But precautions are precautions, after all."

"Indeed," said Zubro. He gazed at the old men

and wondered what it would feel like to be a disenfranchised imperialist. Sad, he supposed. The bottom dropping out of your jolly old world.

"In the list of names you've been given, there are only two I would consider as special security cases," Oblinski said. He raised one hand and picked at the tip of his index finger. "Vassily Kazemayov, for one."

"Why Kazemayov?"

"Simple. The rewards for his particular talents could be considerable here or anywhere in Europe. Something like that might easily enter his mind, after all."

Zubro nodded. This soccer charade, he thought—why had it been nagging at him ever since the meeting with Stepanek? This wasn't entirely a sporting occasion, he was sure of that. But beyond that—well, one resigned oneself at times to the certitudes of ignorance. Now he was thinking of the woman in the wheelchair he had seen at Heathrow. Trainer Charek's wife. It had occurred to him that there was a rather marked age difference between the woman and the trainer; more, that Charek was apparently quite indifferent to the woman—no words, no touches, no ostensible relationship. Still, he thought, who was he to ask questions?

"The second risk factor involves the physician, Domareski," Oblinski said.

Zubro shifted in the uncomfortable armchair. The old boys at the bar, much the worse for drink, were tunelessly singing selections from *The Pirates of Penzance.* One of them, a short, bald man with a weathered face, was slipping from his stool. "Whoopsadaisy," he kept saying.

"Why should Domareski present a special problem?" Zubro asked.

"He is ideologically unsound." Oblinski sat back, his eyes narrow now.

Zubro reached forward and picked up his gin and tonic from the table; the ice in the glass was melting, changing from cubes to opaque, misshapen slivers. Unsound, Zubro thought. "If that's the case, Oblinski, then why has he been sent here?"

Oblinski had produced a ball-point pen from his pocket. On the side of the cylinder were the words "A Souvenir of London." Inside the clear plastic could be seen a miniature figure of a yeoman. Oblinski bit the end of the pen a moment. "I can only tell you that his presence here is necessary," he said, taking the pen from his lips, perusing it slowly. "That comes from the highest authority, Zubro."

Zubro looked at the other man. "Why is the old woman here?"

Oblinski shrugged. "Don't ask me to fathom that one, Zubro."

There was something fabricated in the shrug, something false in the tone of voice. Oblinski leaned closer again, his fingers flat on the surface of the table. "The woman isn't anything you should concern yourself with. I want you simply to keep close in on Kazemayov—but even more, I want the physician locked. Completely locked."

Zubro shut his eyes for a second. Sometimes these little self-imposed darknesses were welcome respites from the pressures of a world of secrets and sealed envelopes. His mind drifted back, and he found himself thinking again of Dubbs, of the connection between Dubbs and the young man Rayner in Grosvenor Square. He had had Dubbs's little flat bugged for the past three days—but the tapes had revealed nothing. As for John Rayner, the dead man's brother, the occasional random surveillance had turned up nothing more sinister than a girl friend in Swiss Cottage or whatever the place was called. It had been a simple matter to wire her apartment also but so far all he had listened to were several incoherent telephone calls, some of them peculiarly maudlin. Rayner went there sometimes and they made love, this much was evident. She had other callers too. A noisy girl, Zubro thought, and wondered if Rayner knew he had rivals for her bed. Or did people still think in terms of rivals in these days of free-for-all copulation? Oblinski was asking him something. He opened his eyes.

"How many men can you put on the physician?"

"I don't exactly have a limitless number at my disposal, Oblinski."

Oblinski looked oddly self-satisfied as he said, "Then you'll have to find them from somewhere, Comrade."

Zubro, touched by a momentary anger that this hack should order him to do something, smiled grimly. "I take it you have the written backup authority for that demand."

"Yes," Oblinski said. "Do you want to see it?"

Zubro shook his head. He was sorry to see the old colonials going out of the lounge. They were huddled together, singing "Good-bye." The revolving door whisked them out into the dark, windy street.

Yawning, Oblinski stood up. He stretched his arms. He paused, smiled thinly, then went across the lounge. Zubro did not watch him go. He picked up his weak drink and stared into it until the ice had totally gone. If one could only melt the mysteries away so easily, he thought: if it were simply a matter of chemistry. A woman in a wheelchair, a suspect physician, a temperamental soccer star; and behind them, like darker shadows forming beyond lighter ones, the snooping Dubbs, the grief-stricken Rayner. Quite a little catalog of woes, Zubro thought.

He went to the bar with his empty glass and ordered a refill. The barman, his red nose suggesting that he did more than merely dispense drinks, mixed the gin and tonic. He smiled at the fifty-pence tip Zubro gave him.

"I understand we've got the Russian football team here," the barman said.

"Indeed," said Zubro.

"Game's on Saturday. You going, sir?"

"I may."

The barman leaned forward in a confidential way. "They haven't got a chance of beating us, between you and me. They haven't got the firepower up front. Where it really matters."

Zubro smiled. *Us,* he thought.

"Anyway, they don't play an individual's game, do they? They're all sort of like robots, if you see my meaning, sir."

Zubro finished his drink quickly.

"Too bloody predictable," said the barman.

"As you say," Zubro said. "Too bloody predictable."

## 5.

She woke in a dark, unfamiliar room, remembering only the airplane flight, remembering Sememko's face in the blizzard at Moscow and how he had pulled his scarf from his mouth and smiled at her as if he wanted to be encouraging. But now, seized by some sudden small panic, she forced herself to sit upright and fumble, with her stiff, thickened hands, for a lamp. They told me, she thought. Israel. You are going. You are going to Israel. And there had been a moment of exultancy when she had been wheeled onto the airplane, a moment of enormous inner peace when the plane rose above the dense banks of gray clouds—but then it had begun to unravel; it had lost any sense. Why would Andreyev and Katya be going to Israel with her? Why would they be going to Tel Aviv? And then she had understood—more lies and obfuscations. Truth: they didn't understand what truth was. And now, having been wheeled through an airport whose signs were unintelligible to her, she understood she was alone in a strange dark room. There wasn't a lamp beside her bed. Struggling, she lay back down and clasped her hands together, feeling a vague numbness between her palms. Why were they continually lying to her? Why couldn't they simply say what they had to say? She could make out the line of a vague light from the curtained window, and more than anything else she wished she could get up and cross the floor and draw the curtain back and look down into whatever street lay below.

But she couldn't move now. It was this, this awful sense of being trapped inside herself, harnessed to her own flesh, that scared her. She closed her eyes and listened, hearing the faint sound of street traffic from far below the room. Other sounds. A hot breeze in an air duct. An elevator rising somewhere with an insistent buzz. There were tiny lights behind her eyes: they were like flies impressed by a lamp. *I must get up,* she thought. *I must get up and leave this place—*

A young girl, she thought.

A young girl could throw these sheets aside and just—

What more do they want of me?

What more can I *give* them?

She opened her eyes. The dark was unyielding. It pressed against her like some terrible fabric, shapeless and rough and uncut. What more? She tried to concentrate, as if by bringing random images into her mind she might contrive to forget the young man called Rayner, whose life—

The door of her room opened. An overhead light was turned on. She squinted, half-blinded, toward the figure of Andreyev, who had stepped into the room. He moved toward the bed as though his whole existence were an apology for some indescribable sin. Blessed are the meek, she thought. But not the cowardly. Slowly, quietly, he approached, in the manner of one who doesn't want to disturb the sleep of a terminal case. She caught his eye, moved her hands, surprising him by her wakefulness. He stopped. He was trembling visibly, staring at his own shaking hands. He sat on the edge of the bed. He can't look at me, she thought. He can't bring himself to *see* me.

Andreyev was gazing at the curtains, his tongue moving against his dry lips. Then, in an unsteady voice, he asked, "Did the trip tire you?"

"It was the wrong trip, Andreyev. The wrong destination."

Andreyev looked up at the ceiling in a gesture of some hopelessness. For a moment she could see him as if he were a transparency, a slight, filmy thing held up against bright light. He wants to speak and he's afraid to, she thought. He wants to tell me something, but he can't. It was the first time she had ever felt anything other than loathing for him—a kind of pity, of sorrow. She saw his hands clench the edge of the quilt.

"I know," he said very quietly.

She tried to sit upright. Andreyev adjusted her pillow, helping her. She felt pain in her chest. When she spoke, her breathing was shallow and difficult. "I sometimes wonder if they ever mean to let me leave. And when I start thinking like that I realize . . ."

"What do you realize?"

She didn't want to say. She stared into Andreyev's face. She saw a strange, flinty sense of purpose in the eyes all at once—a flash, a flare, then it was gone. He is going to do something, she thought. *He is planning something.* But he cannot tell me because he is afraid of speech, of being open, of revelation.

"What are they going to ask me to do this time, Andreyev?" she said. "What are they going to want from me now?"

"I don't know," he answered.

She concentrated, searching him, closing her eyes and feeling herself fall through the scattered clusters of his thoughts, the indistinct flickers of his mind. It exhausted her.

"No," he said, holding the side of his head. He got up from the edge of the bed and walked around the room, reaching the window, drawing the curtains back. "No, no," he was saying again. She shut her eyes and she could feel something slip inside herself, a force draining away. Andreyev stood at the window. She knew without looking. His thoughts, his pains: it was as if his mind were a monstrous edifice supported by a solitary column of fear. *Getting away . . . Running . . . London . . . Escape . . .*

What about me, Andreyev?

What do they plan for me?

He had his palms pressed flat against the sides of his head. He was moving in painful, quick circles by the window.

*What do they plan for me?*

But there was nothing else now, nothing save the silence of some inner scream. She lay back against the pillows, watching Andreyev slump into an armchair at the window. His hands hung loose at his sides. He was sweating profusely, his face white. When he turned his face to look at her, he opened his mouth but said nothing. He means to run, she thought. That's all he knows. He knows nothing of any plans, nothing.

She turned her face away from him, conscious of his labored breathing, of her own unfathomable fatigue. Then she heard him rise, the armchair creak, the sound of his footsteps on the carpet.

He was standing over the bed. He didn't speak.

"There was pain," she said. "I'm sorry for that."

Still, he said nothing.

"I wish you well, Andreyev," she said. "I hope it works for you."

He moved very slightly. His hands touched the edge of the bed. London, she thought. Why had they come to London? Now she remembered, as if through a haze, the young men on the plane.

"Please," Andreyev said. His voice was low, a whisper, hoarse. "I told you I didn't know—why did you have to inflict me with . . ."

She raised one hand slowly, pressing it upon Andreyev's wrist. This gift, she thought: could a thing in itself be evil? She looked up into the man's eyes. A man without knowledge of any future save that of his own complete desperation. What can *he* tell me? She watched him pull his hand away, as if from a hot iron.

"You didn't have to—" His sentence faded. He pressed the palms of his hands against the sides of his head. He sat on the edge of the mattress now, limp, exhausted, beaten. The last privacy, she thought, is no privacy at all. She wanted badly to sleep.

"I had to know, Andreyev, if you were telling me the truth."

He said something that she barely heard. She was thinking of Rayner, a dream of broken glass, of dying. If she felt some distant anger now it was directed less at those around her than at herself: she had become the object of her own rage. But rage took strength, and she had none. Her heart was sluggish, each slow beat suggesting the onslaught of pain. She felt Andreyev rise. His words came from a distance. *You mustn't tell anyone. Promise me that.*

When she opened her eyes he had gone from the room. She stared at the dark window, where Andreyev had untidily drawn the draperies back. Outside, in the distance, there was a neon light pulsing. Tiny reflections, like electrified fish, flashed on and off upon the black glass.

## 6.

It was after midnight when Rayner stepped out of the house in Belsize Park. He paused at the bottom of the steps and turned up the collar of his raincoat. The wind had dragged in its turbulent wake a chilly rain. Sally, he thought. There ought to be a book called *Uses and Abuses of Sex.* His lovemaking, if you could call it that, had been less for her than for himself—an act of anxiety, of self-gratification, a weirdly empty satisfaction. Consider something impossible, he thought: like performing mouth-to-mouth resuscitation on yourself. It had been as meaningless as that. Quick and cold. And she had known she was being used. Lying in the dark, smoking a cigarette, she had said, "There's something to be said for masturbation, Rayner." What could he do? Apologize? Rayner, he thought, you have to pull yourself together. You have to apply epoxy to the dismembered parts of yourself—because it's a long fucking way down.

He stared at the streetlamps and at how the branches of wintry trees beat madly against the blurry lights. He was tempted to go back inside and say he was sorry, but sometimes words were just things you fumbled with. Maybe she understood anyhow. You lose somebody you have loved all your life: there had to be a temporary loosening of some essential screw in the old head. Brave fronts and stiff upper lips weren't his style. He felt the wind in his hair and he shivered. He realized that what he really wanted was a form of revenge—the problem being that he had no object in mind.

He crossed the street, thinking of heading down to Swiss Cottage, or to Finchley Road, where he might find a cab. But halfway across he paused, conscious of some faint movement behind—and he remembered the noise on the stairs, the shadow passing the light. Gull: would good old George go to all that trouble? Would George have a specialist somewhere in pressing ears to doors? Not now, surely; after all, Gull had brought it out into the open. So why would he continue surveillance if Rayner knew about it?

He bent down, pretending to tie a lace, wishing that his shoes were not of the slip-on kind. Who? he wondered. He heard the parting of shrubbery, a damp stick breaking slowly, and he turned around to see a man moving quickly against the low white wall that surrounded Sally's house. Along the street a little way the headlights of a car were turned on. The man was going in that direction. Rayner moved after him, walking quickly, while the car edged forward. The man, who wore an old-fashioned soft hat low on his forehead, swung around to look at Rayner. The horn of the car was sounded once. Rayner moved faster.

The man, tugging on his hat, holding it down against the ferocious wind, went to the edge of the sidewalk as if he needed to remind the driver of the car where he was, but Rayner caught him just as the car pulled up at the curb. The man was middle-aged, flabby, ghostly in the streetlamps. The door of the car swung open, striking Rayner hard in the thighs. Momentarily he loosened his grip on the man. The hat was tugged away, whipped by the wind. Stupid, stupid, stupid, Rayner thought, rubbing his thighs through the folds of his coat. The hatless man was climbing into the car, exchanging some hurried phrase with the driver, then swinging the door again so that it hammered into Rayner's groin. He slipped to the wet pavement, watching the car—a black Saab of uncertain vintage—pull away from the side. Ah, fuck, Rayner thought, squatting there absurdly on his knees and feeling both dampness and pain spread through him. Turning, he watched the car go; and, as if in some surreal comic strip, he noticed the windblown hat dancing down the street over branches, lamps, and telephone wires, and finally vanishing somewhere above the rooftops of Belsize Park like a misdirected homing pigeon.

He got to his feet, still rubbing his thighs and groin. Goons, he thought. He limped to the nearest wall and leaned against it, struggling for his breath. Goons, nighthawks, the clandestine brigade who shared this propensity for darkness with cockroaches, wood lice, and other furtive pests. But they hadn't come from George Gull: he was sure of that. Unless, of course, George had started to use Russian-speaking shitheads to do his dirty work for him.

# 3

A fresh morning, a March sun that had all the suspect vitality of a counterfeit coin newly minted; but somewhere there was spring, a sense of renewal. Of all the English seasons, Dubbs found spring the saddest. What else but rebirth could remind you so forcibly of the running down of your own seasons? He stepped out of the underground station in Chalk Farm, assailed at once by diesel fumes, the roar of hectic traffic, a kind of madness that suggested a headlong rush into various voids. He turned a corner, finding himself on a sleazy street of gray houses and small shops. On the opposite side of the street there was a bar called The Mother Goose, one of those brewery-owned horrors that spend half of their time trying to be discothèques. He shivered and went inside, smelling stale spilled beer, noticing an enormous jukebox standing silent in the corner. Grabowski, whose wardrobe seemingly consisted entirely of soiled raincoats, sat alone at the bar. He acknowledged Dubbs with a slight inclination of his hairless head.

"What will you have, Eric?" Dubbs said. He drew a bunch of coins from his coat.

Grabowski asked for a Vat 69 and a beer chaser. When the order was served, Grabowski threw the Scotch back quickly. Then, with a look of Slavic moodiness, he gazed into his beer glass.

"So," Dubbs said, and smacked his lips, putting his own glass of Bell's down on the bar, "what brings me out to Chalk Farm on such a fine day, Eric?"

Grabowski lit a cigarette, a Woodbine. Dubbs remembered the circular tins of fifty that used to be so common in wartime.

"You've been busy, Dubbs, is what I hear," Grabowski said. His English was flat, accents in all the most unlikely places.

"Never a dull moment, Eric," said Dubbs.

"How I hear it is you've been asking around about a man, a dead man."

"You do make me sound morbid," Dubbs said. He stared at the deep-orange nicotine stains on Grabowski's fingers; an unusual pattern there, every finger covered with the stains.

"A dead man. An American. Is that true?"

"It might very well be," and Dubbs tried to remember his dossier on Grabowski. A Russian of German descent, wasn't that it? Jumped from a trawler in the North Sea. It was somehow disappointing to see the hero so reduced, as if the magnificent flight to freedom and democracy had been undertaken for the sake of booze and Woodbines. I must shield myself, Dubbs thought, from the perils of my own cynicism.

"I have something," Grabowski said. "Maybe we go over to a table."

They carried their drinks to the corner table and sat. A pretty girl in uniform was laying out trays of food for the expected lunchtime crowd. Shepherd's pie and Scotch eggs.

Dubbs watched Grabowski a moment. "What do you have, Eric?"

Grabowski looked suspiciously around the empty bar. He clutched his pint of Watneys and drank. Beer slipped over his lips, down his chin. "You'll pay?" he asked.

"Well, old man, that's going to depend rather."

Grabowski made a face. "I don't have to do this, see. I don't have to help you, Dubbs."

"Of course you don't." Dubbs began to rise, but Grabowski, with some measure of desperation that, Dubbs thought, was in direct proportion to his need for beer money, clutched at Dubbs's coat sleeve.

"I have an item. Twenty-five quid."

"That's somewhat steep," said Dubbs.

"Hear what I have to say first."

Dubbs shrugged. Grabowski emptied his glass with a loud *glugg*-ing sound and then gazed into the emptiness of it with a disgruntled look.

"Okay. Listen. Your place is wired."

"My place is *what?*"

"You heard me, Dubbs. Wired. Tapped."

"How do you know this?"

Grabowski mysteriously tapped the side of his nose. "Hey, Dubbs, what do you want for your money? That I tell you my sources?"

"It helps," said Dubbs.

"Let me put it so you understand. You started to ask some questions. Well, frankly, you don't know how to be discreet. A certain party approached . . . some friends of mine. They are electronical wizards, see?"

Dubbs nodded. "Why would anybody want to bug my place?"

"I'm not the oracle, Dubbs. I only tell you what I know. You go around asking about this American, well, this interests a certain party and so a job is subcontracted. Are you following me?"

"You have a name for this certain party?"

"Are you stupid, Dubbs? I say a certain party and it means only the one thing."

Dubbs was silent a moment. Then he said, "I understand we're talking about the Embassy of the USSR?"

Grabowski fiddled with his empty glass; a conspicuous gesture.

"How many devices, do you know?"

"I understand three," Grabowski said. "My friends, the electronical wizards, they are not exactly pleased to be working for this certain party on any kind of basis. They don't do their *best* work, do you follow?"

"I'll find them, is that what you're saying?"

Grabowski got up, hands in the pockets of his soiled coat. Dubbs wondered how one could accumulate so many disparate stains, unless you were lying under a leaky car, devouring a hamburger smothered in tomato sauce, and simultaneously dropping cigarette ash all over yourself.

"I'm going to the lavatory now," Grabowski said.

"I'll accompany you." Dubbs got up, feeling in an inner pocket for his wallet. He followed Grabowski through into a cavernous room of stained urinals. There was the sound of water dripping from a cistern somewhere.

"Your money," Dubbs said.

"Very fine," Grabowski said. "Can I buy you a drink?"

"I think not," Dubbs said. "Some other time."

*2.*

Dubbs met Rayner in the late afternoon in Marylebone High Street. Dubbs carried a string bag that contained a box of parrot food, two onions, and a piece of porterhouse steak already leaking blood through its paper wrapping. They went inside a Salisbury's supermarket, where Dubbs purchased a couple of green apples, which he slung inside the bag. Then they walked in silence for a while, cutting down a side street away from the noise of traffic. Eventually, in a small square area between blocks of flats, they came to a park—a couple of spindly trees, kids on a slide, a sandpile, mothers looking lonely on benches. They sat down on a bench and Dubbs surveyed the park disapprovingly.

"A veritable oasis," he said. "Courtesy of some benign municipal power. I can just *picture* some idiotic clerk putting his signature to a requisition. *A park? Good Lord, what do they need a park for?* We are overrun with civil servants, my dear. They have bad teeth, poor eyesight, and they take their vacations, under sufferance, in such places as Torquay and Torremolinos. They have white sticks for legs and they suffer dreadfully in the hot sun. Ah, well."

Dubbs bit into an apple, his jaw revolving. He watched a gang of kids come tumbling down the slide. The easy spring of youth, he thought. Bravery and broken bones. Then he turned to look quickly at Rayner.

"I was telling you about the eavesdropping devices," he said. "The first was under the sink. Really, an eavesdropping device in the *kitchen?* The second was more stupid—inside a clock that offers the listener Westminster chimes on the quarter hour. The third, at least, was in my bedroom. Not that I indulge in any great activity in that particular room, John—but it was a better shot than the others."

"The Russians?" Rayner asked.

"As I understand it," said Dubbs, putting the core of his green apple back inside the string bag. He surveyed the bloodied package of meat with some distaste. "The Russians, of course. Which presents us with something of an enigma, my dear. The Russians who savaged you last night—"

"It was hardly that," Rayner said.

"In my book, John, all violence is savage." Dubbs looked brightly toward the sandpile, where a worried mother was removing fistfuls of municipal sand from the open mouth of her infant. "We must assume, I think, that our interest in Richard has intrigued the people at the Embassy. Otherwise, why go to the trouble of tapping my homestead? Why bother with sending their shadows after you? What, one might ask, are they concerned about?"

Dubbs was silent, taking a Sobranie from a box, lighting it. Rayner undid the buttons of his coat in the manner of one taking a calculated risk with the weather.

"Now why would they be so interested in knowing about Richard?" Dubbs said, more to himself than to Rayner. "The man killed himself—are they afraid we might find out something to the contrary?"

"Like what?"

"There's the rub, laddie," Dubbs said. "Like what exactly."

Dubbs gathered up his string bag and began to walk. Rayner followed him.

"Consider what we've got, and God knows it's little enough," Dubbs said. "Your brother jumped from a window. Eyewitness, your brother's wife. A perfect suicide. I trust this isn't painful, my dear? The thing's clear-cut, obvious, no crime to be solved. Because you aren't *exactly* convinced by the situation, we do a little probing, a word here, a question there. And my people are such awful gossips—and frankly some of them are quite untrustworthy—that word gets back to the Russians. Next thing, they're after us. Why? Because there's something we're not supposed to find out? Or because my dear friend Mr. Zubro is himself perplexed?"

"Zubro?"

"Ah, John," Dubbs said. "We work in a hall of mirrors. A Zubro here, a Zubro there. You need to cut your eyeteeth on Friend Zubro, John. He has all the externals of an Englishman, and all the curiosity of a Cheshire cat. One day you must meet Anatoly. To his credit, he knows that the game has its rules."

"And he's behind the bugging, the surveillance?"

Dubbs nodded. "Nobody else, John."

They left the park and walked back in the direction of Marylebone High Street. A cloud pattern passed, like the slender hand of a conjurer, across the March sun.

"What next?" Rayner asked.

Dubbs, shrugging, switched his string bag from one hand to the other. "I suggest you check your own flat for foreign objects. And perhaps even this gal's place in Belsize Park. How can she *stand* it over there?" Dubbs wrinkled his nose, as if a particularly noxious stench had passed just in front of him. They paused at a traffic signal. Cabs and buses roared past: destination hell, Dubbs thought. He glanced at Rayner—young, still wet behind the ears, and out of his depth in the perplexities of the game. What could one do but lend a helping hand when it was needed?

Passing that curve of forty-five on life's wretched graph, Dubbs thought, perhaps you started to see something of your former self in younger men. Besides, Rayner didn't look especially well, healthy: he had developed an uncomfortable expression, a look that one might see on the faces of those who expected something to happen from behind. Jumpy, nervy, a chalky pallor to the skin. Young men, Dubbs thought, ought to appear *vital.* He reached out, touching Rayner on the elbow.

"Can I invite you for tea?"

Rayner hesitated before declining. "My own embassy beckons, Dubbs. But thanks. Thanks for everything."

Dubbs clapped him lightly on the shoulder. "Keep in touch," he said. He watched Rayner turn and lose himself in the throng that moved along the pavement. There were some thoughts Dubbs did not like to entertain—such as those that concerned his own sexuality. For a long time now, ever since a prim little suburban girl called Rita, domiciled in the red-brick jungle of Harrow, had rebuffed his advances, spurned his offer of marriage and respectability, he had considered himself one of those who deserve to be called asexual. But there were times, times in the depths of night, or on rainy empty mornings, when he wondered if he had mislabeled himself.

Ah, well, he thought. And went off in search of a bus.

**3.**

The man sat in the corridor, reading, Andreyev noticed, a copy of the *Reader's Digest,* whose front cover had the provocative question *"What Are the Reds Up to in Ethiopia?"* He glanced up from the magazine as Andreyev passed in the direction of his room. Andreyev unlocked his door and stepped inside the room, going to the window. Late afternoon: a hazy view of an expanse of park, a small body of water, a kite being flown haphazardly in the failing sunlight. London, he thought. Freedom. And all it would take was some simple cunning, some extra surge of courage. He looked at the bedside telephone. Pointless. The line would be listened to—if not by Oblinski then by one of the others, perhaps even directly patched into the Embassy itself.

He sat down at the window, opening a copy of the afternoon edition of *The Evening Standard.* On the inside back page there was a photograph of the Soviet team at practice, together with some prediction of victory by the English team manager in Saturday's game. Saturday, Andreyev thought. He would have to move before Saturday because after that—after that he wasn't sure of anything, if the entourage was going back to Russia or traveling elsewhere. He put the newspaper down and stared from the window. When? When would there be the chance? When would there be an opening in this damned wall? He considered the guard in the corridor, flipping the pages of a magazine whose language he presumably couldn't understand anyhow. Watching, waiting. And then he thought of Mrs. Blum, lying in her room, dreaming of her impossible Palestine, concocting her own Jerusalem from snapshots and letters. What wouldn't he give to have her power—even for a moment?

That power: he didn't want to linger on the memory of it, the way she had slipped, with the efficiency of a surgical device, into his mind, that sense of something sharp touching the furthest recesses of brain, the distant corners of memory, the plunder, the violation, the intrusion—as if what had taken place were a painful defilement of his identity. No, he didn't want to remember the dark humiliation he had felt, brain cells burning, memories going off like brilliant pinwheels, the sure and terrible knowledge that had she so chosen, she could have killed him—

Trembling, he took the piece of paper from his pocket. He smoothed it out, studying the address, the telephone number—anxious memory, like some wasted muscle he couldn't get to respond. Try. Try to get it right. But he couldn't; the numbers came out confused and mixed up. He folded the slip once, then a second time, so that it was nothing more than a tiny square he shoved into his pocket, burying it under a key and some coins. Saturday, it had to be before Saturday. What if he made it anyway? What if he got away? Would the British offer him the asylum he wanted? Or would they just hand him back . . . ?

He was scared. He started slightly when he heard the sound of light knocking at his door. Before he could move he saw the handle turn and the door open.

Katya stepped inside the room—a different Katya, her face made up inexpertly, her dress a bright floral garment, her hair cut and brushed in a new fashion. For a moment he was appalled, disconcerted by the way she looked. The makeup—dear God, the scarlet brightness of the lips, the clownlike touches of rouge on the cheeks, the false eyelashes that created a comic-strip vision, eyeshadow suggesting the appearance of a coal miner. "Well, Victor?" she said, spinning around slowly so that he might have a complete view. "I used up some of my allowance. Does it startle you?"

His mouth was dry. "Yes," he said. "It's very different. I didn't expect it."

She came across the room as if she was dancing, waltzing with a shadow, and she stopped beside him. Even the scent that hung around her was new to him. Sharp, bittersweet, like the juice of an apricot. "When in Rome," she said. "After all, how many opportunities to travel come up?"

Andreyev turned away, pretending to look at the newspaper. But she reached forward and took the paper from his hand. She let it fall to the floor, the sheets separating and fluttering. "Don't you like your Katya, Professor?" The woman, pushing her lower lip forward, was trying to look petulant. He was reminded now of their night in Moscow, their single farcical attempt at lovemaking.

"It takes getting used to," he said. He couldn't look at her. He stared at the window, the darkening sky, the way the sun slipped toward the horizon.

"You haven't been paying much attention to me lately," she said. "I might imagine you were avoiding me, Professor."

He shook his head. The dryness in his mouth: he couldn't swallow. "No," he said. "It's this whole situation . . . it keeps me busy. I don't seem to have a moment when I'm alone." Then he was thinking of Domareski, of the dead man in the snow; Katya—Katya, whose face now looked like some hideous cosmetic mishap—how could he even think of trusting her? There was no one now to trust. Only the name on the slip of paper.

"Don't you like the way I look?" she asked.

"I do."

She closed her eyes, as if she expected to be kissed. But he had already turned away, pretending he hadn't noticed the gesture. There was a burnt-out vapor trail in the sky. He wondered what the young American had felt, standing at a window similar to this one; he wondered about the sharp strokes of pain, the demolition of the will. Katya had her hand on his arm. He glanced at her. Pity. That was all he felt. She began to rub his arm.

"Before we left Moscow," she said, then became silent.

He could feel it; a pressure against his heart. A sense of his own collapse.

"Before we left Moscow—why did you visit Stefanoff?"

Andreyev heard the rush of dark spaces in his head, the turbulent passages of his own blood. Stefanoff. How had she known about Stefanoff?

"What makes you think I visited him?" he asked. Calm, poise. Believe in your own fabrications.

"I followed you," she said.

He turned to look at her again, angry now. "You had no right to do that. You had no right whatsoever."

"It troubles me, Victor. A man in your position contacting a known dissident. And a Jew. Why do you put yourself in such jeopardy?"

"Stefanoff was a student of mine," he said, and his voice was feeble, an untuned instrument.

"Years ago," Katya said. "Why would you visit an old student, Victor? Why would you run the risk of association? It doesn't make sense."

Andreyev watched the flat sun on the glass. It was a cold orange glow now. "It was a social visit. Am I denied that?" Stefanoff's one-room flat. The piece of paper. The name of the person who would help.

"What did you talk about?"

He looked at her face, noticing now a viciousness, feeling as if he were gazing at the blade of an open razor.

"We talked about old times."

She moved away from him to the window, then turned to face him so that the light fell at her back; suddenly she was anonymous, demonic. He put his hands inside his pockets and wondered how much she really knew, how much of this was guesswork. She couldn't know about the paper, could she? Unless—

"You understand that Stefanoff was arrested the day we left Moscow?"

He stared at her, shaking his head.

"He was arrested on charges of treason," she said.

He couldn't feel himself now. There was a curious disembodiment, a sense of free-falling: he was no longer in this room, no longer connected with a known reality, but instead floating indiscriminately through alien spaces. Stefanoff arrested. He sat down, his legs weak. Arrested. With all its implications. How much pressure would they put on Stefanoff? What would he tell them? What would he admit to? There were limits, even for someone of Stefanoff's courage. Would he say he had given certain information to Andreyev? Would he tell them—

"You mustn't look so concerned, Victor," Katya said. "After all, you only visited him for social reasons, didn't you? Perhaps you drank a little vodka, smoked tobacco, talked about the good old days? Perhaps you even listened to some pleasant music, no?"

"I didn't know they had taken him," Andreyev said. "I wasn't aware of that."

Katya smiled. "One ought to be careful of one's social behavior, my dear Andreyev."

She moved to his chair and stood with her hips close to his face. Stefanoff, he thought. Every man has a breaking point, Stefanoff included. *You understand this is going to be dangerous, Victor?* I understand, Alexei. *Don't carry this paper, whatever you do. Memorize it and burn it.* Yes, of course. Dear God. They would break Stefanoff. They would break him as one might a used matchstick. He closed his eyes, conscious of Katya's scent, of her hand in his hair. He got up from the chair, passing her.

Her voice was sharp, hurt. "Don't you find me attractive?"

He stared at her a moment. It was Domareski who came to mind again. Then he thought: *But I am Domareski now.* He was suddenly very afraid of death and dying: a fear of dark heights, of standing on the edge of some cliff that rose above black water. Dying, he thought. Katya, her mouth tight, was watching him. The painted face, the unreal horror of the floral dress, the plastic clasp of yellow that was bound to her hair: a garden of mad colors. *Don't you find me attractive?* He stared at the door, wondering how far he would get if he were to run, dash past the man who sat by the elevator door. Nowhere, he thought. Then you play it differently. You play it with an understanding that the rules have been changed.

Slowly he went toward the woman. He put his hands gently against her shoulders and, drawing her toward him, feeling the lean hardness of her body, he held her against him.

"This is better, Victor," she said. "Isn't this a better way?"

He felt her hand pull at the buckle of his belt and he realized, with a start of self-contempt, that he was already aroused by her.

"This is so much better, so much better," she said, sighing in a way he found dreadful.

**4.**

It was after seven and dark when Rayner reached Belsize Park. A search of his own flat in St. John's Wood had turned up nothing in the way of listening devices. He had poked and prodded in both obscure and obvious places; but nothing. Now, climbing the dimly lit stair to Sally's apartment, he paused halfway up to catch his breath. The problem of Richard, he thought: it wouldn't dissolve. If the Russians were *that* interested, there had to be some good reason behind it— but good reasons were the very things that continually eluded him. What he kept coming back to was Isobel's testimony, her eyewitness account, something he could only explain away as false if he postulated bizarre circumstances. She had been drugged while Richard had been killed: some psychedelic hallucination she now firmly believed to be reality. Hypnotic suggestion was another: look into my eyes and relax and you won't remember anything except the fact that your husband took his own life. But these were farfetched for him. There was also the possibility that it hadn't been Isobel who had been drugged/ hypnotized, but Richard himself. Rayner shrugged, climbed upward, smelling the darkness around him. Some exotic spice was simmering behind a closed door.

He reached the door of Sally's flat and knocked. For a time there wasn't an answer—only a whispered sound from inside, a noise of something being scraped. He waited, then knocked again, and the door was immediately opened. Sally stood there with a glass of red wine in her hand. She looked at him with a dizzy smile, her face flushed. I come in a surprise package, Rayner thought, knowing that there was somebody else inside the flat. Beyond Sally he saw a shadow move.

"This *is* unexpected," she said.

He wondered if he felt hurt or just disappointed. He looked at her a moment, the familiar housecoat, the untidy hair, large earrings in the shape of hoops swaying against the sides of her neck. What the fuck do you say? he wondered. God knows, I haven't been much of a lover lately.

"I guess I should have called," he said.

"It would have been thoughtful of you, John." She swung the edge of the door back and forth nervously.

"I didn't have time," he said.

"The point is, dear, I'm rather occupied—"

He heard low music from inside. Something Eastern, atonal, the music of the gurus: it was as if Sally had missed the Sixties and was doing her damnedest to catch up with them. He could smell incense and, behind it, the perfume of marijuana. *The point is, dear, don't you know, blah blah blah.* He wondered if you graduated from Roedean with callused hands, the hazards of hockey; or if the calluses were inside, deep inside.

"I don't exactly want to disturb anything," he said. "But I need to come in."

"I feel a scene coming on," she said.

"Not from me you don't."

Rayner went inside the flat. The man who sat sheepishly on the sofa—the sofa, Rayner thought, where last night's awkward sex had been engineered—was middle-aged, plump, and somehow faintly familiar. He felt Sally skirt around the room, hearing her make the offer of a glass of wine. Rayner declined.

"John, this is Mark Wellington," she said. "He's one of our authors."

"Nice," Rayner said. Civilized introductions all round. What was he supposed to do? Shake hands? I could try to imagine that I haven't exactly been betrayed. Wellington, of course: the face was familiar from dust jackets of best-selling adventure stories concerning men in submarines, hidden Nazi treasures, cardboard people scaling the sides of impossible mountains. Rayner had read one once. Rugged language, words like *thrust* and *rough* and *jagged.* Sexual passages as explicit, as interesting, as blueprints for turbines.

"Pleasure to meet you," Wellington said awkwardly, half rising.

"Mark and I were sort of discussing his new book," Sally said.

"Yeah? What's it called? *The Matterhorn Connection? The Lost Treasure of the Sahara?*" Rayner hated himself for the adolescent outbreak. You're hurt, he thought. This is a pain.

"You're being silly, darling," she said.

Rayner wondered: Maybe she's an author's groupie, maybe she gets her jollies blowing off masters of basic prose style. Don't let it touch you, he thought. Don't start thinking you're into this a whole lot deeper than you should be. Fuck it. But he couldn't put the pain down. It stuck to him.

"Actually, it's called *The Black Alphabet,*" Wellington said, being awfully nice.

"Hope it sells a million," said Rayner, turning away from the guy, avoiding Sally's expression too. He went into the bedroom, a converted attic with a sloping roof. A room of character, he thought. Screw it. He heard her come after him, closing the door behind her.

"You should have called first," she said.

"It doesn't matter, Sally. I swear it doesn't make an inch of difference who you fuck." He was opening drawers, uncovering piles of crumpled underwear.

"It's one thing to barge in, it's quite another, darling, to work your way through my knickers. If you need a souvenir of our rather ham-fisted copulations, you only have to ask."

Rayner stared at her. He wanted to hit her; the urge came out of him in a way he couldn't entirely understand. He clenched his hands and looked down into the open drawers. She's a slob, he thought. Who needs it? He began dropping her clothes to the floor.

Panties. Slips. Panty hose. A schoolboy's box of delights.

"You don't own me, Rayner. Did you imagine that you did?"

"Look, baby, I recognize the fact I've been relegated to the second division, where all the old lovers play these melancholy tunes. Okay? If you need the fat man in there, good luck."

"You're absurd, Rayner," she said. "You must live in some strange old-fashioned reality if you think I sit round here waiting for you to call. *I think I'll just shove on over to Sally's and dip my wick.* Well, fuck you, Rayner."

He tried not to hear her. He was feeling underneath the mattress that lay on the floor. There's a place, he thought, a place where no such thing as hurt exists. That's where I should be headed.

"What the hell are you fumbling for, anyway?" she asked. She was standing over him, her wineglass tilted to one side, red drops slicking onto the mattress, where they spread like menstrual stains.

"I'll tell you when I find it," he said. "Why don't

you go and sit in Mr. Wellington's lap meantime, okay?''

He heard her go out of the room and slam the door. He sat motionless for a while in silence. Then the outer door was shut. After a while, Sally came back into the bedroom. She watched him, her back to the wall, her wineglass held at the same precarious angle.

"He's gone," she said. "I sent him away."

"Bully for you, dahling."

"All right," she said. "Let's clear the air."

"Let's," he said.

"Fidelity isn't my stock-in-trade, Rayner. And I don't exactly enjoy being made to feel that I'm doing something behind your back. Because I'm not. I sent Mark away because I wanted to speak to you."

"Speak, speak," he said.

"I like him. All right? I like lots of men. I simply refuse to be tied down like some bloody slave—"

Rayner stood up, watching her. "How many, Sally? How many?"

"Oh, Christ, don't be so childish. I don't keep a scorecard beside my bed. I don't keep a diary."

The *Guinness Book of World Records,* he thought. All the old lovers, he realized, were not so old after all. They were still nibbling at the same bait. Maybe she kept a regular reserve team, men she could call on when the first selections were playing elsewhere.

"Forget it," he said. "It doesn't matter."

"Of course it matters. I simply think you're reacting foolishly, that's all. You come in here, you start rummaging around—what the hell *are* you looking for anyway?"

"Hidden lovers," he said. "I'm interested in where you keep them, kid."

"Why don't you check inside the oven? Or look

in the pantry? Perhaps you should start with the freezer compartment of the fridge."

She went out of the bedroom. He could hear her cross the living-room floor: angry footsteps. Mad little noises. It calls for that activity known as "being realistic," Rayner thought. Facing facts squarely. She screws around. Why didn't you suspect it before? Even now, now when you know, does it matter? Ah, shit. *Why does it matter?*

He went into the sitting room. He looked at her for a time. She was lighting a cigarette with one hand, pouring more wine with the other. On the table, beside an unlit candle, he saw rolling papers, charred tapers, a plastic bag of dope. Stoned, he thought. What the hell.

"If it means anything, I'm sorry," he said.

She looked vacantly at him.

"I came here because I have reason to believe that somebody has planted bugs in your flat."

"Bugs? Here?"

"I'll look around, then I'll leave. Okay?"

"Bugs—why here?" she asked.

"It's a long story, Sally."

She put her wineglass down; she laughed, a rather disjointed sound. "Then you *are* a spook!"

He said nothing. He continued his search. When he found the devices they were textbook locations. Under the table, applied with some light putty; beneath the sofa; inside a lacquered Oriental box. They were powerful, high-frequency gizmos.

"Those little things?" she asked.

"Yeah. Those little things," he said.

"But you can't say any more, correct?"

"You guessed it."

He put them in his pocket and looked at her. For a moment he wished he could hear the tapes that would have been made from the gadgets. Lover after lover after lover, the creak of the sofa, the sound of her orgasmic squeals. What was he left with now? *Being realistic,* he thought. Or walking out of the mess. Where did this strange morality come from? he wondered. You run into a free spirit and all you can do is back off and pout like some deprived kid on an unhappy Christmas.

"Bugs," she said. She shook her head. "Something to do with your brother?"

Rayner shrugged. He could still feel, like a stain left behind in permanent ink, the presence of the famous hack. Did she screw all her authors? Was it written into the contract? A sexual advance? She turned away, filling her glass again, her movements unsteady. Deeper than I ever believed, Rayner thought. Otherwise—why the hurt that wouldn't evaporate?

"So—how do you plan to spend your evening?" he asked.

The answer was a crunch. "I'm going over to Mark's," she said.

Rayner hesitated a second before moving toward the door. What was left to say? He felt an absence inside him, a dearth of volition: more simply, he thought, something was crumpling.

"Enjoy," he said, opening the door, stepping onto the landing, seeing the dim light at the foot of the stairs. He closed the door; as he did so he heard her wineglass break. Put your feelings in a rucksack, he thought, then dump it. Dump it.

**5.**

Andreyev woke in the dark, unaware of time, of how many hours had passed since he had turned away from Katya to sleep—now, reaching across the bedsheets, his hand collided with her naked shoulder. But she didn't move. Faintly, in outline, he could make out her face, the open mouth, the closed eyelids. He withdrew his hand and lay perfectly still, thinking not now of Stefanoff's arrest, or of his own immediate predicament, but of what had taken place between himself and the sleeping woman—as if these images were maps of some uncharted region of himself. His quick excitement, his brief elation followed by a sense of his own disgust. Even afterward, she had pressed herself against him, trying to arouse him with her hands and mouth, but all he had experienced then was distance from her, from himself: a tangle of shadows in a dark bedroom, nothing more. Slowly, he sat up. What else could he have done? He couldn't have turned her away, refused her, because he couldn't have afforded to have that viciousness come back, like some remorseless pendulum, against him. Lovemaking. It had bought him time at a rather expensive rate of exchange. It had won him some hours of her silence. She might have gone to Oblinski and said, *He saw Stefanoff in Moscow*—

Quietly he pushed the white bedsheet away from his body. He stood upright, conscious of his own pale flesh as he fumbled for his clothes. The keys and coins in his pants rattled noisily. His feet became entangled in Katya's discarded clothing: the nylon underwear, a lavender slip, the crumpled floral dress. He dressed quickly, silently, crossing the room to the window as he fumbled with his shirt buttons. There was no moon in the city sky. The expanse of park was a dark hollow etched in the night. A starless dark, offering at the very least shadows, places in which to hide. He put his hand in his pocket and, as if it were a rabbit's paw to be stroked for luck, rubbed the piece of paper.

Katya moaned in her sleep, turning to face the wall. Please God, he thought. Don't let her wake. He took his jacket from the back of the chair, struggled into it, then went to the door, conscious of his shoelaces flapping untidily at his feet. *Don't wake, Katya. Sleep. Sleep on.* At the door his fingers curled around the handle; he paused. The man in the chair by the elevator. This is insanity, he thought. You won't get anywhere like this. Where is the logical plan? the precise strategy? the feasible scheme? Instead, you succumb finally to desperation and panic. The need simply to run. How far do you expect to get, Victor? How far?

He opened the door a little way. The corridor was lit badly—a few weak bulbs covered with clam-shaped shades. The man was still holding the *Reader's Digest,* his head tilted sleepily to one side. Andreyev peered through the slit, sweating, exhausted even before he had begun. The man moved his head in the manner of one shaking fatigue away. For a time Andreyev didn't move. Katya turned restlessly on the bed. It comes down to terror, Andreyev thought—to a place that is miles removed from your neat little world of science, your place of scales and balances and charts. He watched the man take out a briar pipe and stuff the bowl with tobacco. The elevator door opened and a couple, walking arm in arm, stepped out and moved off in the opposite direction from Andreyev's room. Move, he thought. Act. But he remained still, clutching the edge of the door, watching the couple disappear, watching the man labor with the pipe, a flurry of matches struck and spent. The man moved his chair a couple of inches, as if he were trying to get out of a draft.

Andreyev waited. Waiting like this, he thought, stuck between Katya and the jailer. How do you solve this? Where are the equations? the formulae? He looked across the darkened room at the indeterminate shape of Katya. How much longer would she sleep? How soon would it be before she reached out for him and found an absence? Do it, he thought. Walk out. Walk out and away. He listened to the noise of the elevator falling in the shaft. He opened the door a little way farther. Then it was as if it mattered no longer, life or death, escape or entrapment; it was as if these opposites had met and merged and there was no difference between them.

"Andreyev?"

When he heard her voice he went out into the corridor.

"Andreyev?"

He pulled the door quietly behind him. The man in the chair looked up from his magazine. Andreyev hesitated. It's not too late, he thought, it's not too late to turn and go back inside the room and forget everything and live the rest of your life with the knowledge that your own nerve let you down and that you were a coward—

The man closed his magazine and got up from the chair and, as if he was stunned by Andreyev's sudden appearance, stood motionless awhile; from behind the closed door Andreyev could hear Katya calling his name in a series of worried repetitions. No, he thought. How could he go back inside the room, *that* room? He stared at the man by the elevator, who had begun, at last, to move toward him. The other way, Andreyev thought: where does the corridor lead? He turned, listening to the man call after him, *"Do-mareski? Where do you think you're going?"*

Then he was walking, hurrying, his heart hammering and his muscles weak, hurrying, expecting the man to shoot him in the back. The corridor twisted at a right angle. When he turned the corner, Andreyev ran. He passed closed doors, an elevator shaft with a sign that read "Out of Order." Then there was a door that opened onto a flight of concrete steps. He rushed through it. His feet echoed on the steps, millions of small fading repetitions. Hurry hurry hurry. He heard the door slam somewhere above him as he went down and then the name was being called again, the dead man's name, but he didn't stop, he couldn't stop and go back now. *"Domareski! Domareski! Stop where you are!"* Katya, Andreyev thought—if she picked up the telephone in time the hotel could be sealed and then there would be no way out. Move, he thought. Don't look back.

How many stairs? How many flights? The man was running above him, clattering over the concrete. *Seventh Floor.* He felt weak again, weak and used, urging wasted muscles into action. He was sweating, damp, his white shirt discolored. But nothing mattered except for getting out, finding a call box, unrolling the precious piece of paper and getting through to the man who would help, the man Stefanoff swore by, but poor Stefanoff—what was he suffering now? Torture, deprivation, the labor camp.

The man was still shouting, still coming down after him. Andreyev paused, stood in motionless indecision. The door ahead of him—or the stairs down? He didn't think now; there was no time for analysis, ratiocination, all the mental tools he had used for so long. He shoved through the door, finding himself in another corridor. *Third Floor.* Had he run this far? He saw an elevator ahead, saw the door slam shut, the numbers light and change on the panel above. But the elevator was the worst kind of trap. He ran along the corridor, passing the elevator door, passing a startled housemaid who was coming out of a room with a silver tray. I could throw myself on her, Andreyev thought. The quality of mercy. Help me.

He rushed past the woman, turned as the corridor twisted at another severe right angle, found his way back to a flight of stairs where a sign read "FIRE ESCAPE." Down, he thought. There's no other way. Down and down and down. Still he was being pursued by footsteps, massive ringing footsteps that seemed to him like monstrous nails being driven into a hardwood box. And then there were no more stairs.

No more stairs.

He went through a swinging doorway and saw, to his horror, that he was in the lounge of the hotel. Two desk clerks watched him. A woman in a feathery hat, her feet surrounded by luggage and trunks, glanced distastefully at him. A man in a tweed suit, sipping a Bloody Mary, raised his face from a copy of *The Times*. Slow, Andreyev thought. Slow. You just pass the desk slowly.

He heard the swing door open and close at his back.

What do I look like? he wondered. A madman in a white shirt, laces flapping; someone on the edge of coming undone? He crossed the lounge.

Oblinski was coming out of the cocktail bar as if he anticipated the sight of Andreyev. He was smiling. "Domareski," he said. The word was quiet, subdued, as if what Oblinski wanted more than anything else was to convince the various spectators that they were witnessing a lunatic. A sick man. You have to have patience.

Ahead, Andreyev saw the glass revolving doors that led to the street. One final rush, he thought. One last dash through the door—and outside there's darkness, shadows, blind streets. Oblinski was still smiling, walking in an oblique angle to cut him off from the doorway. The other man, panting audibly, was at his back. Andreyev paused and then, lowering his head in the fashion of a sprinter, raced toward the revolving door. Oblinski moved more quickly now, trying at the last moment to cut him off—but he was through the door and out into the street and running.

Running and running.

He could hear Oblinski calling from behind: *"Domareski! Domareski!"* Andreyev turned a corner, found himself in a dark alley that ran behind the hotel. Ahead, there was a narrow courtyard filled with garbage cans. He crossed it, hoping with a kind of forlorn pessimism that he hadn't boxed himself in. There was a low brick wall and another alley, darker than before. He wiped his forehead with his shirt sleeve, barely feeling the sting of the cold March night around him. Now, beyond the alley, there were strange little streets with closed and shuttered shops—lonely streets that might only have been traveled along by the hunted, the desperate, the despairing. He stopped and took the piece of paper out of his pocket, smoothing it in the pale glow of a shopwindow: absurd soft toys—stuffed bears, pandas, giraffes—were frozen in glass-eyed malignance, heaped in bundles or hanging from colored wires. A telephone number, an address. He put the piece of paper back in his pocket and dragged himself farther along the street where, on the corner, there was a bar. There would be a phone inside, perhaps—but by the same token he could be trapped in such a place if they tracked him there. No, he wouldn't go inside the bar. How could he? He continued to run until he had no strength left. He had to sit down somewhere. A park, a bench, some miserable patch of green. He found himself moving beneath trees now, disturbing two lovers on a bench—a man and a woman in thick winter coats, fumbling at one another with gloved hands. They stared at him as he slipped past. Like a ghost, he thought, like some terrible specter. When he could go no farther he lay on the grass. Flat on his back, arms spread, he gazed up at the starless night sky: a sheet of unbroken blackness that promised nothing and revealed even less.

A little luck, he thought. Just a little more luck.

## 6.

Ineptitude was to Zubro as a ravenous moth to the wardrobe of a man of high fashion: an irritant whose existence was a matter of some grief. It was bad enough, he thought, that Rayner should discover his surveillance; but what was worse was the very idea of Ernest Dubbs finding and destroying the devices in his flat—for Zubro did not like the idea of Dubbs winning even a minor victory over him. And now this— this dreadful shambles, this calamity. How was it going to look in the thick headlines of those awful London newspapers? *"Red Physician Seeks Asylum in Dramatic Nighttime Escape."* Red, Zubro thought. The color of his own anger.

He did not know exactly what to say to Oblinski, who, pacing up and down his hotel room like a man on fire, was unsuccessfully trying to work off his rage. A little calm, Zubro thought, goes a long way. He ran an index finger along the sharp crease of his pants and watched Oblinski stop by the window. There were times when words were as useless as damp fuel. Such as now, Zubro thought. One could, of course, ignore the fact that the surveillance of Dubbs and Rayner had turned nothing up. After all, he had acted only out of that curiosity of professional conscientiousness—but the flight of the physician: it was quite another kettle of fish, as the English were so fond of saying. *"Commie Doctor Makes Dash for Freedom."* Perhaps one could hope for something more sedate from *The Times*.

He silently watched Oblinski, who was leaning against the dark pane of glass and banging one hand into the other. It did seem to Zubro that the KGB official was overreacting—defections were always possibilities. One learned to live with them. At the least, another physician could be brought from the Soviet Union; at the very worst, the soccer tour could be canceled. But why should Oblinski be so overwrought?

Zubro rose from his armchair and moved to the window. He cleared his throat, lightly rubbing his lower lip with a handkerchief.

"How close is he to the woman?"

Oblinski shrugged. "He isn't close to anybody—"

Zubro stepped out into the corridor. He walked to the door of the woman's room and knocked. Inside, she was standing by the bed—dressed, he noticed, in a maroon dressing gown she might have purchased that very day at Marks & Spencer. Seduced, he thought, by the consumer nightmare. He didn't like the look of the woman—a sharpness of feature, a face of potential cruelty, the kind of person who, in her late middle years, would embrace the philosophy of martyrdom.

He observed her awhile, thinking: If all this is a charade, then what the hell does it amount to? She had her hands in her pockets. A little delicacy, he thought.

A certain tact. She might have fancied herself to be in love with the errant physician, after all. And love, Zubro understood, was what made the world go round.

"I understand that you and Domareski were . . . intimate?"

She said nothing. It was a mean mouth; he couldn't imagine kissing it. Perhaps poor Domareski had felt the same way; perhaps it wasn't anything so profound as a defection, but simply a rather desperate effort to get away from the clutches of this ax of a woman.

"You were in bed in his room when he . . ."

She nodded her head.

Zubro walked up and down the room. He noticed various boxes of clothing, stuffed in bags that carried the labels of Oxford Street stores. C & A Modes. Bourne & Hollingsworth. Selfridges. Doing the town, he thought. A little foreign exchange had burned the proverbial holes in her pockets.

"Why do you think he ran?"

The woman said nothing. She took her hands from her dressing gown and gazed at them. He repeated his question.

"I don't know the answer," she said. "Why did he run? Where did he run to? I've already told Oblinski what I know."

"Tell me again," Zubro said.

She mumbled in a voice so low he had to concentrate to hear it. Shocked, poor thing. Her lover upped and vanished. *"Red Medic Seeks Asylum."* He closed his eyes, inclined his head, listened. They had made love, then they had slept, and when she had awakened he was leaving the room . . . she had called, but he hadn't answered. Silence. Zubro watched her sit on the bed, her knees jammed somewhat primly together. A virginal gesture, he thought.

"It doesn't surprise me," she said suddenly.

"No? You expected it?" Zubro watched the thin face, the movement of some faint contortion cross the tight surface. What the hell is going on anyhow? They send a physician, someone *suspect,* a security basket case—and now this woman says she isn't surprised. It would make sense if, say, there was a *reason* for Domareski to defect, part of a scheme to plant him in the United Kingdom—but why was everybody so damned upset now that he had managed to get away? Twists and turns, Zubro thought rather bitterly; somebody should have told him. Somebody should have told him the truth. After all, didn't he *need* to know?

"I had the feeling he was up to something," she said quietly.

"Why?"

"Well, he was behaving strangely—"

"Like how?"

Now she appeared embarrassed. "We hadn't been lovers for a long time . . . and I was a little surprised when he became so passionate—"

Ah, Zubro thought. The worm turns. The ordinary little physician becomes a sexual fiend. "Is that all?" he asked.

"That—and the fact he visited Stefanoff before we left Moscow."

Zubro sat upright in his chair. There was a change in him now, a rise in his temperature. He felt a faint film of sweat across his forehead. There was a sudden pulse at the side of his skull. Stefanoff, he thought.

"*Alexei* Stefanoff?" Zubro asked.

The woman nodded slowly. "I told him he shouldn't associate with dissidents like Stefanoff—"

Zubro got to his feet. "Why did he go to see Stefanoff?"

"I don't know."

"Didn't he understand the risk?"

"I don't know—"

Stefanoff, Zubro thought, and smiled to himself: ah, there were still those moments of sheer pleasure in which suddenly you could see the shape of the game board. It was a time in which clouds, those same damned clouds that had hung all day long, cleared as if by divine intervention. Stefanoff: of course. He rubbed his hands together. How could it be so easy?

He went to the door, turning once to say he was glad of her help, then walked down the corridor to the elevator, pressed the call button, and waited with an impatience he could hardly restrain.

*7.*

Ernest Dubbs went down the steps to his basement flat, unlocked the door, and stepped inside the darkened room—but he was too late to answer the telephone. He fumbled across the floor and reached the receiver just as the ringing stopped. Damn, he thought. He turned on a lamp, opened a box of parrot food, and stuffed some through the bars of the cage in which the dreaded Rasputin sat, eyeing Dubbs with profound avian contempt. Dubbs, though, was rather fond of his parrot, a bad-tempered old thing who had only ever been able to master the phrase "Piss off."

He opened the kitchen door, surveyed the mess, lamented the impossibility of finding a reliable charlady, then shut the door again as if the sight were too much to behold. He listened to the parrot knock its beak against a tiny mirror—deluded, poor old bastard, imagines it has company, Dubbs thought—then he lay down on the sofa and closed his eyes.

He belched slightly. The parrot fluttered. A single feather, falling from a wing, floated to the rug. He thought of Anatoly Zubro a moment. A worried man, no doubt—going to all the trouble of wiring an apartment and sending his men around after young John Rayner. The problem, Dubbs thought, lay in the fact that people like Zubro couldn't believe the Cold War wasn't quite the permafrost affair it had once been. Now you had a rather hapless *detente;* and the war boiled down to a series of rather pathetic skirmishes. But Anatoly, dodging around the back streets of London, planting his bugs, sending his thugs off on fruitless errands—well, Anatoly could only be disappointed by the politics of the time. They had deprived him of his function, in a manner of speaking. The pulse of things was weaker nowadays, and far less interesting when you managed to find it.

The mysteries, too, weren't quite the fun things they had been once. I wax boringly nostalgic, Dubbs thought, scolding himself. What were the old days anyhow but a bunch of cloak-and-dagger nonsense? The tinderbox of Berlin. Corpses in frogmen suits washed up in harbors where Russian subs had lately been anchored. He turned on his side, feeling fatigued. The only mystery now was that of Richard Rayner—

His telephone rang. He picked it up and said his number.

There was a brief silence at the other end.

"Am I speaking with Mr. Rasputin?"

Dubbs swung around on the sofa. Dear God, he thought. How long since I heard that form of address?

"Who wants to know?" he said quietly.

"We are mutual friends of Stefanoff, yes?"

Dubbs watched the parrot cling fiercely to the bars of the cage. Stefanoff. Dear old Stefanoff.

"Mutual friends, of course," Dubbs said. "Have we met?"

"No. My name is Andreyev. Victor Andreyev."

Dubbs curled the telephone cord around his wrist. "How can I help?"

A further silence. A truck, something heavy, could be heard roaring over the line.

"It is essential that I see you, Mr. Rasputin."

"Did Stefanoff tell you how?"

"He gave me the information."

"Very well," said Dubbs. "When will you be arriving?"

"I think soon. A matter of some minutes."

"I'll be here," Dubbs said.

There was no good-bye. The line was dead. Dubbs held the receiver a moment, then set it down. Stefanoff. It had been a long time since Stefanoff had used the Rasputin connection. Years—not since 1970, when a man called Nankovitch had defected during some trades conference. Dubbs rose, went inside his bedroom, opened the drawer in the bedside table, and from beneath a pile of laundered handkerchiefs took out a discolored .38 revolver. He checked the chamber, then snapped it shut. He walked through to the living room—suddenly nervous now, nervous in a way he hadn't felt in years. He turned off the lamp and sat in the darkness. He held the revolver in his lap, listening, waiting, hearing the damned parrot repeat, "Piss off, piss off, piss off," like a drunk trapped in a repetitive groove of memory.

"Shut up," said Dubbs. "When I want to hear from you, my dear, I'll ask."

The great bird flapped and fluttered and made a noise like an asthmatic old man. Dubbs stood up and wandered over to the cage. In the dark, he put his hands up and the bird swiped at him with a claw.

"Vindictive old fart," Dubbs said. "When you need to be fed tomorrow, you can jolly well *beg*."

Dubbs opened the kitchen door and went to the window, which afforded him a view of the steps that led upward from the basement to the street. There were peeling iron railings glinting dully in the light of a distant streetlamp. Squalid place, Dubbs thought. He stood motionless, fingering the gun, feeling strange to be armed after all this time. He thought about Stefanoff: how had that Jewish madman survived so long? A wild man of the old school: integrity and dignity and a sizable slice of lunacy. Stefanoff didn't know the meaning of the word *risk*.

Dubbs waited. A tap dripped in the sink, splashing on the pile of soiled dishes. Outside, a car passed in the street, lighting the iron railings. Then there was darkness and silence again. *Mr. Rasputin,* he thought. Just as one is pondering the changes in one's world, along comes a whisper from the past.

Now somebody was moving above, a shadow drifting along the edge of the railings. Dubbs saw the flash of some white clothing, a shirt, a jacket, whatever. At the top of the steps, as if he was beset by indecision, by fear, the man stopped. He seemed to be peering down into the darkness, wondering perhaps if he had come to the right address, or if this entire thing was a terrible mistake. Come on, Dubbs thought. Move yourself.

Dubbs opened the kitchen door slightly and, holding the revolver forward, stared up through the darkness at the man. Take no chances, he thought. Wait. Wait for the other fellow to move. But the man stood motionless, his hands hanging at his sides, his whole position curiously purposeless. Come on, Dubbs thought. *If you're coming, come.*

Dubbs opened the kitchen door wider. The lights of a car picked out the man suddenly—a blinding vision, revealing all at once for Dubbs the fear on the man's white face, the open oval of the mouth, one arm rising upward as if he was protecting himself from the lights of the car.

Dubbs leveled his revolver and rushed toward the steps. He looked up. "Andreyev?" he asked.

The car lights dimmed. There was a sound of footsteps hurrying across the concrete. Andreyev moved, balanced on the top step, balanced there a moment as if he were posing for an artist, hands across his face, one leg raised slightly, body turned toward Dubbs.

"Andreyev—"

The footsteps stopped. In the distance, somehow the most incongruous sound in the world, Dubbs heard the whining siren of a police vehicle. Andreyev, reaching for the second step down, appeared to implode all at once. He sat down on the step, holding his hands against his stomach. Dubbs climbed toward him. There was a brilliant flash in the dark, a sharp echo, and Andreyev was rocked against the wall.

"Andreyev," Dubbs said, taking it step by step, seeing still another flare burn a hole in the dark. Andreyev stood up, clutching the wall, moaning—a sound, Dubbs thought, that was more one of disappointment than of pain. As he stood, there was another shot that struck him in the skull, and he put his hands up feebly to his head. Dubbs, peering between the railings, saw a tan-colored car idling across the street. He aimed his revolver badly, fired, heard his own shot whistle harmlessly off into the distance. The car moved away from the curb, and Dubbs, dropping his revolver, leaned over Andreyev, who was still moaning, still clutching his face with his hands. No, Dubbs thought. No. He helped Andreyev to sit on the step—a useless gesture, an act too late to do any good. The man was dying, bleeding his life away on these flaking concrete steps, his white shirtfront soaked with a massive spreading red stain. Dubbs stood over him. Sick, sickening— The hands dropped from what was left of the face: a nightmare mask, a perverse Halloween conceit, all manner of things except those that suggested the human. Dubbs shut his eyes. He heard the man topple over, slide against the wall, then go slithering down the rest of the steps to stop, impossibly jammed, against the half-open door of the kitchen.

# 4

## 1

A dream? But then she wasn't sure because it had become more and more difficult to differentiate what took place from those shifting images she may have dreamed or imagined. It was morning and the bedroom was filled with a soft white light and the woman Katya was standing over the bed, a tray in her hands, the tiny bottles of medication, the syringe. A picture—a picture of Andreyev: a white slash, like that of some vicious lightning, in a black place. She turned her face to Katya; there was a streak of pain coursing from her neck to her shoulders, as if the muscles were aflame. Her throat was dry, her voice hoarse.

*Andreyev? Where is Andreyev?*

Katya filled the syringe, holding it up to the light.

*Where is he?*

She saw the needle, cold and perfect, enter her arm. Something in the woman's eyes, something legible: Andreyev—it didn't work out for him, don't you understand, *it didn't quite work out for him.* Mrs. Blum turned her face to the wall, feeling Katya standing over her, watching her.

"Andreyev had to go back to Moscow," Katya said.

Mrs. Blum shook her head slightly. Reality, those things in the world—such things as walls, rooms, lights, other minds, those things that seemed to some so impenetrable—had never felt quite so flimsy to her before, as if they were all constructed of rice paper through which you could tear a simple hole and see what it was that lay beyond the indifferent surfaces. When had she felt it this strongly before?

"He was recalled," Katya said.

"Don't lie to me. Don't ever lie to me." The old woman struggled, pushing herself upward, grasping at her pillows for support. She stared at Katya: behind the coldness, the eyes as fixed as ancient ice, there was fear. *Don't hurt me. Please. I know what you can do—* Mrs. Blum raised one hand, pointing it toward the younger woman, a shriveled, twisted hand from which a single blunted finger emerged accusingly. The younger woman stepped backward. I can do almost anything now. Anything. I can take the tray and send it rushing from her thin hands and dash it through the window. I can take the structure of her mind and break it down until it has the consistency of a gel. Anything, almost anything now.

*Andreyev is dead.*

Poor, pitiful fool.

The weakling.

She closed her eyes. If only he had asked, she might have tried to help him. If only he had asked—but it was, as always, too late.

"Look," the woman was saying. "I brought these to you."

Now Mrs. Blum could hardly open her eyes.

Squinting, she saw some glossy colored squares pressed alongside her face on the pillow.

"They were sent on from Moscow. They arrived only this morning."

Silence. The soft glow of the room, the color of some distant pearl. Photographs, the old woman thought. She lifted a hand to touch them and then she was beset by a curious feeling of her own unworthiness: I don't deserve them, these beautiful people, these little children; I don't deserve to see them or to love them or to have their love in return. She pushed the snapshots away from the pillow, barely seeing them slip off the edge of the bed to the floor. Katya, a shadow, a pale shadow, bent down to pick them up.

"Don't you want to see them? Don't you want to look at your family, Mrs. Blum?"

No, Mrs. Blum thought. It was always too late. There was always a point of dark regret where, despite what you desired, despite what you most wanted in this world, you realized you were running out of time. She heard the woman's fingers flick the edges of the photographs as if they were a pack of cards and everything associated with them some hideous gamble.

"Soon, Mrs. Blum," the woman said. "Very soon now, I'm sure."

A meadow, from a high place the persistent sound of an invisible lark, a small boy stirring in his fitful sleep, a meadow filled with wild flowers. You are walking across it. The air is sweet. Between the trees, suddenly—like a new construction hurriedly erected in the night—a dark barn, the door an open mouth, an expression of surprise. You go toward it. Seeking—seeking what? Repetition? The replay of the same old horror? The sight of the man hanging—

"I'll come back later," Katya was saying.

The door was closed. But there were other doors.

Old pains, old hurts: even this love you tried to keep alive was an old and wasted thing. She tried to open her eyes but her eyelids were weights that drew her back down into the dreaming.

***2.***

Lord Warsdale—Old Warsy, as Dubbs called him— was a relic of that time when the only efficient diplomacy was the kind you conducted with a gunboat. He had liver spots all over the backs of his hands and suffered from an odd skin disease that caused his flesh to flake and scale like a universal dandruff. When Old Warsy moved, he invariably left behind tiny white particles of himself. His office overlooked the Houses of Parliament; a large picture window framed his pointed bald skull.

"This damned Steperoff business," Old Warsy said.

It seemed to Dubbs futile to make the necessary corrections in Warsy's speech. Stefanoff was Steperoff and nothing on this earth could ever alter the fact.

"You think this fella Zubro rumbled your game, Dubbs?"

Dubbs nodded. "He must have learned, I fear, of my connection with Steperoff, of course. I can't think, my lord, of any other explanation."

My lord, Dubbs thought with disgust. He gazed over at the Houses of Parliament and wondered why Old Warsy wasn't sitting dozing over in Lords instead of concerning himself with matters of international intrigue.

Warsdale tried to stand. He reached for his pearl-handled cane, missed, and slumped back, puffing, into his leather swivel chair. Gloomily he stared at a few specks of his own dry flesh that had fallen to the polished surface of his desk.

"I sometimes wish the Russkis had the decency to stay in their own Embassy grounds, don't you know? Instead, they keep popping in and out and causing bloody mayhem. Messy bloody business anyway. One has to keep the local constabulary from plodding all about the place with their infernal notebooks. And the chaps from Special Branch—well, Lord knows, they don't take kindly to dead Commies turning up in bloody Chiswick."

"Fulham," Dubbs said.

"Quite, quite. It's damned untidy, Dubbs. I mean to say, I warned you before about your association with this Steperoff bod, didn't I? Said it would bring about a damn calamity one day."

Although Dubbs nodded, he couldn't recall any such conversation. Old Warsy, whether from guile or senility, had the habit of inventing past conversations to suit himself. Now, grabbing for his cane again, reaching it successfully, he struggled into a standing position and his bones creaked audibly. He looked out at the Houses of Parliament, his eyes narrow and thunderous, as if he suspected all manner of socialist manipulations going on behind the hallowed walls.

"It's damned unsporting and unreasonable," Lord Warsdale said. "Send over a soccer team like that, pretending this chap is Domareski or what d'you call it, only for him to turn up dead on your blessed doorstep under another name. Soccer—it brings out the worst in a fella, I've always said that."

Dubbs considered the list he had received from the Home Office of the visas issued to the Soviet team and its entourage. The photograph of Victor Andreyev was clearly labeled Fyodor Domareski. It was a small puzzle in its way—even in circumstances where one should not be surprised by deceit—but what troubled Dubbs more was the fact that he had no information in his own dossiers on Andreyev.

Lord Warsdale poked his cane into the thick blue rug. He stared at Dubbs as if he were trying to remember the man's name and purpose. A telephone rang unanswered on his desk. He stared at it awkwardly, then looked once more at Dubbs.

"You say our chaps don't know anything about this Andreyev?"

Dubbs nodded. The poor old dear, he thought, has to be told everything twice.

"I mentioned I was getting assistance from another source, sir," said Dubbs.

Lord Warsdale sighed and went back to his seat. "The Yanks. Well, good Lord, I daresay official policy needn't be too scrupulously . . ." His voice, as it had a habit of doing, faded out. He thumped his cane cantankerously against the side of his desk. "But for that bloody stupid German king, we might still have had a rather nice colony there, Dubbs. Makes you think rather, doesn't it? Instead of a country house in bloody Dorset, I might have had a ranch in Montana." Old Warsy laughed, his face turning lavender. When the fit had passed, he turned once more to look at the Houses of Parliament, as if the real enemy were ensconced therein. "Work it out as best you can, Dubbs. Keep me posted, eh? If I'm not here in the office, you can find me down in the countryside."

Dubbs rose, seized by the ridiculous urge to kiss the back of the old boy's hand: serf to prince. He wondered how Warsy would have reacted—if, indeed, he would have noticed anything at all.

"Good-bye, Lord Warsdale," said Dubbs, going to the door.

"Quite," Old Warsy said. "Quite, quite."

### 3.

It was, Rayner thought, a pointless lunch—an uneasy lingering over fettucine that neither of them wanted particularly to eat but at which they picked for the sake of good form. Besides, the upstairs dining room at Bianchi's was Sally's territory and not his own and he felt an acute disadvantage. When she had come in, some ten minutes late, it had taken her several more minutes to reach the table at which Rayner sat—she seemed to know everybody in the place, literary agents and authors, other editors like herself: she would flit here and there to make a joke or exchange a greeting in a manner Rayner found exceptionally irritating. He was reminded of a queen bee acquainting herself with the denizens of the hive. The outsize broad-brimmed hat, the loose flowing scarf, the short fur jacket that might have been rescued from mothballs, the shoulder satchel overflowing with tissues, bits and pieces of paper, a thin typescript in a purple folder—and he wondered: What could he *ever* have expected from this crazy disorganized lady?

"Pardon my lateness," she said when finally she sat down. A Campari came, even though he hadn't seen her order one. He watched her a moment, wondering in spite of himself how many of the other diners had been her lovers. Impossible games, he thought. You promised yourself to stop. It was all he could do to keep from saying that there was no beef

Wellington on the menu. A kick in the heart—well, that separated the men from the boys.

He sipped his Scotch and surveyed the menu. Why had he even bothered to call and make this date? Was it for an amicable farewell? a form of apology? She lit one of her colored cigarettes and tasted her drink. Irritatingly, she was wearing dark glasses; he wanted to reach across the table and slip them off.

"Here we are then," he said.

"Cheers," Sally said. She raised her glass and knocked it against his.

"About last night—"

"Forget it, Rayner. *C'est fini.*"

"The incident or the whole affair?"

Sally shrugged. "It's a matter of definition, darling. For you, maybe, it *was* an affair."

"What was it for you?" That goddam past tense, Rayner thought.

She smiled. He wished she would take off the absurd black hat as well as the glasses. What was she into today? Femme fatale? Lady of mystery?

"Look, love, I don't think I'm quite ready for you yet," she said.

"You talk in riddles."

"Well, let me turn it around another way, shall I? I'm silly and immature and oversexed and lewd and all the things you can't cope with—"

He waved her words away. "Sally—"

"Let me finish, John. Let me speak my piece, all right?"

He looked down at the tablecloth, the breadsticks in a glass, and saw, from the corner of his eye, a waitress approach with the order of fettucine. He picked up his fork, toyed with it. Immature and oversexed and lewd, he thought. Was that how she really perceived herself?

"The point is, I think you're ready for something a little more substantial than anything I might be capable of offering, that's all. You don't need to look so pained, love."

Betrayed by a facial muscle, Rayner thought. He finished his drink and coiled some of the fettucine around his fork. He had no appetite.

Sally took off her hat at last and shook her tangled hair free. "When your brother died . . . listen, love, I don't want to sound macabre or utterly without feeling, but when he died I rather felt you needed some kind of comfort and that I could supply it. I never wanted you to build it up into something else."

Key words, Rayner thought. Why did they sound like embalmer's terms? Comfort. Macabre. Why did this meeting feel so damned *heavy?*

"What happens now?" he asked. "Do we shake hands? Do I sometimes get to call you on the jolly old telephone, baby?"

"Shit," she said. She dropped her fork on the table, where it clattered. "I'm trying to explain but you aren't exactly making it easy for me."

He looked at her dark glasses, seeing only his own distorted reflection there. Did she really mean all this? He felt just as he had done when he had found the fat novelist in her flat—an emptiness, a disappointment, a slow fuse burning somewhere inside him. Sigmund, Sigmund, he thought, did I see in this careless girl some compensation for my dead brother? Was it so obvious that I was seeking—ah, the word—solace? Was it in my eyes? the way I moved? the words I said? Poor Sally, he thought. She had to suffer through it too—a Florence Nightingale in scanty underwear. Sex as Valium. Sex as medication. Even the best of nurses have other patients, Rayner.

"Okay," he said. "Do we call it a day?"

"John, love." She leaned across the table, touching the back of his hand. "I can't go on carrying the weight of your dead brother. Don't you see that?"

He nodded his head. He looked through the narrow window and down into Frith Street, remembering now how Dubbs had called him that morning after dawn, the request for information, an item that the computer, in its infinite wisdom, might spit out. He remembered, too, the hard look in George Gull's face—

"It's so bloody banal, darling," she said. "But I don't want to lose your friendship."

Rayner pushed his plate of pasta away. His immediate feeling was to get up and leave—go back to the Embassy and deal with Dubbs's request, process the Folweiler material, make good old George a happy man. But what he had come to realize was that in the right circumstances he could have loved this thoughtless girl; he could so easily have come to love her ways. Now he was left with a sense of desolation, an awareness of business that would always be left unfinished. Postcards from foreign places, sporadic letters, irregular exchanges of information. And the curiously lingering sense of sexual jealousy. Mad as hell, he thought. I have to be out of my tree.

He took his hand away from her fingers. She removed her dark glasses. There was, he thought, some small sadness in her dark eyes—but how could you be sure of that? He got to his feet rather clumsily and looked down at her.

"Call you in a day or two," he said.

She shook her head. "I'll be out of town until next week, John. Wait a while, okay?"

"It's your game, Sally. The rules are yours."

He walked across the dining-room floor to the stairs. Somebody—he wasn't sure who—helped him with his raincoat. He went down the stairs and out into Frith Street—a cold March afternoon, a numbing wind, papers blown along the gutters. He thought of her sitting alone at the table in the restaurant—knowing, knowing with certainty, that somebody would have moved already into the vacant chair. *Sally, love, how have you been?*

To hell with it, he thought. Consider it a near miss, a close call, a vague flirtation with disaster. He walked hurriedly toward Shaftesbury Avenue, where finally he found a cab.

## 4.

Stanislav Koprow, sent at the express request of Secretary Maksymovich, arrived at Heathrow from Moscow just after three in the afternoon. He was met by Oblinski after he had cleared customs and Immigration, using a passport that had been issued in the name of Sergei Lefkowitz. The two men went to the snack bar, where Koprow, tired after the flight, fatigued by the sheer need of having to travel abroad at all, drank two cups of black coffee quickly. Oblinski, he thought, looked rather sheepish—but if he knew Oblinski at all, then it was a safe bet that the KGB man would be attributing the blame for failures elsewhere.

Koprow sucked on a Polo mint and rolled the green cylindrical package back and forth on the counter of the snack bar. A little silence, he considered, could go a long way with someone like Oblinski, whose nightmares, he was sure, concerned demotion, banishment, and even imprisonment. There was always enough uncertainty to go around, Koprow thought.

"Your explanation?" Koprow asked eventually.

"Andreyev escaped from the hotel—"

Koprow frowned. "We keep a tight rein on our people, don't we? I like to see that."

"I blame Zubro," Oblinski said, pulling on his lower lip, as if by extending it he might look petulantly innocent. "I blame a certain laxness in Zubro's security arrangements."

"You don't credit him for covering his mistake?" Koprow asked.

"Well, to a degree, of course—"

"Messy. Messy." Koprow picked up his empty coffee cup and gazed inside it. "Instant shit," he said. He crumpled the paper cup and dropped it to the floor. "What else could he do anyway, Oblinski? Permit Andreyev to find safety?"

"Of course not," said Oblinski, his face flushed.

"How much did Andreyev give away?"

Oblinski shook his large head. "Nothing—"

"Are you sure?"

"He was killed before he made contact—"

*"Are you sure?"*

"According to Zubro—"

"Ah, yes, Zubro." Koprow shoved the pack of mints into his brown overcoat. "I still don't entirely agree with the decision not to inform Zubro of what, so to speak, he has in his charge. But that was not my policy to make. However, Secretary Maksymovich has placed me in total control of the situation. I want to see . . . more definite action."

"Of course," said Oblinski.

"First, I want to see Zubro."

"The car is waiting."

Koprow slid down from his stool. He thought of the sickly coffee splashing around in his empty stomach. "And what have our friends in British intelligence made of this dead Russian? Do you know?"

Oblinski shook his head. "Zubro will be trying to find out, naturally—"

"Zubro," Koprow said. "Some things one has to do for oneself, Oblinski. A man can only delegate responsibility when he has the necessary confidence in his underlings. You may be sure that I have no such confidence. None at all."

They left the terminal building, Koprow walking quickly, Oblinski—like a beggar rattling a bowl doomed forever to be empty—hurrying to keep up.

## 5.

Rayner was in no mood to deal with George Gull by the time he returned to the Embassy. Nevertheless, when Gull put his head around the door of Rayner's office, Rayner made a huge effort to be pleasant— even if Gull's expression, like that of a man who has gone to the margins of madness and back, forewarned him.

"I'm working on the Folweiler stuff," Rayner said, looking up from the mess of his desk, noticing how Gull stared at the heaps of paper with significant disapproval.

"I'm glad to hear you're doing something for your keep, John." George Gull closed the door and came slowly across the floor, his hands in the pockets of his trousers. Rayner could hear loose change being rattled; if there was a distant thunder, a harbinger of Gull's mood, it was the noise of the coins rapping against one another.

Silence. Rayner picked up the telexes and tried

to make them look neat. But he was acutely aware now of tension, something locked into George Gull's silence. Gull went to the window and stared out a moment. Coins, Rayner thought. Why doesn't he stop with the coins? Rayner gazed at the little pile of telex material and waited. It was coming, he thought, whatever it was.

Gull whistled a bar of something unrecognizable, then—in a voice that was low, hardly audible—said, "Why did you make a computer-bank request this morning, John?"

Ah, there it was. A little data for Ernest Dubbs and you were made to feel like a candidate for the gangplank. Rayner wasn't sure what to say—but he hated the notion of Gull's prying, the idea of George or one of his secretaries snooping around.

"Is it a crime?" Rayner said. "I ran a simple data-bank request—"

"On a man called Victor Andreyev," Gull said. "Why?"

"Dubbs—"

"Dubbs. Fuck Dubbs, John. I never knew Dubbs was paying your salary. When did that happen?"

Whatever else his gifts, good old George wasn't at home with the heavy sarcasm.

Rayner stood up, folding his shirt sleeves. "Spirit of co-operation," he said. "You're telling me it's a sin, George?"

Gull stared at the desk. The computer print-out, which lay beneath some flimsy sheets, and which Rayner hadn't even bothered to look at, caught his attention; he reached down through the mess of flimsies and scanned it.

"Dubbs asked for this, John?"

"For Christ's sake, George. A helping hand,

that's all. He's extended himself for us in the past. You know that."

Gull dropped the print-out on the desk. "Why do you think Ernie Dubbs is so helpful, John?"

Rayner felt an uneasy sense of expectation; and something else—a presentiment of something altogether nasty. He stared at Gull, at the redness of the man's neck, the short bristles of hair.

"Ever ask yourself that?"

Rayner shook his head. "It's the old thing, George. You scratch my back. You know how it plays."

Smiling, Gull looked at Rayner. "Did it ever strike you that he might have a thing for you, John?"

A thing? Rayner wondered. *A thing?* There was a delicate treading of water going on—something genteel that, if you slashed it open with a good sharp knife, would reveal all the grubby little dark recesses.

"Tell me about it, George," Rayner said. "Is a thing like a yen? Is that what you're saying? Put it in good old-fashioned lingo, huh? Dubbs has a *yen* for me?" He suddenly wanted to laugh.

"I don't like queers, John."

"And that's how you categorize Dubbs?"

"I hear the usual gossip, John."

Rayner sat down and gazed a moment at the print-out. A queer. A fruit. Suddenly you could see all of Gull's shit-kicking prejudices fly out of him like enraged bats—the huge flapping wings of a meaningless bigotry.

"I thought you knew, George."

"Knew what?"

"Isn't it common knowledge that Dubbs and I have been making out for some time now?"

"I don't find that funny. I don't find that funny *at all.*"

"I don't find your prejudices too amusing either, George."

Gull pressed the palms of his hands flat against the panes of the window. A muscle, like some cord tightening in his jaw, began to work. "Sometime, Rayner, you ought to remember your position around here. You ought to keep that in mind. Next time Dubbs wants you to run some fucking errand for him, I'll scream so goddam loud that you'll hear me all the way down fucking Whitehall."

Rayner looked at the print-out again. Was this what had brought on Gull's rage? This simple request? How could it be? You made tiny exchanges from time to time, skirting around the rule book. Everybody did it. Tit for tat. Why the fuck would Gull bitch about this particular deal? Rayner closed his eyes: a flashing image of Sally—then darkness. So what if Dubbs was queer? What the fuck did that matter?

Now he watched Gull pick up the print-out, fold it, fold it a second time, then shove it into the inner pocket of his jacket. "Policy, Rayner," he said. "I can't let you take this out of the building."

He watched Gull go to the door.

There he paused, turned, smiled. "Look, dammit. I flipped my lid, okay? I've been worried about you lately, that's all. Forget this ever happened. Right? Forget we ever had this goddam argument."

Rayner did not move. George Gull—the quick-change artist, a regular Houdini of the emotions.

"Let me hear it, John. Let me hear you say it."

"Okay. It's forgotten. Does that about cover it?"

Gull, suddenly all white teeth and crinkled eyes, grinned. "That about covers it, John. Get back to the Folweiler stuff. See you."

George Gull closed the door and went out. But

he had left something tangible behind, a discomfort that troubled Rayner. A single match, Rayner thought, and I could gladly burn all these damn telexes. *Welcome to the USA, Herr Folweiler.* He sat back, his feet up on the desk. George Gull—good old George, blowing his bloody top. What did it matter about the print-out anyhow? Rayner had seen enough. *Victor S. Andreyev, Parapsychologist.* What was Ernest Dubbs into now? Mumbo-jumbo? Powers of evil? ESP cards and ouija claptrap?

Rayner turned on his desk lamp and stared at the telexes.

## 6.

In Anatoly Zubro's office at the Embassy, Koprow had assumed, quite as naturally as breathing, Zubro's chair behind his desk. The usurpation and its possible connotations did not escape Zubro, who thought that of all men only Koprow could instill such a sense of fear into him. In part it was the man's reputation; in part, too, it was his extraordinary physical appearance—a sharp thing, as if he were delineated all around by thick black lines. Although they had met only once or twice briefly in the past, Zubro hadn't forgotten that Koprow had the power to return him to Moscow if he ever thought it necessary. It was not, Zubro thought, the most scintillating prospect in the world.

"When the name Stefanoff was mentioned, I surmised at once that Domareski intended to make his defection through the good offices of Ernest Dubbs," Zubro was saying, trying to still the quietly persistent sensation that he was being interrogated.

Koprow smiled. He was a patient man, or so it

seemed. But Zubro was not deceived by the expression.

"I went to Dubbs's residence. The rest . . ." Zubro shrugged.

"How long have you known of any connection between the Jewish dissident and this man Dubbs?"

"For some years," Zubro said. "There was another defection once."

Koprow placed the palms of his hands flat together on the desk and looked across Zubro's papers for a time. Then he raised his face and smiled again. "Unhappily, Domareski was literally exterminated on Dubbs's doorstep, as I understand it."

Zubro nodded. He was conscious of waiting; it was rather as if he expected an injection from the good doctor Koprow. *This will be painful but, of course, it's for your own ultimate good.*

"The problem now, Anatoly, is that Dubbs and his friends in British intelligence will be excavating here and there, looking for whatever riches might be hidden. No?"

Zubro thought of Dubbs and the association with John Rayner and realized that the death of the defector might not simply be limited to British intelligence. He could easily imagine the wires humming over in Grosvenor Square, a noise that buzzed, like a trapped fly, in his head. Should he tell Koprow of this? Of the meetings between the two men?

"You aren't a stupid man, Anatoly. It has presumably crossed your mind that our physician was a little more than what he seemed to be."

Zubro contrived to look suitably surprised. He shrugged.

"The authority for his presence here came directly from Secretary Maksymovich. I argued, without success, that you should be made fully cognizant of

Domareski's real identity and the purpose of his visit. Containment, however, was thought to be the best policy. The fewer people privy to a certain secret, the more that secret stands a chance of success."

"Indeed," said Zubro.

"This policy, despite Domareski's death, remains in effect."

There was a momentary silence in the room. Koprow, rubbing his hands together, created a faint friction that suggested to Zubro the scampering of a mouse behind the walls.

Then Koprow said, "My immediate problem is to ascertain how much British intelligence may have discovered concerning Domareski's real identity. If they have gone too far, then the matter will have to be aborted. If we can, as it were, clear our tracks, then we can continue with our purpose."

Purpose? Zubro wondered. He was remembering now a strange absence of purpose in killing the physician—how perfectly the man had made a target in his white shirt caught in the lights of the car. Frozen, immobile, simply standing there at the top of the steps like someone anxious to welcome death. The sitting duck. Who was he? Who was this dead man? And why was anything so important that Koprow himself had to make an appearance in London?

Zubro sighed and got up from his chair and stood by the desk. It was as well to say what he had in mind now. "It had been brought to my attention, Comrade Koprow, that Dubbs was keeping company with a young American, connected with the Central Intelligence Agency, called John Rayner."

Koprow's expression underwent a quick, dramatic change. He glared at Zubro, and for a moment Zubro wondered if he was to witness Koprow's infamous wrath. "Rayner?"

"His brother, it seems, committed suicide in Moscow."

Koprow took a silver pencil from his pocket. "The apparent association between Dubbs and Rayner troubled you?"

"It made me curious that Dubbs would ask questions about the dead man."

"What course of action did you take?"

"Surveillance. Eavesdropping devices."

It was like an examination, Zubro thought, feeling himself perspire; he might have been a candidate taking the preliminary entrance test for the university.

"What did you discover, Zubro?"

Zubro shook his head. "Nothing."

"There are tapes, I assume?"

"A few. Harmless things. The young American had a girl in North London. A mistress. Unfortunately, he discovered and destroyed the devices. As did Dubbs—"

"Careless," Koprow said. "Damned careless."

"Unavoidable—"

"No, Zubro. Nothing is unavoidable." Koprow, still tired from his journey, stretched his arms and yawned. He tapped his silver pencil on the desk a few times, creating a small drumlike noise. Then he rose and stared at Anatoly Zubro. Suddenly he smiled. "You have a good nose, Anatoly. I have often thought that your detailed work left something to be desired. But your intuitions are good ones."

Was this praise? Or was damnation about to follow? Zubro wondered. But Koprow said nothing more. He went out of the room slowly, closing the door behind him without a sound.

## 7

"The man who died," Dubbs said, lighting a cigarette, looking across the failing light in Regent's Park, "the man who died was Victor Andreyev. A parapsychologist."

Rayner thought he felt a spot of rain in the air. He turned up his coat collar. He watched the little man shield his colored cigarette from the moisture. Dubbs was silent for a time. Across the park some enormous spotted hound was bouncing after a tennis ball. A woman was calling in a shrill way, "Over here, Randolph! This way! There's a good lad!" Her head scarf flapping, her solid brogue shoes pattering the turf, she went off in a headlong chase of the silly animal.

"The English have a traditional love of mutts, my dear," said Dubbs. "But once upon a time, you know, parrots were more popular than they are now. Something about a parrot has always appealed to me. Of all birds, they most resent being caged. You can see it in their eyes."

Dubbs was walking now. For a time he puffed his cigarette quietly, then dropped it underfoot and crushed it. "Victor Andreyev. Odd you couldn't contrive to pilfer the whole print-out. Still, your bloody Embassy's like a fortress, Rayner. I can't understand how you manage to leave at night without having to show several passes, turn various electronic keys, and know the Marine sentries on a first-name basis."

They were moving, Rayner saw, in the direction of Bedford College. Dubbs paused; a few raindrops sparkled on his astrakhan collar. "Why would a parapsychologist come to London dressed as a physician, my dear? Don't even *bother* to answer. You'll catch a headache. Sometimes, with the Russians, you wonder if they can fathom even their *own* deviance. I'll say this—they take their parapsychology seriously, which always strikes me as a paradox, given their political system. Religion is *kaput,* but not the possibility of the ghost in the machine."

"Why are we going to Bedford College?" Rayner asked.

"To ask a few questions, John."

They walked a little way in silence. Rayner wondered now about the dead man who had come to Dubbs's home the previous evening. It didn't seem to have had any profound effect on the little man, but there were times when you couldn't tell what was working inside Dubbs, what was ticking away at the deeper levels.

Outside the gates of the college, Dubbs stopped and smiled at Rayner. "That other matter—"

"Which?"

"The one you were mentioning about this young lady giving you the old heave-ho," Dubbs said. He appeared sympathetic, frowning slightly. "Passé, I daresay, but time is the great physician. Remind me to recount the saga of a rather boring affair of the heart I once had with a girl whose name—of all possible names—was Rita Happeny. It sounds like a name that *should* be filled with the possibilities of joy, doesn't it? *Happeny.* However, she gave me a rather hard knock and eventually settled down with a mechanic called Charlie. They live, as I understand, in Radnor, surrounded by a brood of nippers. In other words, don't take it too badly."

Dubbs put his hand on Rayner's shoulder a moment; a tender gesture, reminding Rayner of Gull's outbreak earlier. Rayner felt the sincerity of the little man's sympathy: it was for real, it was on the level.

Fuck Gull, he thought. Gull, who didn't know an expression of sympathy from a hole in the head.

They went inside the grounds of the college. In a corridor Dubbs approached a porter and asked the way to Professor Chamber's office.

"You'll like Maggie Chamber, I think," Dubbs said. "Her colleagues think she's batty, but I know better. At a time when everybody is so damnably *busy* measuring gloop in test tubes, Maggie is pursuing immeasurable things."

They paused outside a door and Dubbs knocked, then without waiting for an answer went inside the room. Rayner followed, seeing a middle-aged woman with thick glasses look up from behind her desk.

"Dubbsie," she said, smiling widely. "What brings my favorite civil servant to these halls of higher learning?"

Dubbsie, Rayner thought. It sounded funny.

"My dear Maggie. Meet my young American amigo, John Rayner."

"Any friend of the little Dubbsie person is a friend of mine, of course. Why don't you both sit down? I can get you some utterly insipid tea, if you'd care for that."

Dubbs shook his head. "I wish the call were social, my dear. But the business of running the country goes on at such a *wretched* pace that even a break for tea does seem a needless luxury."

The woman took off her glasses. She had eyes that were so brown as to be almost black: eyes, Rayner thought, of some rare intelligence. She glanced a moment at Rayner, then returned her gaze to Ernest Dubbs.

"In your line of work, have you ever run across the name of Victor Andreyev?" Dubbs asked.

"Of course," the woman said.

"You see, Rayner. Professor Chamber has encyclopedic knowledge and a memory that is nothing short of photographic."

"I wish," the woman said. "What can I tell you about Andreyev?"

"Oh. Publications. Line of professional interest. Anything."

Maggie Chamber looked at her glasses, blinking. "I never met the man. Something of a recluse. He was supposed to address a symposium I attended in Moscow in 1968, but for reasons that were never explained he didn't show up."

"His line is parapsychology," Dubbs said.

"That would be rather like saying that Newton's line was apples," the woman remarked.

Dubbs made a strange little snorting sound, as if he were deeply impressed.

"If any one figure has contributed to the new respectability of what you call parapsychology, Dubbsie, it would have to be Andreyev."

"Despite his reclusiveness?"

"Despite, too, his lack of publications. There's one monograph, available only in a Russian-language edition, concerning the results of his experiments in psychokinesis. An enterprising publisher should bring it out in English, if you ask me."

Someone like Sally, Rayner thought.

"Why is he so wonderful?" Dubbs asked.

"I can answer that easily. For one thing, he had some of the most remarkable subjects any researcher could wish for. For another—unlike some of his Western colleagues—he was more interested in results than in analysis. You know how it goes in the old ivory tower," the woman said. "This works. Let's have fun and take it to pieces and see just how it works. I find it somewhat boring. Andreyev *accepted* the phenomenon. Measurement didn't enthrall him. Only possibilities. Only how far it might lead."

"Have you any idea what he's been working on recently?"

Maggie Chamber shook her head. "I haven't heard about Andreyev in five or six years, Dubbsie. So far as I could understand it, he had either fallen from favor and vanished inside some Soviet black hole, or else he had become involved in something rather hush-hush."

"Like what?" Dubbs asked. "Something that might have strategic significance?"

Maggie Chamber laughed. "Your guess, my dear, would be as good as mine."

Dubbs put his hands in his pockets and looked around the office. "What are you working on these days, Maggie?"

"Did you come here for a laugh, Ernest?"

"Of course not—"

"Well, if you really must know, I'm examining the relationship between ESP and the effects of marijuana."

Dubbs smiled. "Am I to believe in such a relationship?"

"Why shouldn't you?"

Dubbs was silent for a time. He took his hands from his coat and said, "You must turn me in sometime, Maggie."

"I understand the expression is turn you *on*, Ernest."

"Whatever," said Dubbs, looking at Rayner. "Time, my friend, to hit the road."

"Why all the questions about Andreyev anyway?" the woman asked.

Dubbs winked secretively. "Idle curiosity, whatever else?"

## 8.

Koprow, who never felt entirely easy outside of the Soviet Union—for reasons that had more to do with his social distaste for English life than his problems with the language—stepped out of the Temple underground station and walked away from the Law Courts in the direction of the Embankment. It was dark now. He stood and gazed down into the Thames, watching the play of lights on the water. A barge, long and flat, skimmed downriver; a single figure could be seen standing on deck, a lantern in his hand. Koprow broke open a new packet of Polos and put one into his mouth. There were considerations here, he thought. Maksymovich's scheme, for one thing, was the most important. Abandonment would most assuredly put the old man in a bad light; it was his baby, after all— and there were those, amongst them the doves, who had considered the matter preposterous to start with. No, Koprow thought, abandonment would be a last resort. For the present, it only mattered how much of Andreyev's identity had been revealed—and whether the breach was narrow enough to be healed with a minimum of effort.

He looked toward the monolith of the Battersea Power Station; a pall of gray smoke hung over it. Beyond, the lights of South London shimmered through smoke and trees. Elsewhere in the night he could see the floodlit pylons of a stadium, blinding globes of white light. He tapped his hands rhythmically on the low stone wall, then turned his face along the Embankment. Cold now—a splitting March wind that stung his face and eyes. He bit on the white mint, swallowed, and then saw a figure come down toward him from Temple Station.

He listened to the clack of footsteps coming across the concrete. Then they stopped. Without turning, Koprow said, "It has been a long time, my friend."

The other man, dressed in a lightweight raincoat that had a blue sheen in the lamps, coughed into a handkerchief and leaned against the wall alongside Koprow. "Long time," he said.

"You heard of Victor Andreyev's death, of course?" Koprow asked. Grinning, looking ghastly in the lamplight, he swung around to stare at his companion. "The years have been good to you, I must say that."

The man shrugged. "I live on my nerves. It keeps me fit."

"In the matter of Andreyev's death . . ." Koprow was silent a second. He could hear, in the distance, the mournful sound of a horn. The barge, trailing a thick wake, was going out of sight. "What do the British know?"

The man shook his head. "Next to nothing."

"Next to nothing is not quite nothing," Koprow said.

The man reached into the pocket of his raincoat and took out a folded piece of paper, which he gave to Koprow. The Russian smoothed it out and looked at it, holding it obliquely toward the nearest lamp.

"If they knew anything, they would hardly be asking for this information," the man said.

"Perhaps," Koprow said. "Tell me about John Rayner."

The man groaned. "That was a bad mistake, Koprow. Didn't it ever occur to your people that Richard Rayner's brother works, in a sensitive position, in the United States Embassy? If you had to test this woman, why was Richard Rayner chosen?"

"I am not here to debate the decisions of Secretary Maksymovich, my friend."

The man was quiet for a time. Again, the horn sounded downriver. The smoke, rising from the power station, was disintegrating.

Koprow shredded the sheet of paper methodically and let it slip from his hands toward the dark water. It fluttered away in the manner of small, dying seabirds. "Did John Rayner see this paper?"

"He must have."

"Did he pass the information on to Dubbs?"

"One can assume that. They met tonight."

"What else can one assume?" Koprow asked wearily, in the fashion of someone sick unto death of a world where assumptions replaced verifiable facts. "Did he speak to his young woman about it?"

"It's possible," the man said. "They had lunch together."

"Bad, bad, bad," Koprow said. "It could be worse."

The man stepped back from the wall.

Koprow looked at him curiously for a time. "You're scared, no? It scares you to meet like this?"

"It puts me in a bad place, Koprow."

The Russian smiled cheerlessly. The wind, throwing itself up from the river, blew at his collar. He stamped his feet a couple of times for warmth. "We can *assume*, Mr. Gull, that at least three people may have information concerning Andreyev's real identity?"

George Gull nodded. His nose, blistered by the wind, was a deep red. He appeared anxious, ready to leave as quickly as Koprow dismissed him.

"You've been very kind to us in the past, George. Very kind and helpful. Naturally, you haven't gone unrewarded."

Gull looked this way and that up and down the Embankment. "What do you do now?"

"We save the day," Koprow said. "Isn't that how the saying goes? We save the day."

"Something like that," George Gull said.

"A world of assumptions," said Koprow. "Then we work on the assumption that we can contain this thing. What else?"

George Gull was already moving away. "This is the part I don't need to hear about."

Koprow shrugged his shoulders lightly. "You'll read about it in the newspapers, no doubt."

# 9.

Despite his bulk, Mark Wellington was a tender and considerate lover. Sally was not passionately aroused by him, but she enjoyed his attentions. Simple things. The way he would get out of bed and fetch glasses of wine; the way he always made sure there was a supply of good dope on hand for her. Now, as she lay beside him, she was trying to get John Rayner from her mind. How long could you carry an invalid around? That was how she had come to think of Rayner: an emotional invalid. She struck a match and lit the thick joint Wellington had just rolled.

"Don't know how you can *do* that stuff," he said.

"Here. Try it."

Mark Wellington shook his head. Sally puffed on the joint loudly. "Higher and higher," she said, turning her face against the author's chest and giggling at something she couldn't have explained in a million years.

"What's so funny?" Wellington asked.

"I don't know. Lying here, I suppose. Your bedroom. All those funny little things you collect."

"The china pieces? They're an investment."

"Poor Markypoo. I hurt your feelings." She tickled him under the armpits and he turned, laughing, away from her. When he was silent again, she said, "Do you know we're going to print fifty thousand copies of your new book? Have you considered the enormity of that? All those glossy books all piled up in a warehouse, waiting to go out to bookstores and libraries. Isn't that amusing?"

"You're stoned, my sweet."

"Well of course I'm bloody *stoned*."

Wellington propped himself up with a pillow. Sally, burying her face in the sheets, couldn't stop laughing.

"I say, was that chap Rayner put out the other day?"

"Put out? You make him sound like a cat, Markie."

"Oh. You know what I mean."

"I disappointed him," Sally said. "I hurt him, I think."

Wellington sighed. "These things happen, after all."

The author rose, rings of spare flesh falling around him, and went across the room to the table, where he poured two glasses of wine from a decanter. Sally watched him outlined against the glass door that led to the living room. A faint yellow lamp burned; he looked monstrous in silhouette, like a whale. He came back across the floor.

Sally took one of the glasses unsteadily. A little wine slicked down her chin to her breasts. "Oooh, it's so cold," she said.

"I'll lick it off," Wellington said, and proceeded to do just that.

She watched his head bent over her breasts, feeling his damp tongue against her nipples. Beyond the glass door, a shadow moved. For a moment she couldn't make a connection; ridiculous thoughts rushed through her head—mainly, that Rayner was out there spying on her. She pushed Wellington away from her.

"Is something wrong?"

The adjoining door opened. Somebody stood there.

"You didn't say anything about a *ménage à trois,* Markie," she said. "I agree in principle, but I like a little forewarning."

Mark Wellington, surprised, turned to the glass door. The figure was dark, shadowy.

"I say," Wellington remarked.

Sally pulled the bedsheets up over her breasts. She saw Wellington step toward the door and then, in a frightful moment, his huge shape was blown backward across the bed. Sally let the joint slip from her fingers and tried to rise. She experienced a searing pain in her ribs, a searing, spreading pain that caused her to twist to one side, as if she might find relief in this position—

The figure moved again. Sally slipped from the bed to the floor, an unpleasant rush, a turbulent sensation of darkness moving in on her irrevocably.

## 10.

It was a blustery afternoon; an uneven wind, forever shifting direction, swirled around Wembley Stadium.

The crowd was low, about fifty thousand people with an inbred suspicion of the weather. Dubbs, panting up the terracing steps, followed by Rayner, clutched the ticket stubs in his hand. When they reached the top, seeing the expanse of the terracings below them, the grass seemed an impossible green, the markings on the pitch a brilliant white. Rayner realized that he was expected to stand throughout the game, a fact that struck him as curious. He followed Dubbs down through the throng to a position near the front.

"The only way to understand this odd ritual is to stand for the entire ninety minutes," Dubbs said. "If you take a seat in the place paradoxically known as the *stands,* I have the feeling that you lose touch somehow. Self-imposed isolation."

They leaned against a crush barrier. Dubbs said, "It could be, of course, that the Russians intend to play a psychic game. One never knows. Perhaps they practice mind rather than ball control."

Rayner looked across the crowds. There were yellow flags waving; the lion rampant on a yellow background. An odd sort of chant had begun to echo around the huge stadium bowl. *Eng-land. Eng-land.* It grew deafeningly, then died, only to grow louder than ever before. It had been Dubbs's idea to come to the game, attracted by the mystery of the dead parapsychologist. But what did he expect to find? Evidence of telepathic communication among the Soviet players? Rayner felt decidedly claustrophobic in this crush. Dubbs, he noticed, wore a black-and-white rosette in his lapel.

"I didn't know you were an aficionado of the game," Rayner said.

"Normally, no. But the circumstances are somewhat peculiar. And I may as well exercise a little patriotism while we're here." The little man craned his neck forward, staring across the empty field. Two men in overcoats strolled across the grass. They appeared, at least to Rayner, to be looking for potholes.

Dubbs watched them go out of sight. "A parapsychologist," he said. "Why go to all the trouble to bring a man like that into England only to kill him as he intends to defect? Trifling puzzles bother me, my dear."

Rayner leaned forward, catching bits and pieces of conversation from all sides. "I reckon it a bleedin' cakewalk." "Yeah, except for this Kazemayov bloke." "We ain't got nuffin' like the forward penetration we need, this fackin' defense is like a bleedin' brick wall." It was incomprehensible—yet he felt something of the growing tension around him. He watched Dubbs now, who was still trying to peer down toward the field as if he might catch something of interest. But what exactly? A floating piece of ectoplasm? Rayner had never given much credence to parapsychology, perceiving it in terms of card tricks, guesses, coincidences. But Dubbs was behaving as if something unusual was about to take place—

Suddenly there was an enormous roar. Below, Rayner saw a group of white-shirted players come running onto the field. The English team, he thought. How else could that roar be explained? He realized that in all the time he had spent in London, he had never before felt quite so foreign.

Now the Soviet team appeared. The silence that greeted them was enormous. In red shirts and white shorts, they lined up in the center of the field and bowed first in one direction, then in another.

Dubbs nudged him. "They tell me that this Kazemayov chap is the one to watch," Dubbs said.

"Which one is he?"

"He wears the number nine. See him?"

Rayner looked, but the referee was already calling the captains to the center of the field. A coin was tossed, and for some reason the crowd roared again.

The man who stood next to Rayner, a toothless figure in a checkered cap, appeared beside himself with excitement even before the game had begun. "Here, you a Yank?" he asked.

Rayner nodded. He felt his hand being shaken vigorously.

"Bet you'd like to see the Russians hammered, eh?" The man poked his elbow into Rayner's ribs. "Bet you'd like to see them fuckers *demolished,* eh?"

Politely Rayner nodded. The man took off his cap, wiped sweat from his forehead, then screamed a sequence of abuse at the referee, who, so far as Rayner could tell, had done nothing except blow his whistle for the game to begin. The ball was kicked upfield, hanging in the wind. The Soviet goalkeeper came out and gathered it up safely. When he kicked it back downfield, the wind carried it directly into the English goal area. A scramble took place, a shifting mixture of red and white shirts.

"Fuckin' hell, look at this, look at this shambles," the man was saying. "You'll see them bastards get a goal before the game's hardly even started. Watch it. Mark my words."

The ball had broken free and Kazemayov, shuffling forward deceptively, went around an English defender. Rayner could not see how it had happened, but the Soviet player was clearing a path toward the English goal, avoiding a series of wild tackles. The goalkeeper, a blur of yellow, came forward and plunged at Kazemayov's feet—and somehow the ball went bouncing off his arms toward an English player. The noise was deafening: it was like the opening of one massive mouth. Even Dubbs, standing on tiptoe, was excited.

"Fuckin' lucky," the man said. "They nearly put it away then."

But now an English counterattack had begun. The ball was moved from one side of the field to the other, passing accurately among players. The Russians fell back into a defensive pattern.

"Fuckin' hell," said the man, taking off his cap again. His face was covered in perspiration, despite the wind that made ball control almost impossible. "C'mon, Woodsy, you fucker—do something! Fuckin' do something!"

Woodsy, who was clearly an English attacker, had stopped on the edge of the penalty area, where he was faced by a mass of red shirts that blocked his way to the Russian goal. The crowd screamed for Woodsy to move the ball—"pass the bleedin' fing, pass it, you blind fackin' arsehole"—and the Englishman, slipping on the greasy turf, tumbling like a clown, lost his balance and the ball was kicked back down toward the center line. Even Dubbs, waving his arms comically, was shouting now.

"Bloody Woodsy," said the man in the checkered cap. He took a bottle of light ale from his pocket and opened it, offering it to Rayner. "That bloody Woodsy—he don't know his arse from a hole in the ground."

Rayner sipped some of the ale, which was warm and almost flat, then passed the bottle back. The action had become concentrated in midfield in a series of untidy skirmishes, players colliding with players, the ball rising and falling on the wind.

Dubbs, turning, said, "Whatever our old friend Andreyev was supposed to do with this team, he obviously didn't manage to improve their reading of a game. I haven't seen so many misdirected passes for ages."

Below, the referee was blowing up for an infringement that the crowd didn't like. A free kick was awarded to the Soviets a few feet from the English eighteen-yard line. White-shirted defenders formed a wall as the Russians moved into some prearranged pattern of play. The free kick was taken, lofted over the defenders, and Kazemayov—flashing, hair blown, arms held wide for balance—rose up, entangled with the leaping English goalkeeper, and somehow managed to glide the ball with his forehead into the back of the net.

"Fuck me," said the man in the checkered cap. "You see that? Did you bloody see that? Pushed the fuckin' goalie clear as a bloody bell."

The jubilant Soviets crowded around Kazemayov, who raised his arms upward in triumph. The man beside Rayner took off his cap and scratched his head. He was shaking his face from side to side with disbelief. Rayner mumbled something sympathetic, noticing that Dubbs—even Ernest Dubbs—looked dispirited.

At half time, the score remained 1–0 for the Soviets. The players ran off the field toward the dressing rooms. The man in the checkered cap drifted away.

Dubbs blew his nose with an outsize handkerchief and surveyed the empty field. "What you see before you, my dear, is the culmination of English culture. Wordsworth, Constable, Pope, Milton—the very essence is distilled in a game of football. Have you seen enough?"

There was a touch of rain buried in the wind now. Rayner looked up at the gray sky. "You want to leave?"

Dubbs shrugged. "Might as well. I doubt that

we're going to find any explanation of friend Andreyev by hanging around here. Besides, it's a poor game. The second half will be one long struggle by the English forwards against a team that has absolutely no desire to adventure out of their own half of the field. Let's go.''

Following the little man, Rayner began to climb the steps to the top of the terracing. Dubbs moved quickly, pushing his way through. Here and there groups of men drank from metal flasks or balanced cardboard cups of hot Bovril. There was martial music, shredded by the wind, coming across the loudspeaker system. At the top, Dubbs stopped. He turned to make sure Rayner was immediately behind him, then continued down the stairways that led to the exit. Crowds milled around the entrances to toilets; mounted policemen sat on gigantic brown horses; brigades of officials from the St. John's ambulance service stood beside piles of empty stretchers. It was all odd somehow, Rayner thought: the whole ritual that, played out in a vast bowl, had something almost gladiatorial about it.

Halfway down the steps, Dubbs paused. For a moment, Rayner thought the little man had suffered a heart attack or that some savage twist of indigestion had caused him to double over, hands pressed to his midriff, moaning. Rayner reached down and caught him as he began to fall. Slippery, a sense of wetness, his own hands covered with blood, an awareness of the crowd roaring in the stadium as the teams ran out once more to resume play—these impressions surged against Rayner as he tried to keep Dubbs from slipping, as he held him against himself, forced him to sit with his back to an iron rail. And then he understood, with a comprehension that was distant from him, with a recognition that blinded him, that Dubbs had been shot.

He opened Dubbs's shirt collar. The little man's eyes were blank. Through the crowd now a mounted policeman was forcing his horse.

"Dubbs. Dubbs."

Dubbs opened his mouth a little way. "A rough sport, John. I've always thought it a rough sport."

"Dubbs, keep your eyes open, don't move—" Rayner shouted toward the mounted policeman, aware too of several men running with stretchers through the crowd.

Dubbs smiled. "Damn funny how there's no pain, my dear. I always imagined it would be terribly sore, but . . ."

"Please, Dubbs. Please don't speak." Rayner felt a horrible panic: it was as if he were hauling someone out of a rough sea with a rope frayed to breaking point. "Don't say another thing, *please.*"

"Twice," Dubbs said. "I felt the damn thing twice."

Transfixed, Rayner stared at the blood soaking through the dark overcoat, at the streaks running across the astrakhan collar.

"Two shots," Dubbs said. "And the funny feeling I have, John, is that the second one . . . wasn't . . . meant for me."

Rayner watched the ambulance men come up the steps with a stretcher. He looked up. The wind, the flags flapping, furling, unfurling, as if what they signaled were a coronation of death. He clenched his hands so tight that the nails brought blood to the palms.

The ambulance men raised Dubbs, with strange gentleness, onto the canvas stretcher. One, skinny and bespectacled, with a face Rayner realized he would never forget as long as he lived, said, "You know this fellow, sir?"

Rayner tried to speak. Shock. What did shock do to you? Numbness. A weird indifference. The defensive system of the emotions. He nodded his head vacantly.

The ambulance man said, "It doesn't look good, sir. It doesn't look good at all."

## 11.

Sometimes, Rayner thought, there is a perversity in nature that maliciously fails to take into account the feelings of men. Funerals in the sunshine, weddings in the rain, the final parting of lovers in a heat wave, babies born in blizzards. It was as if whoever had been the architect of the system had built into it a magnificent indifference. This Sunday, for one thing—the sweet sense of spring in Grosvenor Square, the warmth in the breezes that rushed across Hyde Park and flowed through the narrow streets of Mayfair. A beautiful morning: if you weren't dead. If you weren't in that place where Ernest Dubbs was. If you were alive and breathing and holding your own against whatever forces, natural or otherwise, conspired against you. He could not believe in Ernest Dubbs's death. A magician might have fabricated a rabbit or an eagle out of thin air and claimed the act as a direct result of spiritual materialization, and he would have believed in that before giving credence to the little man's death. It was more than a sense of absence, of some hollow in experience: it was the feeling he entertained that Dubbs was *not* dead—that he was alive somewhere, standing in his favorite bar, drinking his

Scotch, smoking one of his ridiculous cigarettes. Explain it to me, Rayner thought. Explain it to me, somebody.

*The second one wasn't meant for me . . .*

He went up the Embassy steps. The Marine guard, unaccustomed to Sunday duty, fresh from some impossible place like Des Moines, smiled; a gesture Rayner didn't return. He rode in the elevator, newspaper tucked under his arm, and went directly to his office. Inside, he closed the door, crossed the room, threw *The Sunday Telegraph* down on his desk. Why had he come here anyhow? Hour after hour he had spent at the hospital in Wembley. Transfusion followed transfusion; but all the plasma in the world wouldn't have restored Dubbs.

Two shots. Two direct hits. One had passed through a lung. The other had blown a kidney away. *The second one wasn't meant for me . . .* Rayner sat down, tired, his eyes shut. He had waited for the announcement of death, then had gone to his flat in St. John's Wood and slept, a deep sleep, dreamlessly still on an ocean floor. He opened out the newspaper. The dark newsprint angered him. Even the feel of the paper. They reminded him of the continuum of things, of how little a life mattered, how little even a death mattered; there was news to print, there was a world running on like some fucking great machine. But not for Ernest Dubbs. There wasn't even a mention of the little man by name—the bizarre protocol of security. Boxed, a couple of sentences, a couple of flat phrases: "An unidentified man was shot yesterday during the football game between the Soviet Union and England at Wembley. His assailant is unknown. The identity of the man is being kept secret until close relatives are informed."

Like Dubbs himself, the story would die there.

Period. No more. Who fucking cared? Rayner gazed at the paper . . . "man was shot yesterday . . ." On the bottom line of the story, an added extra, there was the phrase: "The game ended in a 2–2 draw (for a full match report turn to page 24)." Rayner slung the paper down and got up and turned to the window. What did it come down to? Somebody meant to kill both Dubbs and him, the common denominator being Victor Andreyev. Victor Fucking Andreyev. I should count my lucky stars, he thought. A poor marksman: he could pick off only one of us. Back to target practice, motherfucker.

   *. . . being kept secret—*

Somebody buries the story. Somebody buries Dubbs.

He watched the gorgeous sun aflame on a red-brick building. Then he turned back to the paper, idly turning pages. You keep running into questions, he thought. Never the sight of a plain old answer. Richard Rayner. Andreyev. Dubbs. Were they parts of some illogical whole? Or simply splinters? Take any old kaleidoscope and give it a shake and you never get the same pattern twice. It was easy when you were innocent and unsullied—two plus two always came out the same. But not now, not in a world in which mathematics and death were conjoined in a terrible mismatch.

He listened to the great silence of the building. Then he heard the whining noise of the elevator moving in the shaft. It stopped. Faintly he could hear the door slide open. And then the silence came in once again. He looked back at the newspaper where, momentarily, a headline caught his eye: *"Police Puzzled by Murders"*—

He had begun to read it, drawn not by the headline but by the curious suspicion, the uneasy presentiment, that something in this story was familiar to him—as if he had noticed, without really seeing it, a name he knew, a person he knew—he had begun to read it when the door of his office opened and he looked up to see Ambassador Quarterman standing there. Sunday suit, fresh flower in the buttonhole, the face of an old charmer, a faded film actor, perhaps, who has bought himself into a nice diplomatic situation.

"I heard you were here, John," the Ambassador said. He slid across the room, a man on wheels. You couldn't imagine Himself in his underwear, or making love, or defecating: he was not of this world.

Rayner, torn between the Ambassador and the newspaper article, stood up.

Schoolboy time, he thought. Quarterman, picking at his carnation, always reminded Rayner of a face in a credit-card commercial, but he wasn't sure which one.

"I don't normally drop in on you people," Quarterman said. "The business of the Embassy isn't always on a par with what you people do. More often it's a collision course."

Tell me, Rayner thought. Tell me more.

The Ambassador frowned now: a piece of play-acting. He might have been faced with a lunch of jellied eel during a goodwill visit to the London docks.

"This terrible business with the Englishman yesterday," Quarterman said. "It must have been a great shock to you, John. I can understand it."

Speech, Rayner thought. You stand *that* close to death, you're bound to get a little upset. He glanced down at the newspaper again, seeing, not seeing, her name. *Her name.* He couldn't get it into focus, as if there were two realities running, like a pair of amok battleships, into one another. *Her name.*

"I've been having a word with George," said the Ambassador. "Naturally, this isn't my business, I'm not officially a part of George's team, after all . . . but we think, George and I, that after all you've been through—your poor brother, now this awful incident yesterday . . ."

Sally Macnamara. *Leave would be in order for a month or so. Sally, Sally. Spend it where you like, John. George suggests Europe. But it's up to you, of course.*

Rayner saw his own hand fall across the newspaper article.

*Puzzled by the apparent lack of motive, police officials*

He saw how white his knuckles

Quarterman was laughing at something. Some goddam story. Some fucking pointless reminiscence about a cycling tour of the Camargue—

*Wellington, 47, was the author of several well-known*

Flat tires all the way from here to the Bay of Biscay, I swear it.

*Ms. Macnamara was employed in an editorial capacity at*

Rayner, unable to see clearly, looked up at the Ambassador and heard himself say, "I'm sorry, sir. I'm sorry. I don't know what to say except I'm sorry."

"Sorry?"

Quarterman, who looked as if death and disease were as much occasions for speeches as the launching of ships, opened his mouth and, with a tone of dismay, repeated his question.

*Sorry?*

*apparently entered by the front door while the couple were in the bedroom*

"I'm sorry," Rayner said again. "Really sorry. I mean, about everything. Really."

"John, John." The Ambassador stood by the desk

and put his hand on Rayner's sleeve. "The shock, the shock must have been terrible."

"The shock?"

"Look. Sit down. I'll get you some water or something. Better still, I'll call my physician."

Physician. Parapsychologist. Nerve pills. Voices from the Great Beyond.

Rayner sat down, his eyes shut, conscious of Quarterman fussing with the telephone, shouting down the line at somebody—*get your ass over here, I don't care a damn if you're having breakfast*—

*also worked closely with Mr. Wellington*

worked closely, closely, very closely

*two of his books were made into*

Rayner opened his eyes. You could wish your way out of the world. You could long so badly for a better place that people came and locked you up. You were safe in rooms with soft cushioned walls and all your friends wore nice white coats.

Oh Sally

Quarterman slammed the telephone down. "He'll be here soon, John. I'll wait with you until he comes. Don't worry. Don't worry."

Don't worry, Rayner thought. Bit by bit they're killing my world and I'm not to worry. He stared at the Ambassador for a time. But there was nothing else to say and he had run out of apologies and explanations and reasons—and even grief, even that.

# PART III

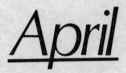

*April*

"Do you want to have power over something?
Be more nearly real than it."

—CHARLES FORT, *The Book of the Damned*

# 1

It was George Gull who suggested Europe as a suitable place in which to spend a month's leave; and it was George Gull, smiling, strangely subservient, as if Rayner were a bomb about to explode, who brought in travel brochures proclaiming the merits of this or that Greek island, of Venice in the spring, Munich—"the sweet jewel of Bavaria." Rayner, sick of being treated like an invalid, lied about his itinerary; that way, at least, he could get George Gull off his back. He could rid himself of Gull's relentless platitudes: "We all need a break from time to time, John. You'll come back a new man. You'll see." Rayner promised he would go to Germany but instead spent four days in a rainy Scotland, driving from one dark loch to another in a hired car, wandering through ruined keeps and broken castles, immersing himself in a history he felt no attachment to: a stranger in a strange heritage. Glasgow, a huge dark slum on a grubby river; Edinburgh, where he visited the Castle and looked from the battlements across a damp gray vista; Perth, bleak in the cold April rains.

He took to driving circuitous routes, imagining that whoever had fired the shots at Wembley would be following him around still. Or maybe both shots had been meant only for Ernest, after all; how could he know? He drove south from Glasgow along the Ayrshire coast, barren little seaside towns. He was tired of the absences in himself, tired of death, of dead seasons, of going nowhere.

At Prestwick Airport he booked a flight to New York. He checked in his rented car, spent a sleepless night in an airport hotel, listening to the noise of the Atlantic. He realized he should have told George Gull, as his superior officer—and therefore someone with a right to know—that he was going back to the United States. To hell with him, Rayner thought. To hell with all that he stands for. *I'm going back home.*

The long Atlantic crossing was turbulent. The ocean was raked by great electric storms. The plane came down in New York City—a humid darkness, a tightness in the air. Rayner passed through customs and Immigration uneventfully, yet somehow suspecting that he would be questioned: an absurd feeling altogether. *This man must be stopped.* But he was free, after all. Who could stop him from reentering his own country? From the airport he tried to place a collect call to Isobel's number in Georgetown, only to be told that the line had been disconnected. She had a different number now, the operator said, and gave him a number with an area code of 804. When he had hung up he checked the directory, discovering that 804 was Virginia: Norfolk, Richmond. He put through another collect call. The number rang for a long time before he heard her voice. Then there was silence before the operator said that Rayner could speak.

"John? Where are you, John?"

Rayner said, "More to the point, where are *you*? I called the Washington number and—"

"I moved, John. Sometimes you get sick of an empty house."

Rayner was silent a moment. He hated airport terminals, the transiency; even the loudspeaker announcements were terse, abbreviated, as if there was no time to spare for anything. The essence of things; the absence of the superfluous.

"I have a little place on the beach," Isobel said.

"Beach?"

"Virginia," she said. "When are you coming home?"

"I don't want to shock you, but I'm presently standing in a phone booth at JFK—"

"What happened? What happened to London?"

"Euphemistically they call it leave, Isobel."

"Does it have another name?" she asked.

"I'll tell you about it."

"Can you get a flight to Norfolk? I'll pick you up," she said.

"I'll try. Call you back."

Somehow he didn't want to hang up; it was as if this connection was more significant than a simple electronic conjunction—an emotional skein, he thought, something attaching him to his dead brother.

"Call me back just as soon as you know," she said.

He heard the line click dead. He stood a moment in the booth, unwilling to move back out into the concourse, the crowds, the madness of motion and noise. Maybe they were right, he thought. Gull, Quarterman, Quarterman's personal physician, a Harley Street man with a cold touch and a quick prescription pad—maybe they were right, all of them, and he did need to rest. *Shock will sometimes be a delayed thing, Mr.*

*Rayner.* Yeah, he thought. *I have personally known people who didn't feel the aftereffects for years.* He looked through the glass, feeling in his coat pocket for the pills that had been prescribed. Two kinds. One that brought sleep, dreamless unsatisfying sleep, the other—Quaalude—that was meant to relax him. Shock, he thought. He had gone to Dubbs's funeral, standing in the stupid spring sunshine and wondering, *Who's going to feed the parrot, the fucking parrot?*

He stepped out of the phone booth and went in search of an airline desk. Make arrangements, comprehend timetables, catch flights. It was called Going Through the Motions. And if that was what it took to hold himself together—in a place where he wouldn't need the salves of a Harley Street doctor—then that was what he would do.

## 2.

He couldn't get a flight until morning and was obliged to spend the night in a motel room. He was in Norfolk by noon. A new Isobel met him, somebody he didn't recognize at first, a different woman: not the glacial hostess who had looked more like an elaborate birthday cake than a human being, but someone less gaunt, more vibrant, wearing her clothes with casual indifference: faded blue jeans, a shirt smock tucked untidily inside the belt, cracked leather boots. Her hair had grown down her back; there was a simple center parting, combed unevenly as if there were no longer mirrors in her life.

When he embraced her, feeling her face pressed against his cheek, he could sense her *aliveness;* if there was a memory of death in her, it belonged to another season. He wondered at first if perhaps there was a new man, a new love. Hand in hand they went across the parking lot to a 1968 Ford station wagon, a rusted-out vehicle with broken upholstery. Where was Richard's beloved Jaguar? Where was the low-slung British sports car on which he had lavished such inordinate attention? A vehicle, Rayner thought, that was like a surrogate wife to him. Now this beat-up old Ford that looked as if it should be crammed with grubby kids and shopping bags and all the paraphernalia of a crazy family.

"Don't look like that," Isobel said. "It works. Really. Runs like a sweetheart."

"Are you sure?"

"Want to drive?"

"When my nerve comes back," he said. He slung his suitcase in back, noticing how the rear seats had been removed. There were cardboard boxes, flowerpots packed with dirt, balls of string.

"The door doesn't work on the passenger side," Isobel said. "You have to climb across the wheel. If you don't object?"

Rayner scrambled in. Loose wires hung raggedly from the dash. "Aren't you afraid of being electrocuted?"

"Nope. None of the instruments work anyhow. The whole point of a car is transporting your body from A to B, right? And that's what this one does." She smiled at him. Even the smile—when had he seen it so warm? so welcoming? Changes, he thought, changes in all of us.

On the Norfolk–Virginia Beach Expressway, he said, "I can't get over how . . . well, different you look. And all this. I mean—"

"Words fail you, huh?" She hunched over the wheel, swinging the car into the outer lane of traffic.

"Words fail me," he said.

"We'll talk about life-styles sometime," she said.

Sometime. The sky, a marvelous unclouded blue, suggested the ocean, as if it were all one vast expanse of mutually reflecting mirrors. You could run a long way from death in a place like this, under a sky like this one. He closed his eyes; a warm breeze floated in through the open windows.

Isobel drove off the Expressway, turning the car through the streets of Virginia Beach, past the monstrous hotels that straddled the sands like purposeless concrete slabs. She was driving left on Atlantic Avenue, heading toward the edge of town. Then they were going down a sand-strewn lane that led to the shore—and the sea, drawn far back by the tide, looked impossibly distant. She stopped the car outside a cottage. It was small, awkwardly angled, as if a series of residents had whimsically added to the original structure.

"Home," she said. She got out of the car. "Do you like it?"

Rayner slid across the seat. The breeze, smelling of salt, a clear, stinging scent, blew random patterns in the sand. "I like it," he said.

She took his hand and led him inside the house. A dark cool room, barely furnished: a room of spaces, dim corners, plants. She lives here, he thought, where there's no clutter. Where there's nothing of the past. She lives, he understood, with an exorcism of her own history. Plants, climbing ivies, hanging ferns: a dark green cool room.

"No chairs, John. Help yourself to a pillow."

He squatted on a fat embroidered pillow. Too much, he thought, too much to absorb at once. Take it slow, in stages. She reclined on a pillow opposite, her head propped up by her hand. He could hardly see her: his eyes were still filled with sunlight.

"Made it myself," she said. "The very pillow on which you sit. With my own little hands."

"I didn't know you had such talent," he said.

"Oh, there's a whole bunch of things you don't know, John Rayner," she said, laughing very lightly.

He realized he had never heard her laugh before. A musical sound, as if she meant it. He looked around the room, the darkness beginning to take shape. Drawn blinds, an absence of pictures, of photographs. There wasn't, as far as he could see, a TV. A small portable record player, of the kind one might find in a child's bedroom, sat on a shelf—but even this gadget was surrounded by some massive philodendron. Growing things, he thought. She's taken her life, erased her past, crowded her energies into *growing things.* And she looked—well, beautiful, even if he had some trouble in thinking of his brother's widow in this way.

"Are you intending to stay for a time?" she asked.

He wasn't sure how to answer. Coming here, coming to see Isobel, had seemed the most logical thing; but he hadn't given any thought to time, to movement.

"Can you use a guest?" he asked.

"Sure. Sure I can use a guest."

He smiled, closing his eyes. Here it was easy to imagine that nothing had ever happened; events dwindled, diminishing into nonoccurrences. *Richard hadn't died. Richard was still—* He opened his eyes and looked at her. Leave it alone, he thought. Put the questions aside. All the asking in the world wouldn't bring any of them back. Not Richard, not Dubbs, not Sally.

"So, John. How come the leave? Did you do

something terrible? Trade a few secrets with the Russians or something?" She was leaning forward, her face hardly visible in the gloom, but he knew she was watching him intently. He said nothing. The silence was like a pool in the room. There was, he thought, an edge of slight bitterness in her voice. But what could he expect? She was still staring at him. "I've come to the conclusion, the hard way, John, that it's all a crock of shit," she said. "Your world, the world *he* lived in—it doesn't mean a goddam thing. It never meant anything. They give you badges and ID cards and special passports and secret telephone numbers you can call. It's hilarious. I was in a toy store yesterday and they had this kit you could buy. Secret Agent Kit, it was called. Imagine little kids pretending to be people who're pretending to be something else—"

She stopped, turning her face to the side.

"I sold it. The house. The two cars. The furniture. Every goddam thing I could see I sold. The junk of my life. And I came down here because all I wanted was peace. It's not so much to ask for in life, is it? Is it, John?"

"No. It's not much," he said.

"You find other things. You go on. After a time it isn't so difficult. You accept easily. New pastimes. New friends. New things to dabble in."

Rayner had an image of Richard: obscure, fuzzy, like a face seen through mist. Broken glass, the fall. He looked away from Isobel, noticing now the row of books held in place with cinder blocks. He moved nearer to them.

"Don't mock it," she said. "When the physical world's a huge pain in the ass, what do you turn to?"

Rayner said nothing. He stared at the titles on the paperback spines. Strange—strange how damned hard it was to get away from reminders. Books and Sally.

Books and Andreyev. *Keys to Inner Space. New Frontiers of the Mind. The Third Eye. The World Beyond. Many Mansions. Make Parapsychology Work for You.* He touched the spines; how could he laugh at it all? You come, like Isobel, to some hard, cold place and all you want is the reinforcement of a belief. Powers of the mind. Extrasensory perception. Life after death. How could you make fun of her?

"Okay. Call them comforters. Nipples for babies," she said. "It's a growing process. When I finish with that, I move on to something else. When I finally understand what a shitty woman I was, what a terrible wife I was to him, then I can grow."

"Do you . . ." He hesitated. He was uneasy now. "Do you want to talk about that night?"

"Do you know how many goddam times I was asked that same question? 'We must know, Mrs. Rayner. We must know everything, Mrs. Rayner. Would you please go through it again, Mrs. Rayner?' Then I stopped believing in what I was saying. What really happened anyway? A man committed suicide."

She got up and lit a lamp. In the soft glow of the light she looked sad now. I shouldn't have come, Rayner thought. I intrude. I bring it all back home. He picked up one of her books and flipped through the pages. He read one sentence absently: "*. . . unlike most people plagued by a poltergeist, Nelya suddenly realized the 'force' was coming from her.*" He closed the book, wondering why these things spooked him as they did. *The force.* What force? Exactly what? Visible by X-ray? by brain scan? Could you find it in the course of a postmortem?

Isobel said, "Keep an open mind, John. Sometimes you're too much like your brother."

Rayner stood up. He wanted to go outside. He

reached out and touched Isobel's hand lightly. Had she seen the incredulity on his face?

"Want a guided tour of my garden?"

"I'd love it," he answered.

Still holding her hand, he followed her outside to the back of the house. The small walled garden was filled with stakes that had been driven into the ground. Each stake was labeled.

"I'll have all kinds of goodies coming up," she said. She wandered among the stakes as if she were crossing a minefield. "Sweet corn. Runner beans. Beets. And the great secret, John Rayner, is solar power and TLC—tender loving care."

Rayner watched her bend to pat the soil. It was a strange, unsettling feeling to find your own brother's widow attractive; and, in its way, almost unnatural. But there was something in how she moved, in how deeply involved she appeared in her surroundings, that touched him.

Kneeling, squinting into the sunlight, she was smiling at him. "Come and see these tiny shoots."

A dead marriage; living plants. There was an association here that troubled him, a sense of dislocated identity. *Who is this Isobel?* he wondered. *How can she touch me now?*

## 3.

"I want you to understand what this is. I want you to understand what these papers are," the man called Koprow was saying. He was holding several sheets of flimsy paper of different colors toward her—pink, yellow, white.

She nodded her head: she understood.

"I want you to understand, Mrs. Blum," Koprow said. "When I sign these papers, you are free to go to Israel."

She watched him. The bald head that so reminded her of an egg, a distorted, misshapen egg.

"Do you understand, Mrs. Blum? Do you understand how *important* my signature is?"

Fools, she thought. A world in which a man can crush a city at the stroke of a pen. Did he really think he mattered? Did he really enjoy the notion that history would enshrine his name? She looked bitterly at him. "I understand," she said.

"I want you also to realize that if anything happens to me as a direct consequence of your interference, two things will follow. The first is that you will not be allowed to go to Israel."

She waited. Afraid, upset, for she already knew the second threat.

"The other, Mrs. Blum, is that your family will be killed." He rose from her bedside, tucking the papers inside his jacket. She watched him cross to the window, hands folded behind his back. Beyond, there was a view of dark-green hills: a cold view. Nobody had troubled to tell her where she was but time after time she had caught the word *Pennsylvania;* and she thought: America, where else could one go that would take such a long time on a plane? America. A country of fable. An enchanted place. Now she stared at Koprow, wondering at the depths of her own hatred. She wanted to reach out and hurt him, but she was afraid— afraid no longer for herself, for her own future, but because of the children. Little children, she thought. I bring death and destruction, but not to them. *Of all people, not to them.*

Koprow turned and smiled at her. In that smile

she could already see Israel fading. She could already see her own Palestine vanish, as if it had never existed in the first place. Perhaps that was it; it was all illusion, every aspect of it was illusion—all the way down the line. In that smile she could see all the dying, all the despair.

He stands there. Smug. Despicable. *I could kill him now.* She turned on her side, feeling aches in her wasted limbs.

"We want one more task from you," he said. "One more. Then you're free."

She twisted her neck, seeing his shape outlined against the window, against the cold black-green hills. "Every task is the last one," she said. "How can I know that you'll ever keep your word?"

"You have to trust me," Koprow said.

"Trust?"

Koprow nodded. "Consider the consequences, Mrs. Blum, if you *don't* trust me."

Consequences, she thought. His mind was a labyrinth, passages and corridors and locked doors. In this labyrinth there was neither trust nor suspicion because opposites had ceased to exist: words meant only what he *needed* them to mean. She flinched—there was pain in her arms, legs, pain all across her chest. Wasted, flabby breasts; a heart whose every beat threatened to be the last one of all. I could welcome death, she thought. An old friend, an ancient love that lived in damp familiar chasms—I could welcome it. But the children, she thought. The children. I have to live that long.

Now she reached for the most recent photographs, the ones Katya had given her in London. There was something about them, a different quality: the faces were sad in the white sunshine, as if the pictures had been taken by force, as if the subjects were unwilling.

"Remember," said Koprow, approaching the bed. "One more task. Then I sign your papers. Do you understand me?"

She reached up, her hands shaking, her fingers trying to grip the lapels of the man's jacket. "You must promise me," she said. "Promise me!"

Koprow gently took her hands in his own. "You have my word."

The old woman lay back down, breathing heavily, hard. "Send the woman in. Tell her . . . tell her I'm in pain. Will you do that?"

Koprow was smiling as he stepped to the door. "For you, Mrs. Blum, anything. Anything at all."

She watched him go out and she lay motionless a long time, her mind empty—her mind empty as a well from which every last particle of water has whirlpooled away.

**4.**

The Lehigh Lodge was a timber construction designed to impersonate a vast log cabin in which, during the fall, amateur hunters might feel that they were roughing it. It was usually filled with men in plaid jackets who carried shotguns and rifles, but now it was occupied entirely by the soccer team of the Soviet Union and a small entourage of curious journalists who perceived themselves as pioneers of a sport that had never quite taken root in American soil. They were, by and large, fatalistic men accustomed to having their copy butchered and condensed by sports editors who needed to make room for the latest in baseball or football.

In a field behind the lodge they watched the Russian team at practice. The trainer, Charek, occasionally shouted instructions from the sidelines; sometimes a man named Oblinski, seemingly the official interpreter, answered the reporters' questions in stilted English. When it suited his purpose, he appeared not to understand what was being asked.

—Why didn't you win at Wembley?

—We were robbed by a late penalty goal.

—Is the American team strong, in your opinion?

—Extremely so.

Question and answer. The journalists watched the Soviets practice dead-ball strategies of the kind that had brought them their first goal against the English. The chip across the opposing defense and the accurate running of Kazemayov. But the brilliant Kazemayov wasn't the only attraction of the morning. The Soviet Ambassador, Leontov, had driven from Washington to watch the players. But Leontov, whether from the inscrutable needs of protocol or from a basic ignorance of the sport itself, refused to be drawn on any questions. Hustled by his own small entourage, he went inside the lodge—every part of which, with the necessary exception of the bar, was off-limits to the American press. A small man with a goatee, he looked more like an actor playing a diplomat than the real thing. Inside the lodge, he climbed the stairs hurriedly to the first floor and, leaving his entourage in the corridor, entered Koprow's room. The two men shook hands, and Leontov, unbuttoning his woolen coat, sat down in a wicker chair at the window. For a time, the Ambassador watched the players beneath the window; then he turned to look at Koprow, who was standing with his back to a well-lit coal fire.

"I would prefer not to talk here," Leontov said.

"The room has been vacuumed," Koprow said.

"Nevertheless." Leontov stood up now, fidgeting with the buttons of his coat. Koprow watched him a moment. What did he know? What did this little man, fresh from his world of meaningless parties, glasses of claret, his tiny universe of pomp and circumstance—what did he know?

"We can walk, if you like."

Leontov nodded his head, a sharp little gesture; it was as if he had no time in the world to spare, as if all his experiences were measured in terms of some internal schedule. They left the room together, Leontov indicating to his entourage that they should wait for his return.

It was chilly outside: a bright Pennsylvania spring morning. Both men walked in the opposite direction to the soccer players and into a small fir wood. Silver bark threw the sunlight back in the fashion of dulled mirrors. Koprow broke open a packet of Life Savers and slid one into his mouth. It tasted rather bland to him.

When they had gone a little way, Leontov stopped and looked through the skinny trees. "Pretty countryside."

"It makes my heart sing," said Koprow. He spat the candy out: two broken half-moons.

Leontov looked as if this minuscule act of pollution annoyed him. He gazed at Koprow and said, "I understand that the so-called neutralization process failed in London."

Koprow saw a plump bird wing it through the trees. It flew clumsily, with a motion that suggested its first jaunt from the sanctity of nest. "Zubro's marksman failed, if that's what you mean," he said. "Two down. One to go."

Leontov appeared surprised. "Are you trying to tell me that this scheme has not been aborted?"

Koprow, momentarily angry with the diplomat, laughed. "I don't exactly have to tell *you* anything, Leontov."

"It's preposterous, Koprow. I want this on record—"

"Let me adjust my portable tape recorder," Koprow said, reaching into his coat.

"I hardly think it's a matter you can take lightly, my friend—"

"I hardly think, by the same token, Mr. Ambassador, that the affair should concern you."

Leontov sighed, leaning against a tree that had been tilted sideways by the weather. Then, as though he was thinking that he might stain his coat, he stood upright. You little tin soldier, Koprow thought. A diplomat was about as valuable as a fart in the breeze.

"Koprow, consider this. You have been working on the notion that only three people knew Andreyev's identity—"

"Perhaps only two, Leontov. The girl was simply the cashing-in, so to speak, of an insurance policy—"

"What if there were more? What then?"

Koprow placed a hand on the small man's shoulder. "Poor little Leontov. You worry. Look at yourself. All those little lines on your small forehead—"

The Ambassador stepped away from Koprow's touch. "Answer my question, Koprow. What if there are more?"

Koprow shook his head, staring through the trees. From somewhere he could hear the sudden rush of water over stones: a brook, a stream. The same fat bird circled overhead like a flying grapefruit.

"The game, Leontov, is truly worth the gamble," he said.

They walked a few yards farther into the trees. Suddenly they came upon the stream: white froth surging over smooth pebbles, a dark-brown trout basking in the shallows. In silence they watched the trout whip out of the shadows, glimmer dully in the light, then disappear downstream.

"The young American," Leontov said, looking at Koprow in a sideways manner. "I understood he was to be neutralized in Munich."

"Ah," Koprow said. "Our American associate reserved a room at the Hotel Ritzi in Munich. Young Rayner was supposed to arrive there to take up the booking—but, for reasons best known to himself, he didn't make it. In fact, he didn't go to Germany at all. Pity. We had a man waiting for him there."

"Where did he go?"

"Scotland."

"Scotland?"

"And now he's back in the United States," Koprow said.

"Here? *Back here?* And you're going ahead with— You must be out of your mind, Koprow. Crazy."

"I don't think so," Koprow said. "I believe in insurance, as much insurance as I can gather around me. There are more ways than one of neutralizing a person, Mr. Ambassador. For one thing, our American associate has given me certain assurances."

"Such as?"

"You needn't concern yourself with trivia." Koprow reached inside his pocket and took out a piece of paper, which he handed to Leontov. "For another thing, you will be good enough to send one of your people to that address. My second line of insurance, you might say."

"One of *my* people?"

"Don't tell me, Mr. Ambassador, that you don't grasp my meaning, please. You have human resources."

"You're asking me to send a man—"

"You know what I'm asking. Let's not labor the point."

Leontov looked upset. "Is this where Rayner is to be found?"

"It's a logical deduction," Koprow said. "If your man fails, if the Americans fail too, I still wouldn't worry myself sleepless over Rayner. Imagine, by some slight miracle, he finds out what's going on—what do you think? Do you think people are going to believe him? That they'll be falling all over themselves to believe his wild tale?" Koprow laughed. "No, the young American isn't even a *nuisance.*" Koprow picked up a pebble and threw it into the stream. It was meant to skim the surface, but it sank at once. He looked at the Ambassador. "Don't concern yourself, Leontov. Accept my word. Your main responsibility was that of issuing an invitation and of making certain it was accepted. Have you done that?"

Leontov took off his gloves and scratched his beard. He was shaking his head from side to side, as if to rid himself of an ambassadorial migraine. "The invitation has been issued."

"And?"

"So far as I can tell, it will be accepted."

*So far as you can tell,* Koprow thought. *Which isn't very far at all.*

"I want assurances, Ambassador," Koprow said. "You can save your twisted diplomatic bullshit for state functions."

Leontov studied his leather gloves for a moment; they might have been the open pages of a book written in an inscrutable language. "We do what we can, Koprow—"

"No," Koprow said. "We do *better* than that. Don't we?"

## 5.

On his second night at Isobel's it rained—a sweeping rain that fell in wind-driven patterns from Chesapeake Bay all across Tidewater. They had eaten a supper of salad, watching the flow of rain from the window of the kitchen. Now, with a single lamp barely illuminating the kitchen, they were drinking Californian sauterne. Rayner could hear the tide, not as some intermittent rumble crossing the sand but as a constant symphonic thing. Amongst the leftover food there lay a scattered deck of ESP cards; they had been testing each other, lost in the circles and squares and stars of the pack.

Rayner's best score had been eight out of twenty-five, after a half-dozen runs through the deck; Isobel had managed ten on her first run, but nothing more than five afterward. Rayner poured more wine, rose, went to the kitchen window, and watched the rain run down the glass. He understood he was vaguely drunk, slightly distanced from himself—and yet not absolutely so: some small area of his brain was clear and hard and brilliant. In the distance, by what little moonlight lay behind cloud, he could see the surf rise in broken white walls.

"But you've no idea why she was killed?" Isobel asked.

Rayner, turning, shrugged. "Not really. Somebody . . . What the fuck. A jealous lover? A lunatic? I don't know."

Isobel was silent a moment. She picked up the deck and shuffled it slowly, quietly. "I'm sorry," she said. "I'm really sorry."

Rayner walked back to the table and sat down, looking at his sister-in-law, thinking of Dubbs, wanting to say something about the death of Dubbs. Security: even this blind wall remained impenetrable in front of him. Talking of Sally was a way of talking about Dubbs too, as if in his mind they had become one corpse.

"From what you've told me, she sounds . . ." Isobel, smiling, something a little sad in the expression, paused. "She sounds like the kind of person who would have led you a dance, John."

"Maybe," Rayner said. He touched the rim of his wineglass. "Maybe what it comes down to is my pride was hurt. Maybe I thought I was of some importance in her life. Then to find out otherwise . . . It doesn't make much sense to talk about it now."

"I guess," Isobel said. She began laying the cards out in random rows—stars and boxes and squiggles and circles and pluses. As if they were a form of tarot deck, she looked at the design for a time. "There's a kind of woman who is known commonly as a cunt. I think your friend Sally and I had that in common, John."

Rayner started to say something, to protest in some feeble way, but she interrupted him. "What kind of life did I give Richard? Did he ever really tell you? I guess he didn't. I guess he was too discreet, too polite, too well-bred. When we were married, I used to think of my body as a system of rewards. When he was a good boy, he got a shot at it. When he was out of favor—wham, down came the old portcullis. I had more headaches of convenience than there are Bayer aspirin in the world."

There was something in this confession that Rayner found slightly embarrassing. She was turning the cards over and over in meaningless gestures. He reached over to stop her, feeling that somewhere at the back of all this empty behavior there were tears— but not the kind that might be shed openly. Momentarily he held her hand; the cards slid on the table.

When she took her hand away, she smiled. "I'm glad you're here, John. Really. I think I wanted somebody to look at me and say, Jesus Christ, you've really changed. And then you wonder if the change is anything more than just a few different behavioral attitudes. Skin-deep? I don't know."

Rayner listened to the rain again. Squalls, breaking off the ocean like cannon shots, rattled the glass panes. He said, "Jesus Christ, you've really changed."

She laughed quietly, then began to gather the dishes to dump them in the sink. "In the house in Georgetown we had a dishwasher," she said. "A woman came in every morning to vacuum. My whole goddam life was a clutter, when what I really needed was space and light. Does that make sense?"

Rayner waited as he felt he had been waiting now for two whole days to hear about Richard, about what had happened that night. He watched Isobel dry her hands with a dish towel. The knuckles, he noticed, were slightly red. *Tell me,* he thought, *tell me what happened.*

"Do you like walking in the rain?" she asked.

"Sure I do."

"Without umbrellas?"

"Any way you want it."

"There's something good and clean about seaside rain," she said.

He put on his raincoat. She wore a plastic mac, blue jeans, no shoes. Outside, wind and rain had conspired to fill the air with grit that stung their eyes. They walked toward the beach, where the spray was violent, vicious. In the distance, far beyond the lights of the Chesapeake Bay Bridge, a crack of lightning opened a hole in the night sky; thunder drummed miles away. Rayner could feel the salt in his eyes. In a blurry way he saw a thin figure sprinting along the edge of the rough tide. A middle-aged man, arms and legs pumping, was jogging his way out of the coronary season of the heart.

"Didn't anybody tell you about Virginia Beach, John?" Isobel asked.

He could hardly hear her words. They were torn by the wind. Like the music, he thought, the music through the loudspeakers at Wembley, ripped by the wind and blown away. . . .

"The place is filled with mind readers, palmists, spiritualists, UFO believers, psychics, food fanatics, health nuts. It's the freak capital of the eastern seaboard, I swear it."

Rayner watched the man turn some distance away. He was barely visible now, far beyond the reach of the lights that burned in the huge hotels. He stopped, lay flat on the sand as if to do push-ups, then jumped once again into a standing position. He began to jog back again in the direction of Isobel and Rayner. He passed them, close to the ragged edge of the tide. Then he was gone down the beach and out of sight.

"I feel damn tired just watching him," Rayner said. "Is there someplace we can sit?"

They found shelter alongside a broken seawall.

They sat on the wet sand, and Isobel tried, wasting match after match, to light a cigarette against the squall. Rayner watched her flip the sodden, broken cigarette into the wind.

"Tell me about this ESP business," he said. "The cards, I mean."

"What can I tell you?"

"Do you believe in it all?"

She was quiet for a moment. "A month or two ago I would have said it was garbage. Even now, for someone like me, it's just a kind of parlor game. I don't have any talent for it. I play with the cards, like some kind of solitaire or whatever. But I've met people who can predict them accurately—"

"You mean *guess* them, don't you?"

She shrugged in the dark. "No, not guess. It isn't guessing when you can predict with terrific consistency, is it?"

Rayner thought for a moment of Dubbs's friend Professor Chamber. And then of Andreyev. Worthy academics in hot pursuit of the indefinable: the magic of mind. "You say you know people who can predict the cards?"

He felt her hand touch his sleeve. "One day I'll arrange a demonstration for you, if you like."

He wasn't sure suddenly; he wasn't sure if he wanted any such demonstration, any kind of proof. The idea of Andreyev nagged him again, the unsettling intuition that if he hadn't acquired a certain computer data sheet, Dubbs might still be alive.

He laid his head back against the damp wall, conscious now of the runner coming back along the tide. There was no holding the guy back, he thought. A gluttony for punishment; or fear of an early eclipse? Rayner watched him through the dark. Another sliver of lightning, forked, misshapen, broke above the bay.

In the stunning silvery light, brief as the flash of a malfunctioning firework, Rayner could see the man's face—the gaunt jaws, the shadows of the eyes. It didn't make sense to him all at once: there was something absurdly out of place, so ridiculously incongruous that he wondered if he were hallucinating. He reached across to touch Isobel. "Did you catch a glimpse of that guy?" he asked.

"I couldn't help it exactly—"

"Did you ever see somebody jog in a suit before?"

"No—"

"I mean, an average two-piece off-the-peg behind-the-desk suit? Did you ever see that before?"

Isobel shrugged. "I told you, John. It's a funny town."

"Yeah. Yeah, maybe it is."

He watched the man, still running, disappear in the spray ahead. No, he thought, it doesn't make the best possible sense. Figure, maybe, a drunk. A guy who's just had a knock-down rolling-pin fight with the wife. Somebody working off the heat, the anger. He narrowed his eyes and tried to see through the spray—but the figure was out of sight now, and so far as he could tell, the beach was empty. Relax, Rayner. Too many deaths make you suspicious. Too many upsets and sadnesses and you dwell on them—which only leads you to reach for Dr. Whatsisname's downers. He took Isobel's hand and hauled her to a standing position. A fraction away, he thought, from an embrace. *That close.* He stepped back, feeling wet sand clinging to his hands, inside his shoes. The wife of your dead brother, for God's sake. Okay, she isn't the old Isobel, she's going through the changes—but some things you don't touch, after all.

"You want to get back?" he asked.

"If there's wine to finish," she said.

"We've got lots of wine," he answered. *We*, he thought. Don't take it this far; it's almost as if you've moved in on the ghosts.

They walked back quickly, bent against the rain, toward the house. Shivering, Isobel opened the front door and Rayner followed her inside.

"Don't you ever lock up when you go out?" he asked.

She laughed. "What's to steal? A few plants? Some cushions? I don't even have a key for the place."

They went into the kitchen and opened a fresh bottle of sauterne. Isobel poured two glasses and they sat at the kitchen table. They knocked their glasses together and she said, "I forget, don't I? Your world's filled with keys and locks and secret combinations. Like Richard's used to be. You know, he had this briefcase with a combination lock. I'm not laughing at him, John, just at the world that makes these things so godawful necessary."

"Sometimes—"

"Ah, sometimes, of course, the other team might actually filch a few of the game plays, right?"

"Something like that," Rayner said. He wondered why he felt a sudden sense of shame. It was as if she had punctured the surface of him, revealing something of almost inestimable worthlessness. Or was it what he had felt a moment before on the beach—the closeness of her, a nearness that in itself had seemed immoral to him? He looked across the kitchen, thinking again of the running man on the beach. And then he was beset by the strange feeling that there was somebody else, other than Isobel and him, in the house. No, he thought, you're trying to get away from that world of bugs and eavesdropping devices and gadgets. Why the fuck can't it leave you alone?

He stood up. Isobel opened her mouth to say something and he pressed his index finger against her lips for silence.

Puzzled, she pushed his hand away. "John—"

"It's nothing," he said. The layout of the house, he thought. Remember it. A living room they had just come through. This kitchen. A bedroom. A bathroom. The basic accommodations of life. Shit, Rayner, there's nowhere for someone to hide.

"What's up?" she asked.

He shook his head. A man running in a storm. A man in a two-piece suit. Street clothes. The equations that never made sense until the last possible moment. Someone on the stairs outside Sally's flat. Figure it out, he thought. Make it work somehow. Why was Dubbs killed at Wembley? Why had they been followed to Wembley? And by whom? You know a man's name, his identity, you understand he wants to switch sides. Where does that take you?

"John, for God's sake," she was saying.

It was against the glass, briefly, quickly, nothing more than a shadow that interfered with the dripping of rain upon the pane. He had forgotten how quickly he could move. He pushed the woman out of her chair and lay on top of her, all this in one fast move, one continuous chain of activity. He heard the glass shatter and then he rose, ducking, rushing to the kitchen door, feeling the rain break hard and cruel against his face, blinding his eyes. The running man. Now, turning, barely visible in the light, the man fired a second shot. It was with a silenced weapon, an automatic that in the reflection of the kitchen light looked like stainless steel. Rayner threw himself forward but the man was moving backward already, retreating across the garden, trampling over the wooden stakes, breaking them, clumping through the shrubbery that lay beyond the vegetable patches. Rayner watched him go, then hurried inside the kitchen again, where Isobel was standing beside the fallen chair. There was an expression on her face: not fear, for he would have recognized fear. Not anger. He could read it anyhow: *When does it ever stop? Does it ever stop?*

All she was looking for, he thought, was peace. Peace and sand and withdrawal. And I bring something else, something as rank as a dead dog, as grubby as a piece of some old skeleton, into her dark cool green world.

He went across the floor and put his arms around her. He wondered how sorry you could ever really say you were.

# 6.

Patrick Joseph Mallory liked to conduct his Cabinet meetings before breakfast but immediately after taking a brisk swim in the White House pool. He arrived at these sessions—a young man, his black hair wet and slicked back—with a kind of brightness that the older members of the Cabinet found irritating. Invariably, these were men who had risen late and managed to gulp down coffee before making it to the White House, men who sat in tetchy silences, fidgeting, wanting to smoke, wanting to eat, while the President, with that firmness of purpose which had first endeared him to the electorate, ran speedily through the agenda. It was rare for Mallory to encounter any genuine opposition to this or that statement of policy because he had close and workable relationships with both the House and the Senate; there was a charm to Mallory as well as a certain strength of mind. Even the skeletons in his closet were said to be so well greased that they never once creaked.

On this morning's agenda there were several trivial items that he dealt with summarily. He also passed out copies of Kimball Lindholm's report—belatedly written—on his visit to the Soviet Union. Mallory had not himself read this ninety-eight-page document except to glance at it for *tone*, which, as he had suspected, was predictable. "There is very little difference," the Vice President had written, "between a Russian farmer and one from Kansas." There was a sense of universal brotherhood. There were the same concerns with soil and climate and fertilizer. (In fact, so much of Lindholm's report concerned fertilizer that it became known in inner circles as "The Shit Manifesto.") The President passed the documents out and advised his Cabinet members to read the Vice President's report as soon as possible.

The final item on a short agenda concerned the activities of the Central Intelligence Agency in supporting the push for human rights in the countries of Eastern Europe. It was the opinion of the Secretary of State, Rieckhoff, that while the effort should be continued as a matter of simple humanity a line ought to be drawn between the kinds of matériel the United States should supply to Communist dissidents. Furthermore, he had obtained new information from the CIA concerning the presence of Soviet "advisers" in the Republic of Ivory Coast, in the Republic of Botswana, and in the United Republic of Cameroon. The suggestion was made that various pressures—mainly economic—be brought against these African nations. It was Rieckhoff's opinion, and one supported by Mallory, that "Soviet advisers" had the odd habit of transmuting into "Soviet military experts."

Kimball Lindholm was the only dissenting voice. He didn't personally give a damn about some sandy wastelands halfway across the world and he didn't give a damn what other people thought of him for holding that opinion. Mallory smiled at his Vice President with an expression that might have passed for one of tolerance. The old fella's entitled to his opinion. What the hell. But Mallory perceived more than a simple insularity in Kimball Lindholm; he saw what he thought of, on the bottom line, as an extreme form of prairie asshole. And on those few occasions when he had taken one Martini more than necessary, he had been heard to speak both badly and indiscreetly of his Vice President. But there were times when the price you paid for votes was higher than you might have liked. Kimball Lindholm bullshitted, Mallory thought, ergo, he existed. A Cartesian travesty, perhaps, but he was saddled with a philosophical reality for the next three years in the form of the little man whose opinions had been formed, somewhere around the age of ten, in the shadows of Kansas silos.

The President proposed that the Secretary of State direct the Central Intelligence Agency to consider new ways of assisting Eastern European dissidents; after all, if the Soviets were scrambling around Africa with "technical advice," why shouldn't the United States of America, in a game of global tic-tactoe, offer "technical advice" of another kind to those people who wanted to shape democracies in countries resistant to the notion?

At the close of the meeting, the various Cabinet members left. Only the President and his Chief of Staff, Callaway, remained behind in the Cabinet Room. Callaway had been with Mallory since the early days in Maine—the State Senate, the gubernatorial campaign, the House of Representatives, and now 1600 Pennsylvania Avenue. Of all his virtues, fidelity was the greatest. There were those who said that if Mallory were to go blind, Callaway would go on his knees to beg that both his corneas be transplanted into the President's eyes.

Now, in the empty Cabinet Room, the President said, "Do you ever have nightmares, Jim?"

"Sometimes," Callaway said.

"Real bad nightmares?"

"You're getting at something," Callaway said. "I don't need two guesses at it, do I?"

Patrick J. Mallory clasped his hands together in front of him on the table—it was as if he meant to pray but had changed his mind. He stared at his Chief of Staff for a time in silence, then said, "I'm watching my own funeral. Okay? I'm with the angelic band up there somewhere. It doesn't feel so bad. After all, I'm not stoking the old fires, right?"

Callaway, smiling, nodded.

"I'm floating on a nice old cloud. I see them lowering the box into the grave. I don't feel too bad. It isn't all blackness and horror."

"Then it changes?" Callaway asked.

"Damned right, it changes. Because all of a sudden I see Kimball Lindholm being sworn into office and I wake up and it's cold sweat time. It's cold, cold sweat time."

"I wouldn't worry, Mr. President," Callaway said. "You'll outlive him."

"I wonder if it's a contradiction in terms to say that anybody can outlive Kimball Lindholm," Mallory said. "Ah, what the hell. You pay a certain price. And Kimball comes with the property."

Callaway, gathering his papers, turned toward

the door. There he paused and looked back at the President, as if suddenly remembering something. "You haven't given a reply to Leontov yet, and his office called this morning."

Mallory stood up now, hands in the pockets of his dark suit. He rattled a key loosely for a time. "That's the game where they have men in shorts who kick a ball into a net?"

"Yes," Callaway said.

"What do you think?"

"It's your decision, Mr. President. It's the first time a soccer team consisting entirely of native-born players will be playing a full international against the Soviet Union."

Mallory thought for a moment. "What I can't stand is saying yes to anything, *anything,* from that little shit Leontov."

Callaway shrugged and turned toward the door. "I'll do the regrets then."

"No, wait." Mallory looked across the room at his Chief of Staff. "Accept. I'll go. Tell Leontov that I'll go. If Kissinger could sit through soccer games, what the hell. Besides, there's the patriotic angle."

Callaway smiled. "I'll tell Leontov."

"Do we have a chance of winning?"

"According to the press, no. According to the team coach, yes."

"It would be a drag to have Leontov turning smug on me if his side wins," Mallory said. "It would be a real drag."

# 2

## 1

Shortly after dawn he woke and went out onto the balcony of the Ramada Inn and looked at the calm Atlantic—hardly moving, gray and sluggish, lifeless after the night's storm. The morning air was chill against his skin. He slid the door closed, reentered the room, and watched Isobel as she slept. He sat down in the chair by the balcony door. The sea was a whisper. Last night, he remembered, it had been his idea to move here out of the cottage; it had been his idea to park the old station wagon several streets away and check into the Ramada in the hope that somehow, in all its gaunt plastic splendor, its curiously lifeless quality, you could contrive to lose yourself. . . .

*Other people go to the police, John. Don't they? Isn't that what they do when they've been shot at? Isn't that what ordinary people do?*

Ordinary people. He had forgotten the ordinary, the banal. He watched her as she slept and he kept thinking of Dubbs dying on the steps at Wembley. The second shot. *The second shot, my dear.* He closed his eyes and rubbed his face with the palm of his hand: cold, chilled.

*But I forgot, didn't I? You don't go to the police, do you? You have funny little numbers you're supposed to call, right? You dial some funny little number and ask for some anonymous extension, don't you?*

Bitter. Hadn't she every right in the book to be bitter? He opened his eyes, rose wearily from the table, went back out onto the balcony. Out on the ocean, like some ancient dowager trying to keep up with changing times, an old battleship performed perfunctory maneuvers. A pall of light smoke hung over it. An attendant launch, white and sparkling as a new seabird, created a rich wake around the vessel.

The second shot, he thought.

Think.

Go over it. Say it line by line. See what you can dredge up from that burnt-out memory. Dubbs died because of Andreyev. Okay. Because he knew Andreyev's identity. That leaves me—that leaves me and I must die for the very same reason. Okay. Okay. Okay. What in the name of God was so damned important about this Andreyev anyhow? And Sally—was that just a fucking coincidence? A parapsychologist. Things that go bump in the night. No. It was no spooky séance, no half-assed deal in the dark, flying cigarette butts and ringing bells and voices coming at you through trumpets.

*People don't die on account of parlor games.*

He watched the old vessel turn laboriously, as if it were a wounded whale. The plume of smoke drifted away, forming a cloud. The sea threw up a bluster of wind all at once and he went back inside the room. Isobel was awake, sitting propped up on her elbows. He was suddenly furious—not with the intruder, whoever he was, but with himself for dragging a familiar old darkness into this woman's life. Death follows some people, he thought. It comes on like a black magnet. What the hell do I know that makes me worth killing?

"Do I say good morning? Thank you very much for the hotel room?" Her voice was faintly hoarse and she was staring at him accusingly; and he thought, I deserve it, all of it.

"I didn't know it was going to happen," he said. "Do you think I would have endangered you? Do you think that?"

She closed her eyes impatiently. "I'm trying to work out the difference between you and your brother, John. I think it's one of degree. In your world it's guns. In his world it was paper. Cut it any way you like, one's as dangerous as the other."

She rose from the bed, clutching the sheet to her body. In the bathroom doorway she stopped, turning to him. "All I know is I was beginning to get better. I could see it, okay? Light at the end of the proverbial tunnel? I could see it. I was working my way out of being a bitch—or what I more colloquially called a cunt last night. I was beginning to understand the bits and pieces of myself. Shit!"

She slammed the bathroom door, locked it.

He stared a moment at it. Oh, Christ, he thought. What was there to say? That look in her eye, that ice-like look which seemed to throw reflections up from far within herself—he was reminded of Richard's Isobel. *The bits and pieces of myself,* he thought. She could read the books and work the cards and delve into spiritualism and learn how to grow plants and catch the latest manuals on how to be your own best friend—and in a flash, in a sweep, he could make a ruin of it all.

He could hear the sound of the shower running

now. He walked up and down the room, hands jammed in his pockets, his steps quick and angry. He picked up the key, locked the door behind him, and went down in the elevator to the lobby. He bought a copy of *The Richmond Times-Dispatch* and two cardboard containers of coffee from the empty coffee shop. When he got back to the room Isobel was already dressed, toweling her damp hair. He set the coffee and the newspaper on the table.

"Room service too?" she said. "Busy beaver, aren't you?"

That tone, he thought. "Look—"

"*You* look, John."

"No—"

"I want to say this once and once only. I don't know what kind of goddam mess you've got yourself into, and I frankly don't give a flying fuck, but don't drag me through it. Okay? Sometimes, sometimes I feel a total hatred when I hear the name Rayner. Is that strong enough for you, John?"

He sat at the table and pried the plastic lid from the coffee. It was too hot to drink. He watched her sit down opposite him. She picked up the newspaper, surveyed the front-page headline, threw the paper down; it was as if she wanted no knowledge of what was happening in the world, as if, no matter what, it was destined to sicken her. She sipped her coffee and made a face. The silence was unbearable to him now. Words he might have spoken—but he recognized their uselessness as soon as they entered his mind. He went out onto the balcony. Dial your funny little number, ask for your anonymous extension, he thought. The door slid open behind him and he heard her step out, shivering in the cold, standing against the rail a few feet from him. He looked at her and was caught once more with his own uneasy desire.

"Okay," she said. "I withdraw. I take it all back. Friends?"

"You have every right to be angry," he said.

"Forget it," she said. "Let's just forget it."

He watched the battleship plowing, like some cripple on its last run, back toward Norfolk. His call, he would have to make his call. He would have to report the gunman. He turned to her and smiled, a look she didn't return. Instead, he saw something serious in her eyes, something strangely purposeful—and he wondered if she had felt the moment of his desire, if it had somehow communicated itself to her. He turned to the door, slid it open, went back inside the room. He picked up the telephone.

"Who are you calling?" she asked.

"My funny little number," he said.

She came in, sliding the door shut. "Before you make your call, John—"

He paused, looking at her.

"It's too soon," she said. "Do you know what I'm saying?"

"I know what you're saying," he answered. He watched her a moment, then dialed his number. The line was busy. He put the receiver down. Isobel was standing motionless, withdrawn, by the table. Too soon, he thought. How could the time ever be right? Could you make love with this woman and not think of Richard? Could you lie in bed with her, hold her, enter her, and not have images of the dead? A morbid maze, he thought. In time—could you find your way through it?

He walked over to the table where Isobel was idly scanning the pages of the newspaper, turning them in a listless, disinterested way. He saw how, when she reached a certain page, she flinched slightly, as if she had seen something she didn't want to see, something she couldn't handle. What? he wondered. What had touched her? He reached over and picked up the paper, noticing that it was open at the sports pages. The sports pages: what could be so terrible there?

She was smiling now, still looking at him in the manner of someone who has posed a difficult question and is waiting for a response. The sports pages, he thought. He glanced across them and saw, buried amongst horse-race results, baseball scores, and an item concerning the heavyweight champion of the world, a simple headline: "Soviets Plan Soccer Victory over US." He stared at the article for a long time, not really reading, not really seeing, but remembering.

"Stupid," Isobel said in a hollow way. "I still can't read something about Russia without thinking . . . thinking in a way I don't much like."

He looked at her.

*"Soviets Plan Soccer Victory over US."*

He went to the telephone and tried the number a second time. This time he got through.

## 2.

At first it was the sense of an impossible victory over her body that kept her trying to rise. Each muscle, each fiber, every part of her rebelled against the notion of movement but when she had thrown the bedsheet back and touched the floor with the soles of her feet she felt an awareness of triumph that overcame, if only momentarily, her pains. But her weak legs would not support her and she slid to the rug, thinking: The window, if I could get to the window. She began a slow crawl, padding forward in the fashion of an injured animal, toward the rectangle of pale light. From outside, there were sounds of voices—some of them Russian, others speaking what she assumed to be English. She wasn't sure exactly why she had to move now. Only the idea of reaching the window was of any real importance to her. Light filled the glass like sweet clear water and maybe, somewhere at the back of her mind, she had an idea she might immerse herself in this cleanliness, a form of purge, of renewal. Her swollen fingers throbbed from the effort of supporting her own frail weight. Her knuckles, solid blocks of pain, seemed no longer a true part of her. The veins in her pale legs were blue and raised. But it was the window that drew her still, magnetizing her, forcing her across the floor. She felt sweat form on her forehead and tried to lift one hand to wipe it away before it fell on her eyelids and blinded her; but even as she did so, even as she lifted a palm upward, she lost the slight balance she had and sprawled face down on the floor—and found, to her horror, her humiliation, that she could no longer force her body forward.

Youth, she thought. Youth was a bird you could not trap and cage no matter how hard you tried. Her neck slightly twisted, she stared at the distant window—a cross of wood supporting four panes. The wood was fragile, flaking, the glass bright and sparkling. All I wanted was to see, she thought. All I wanted was to make this wasted body move so that these eyes might look down and see.

She moaned slightly. Saliva gathered in white flecks at the corners of her lips. She edged forward very slightly, her eyes fixed still to the window, where the light by now had become a translucent blur, a hallucinatory aura.

Again, she could hear voices from below; she could hear the sound of people running back and forth, the noise of a ball being kicked, someone's name being called.

And then the door of the room was opened and Katya was hurrying across the floor toward her, hurrying, flapping, bending over her and drawing her upright by her armpits.

"The pain," she said to Katya. "Please—"

The woman was dragging her back toward the bed, dragging her roughly, hauling on her. She could feel her heels scrape the hard fiber of the rug. The window. All she wanted was to look out of the window and now this woman, this terrible woman, was hauling her away.

*I can't let it.*

*I can't let her.*

"You shouldn't have tried to get out of bed—"

*I can't stop myself now—*

In faint spidery lines the windowpanes cracked, cracked slowly and audibly, cracked in fibrous whorls of split glass; the wood frame snapped loosely and hung inward; and the woman, Katya, as if she had been stung, spun backward against the bed and lay there motionless, her arms limp, her legs useless.

No, she thought. What have I done? The broken glass. The woman. What have I done? They warned me. What have I done? She strained, dragging herself upward onto the mattress, and looked at Katya's face, white, sightless, the mouth a damp open hole. *What have I done?*

She crawled, aching, on top of the woman. She put the palms of her hands upon the sides of Katya's face, feeling the cold skin. *A witch? Is that what you are? Aaron, love, O my love, why did you*

Katya blinked, the whites of her eyes showing,

then slowly the irises appearing, like someone brought back from a trance, from a minor death. She stared at Mrs. Blum and then, as if she was horrified by the sight of the old woman alongside her on the bed, she pushed her away.

*"What did you do? What did you do to me?"*

Cracked glass and broken wood and the enraged woman. I should have done nothing, nothing, I should have spared myself any of this, now the pain begins and grows and then it reaches a crescendo I cannot tolerate every nerve end aflame every muscle cord snapping every heartbeat a hammer against the ribs I shouldn't have done this the cracked glass and the broken wood and the enraged woman.

Katya was standing by the bed, looking down at her.

"Please," Mrs. Blum said. Please. Hear me beg. *Hear my pain.* "The medication. Please. Help me."

*"Help you?"*

Katya went to the bedside table and took the small plastic tray of medication to the sink in the corner of the room, where she opened the bottles and poured the precious liquid away. "Help you? Help *you?"*

The old woman sat up. She wanted to bring the hurt back into the other woman again but now she hadn't the strength for it, now she had nothing left. She lay back down against the pillows, unable to catch her breath, gasping, holding her hands to her throat. *What have I done?* Light, fractured, altered as if it fell now through stained glass, was no longer a pure clean thing upon the window, but a series of broken lines, ruptures, suggesting that what had passed this way was a terrible storm.

"Help *you?"*

"Please—"

Katya turned on the faucet and broke the glass syringe upon the porcelain side of the basin.

"Suffer," she said. "Suffer the way you make other people suffer."

**3.**

"You mean I have to kick my heels in this goddam room?"

"For you," Rayner had said. "For your own safety."

Rayner had called Chip Alexander in Langley and then gone downstairs to the coffee shop of the Ramada Inn. Three hours, he thought. It would take Chip at least three hours. He sat where he could watch the doorway. A few early diners were scattered throughout the room, picking disconsolately at their food in the fashion of those who regret having taken premature vacations. He turned the newspaper to the sports pages, read the brief article, read it again, then a third time, as if it might be made to yield some deeper meaning. There was a photograph of two Soviet players rising, in some awkward defiance of gravity, to head a ball. But it was Dubbs he kept seeing, Dubbs slipping on the steps, Dubbs bleeding, leaning against the iron rail, Dubbs trying to joke as if death were simply the final theatrical merriment or some atrocious last pun. He ordered coffee, sipped it, tried to think his way around the series of puzzles. "The Soviets, according to their trainer, expect to win by at least a two-goal margin." He folded the paper flat, his brain seeming now to race, to fly, as though somewhere in this tangle of vague threads there was a core, a center, a meaning. A parapsychologist. The markings of a deck of ESP cards. Make parapsychology work for you. . . . And someone in this seaside town with a stainless-steel automatic pistol is looking for you.

He had gone through a pot of coffee and half of a sandwich before he saw Chip Alexander come in by the front door. He raised his hand, noticed how Chip hesitated, then how his step quickened as he walked across the floor and took the vacant seat at the table. Momentarily Rayner felt a surge of deep relief. There was a comfort in the sight of Alexander—old colleague, friend, a man of solid weight and even more solid emotions, Chip Alexander was never convinced of anything unless he could hold it up to the light and shake it and be sure of what it contained. The reddish hair, the gingery eyebrows, the light moustache— there was in all of this, for Rayner, the pleasure of confidence. Alexander undid the buttons of his coat and smiled at Rayner; and for the first time Rayner detected an uncertainty in the other man, a vague unease.

"The message I got is that somebody has your number, John," Alexander said. He fiddled with the menu but nothing he saw there appeared to appeal to his appetite. "Who is it, John? Who has your number?"

Rayner lifted his half-empty coffee cup. "You heard about Ernest Dubbs?"

"John, look, I hardly know your London pals. I saw a bit that came over the wire, that's all. The guy got it at some sports thing. And you were there. The rest—I don't know the rest."

"Look at this." Rayner handed the paper, sports page folded over, to Alexander.

The other man barely glanced at it. "I see a few race results, something about a baseball trade—"

"The Soviet thing," Rayner said. He could hear the irritation in his own voice.

"The Russian soccer team. Yeah. I got it." Alexander placed his hands flat on the table and stared at his knuckles. Faintly reddish hairs, barely visible, grew along the backs of his fingers. "Okay. Okay. Now start explaining."

Rayner said nothing. There was something wrong here, an edge he couldn't exactly fathom; it was almost as if this were not Chip Alexander but an impostor, a lookalike—and he had the unsettling feeling that if he were to reach for the other man's face and pull at the skin some dreadful mask would come away between his fingers.

Alexander said, "Look. I get a message. You've got some trouble. A guy with a gun? So I drive down here, breaking various federal laws concerning behavior on the freeway, and you start in with the puzzles. You mention Ernest Dubbs. Then you show me a picture of some Russian jocks. I mean, John—for Christ's sake."

A babble, Rayner thought. A madness. He looked into the other man's eyes, seeing there an expression of helplessness. "Did you run a security check on the Russians?"

Alexander smiled grimly. "No, we let them in the country without visas or passports, John. What the fuck do you think?"

Exasperated, Rayner leaned across the table, one hand going out to touch the lapel of Alexander's coat. "Did the check turn anything up?"

"I didn't do it personally. There's one KGB goon, so far as I know, but that's par for the course. They don't let their jocks come and go, you know? The guy's down as an assistant at the Ministry of Sports, which is the usual ploy. He's only a security buff. Ob- somebody or other. I don't know. If there'd been anything unusual, John, it would have come across my desk."

Silence. Rayner tapped his fingertips on the surface of the table. It wasn't making sense. It wasn't adding. And this oblique quality to Alexander, this edge that was almost abrasive—how was he supposed to explain that?

"You know why Dubbs was killed?" he asked.

Alexander impatiently shut his eyes. "Yeah. What I hear is some Czech malcontent took a potshot at him. A loony. It was on the wire. I didn't pay much attention—"

Rayner shook his head. "Then you didn't hear about Andreyev? Victor Andreyev?"

Alexander shrugged. "Means nothing."

Rayner pushed his chair back. It occurred to him suddenly that he couldn't trust Alexander, that the safety he thought he could turn to was nonexistent, a detour leading to some false place on a highway, nothing—

"John, I don't know what you're getting at. I knocked my ass off getting down here to *help* you—and, Jesus Christ, you come up with some doubletalk."

Rayner paused. He could get up. He could walk away. He could go back upstairs to Isobel, to the room, sit on the balcony, watch battleships—but he understood that beneath his feet the wind was blowing sand in all the wrong kinds of patterns.

"Andreyev was with the soccer party in London," he said. "He tried to defect through Dubbs. It's the old Stefanoff card. He was shot. Because Dubbs knew the real identity of Andreyev—that was the end of the line for him. Because I also know—"

Alexander interrupted. "Stefanoff card? This is

double Dutch, baby. Okay. So who was Andreyev supposed to be?"

"An eminent parapsychologist."

Alexander took a moment over this before he smiled. It was a cheerless smile. He scratched his head, gazed at the menu, folded it, and put it back in its little metal slot. "John, we've been friends for a time. Right? I mean, we go back a few years together. And that's a problem. That's a real damn problem."

"You don't believe me, Chip? Is that it?"

"John, look. I believe you. Okay? I believe you think you're telling the truth, okay? That's what I believe."

Rayner stood up. He turned as if to leave, but Alexander had grabbed his wrist across the table.

"I heard about your brother, John. A bad business. A really tough break, *really.*"

Rayner could feel the grip tighten. He sat down again, watching the other man's smile as one might keep a cautious eye on a cocked weapon. He saw it coming, he saw it coming from a long way back, he could hear its reverberations already, even before Alexander went on talking.

"Then this business of being with Dubbs when he bought it." Alexander shrugged. "That's a lot of real hard tension, John. Anybody could break, you know?"

"Is that what you think?"

Alexander in short, quick gestures was patting the back of Rayner's hand. It must have been more of a signal than a kindness because Rayner saw a second man come through the doorway and stand there watching the table, hands in the pockets of his coat, his face sullen and dark.

"A friend of yours?" Rayner asked.

"You might say. I'm training him."

"What happens now?"

Alexander rubbed his moustache lightly. "Yesterday I got this message from London. You want to hear about it?"

Rayner didn't speak; he understood.

"Well, Gull—our old friend Gull—said you'd had what is commonly known as a nervous breakdown."

Gull, Rayner thought. It was growing louder now, like a terrible ringing in his ears, like some far thunder in his head.

"A nervous breakdown," Alexander said. "Now in my book that could mean a whole lot of things. I guess, on the lower end of the scale, you need a couple of weeks' rest. Right?"

A dream, Rayner thought. It was the noise you heard in a dream.

"Higher up, of course, it could be worse. It could, for example, indicate some pretty heavy-duty medication. Right? You following me, John? It could mean—well, a guy's head might be more than just a little fucked up."

Rayner looked toward the doorway. The other man, like someone posing for a statue, hadn't moved. So good old George had put out the bad word on him: the blacklist effect. *Fucking Gull.*

"I understand Himself's private doc put you on some real dope, John," Alexander said. "That's what the old wire said yesterday. Bad case of the breakdowns. And something worse."

Worse? Rayner wondered. What could be worse than this plethora of lies? this bullshit? What could be worse?

"According to Gull, you took classified material from the Embassy. Some computer print-out concerning a Russian dude."

"You believe that? You really believe that?"

Alexander shrugged. "It's a serious charge—"

"Gull's a liar—"

"Who knows? But the brief I got on you, John, was to apprehend for hospitalization. Sorry, I mean. But that's the chit that came down after the message from London. Look, it won't be too bad. At least you'll be safe from this character running around this nice old seaside town with your number written on his heart, right?"

Apprehend. Hospitalization. The theft of classified material. The Ambassador's private doctor. Alexander must think it—he must really believe it. *Rayner's gone off the fucking deep end. Nice guy, couldn't ask for a nicer one, but the death of the brother, well, took it damn hard, then the killing of the old pal Ernie Dubbs, it was insult to injury, poor fucker.* But George Gull—why had Gull lied? What was George concealing?

"You think you're taking me, Chip?"

"Got to, friend. No options in the matter."

"You think—you think I've flipped?"

"Flipped?" Alexander shrugged. "I think you need a good long rest. And the facilities are just downright terrific, John. Terrific."

Rayner stood up, pushing his chair back from the table. Pointless, he thought. Pointless to plead, beg for some time, ask for a break, explain. Explanations would only take you back to one dead Russian parapsychologist. Mumbo-jumbo Boulevard. *Oh, sure, John. The guy had a trick deck.*

"You'll have to stop me, Chip."

"Ah, the macho route," Alexander said. "My young associate over there is armed."

"You'll still have to stop me, Chip." Rayner stepped away from the table. The young man moved slightly in the doorway. "You're going to have to give

that friend of yours the order to shoot. Are you prepared to do that?"

"Yessir," Alexander said. "I make one piddling
little signal and you're broken, John. No halfway
measures. None at all."

Rayner paused. He could feel the fluorescent
lights overhead: electronic pulses trapped in tubes. He
could hear a plate smash in a distant kitchen and the
sound of a man's voice bitching, "Comes outta your
wages." He could feel Chip Alexander's sense of purpose, a tangible thing. Apprehend. Hospitalize. The
madhouse. Some nice little compound in West Virginia, where all the freaked-out, burned-up espionage
fellows went when their nerves were shot or they
were security risks or they were too juiced or too
doped to be any good—the ruins, the sad and miserable wreckage of this business of thinking you can secure a world and make it safe with ribbons of blood-
red tape. He stared at the young man in the doorway.
Hands bunched in the coat pockets. Gull, you fucker.
What were you playing at all along? Were you dicker-
ing with the other side, getting your palm nicely
greased? Was that it? Did that explain your outrage
over the Andreyev print-out? Dear Christ, was that
why you had me followed—because you wondered
what Dubbs was up to? George, George, George,
how long? How long? How goddam long?

"Be good to yourself, Rayner," Alexander said.
"Be a good kid and come along with me in a nice
peaceful manner, huh? It stinks if we have to shoot
a joint up."

"Give your signal, Chip. Go on. Give your dip-
shit over there the signal. What is it? Do you drop the
menu? Wave your handkerchief?"

"No. I lift my left hand. I put it against the back
of my neck."

"Let me see you do it, Chip." Madness, Rayner thought. Well, maybe. Maybe. Maybe there wasn't a line you could inscribe in the world and say, *All you sane ones this side, all the crazies over there.* He stared at Alexander's left hand. It was motionless, upturned, on the table.

"You don't really want to see it, John," Alexander said.

"Don't you fucking understand, Chip? Gull's with the other side. Don't you understand that?"

Alexander laughed. "Now tell me that Ambassador Quarterman is also a Soviet agent."

Rayner sighed. "I'm walking out of here. Over there. You see that elevator? That's where I'm going."

"Be my guest, John."

Again, Rayner hesitated. "One chance, Chip. Give me one goddam chance."

"It's not like I'm on my own, John. If it was just me—maybe I'd think it over. But my young friend over there, well, he's *keen*. Remember what it was like to be *that* keen?" Alexander shifted his left hand slightly, crumpling a paper tissue, dropping it in the ashtray. He looked at Rayner, and almost as if a moment of regret touched him, he said, "The car's just outside. Let's get it over with. Okay?"

"Chip, call him off. For a moment. That's all I need. You can do that."

"Then what? We'd still have to come after you. I told you, kid, he's goddam eager." Alexander gazed at the crumpled tissue. "Then you got to consider how bad I'd look if I let you slip. Right?"

Rayner looked at the face of the young man.

A killer. The sullen, unadorned face. It wouldn't even flinch. It existed only for Chip Alexander's ridiculous signal. Rayner thought of Isobel: how she would laugh at that—signs, signals, little gestures that meant death: the freemasonry of assassination. Walk, Rayner thought. Just turn and walk to the elevator. *Do it!*

From the corner of his eye he saw the elevator door slide open. He thought: Christ, no. Not now. Why now? But she was coming across the floor toward him with that graceful walk of hers, that high strut, as if even the most casual of clothes deserved to be worn with grace. She approached, sliding her arm through his, smiling, smiling at Alexander—and yet the smile was tense, suggesting she had intuited the dark edge of the situation.

"I got lonesome," she said.

"I didn't think I'd be gone this long," he said.

"Anyway, I'm hungry. How about some lunch? Can you afford me?"

Alexander, even as he returned her smile, looked momentarily distressed, confused. The hand that held the Kleenex was tight now, the knuckles hard and up-raised. Rayner wondered: Do we both die? Isobel and me? He realized she was pulling on his arm gently, drawing him away from the table, away from Alexander. She was drawing him toward the doorway, to-ward the young man, whose own expression had become one of mild bewilderment as if his internal clockwork, already preset, had come unsprung.

"Good to see you again, Chip," Rayner said.

"Likewise, I'm sure," Alexander said, turning in his seat to look toward the doorway. Is there a signal, Rayner wondered, for two killings? Does he have to rub his neck twice? Does he have to do something as fucking stupid as that? Isobel was pulling him into the doorway, where the young man sidestepped and stared toward Alexander for guidance, for fine-tuning of his blown controls.

They stepped into the lobby. The young man

moved just behind them. Any moment now, Rayner thought, straight through the back. But Chip Alexander obviously hadn't made his gesture because now they were going through the front door to the street— the overcast midday sun, passing traffic, the blown and beautiful perfume of the sea that seemed to Rayner just then a magnificent creation.

They ran toward where the station wagon had been parked; then Rayner—remembering the man with the pistol, remembering how like a flag the sight of the car would be—drew Isobel inside a shop doorway; he held her against him, hearing a small bell ring above his head as he shoved the door open with his foot.

"Trouble?" she asked.

"There's got to be a stronger word than that," he said.

He looked around the store. Of all places it was a wild candy emporium, a paradise of rainbow stripes and polka dots, saltwater taffies, monstrous lollipops that lay in huge glass jars like primitive art forms, reds and greens and splashes of brilliant yellow. Rayner stared toward the back of the store, where, through an open doorway, a man in a white uniform was mixing a sugary paste in a large metal vat. "Let's get the hell out of here."

He pulled her into the back room.

The man said, "Hey—"

"My apologies," Rayner said.

"There's a sign says employees—"

"I know about signs," Rayner said. Beyond vats, jars, rows of chocolate bears and jelly beans and licorice delights, he saw a glass-paneled door. "Where does that go?" he asked.

"The seafront, but—"

He hurried toward the door, hauling Isobel after

him. The beach, the backs of the large hotels, an expanse of shell-littered sand dotted here and there by windblown umbrellas and shades.

"Okay," he said. "To put this whole deal mildly, we're in a bind—"

"We?"

"I don't think it's time to start arguing—"

"Let me guess, Rayner. You need a safe place?"

"You and me both," he answered.

She looked a moment out toward the ocean. Seabirds, tossed on currents of air, hovered above the gray water. She seemed to think a moment, then said, "Okay. Okay."

## 4.

There was a great darkness behind her eyes. Her body shuddered; her flesh was damp, a sheet of cold sweat. She could barely hear the man's voice, which reached her as if he were calling to her from across a valley through which a river rattled and roared—but the roaring, she realized somehow, was in her own ears.

*It was stupid to get out of bed. Don't you realize that? How can you expect me to trust you if you don't obey me?*

She tried to say something: *Yes.*

But her mouth was parched and she couldn't even ask for water. Cold: *she was so cold.*

*I had even prepared a special treat for you,* he said.

She forced her eyes open. Sometimes it seemed to her that she wasn't hearing things properly. Words became scrambled, disjointed, obscenely meaningless.

*A special treat.*

She opened her mouth. There was no moisture on her tongue, on the roof of her mouth, in her gums.

Water. If they could give me water. But I'm being punished. For what I did to the woman. For the silly trick with the window. I'm being punished for all this now. A violent muscular spasm went through her and then there was more cold sweat pouring from her body and she wanted so badly to find the strength to say simply, Water. Please.

*You can't have the treat now, of course.*

In this old age there's nothing, nothing, one by one they leave you, old friends, old loves, one by one they die out like yesterday's fires—what keeps you going on, what makes you want to

*I had arranged for a telephone link between here and Tel Aviv. You could have spoken to your family. Not now. You've made me very angry.*

In this old age they speak as if you were a child again. Scold. Punish. Reward. Her sweat was so cold it seemed to freeze her to the bedsheet. There was a vicious muscular contraction in her body and her legs began to shake. She opened her eyes a little, hardly more than a slit, aware of some vague and distant light. A telephone link. It didn't make sense. A telephone link to Tel Aviv. These were words. Words.

*Now I have had it canceled.*

Please, she wanted to say. Please, no.

*Furthermore, you won't receive any medication until morning.*

Stop shaking, she thought. I can't. I can't stop it now. A telephone. I would have heard their voices. Instead. There is to be nothing. Punishment. It went on. It would never stop.

*You could have talked with your grandchildren.*

Yes, the grandchildren, that would have been something, a wonderful thing to happen, the sound of their young voices coming across all the distances of our lives but not now, not now—

*Cooperation,* he said. *You'll have your photographs returned when you've decided to behave—*

The pictures too? When could they stop taking things from her? She understood, without really feeling it, that there were tears coming from between her half-shut eyes. The pictures. The photographs too. Stripped. Humiliated. They couldn't take anything else away from her. There was a severe wracking pain crossing her chest—

My medicine, she tried to say, but her mouth opened and closed dryly. Now the man was moving around in the room. She could feel his movements. She could hear the door shut as he went out. The light was turned off.

But that didn't matter. No, that didn't matter now.

For within one darkness you will only find another: the shadows that grow deeper in the hearts of flowers. Flowers? When had she last smelled flowers? She could create them, she could make the scents for herself if only the pains would stop but the pains wouldn't stop because hadn't he said there would be no more medication until morning? And wasn't morning a long time away? Wasn't everything such a long time away?

Help me.

Help me.

**5.**

When Koprow went to his own room, after leaving the old woman, he dialed Leontov's number in Washington. The conversation was conducted in an innocuous code. Leontov mentioned that a certain invitation had, happily, been accepted. He also informed Koprow, less happily, that the trout fishing wasn't all it was supposed to be, both upstream and down. Koprow understood this to mean that the errant American, John Rayner, had evaded the attentions of an associate of Leontov's as well as the promised "arrangements" of his own ally in Grosvenor Square.

After a short silence Koprow said, "I suggest you pull your own angler out of the situation."

Leontov sounded relieved. "I accept the suggestion."

Koprow stared out of the window at the impenetrable Pennsylvania darkness—unrelenting, merciless. "There's a certain neatness in letting the Americans fish in their own waters, don't you think?"

"Definitely," said the Ambassador.

When he had hung up Koprow pondered the young American for a time, enjoying the idea that he would be caught by his own side. It should never have happened in the first place, of course, the test on Richard Rayner—it could have been conducted on almost anyone. But that had been Maksymovich's choice. Maybe the Secretary still liked the notion of a good-looking woman, especially a widow, for it at least afforded him the chance to offer his condolences—a brief embrace, a kiss placed on the back of the cold hand. In such trifling ways, Koprow thought, do we exercise our sexual inclinations as we reach beyond the possibilities of more active outlets. Old age, he thought.

John Rayner. John Rayner could do nothing. He was hardly worth considering now. He was something to be relegated to a quiet corner of the brain, something to forget.

He stared morosely at an unopened pack of peppermint Life Savers and wondered if the old woman had picked up on the lie about a telephone call to Israel. It didn't much matter now anyhow. She was under control, firmly so, and that was a good feeling. A very good feeling.

# 3

## 1

It took them hours to reach the place where Isobel thought they would be safe. A safe house—a phrase Rayner had always found faintly absurd, as if its opposite, an unsafe house, were a bad joke concerning gas leaks in basements, rotting timbers in attics, a bomb ticking away in a concealed closet. It took them hours of turning this way and that, going from beach to alleys among hotels, wandering hotel lobbies, dimly lit cocktail bars. If you had drawn a graph of their movements, Rayner thought, it would have looked like a crazed series of loops forged in string by an insane Boy Scout. The house, set back from the road behind a glade of trees, had a rear lawn that ran down to a narrow inlet of water where willows skimmed the quiet, glassy surface. It was a dark and cool place of long corridors and stained-glass windows; once it must have belonged to a family of some wealth but now it was run-down and flaking, occupied by a man Isobel introduced simply as Fox and his teen-age daughter, Fiona. A space duo, Rayner thought. Fox with his thick-lensed spectacles, eyes unblinking and distant; the girl, shy and indifferent, with that sullen quality that you sometimes find in adolescents. But there were no questions asked.

Isobel led him upstairs to a small room with a single bed and a dresser with a rusted mirror. He lay down, exhausted, trying not to think of Chip Alexander and his young friend, trying to forget the man with the stainless-steel pistol. Trying, instead, to make sense of things. It was like listening to a series of echoes in reverse order; a guessing game in which you were to find the original word. A crossword puzzle in which you hoped simple repetition of an elusive clue would somehow unconsciously release the answer you wanted. The flash of insight, he thought. The penny that must one day drop. The soccer team. The soccer team. And why had Andreyev come to London in the first place?

Isobel was standing at the window. A thin muslin drapery was drawn halfway across the glass. From outside, a distant streetlight illuminated her face. He sat up, tired, barely managing to keep his eyes open. Holding the drapery in her hand, bunching it, she turned to look at him and asked, "Why did they want to harm you?"

Harm, he thought. A curious word, its sound somehow soft and whispered and *harmless.* "I think what they wanted was to put me on ice, in a manner of speaking."

"You have to hand it to me, Rayner," she said. "I must have a knack of being in all the wrong places at the right times."

He massaged his face softly for a time. He swung his legs off the bed; he could imagine lying in a Jacuzzi. "Lucky for me," he said, wondering if luck was any part of it, if perhaps Chip Alexander had mo-

mentarily relented, given him the time he had begged
for. Time, he thought. *Tempus fuckit.* Time for what?
Time—to do what with? He watched Isobél for a moment. Suddenly, throughout the house, there was the
sound of a harp being played to the accompaniment
of a flute. It was an odd rippling sequence of sounds—
and visual rather than auditory, as if he were watching
a school of silver-skinned fish just beneath the surface
of black water.

"Fox and his daughter," she said. "They're heavily into their music. I think it sounds good."

"Where did you find them?" he asked.

"Are you worried about trusting them?"

He stared through the darkness at the outline of
the closed door. Trust? Who could he trust now anyhow except for her?

"Don't worry about them," she said. Even
though he could not clearly see her face, he had the
feeling that she was smiling. "They don't know about
your world, John. And even if they did, they wouldn't
understand it. All they want is to play their music."

The sweet life, Rayner thought. A little inno-
cence. You cut yourself adrift on a raft of ignorance
and you just floated, mindlessly, away. "How did you
meet them?"

"We have some common interests," she answered. "I met them at this group I sometimes go to.
You'd find it funny, I'm sure."

"Funny? Like how?"

"A bunch of psychic freaks. Remember I told you
I had seen the ESP cards done consistently? The girl
you met. Fiona. She's the one I saw do it."

Rayner closed his eyes. The music stopped. Then,
when it started again, it was different, rather dark and
frenetic and atonal. An unhappy music, bleak and dismal, rising upward through the house like a scythe

awkwardly angled. It was beginning to irk him. He sat with the palms of his hands pressed to the sides of his head, the classical disposition of the thinker, except he was thinking of nothing. His head was a stalled engine. What have I got? he wondered. Exactly what have I got stuffed into my own burnt-out computer?

A man defects. Okay. He usually has something to sell. What did Andreyev know that was so goddam important he had to be stopped? Why did Ernest . . . Isobel came and sat on the mattress beside him and was silent for a time, as if she was listening to the music.

"What makes you so dangerous?" she asked. "What do you know, John Rayner, that makes you such a menace?"

*What do I know?*

He reached out and held her hands and heard the mattress creak as she shifted her weight around. Her skin was chill. Desire, he thought—was there ever a more incongruous moment for it? And then he was thinking of his brother again: the unavoidable presence of the ghost. Blood relations. Even the grave didn't put them out of your mind.

"What do you know?" she asked again.

He shrugged. She had moved her hands away. Too soon—wasn't that what she had said? Too bloody soon. He gazed at the darkened outline of her face for a time.

"There's something I want to ask you," he said.

He heard her sigh. "That last night with Richard?"

"That last night."

"Don't you think I've asked myself a hundred times about that damn night? Don't you think I've gone through all kinds of shit trying to understand it?" She rose, wandered to the window, looked out into the dark. "He said he had a headache. Then he lost it. Whatever makes you work as a human being just . . . snapped in him. He lost it totally. He looked at me. The way he looked—it was like he had never seen me before. What's the word? *Emptiness* would be close. But it wouldn't be good enough. It wouldn't be strong enough. He didn't know me."

"Then what?"

"You want blood, John," she said. He could hear a slight friction as she rubbed the palms of her hands together. "I'll give you blood. He wasn't Richard any longer. That's how it was. It wasn't Richard. It wasn't my husband, your brother. He wasn't anybody we knew. And then he . . . The rest you can read about in the official report, right?"

Rayner went toward her. Lightly he touched the nape of her neck. Comfort, he thought. Comfort, ease.

"It's okay. It's okay," he said.

But it wasn't. It wasn't okay. It didn't make any more sense to him than it had before. He was aware now that the music had stopped, that somebody was coming up the stairs. He turned quickly to look at the door and he thought: A gun. I don't even have a gun. There was a knock on the door. It opened and the girl, Fiona, stood there, her hands thrust into the pockets of her blue jeans. She didn't speak for a moment. Rayner had the feeling that she was staring at him in the way one might scrutinize a textbook problem in algebra. He was uneasy. *She can do the cards,* he thought. Why would that unsettle him? Was it that world of darkness and poltergeists that broke bone china and trumpets that floated in midair—the remnant of some childhood fear, the shapes that became manifest on drawn curtains and the sound of the wind and the flickering night-light plugged into the wall? It was Richard, he thought. Richard had loved ghost stories. Richard had loved to scare him with indescribable monsters that lay, hungry and fanged and waiting, in the shrubbery beneath the bedroom window. I'd forgotten all that, he thought. Time slips.

The girl suddenly asked, "You guys want to eat?"

Food, Rayner thought. The flood of the ordinary, the return to earth.

"It's ready," the child said. "If you'd like some."

## 2.

A vegetarian stew, but Rayner was hungry anyway and ate two portions. When he was through he thought how it would be the simplest thing in the world to imagine only a pristine domesticity—sitting in this kitchen with its curtains drawn against the darkness outside. But it was the darkness that kept coming back at him, the idea of people moving out there, the hunters, the haunters, those who needed his silence.

He put his fork down on his empty plate. Fox, who wore an old-fashioned pinstriped vest over a collarless shirt, was watching him. The large unblinking eyes, magnified by the glasses, embarrassed him in some way. It was as if he felt the need to converse with Fox but understood that there wasn't a point where their levels of language would coincide. And the child—she was worse somehow, staring down at her plate secretively, pushing back and forth a piece of zucchini she hadn't eaten. Maybe, Rayner thought, she has come to some understanding with that particular piece of vegetable matter, a truce of sorts. I should be thankful for sanctuary, but where did Isobel dig these people up? He watched her a moment, wondering at how relaxed she appeared to be: a certain tranquillity of expression. Perhaps it had gotten through to her finally—a retreat from the physical world to the psychic, a change of her elements. Run down one battery, he thought, replace it with an altogether different kind. Why the hell not? *He wasn't Richard any longer.* If the physical world was so shifting, so treacherous, so damnably unstable, where would you go for consistency?

"I liked the food," he said. "Thanks."

Fox stared at him, saying nothing. The girl looked up from her plate a moment. Dear Christ, he thought. They have this way of doing you over, kicking at the foundations of your politeness. Be grateful, Rayner. Thank whatever lies in your stars.

"Isobel says you can do the ESP cards," he said to the girl.

"Yeah. Sometimes." She picked up the zucchini and let it flop around in her fingers. "Like when I'm in the mood."

"Don't be so modest," Isobel said. She smiled at the girl, then looked at Rayner. "They tested her at Duke. She blew their minds away."

Rayner looked suitably impressed. The girl gazed at him and he had the distinct feeling she was, in a fashion, deriding him for his own obvious lack of extrasensory perception. Fox got up from the table and brought a bottle of elderberry wine from a cabinet. It's the whole trip around here, Rayner thought. The weird music, the vegetarian bit, the homemade wines, the voices from the ether. He sipped some of the wine, but it was bitter and vinegary.

Fox said, "You don't believe, do you?"

"Believe in what?"

"In other modes of perception?"

"I try to keep an open mind," Rayner said.

"Ah. The skeptic. I was like you once. But you can't fight it." Fox smiled, an odd rubbery expression, as if he had no full control of his lips. "Take the narrow view of reality, and what have you got? Is that a glass of wine in your hands?"

Perplexed, more than a little irritated, Rayner wondered about perpetual trees falling in forests and whether anybody could hear them fall. Sally's unanswerable questions.

Fox said, "It isn't a glass of wine. If you had another view, if you weren't such a *limited* man, Mr. Rayner, you would understand that you hold only the illusion of wine there. From the viewpoint of eternity, you're holding something that is already decaying and disintegrating—only you don't see it. Fixed, you think. Substantial. But no."

Isobel, dear Isobel, Rayner thought, how did these people grab you? How did they take hold of you? He watched her now as she nodded her head up and down seriously. The man's gobbledygook enthralled her, you could see.

"My daughter's gifts," Fox said, staring at Rayner as if he meant to blind him with his large eyes, "my daughter's gifts have taught me to open up my head."

Let it all hang out, Rayner thought.

The child groaned, as if this praise of her father's annoyed her. What is she but some typical teen-ager? he wondered. A child tired of whatever prodigal talents had been ascribed to her? She got up from the table, scraping her chair, and went to the kitchen window, where she pulled back the curtain and looked out. From somewhere, perhaps from a pocket of his vest, Fox had produced a pack of ESP cards and was shuffling them quickly. He slid them down the table to Rayner, who stared at them, wondering what was expected of him.

"Go ahead," Fox said. "Cut them. Shuffle them. Then take one off the top without letting Fiona see."

By the window, the child moaned. "I don't think I'm up to this," she said.

"Do it," Fox said. "Just do it."

Rayner cut the deck. He raised the top card: a star.

"Star," the child said.

He raised the second card and looked at it. A square.

The girl was quiet a moment. "Square. Square, I think. Yeah."

Fox, as if something had been confirmed to his great satisfaction, watched Rayner with the expression of a true believer turning a new disciple. The next card was a plus sign, a cross.

The girl said nothing.

"Well, Fiona?" Fox asked. "Well?"

The girl, her back to the room, didn't move.

Something all at once was different here, something—at a level Rayner couldn't absolutely comprehend—had changed. A mood, a certain ambience; he wasn't sure. He could feel the change as surely as a draft coming through an open door. He felt a pulse of a strange alarm within himself: it was as if, having sat down jokingly to tinker with a ouija board, he had received a message of utter malice. The girl turned around and stared at him.

"What is it, child?" Fox asked.

The girl was still staring at Rayner. He couldn't keep her eyes in focus, couldn't look at her, didn't want to see her expression; his hands trembled slightly on the deck. Come on, he thought. Control yourself. She just can't get it, that's all. She just can't see this one, that's all it is. A flaw, a failure, a breakdown. The girl had moved toward the table. Her mouth opened, as if she was about to speak, but she said nothing. Fox was standing up now, touching his daughter on the shoulder.

A difference, a change: something unraveling, coming undone. Rayner didn't want to hold the deck any longer. It felt hot in his hands. He wanted to drop it. A game, he thought. A game of cards.

"Can't you see it?" Fox asked.

The child shook her head.

"The next card," Fox said. "Pass to the next card."

"No," the girl said. "No. Don't pass. Don't."

"Pass," Fox said, glaring at Rayner.

"No!" The girl was panicked suddenly. She came closer to Rayner. "I know what it is. I know what it is. Don't pass to the next one. I know."

"Tell us," Fox said.

"It's a frame of wood," the girl said. "It's a frame of broken wood."

## 3.

Koprow, dozing in the armchair by the dying fire in his room, was awakened by the woman touching him lightly on the shoulder, shaking him. For a moment he was uncertain of his surroundings. Katya was looking urgently at him.

He stirred in the chair, half rising. "Is something wrong?" he asked, wondering if perhaps she had caught him talking in his sleep, an embarrassing prospect altogether. He stared up blearily into her thin face.

"It's the old woman," Katya said. "I think you should change your mind about the medication."

"Why? Whatever for?"

The woman hesitated a moment. "Come and see for yourself."

Koprow, irritated, rose. He shuffled after the woman and out into the corridor. His limbs were numb from the position of his sleep; needles and pins, slight aches. He saw the woman hurry ahead of him to the stairs. Climbing, trying not to pant, he reached the upper landing, where Katya was already at the door of the old Jewess's room, opening it so that a rectangle of light fell through the dark. He went in after her.

"I think she needs medication now," Katya said.

"Do you? Do you indeed?" Koprow went closer to the bed.

She might, save for the way her head rolled from side to side, her mouth opening and closing silently, she might have been dead: the skin was white, beneath the eyes there were fleshy circles of dark purple—and sweat, everywhere the glossy covering of perspiration. Momentarily Koprow felt an unusual sense of panic: if she were to die, if they were to lose her now . . . He leaned closer to the old woman, seeing how the eyelids flickered, sometimes barely opening to reveal expanses of white flecked with blood—and he realized that she was not silent at all, but that in a voice that was a whisper she was uttering some kind of gibberish.

"What's she saying? What's she talking about?"

Katya shrugged. "I don't know."

"Is it some kind of Hebrew nonsense?" Koprow asked. "A prayer for the dead, or the dying?"

"I think she's in terrible pain," Katya said. "And withdrawal—the shock."

"Yes, yes," Koprow said impatiently. He stood

upright, feeling coming back to his legs. "Very well. Give her her damned dose. Do it now."

The woman broke the plastic seal of a new syringe and filled it from a small bottle, then shoved the needle into the old woman's arm. Koprow winced at the sight of the puncture. Did it have to be done so roughly? with such a lack of care and concern? with such an obvious look of triumph? The old woman continued to turn her head this way then that on the pillow. Watching, Koprow caught the unmistakable scent of excrement. He stepped away from the bed.

"And for God's sake, change her sheets," he said.

"I'm not a nurse—"

"Change the sheets," he said again. He hated it— that trifling defiance, the hard little light in the eye.

The woman pulled the surface blanket away. Beneath, the white sheet was stained with blood and excrement. She stared at him as though to say, *You'd have me do this?* He turned—he could look no longer—then went toward the door. When he had reached the corridor he felt he was gasping for air, choking, as if he had stepped into a vacuum.

### 4.

A sense of touching, of feeling: reaching across darkness to the single point of light. Like being inside a camera. If you concentrated on the light the pain would go away and everything would be well but the light was so small, such a tiny hole in space, just an absence of all the dark. Then the pain came back, waves, hot waves, a tide of lava running in every vein, in every muscle, every fiber; then you tried for the small hole again. Dear God. It was only a whisper any-

how and you couldn't really catch it because it was so
weak so thin so faraway, this touching, this reaching
*How can I help*
You don't know. You can't help whoever you are be-
cause you don't know and you don't have the reach
*Reach help me reach*
Impossible
*Help me          what do you want*
Pain all the fires all the hideous infusions of blind-hot
wires running through me          no you couldn't
help me because you don't have the reach
*The reach?*
It goes on through the mind          a picture repeats
and repeats          you are too young to know
          if the sweetness of youth dies and it dies at
the end of a rope in a barn stinking of old hay and
rotted manure          only if the sweetness goes will
you know and understand          but you must close
your mind to me
*No*
You must
*Where are you? Who are you?*
There are no measurements for these distances
          inches and yards and meters they don't matter
          you're too young and you must kill this thing
you must kill it inside you the way you would kill any
disease do you understand me do you understand me
the way you would any disease
*You asked for help*
no          there's no help          trapped
*Trapped where? Trapped how?*
no          questions          answers wouldn't help
you
*Danger?*
danger death          please leave leave now
          you don't want to be in this room with this

pain      and know who I am
*Don't make me leave*
the reach fades
*You're old, I can feel it*
you don't feel anything      you dream this
      you dream the wrong dreams for yourself
*Who are*
none of this happens don't you see
*A friend I could*
you can't be anything      if you listen it's going
already      I know      listen closely and I
know you can hear the sea
*Please don't make me leave you*
we don't have those choices you and I      none
of this is what we choose      before it's too late
you must kill it in yourself
*Kill what?*
No more      she comes with the needle
      with the needle      the dreams are better
when the pain is gone      and when you tell them
      what you can do      what you are capable
of doing      they'll make you kill and kill and go
on killing
*Killing who?*
names      names are nothing
*Please?*
no more      nothing more      nothing more
now

**5.**

Fox carried his daughter, saying she needed air,
through the kitchen door and out to the lawn, carried
her—out of breath, straining—to the willows that

hung above the inlet of water. He laid her on the grass, gently stroking her hair with one hand, massaging her fingers with the other. In the light that reached through the open kitchen doorway Rayner watched: cold, a chill rising from the slow water that pierced his clothing, but colder still in ways he couldn't quite describe, in places he couldn't exactly name. He heard Isobel beside him. She stood with her arms folded, staring down the slope of grass to where the girl lay.

*Fiona. Fiona. Everything is fine. Fine.*

The father's voice, filled with an almost hopeless concern, carried up from the water's edge. Rayner could hear the motion of willow leaves. They were like soft hands dangling in the quiet stream. What happened? he wondered. How would you describe what had happened? In the space of minutes, moments— how could you say? Isobel, shivering, moved nearer to him; he put his arm loosely round her shoulder.

*Fiona. Fiona.*

A trance, Rayner thought. But that didn't do it. You would have to make that one work harder to carry the load. No, not a trance. Then what? I saw a child, he thought. A teenage girl. I saw her suddenly pause in the middle of her guessing game—*no, goddam, it wasn't a game*—I watched her fall to the floor and lie there motionless. And then what? Then what did I see? What did I hear?

Upward, through the branches of the willows, the night was starry and somehow complete. He saw the moon, faceless, a flat anonymous disk, drift. What did I hear? He shut his eyes. *Fiona. It's all right. Everything is all right.* Isobel was shivering still, huddled against him. A trance, he thought again. She was talking to somebody who wasn't in the room, talking in words he couldn't understand, in meters he hadn't heard before—a language that wasn't a language at all, but something else, something more basic, more primitive: as if you were hearing, he thought—amazed by his own sense of the ridiculous—the first forms of communication that had ever been uttered anywhere. A thing comes out of a swamp, rises out of the vapors, and speaks. But it was a language nevertheless because the *form* was there, the intonations of questions uttered in faint, breathless whispers. Questions. *Where the hell were the answers coming from?*

And then. Then what?

*Open your eyes, child. Come on.*

He had heard only the questions, watched the fluttering motion of the eyelids, the grotesque stiffening of the child's body as she had lain on the floor, the palsied twisting of her hands and fingers and her limbs. She had been in pain, he had no doubt of that. Real? Imagined? Some distinction there; did it matter anymore?

The real. The fanciful. What did I really see?

He watched the shadowy outline of Fox, lifting his child up; he watched Fox begin to move slowly across the lawn toward the house. Questions. No answers.

How did it work? Did it come out of the ether? Was it some magical form of telegraph? News from nowhere? How did it work? Or was it just another kind of deceit? A child playing? *How can you think that now?* She had stood up in her twisted way, suddenly a grotesque figure, suddenly as white and as awful as some broken Victorian doll; she had stood up and, clutching the edge of the table with her disfigured hands, had opened her eyes. The whites. Nothing but the whites. A travesty of sight, he thought. But how could you say even that? You don't know what it was she was looking at, do you? You don't know what she was seeing, do you?

Then she had lost control again, slipping, clattering downward, broken dishes and bits of cutlery and half of a table linen wrapped, like some haphazard shroud, around her body. Even now he could see the linen stretched out on the lawn by the water where Fox had left it.

Isobel said she was cold. But he didn't want to go back inside the house, not yet. Too soon, like everything else. He had the feeling that something intensely private was passing between father and daughter and he didn't want to intrude. He slipped off his jacket and draped it around Isobel. They stood together in silence and listened to the water touching the willows. He drew Isobel's face against his shoulder and looked down through the dark, hearing the sound of her quick breathing. I need to know, he thought. I need to know what I saw and heard. Sometimes you just can't ask because the time is all wrong. And sometimes the time doesn't matter. There was a skein of things here, concentric circles of coincidence that stretched back to the impossible death of his brother, to the mystery of Andreyev: too many deaths, too much dying.

The moon was sucked behind cloud. The night darkened. He turned and looked at the light in the kitchen window. The shadow of Fox passed in front of the glass. He took his arm from Isobel and went toward the house.

He stepped inside the kitchen. Then he stopped, thinking again of the way the child had spoken, the incomprehensible sounds of that language, and he realized that what it reminded him of now was the broken language of the dreamer, the outbreaks of meaninglessness you heard in the sleep of other people. Conversations that were not conversations, talk that wasn't talk, cries that could mean something only if you had the ability to step inside another person's dream.

Was that what she had done? Was that what he had listened to? He heard Isobel come inside the kitchen behind him. She reached out and touched his arm, as if to delay him, to stall him, as if this were a way of saying, *It's enough, leave it for later.* He looked at her apologetically. It couldn't wait now; not now.

He was suddenly tense, tense as he had been when the child had—language, where was the goddam language—when the kid had just *slipped away from things.* Slipped away from things, he thought. It could never be enough. Okay, he thought. A time comes, Rayner: either you do a thing or you don't. Either you go ahead or you hang back, and sometimes you hang back too long and the clock has moved on and all at once you're in another place. The Land of Lost Opportunities. The Plaza del Might Have Been. He stepped away from Isobel, thinking of the darkness outside, of how, without her, there was only the cold isolation of knowing that nobody much cared if you lived or died. A man with a gun, smiling faces in the mad room of some company hospital—it was the same card, the same deck.

He crossed the kitchen. The child was stretched out on an old velvet sofa. Fox stood over her, turning his face when Rayner came into the room. The huge eyes were like those of some staring night bird accustomed to the crazy predatory things that lie in the foliage.

"She's going to be all right," Fox said, answering a question that hadn't been asked. "I think she's sleeping naturally."

Rayner stood beside the sofa and looked at the girl. He had seen her face before in a million places—drive-ins, fast-food outlets, supermarkets, catching yellow school buses; it was an ordinary teen-age face and sullen in sleep. Then he gazed at the father. "You want to explain?"

Fox took off his glasses. The eyes, without magnification, were like tiny stones you might find on a beach. He rubbed his eyelids and sighed. "Isn't it obvious, Mr. Rayner? Isn't it obvious to you what happened? Can't you overcome your *limitations?*"

Fuck my limitations, Rayner thought. I am sick and tired of hearing about them. Especially from you, Jack. Especially out of your mouth. He tried to be patient; he tried to catch his patience like a swimmer coming up from a deep place and lurching for air. "Obvious to me? Uh-huh. You tell me, Mr. Fox. You explain it."

"It's happened before," Fox said. "Not often. But it's happened."

"What's happened?" Rayner asked.

Fox, like a priest who alone has had revealed the arcane name of the deity, smiled benignly. "She had an encounter."

"What does that mean?"

"I could explain for days and you still—"

"I don't have days, Fox."

Fox put his glasses back and said, "I tolerated you because you're a friend of Isobel's. I don't have to put up with your rudeness—"

Rayner thought: A velvet glove, something soft. "I don't mean to be rude but I don't understand, that's the problem." Slow and nice and a snow job: the brown-nose route.

"Understanding isn't always easy," Fox said. "It was hard for me too, Mr. Rayner."

Good, Rayner thought. Now we have established a common denominator. "What's an encounter? That's what I don't get exactly."

"She talked with somebody, that's all."

"Talked with somebody. Okay. But not somebody in this house."

Patiently Fox shook his head. "Somebody elsewhere, of course."

"How? How does that happen?"

Fox stared a moment at Rayner. Rayner thought: This isn't my world. Processing Eastern Europeans through intelligence computers and security data: *Is Herr Folweiler really a stonemason from Dresden?* You pressed a button. Decoded a telex or two. Checked birth certificates. Records were available; information could be turned up. This is some other place and I don't believe I like it.

"I could throw words out, Mr. Rayner. I could talk of telepathy. But that would only be a beginning—"

"Okay. Let me see if I've got it. The kid had a telepathic encounter? That's what you're saying?"

"An encounter of minds, yes—"

"Then what about the things she was saying?"

"I could talk about a kind of linguistic overflow, if you liked. I could tell you that even though she wasn't communicating in any way *you* could understand—she was using channels of mind—nevertheless she's a creature of the habit of speech—"

"Speech? That wasn't speech. I didn't hear—"

"You heard, Mr. Rayner. You just didn't understand."

Linguistic overflow. Crap, Rayner thought. You could smell it around Fox and it was yards thick and highly fermented. What could he extract from this nut? He had to get the girl. He had to wake the girl. He reached down and shook her quietly, repeating her name over and over.

"Leave her," Fox said. "She needs to rest after her experience."

Isobel had come around the sofa and was staring at Rayner in an alarmed way. She doubts my mind too, he thought.

"John, please. The kid's exhausted."

"I want to talk with her, that's all."

"No," Fox said. He tried to step between Rayner and the girl. Rayner, angry, impatient, shoved him aside.

"John, for Christ's sake," Isobel said.

Fox's glasses slipped down his nose. Preposterous, upset, he tried to push his way back between Rayner and the kid.

"Look, Fox. I want a couple of minutes, okay? I'm not going to hurt her."

Fox looked at Isobel and said, his voice a whine, "I don't know why you brought this man here, Isobel. For the sake of our friendship, I must ask you to take him away from my house. I offered him my hospitality—"

The girl had opened her eyes and was looking up at Rayner. There was a faint smile on her mouth, as if she had come out of some pleasant dream. Pleasant, Rayner thought: stuck in this house with the harp-playing madman, poor kid, stuck here with his mysticism, forced to perform her mind tricks for all and sundry, dragged around psychic research circles like some freak, probed and prodded by idiot professors—Jesus Christ, he *hoped* she had some pleasant places of escape, even if only in dreams.

"Are you tired?" he asked.

"A bit," she said. "I guess I flaked out, huh?"

"Fiona, you should rest," Fox said.

She sat upright, hugging her knees, looking at Rayner. "I don't want to rest." She glanced at her father. It was a defiant *Screw you* look. "I swear, I'm okay."

"Can you tell me what happened?" Rayner asked. "Can you remember?"

She watched him a moment. She had a plain face; only the eyes suggested something other than plainness—light, alert, alive now.

"What do I remember?" she said. "Let me think. Let me get it straight in my head."

Rayner saw: she was playing a little game with him, a form of teasing, a vaguely coquettish thing. He had the absurd feeling that he had just invited her to the high school prom and she was stalling her answer. *I gotta check my calendar first.* He was trying, desperately, to hold on to his patience again: a matter of nerve, of doing that strange thing people described as *steeling yourself.* He leaned down, a supplicant, and smiled at her. Bait, he thought. Play her little game. Please come to the prom with me, only me.

"A woman," she said.

"What woman?"

"She was trying to lose me. I can't explain that. She was like trying to say something but she was trying to lose me at the same time. She wanted to fade me out." The girl paused. "She was having a real hard time. That's what I got. A lot of stuff about killing."

Killing, Rayner thought. He had the unsettling feeling of having stepped through some curious barrier, of having drawn aside a curtain, expecting daylight, but finding instead a black window, a world suddenly without sunlight.

"Killing who?" he asked.

The girl shrugged. "I don't know."

"What did you mean when you said something about a broken frame of wood?"

"I don't remember saying that," the kid said.

"She was too much, whoever she was. She was about the heaviest thing I ever ran into. All this power, I mean."

"What power?"

"She was strong, I mean. I couldn't reach her. She could block me out anytime she liked."

Rayner paused, looking at Isobel. This conversation, he thought—the underlying absurdity of it touched him strongly. What the hell are we talking about? A faulty telephone connection? *All this power, I mean.*

"What else?" he asked. "What else do you remember?"

"I know she was bleeding—"

"How do you know that?"

"I just know it. It wasn't like she was cut or anything. She was bleeding. Not a period." The girl blinked at him: *I'm older than you think.* He could feel it, the undertow of teasing, of how she was coming on to him, the casual reference to menstruation. Okay, he thought. You're a big girl. You're a big girl, love.

"If it wasn't a period what was it?"

"It was from inside, I guess."

"Like how?"

"I don't know. A rupture? Does that make sense? She was in bad, bad pain, I can tell you that. And I got this real lonely thing."

Rayner waited. Maybe the madness was a complete thing, a circle fully formed. Maybe you didn't even know you were long gone until the circle had snapped shut all around you. A broken frame of wood. Imagine a window breaking, your brother—

"A young woman? An old woman? What?"

"Real old," the girl said. "Real old."

Fox, who had been sitting on the arm of the sofa as if to protect his daughter from the obvious menace of Rayner, said, "I think that's enough, Rayner. She's tired. Can't you see that?"

Rayner ignored the man. He reached out and held the girl's hand, stroking it lightly. She looked down with a kind of artificial coyness and he suddenly imagined her in the back of a car at some drive-in, her knees angled in the air, a pimply kid trying to stick it inside her.

"This old woman," Rayner said. "Where is she?"

The girl took her hand away from Rayner as if to say, *That's enough intimacy for now. Check me out later, baby.* Sweet little thing, Rayner thought. You could blow your old man's fuses if he really understood you.

"I don't know where she is. I get the feeling of a lot of trees. Hills. Cold. I can't say where she is exactly. But I know she's pretty damn miserable wherever she is and there's some people trying to get her to do things. She doesn't want to do them. Oh, yeah. She had something about a Chinese soldier. And a young American. But I didn't really catch that too clear. See, she was fading me out, like I told you. She didn't want me to keep coming in."

A Chinese soldier, Rayner thought. A young American.

"What did she say about the soldier?"

"I didn't get that bit—"

"The American?"

"I don't know."

Rayner realized he was extraordinarily tired now, that he had come to the dark bottom line of fatigue. A Chinese soldier, a young America, an old woman: if you could put that lot together in a way that made sense, they would have to certify you incurable. Killing. What killing?

"Another thing," the girl said, as if she perceived

she was losing Rayner's interest. "She was foreign. She wasn't American."

"Foreign?"

"Yeah—"

"Like how?"

"I don't know. European. I can't really say."

"Europe's a big place," Rayner said. "Where in Europe?"

The girl closed her eyes for a time, trying to think; then she opened them, smiling slightly at Rayner. "I don't know where in Europe. But there was somebody who had a needle. I got that. Somebody else with a needle. I don't know what it means. I mean, she's real old and pretty damn sick, so maybe it was a doctor's needle, you know? It made her dream, so I guess that was it. And something about a barn, a lot of stuff that didn't really mean anything. I don't know what else."

Rayner stood up. There was an expression of disappointment on the kid's face. She didn't want to lose him now; she didn't want to give up the brief, curious flirtation she had going. "Her power, though. That's what I got. With that kind of power, well . . ."

"With that kind of power—what do you mean?"

"Somebody's making her use it," the girl said.

"Use it how?"

"For killing people."

"Killing people?"

"Blowing them away."

"You're making this up—"

"I swear. I wouldn't put you on."

"How can she kill people?"

"She can make them die because of this power—"

Power, Rayner thought. Force. Okay—it was one thing to admit that some kind of communication, call it telepathic, could exist; but this was a whole new game. Killing people.

"How does she do it?" he asked.

"Look, when you're strong as she is, you can do anything you like with somebody's head. Because nothing, *nothing* is gonna stand in your way."

"She forces them—"

"It's more than that," Fiona said. She folded her hands in her lap, looking down at them. "She wrecks their heads."

"I don't follow—"

"She can make them do anything just by thinking it. Don't you understand what I'm telling you?"

"I understand." Rayner glanced at Fox, as if from that source there might be confirmation of this claim. But Fox, caught up in his daughter's world, made no gesture, said nothing. "I understand," Rayner said again. "It's just hard to believe."

The girl looked at him, sulking now. "Believe what you want. I'm only telling you what I got."

She got up from the sofa and picked up her flute from the table and blew a couple of random notes. It's like nothing ever happened, Rayner thought. Change worlds as easily as changing shoes. Skip from one side of the barrier to the other at will. How could you live with that kind of insight? How could you ever possibly consider it a gift, a talent? He looked at Isobel, who was watching him in a cold way, distantly, her face without expression.

He listened to the discordant sounds of the flute and he was reminded of the cries of birds in pain. She stopped playing after a moment, and tilting her head to one side, looking across the room at him, she said, "I get the feeling she's going to kill again."

Rayner watched her. She tapped her flute against

the side of her leg; a single drop of saliva fell against her jeans, glistening.

"Kill who?"

The girl shrugged. Rayner was cold again, feeling the draft that came in through the open kitchen door. He shivered.

"Kill who?" he asked again.

"If I knew I'd tell you, wouldn't I?"

She blew on the flute once more. He recognized the opening phrase of "Yankee Doodle Dandy"; incongruities, he thought. A mad mixture of the darkness and the light. An old woman who can kill with her mind, a few notes of an irrepressibly happy tune. The fine line dividing things, the normal from the abnormal—where had that line gone?

He watched as she put the instrument on the table, where it rolled a few inches before stopping.

Fox, rising from the sofa, said, "You should get some sleep, child."

"I was thinking that. Funny coincidence."

Fiona smiled at Rayner, went to the door, then turned on her way out. The smile was still there, as if she had known all along that there was something to be saved for the very last, for the final curtain; as if, with the instinct of an actress, she knew how to make her exit. "I got the hills and the sense of green and cold," she said. "And the feeling it was a place like Pennsylvania. That was the strong impression I got."

She paused.

Rayner stared at her.

"I can't figure you out," she said. "You don't want to believe any of this stuff, do you? You just wish it would all disappear. Like go up in a puff of smoke."

He said nothing. He watched her as she closed the door. And then he felt Isobel come up alongside him, touching his arm, drawing him toward the kitchen. Pennsylvania, Rayner thought. He looked at Isobel, who was still wearing his jacket. In the kitchen she said, "You really fucked it up as far as your safe house goes. What are you, John? Self-destructive?"

Me and Richard both, he might have said. He might have come out with a morbid joke like that, but he let it go. He was thinking of the dark outside now. He was thinking of the sports pages of the newspapers. There were equations but only if you could accept the symbols on either side of the plus sign. Have I come this far? he wondered. Am I ready to accept them?

"We're not exactly welcome here as of now," Isobel said. "What do you propose? A night on the old beach?"

He said nothing. Links in a chain, cogs that turned wheels. It could all flash suddenly through your head but you had to grasp it before it finally evaporated. The sports pages of a newspaper, a newspaper he had left behind somewhere. Think think think. The soccer team. The goddam soccer team.

"I remember a time when I had this garden growing," Isobel said. "I was looking forward to the harvest."

She sighed, putting her hands inside the pockets of his jacket.

**6.**

It was just after dawn when the bus rolled up in front of the Lehigh Lodge—a gray morning light, everything green touched with frost. Oblinski ushered the sleepy players onto the bus. Their breath hung on the chill air; they grumbled about having to get up so early to go to the airport. Charek made his head count, ticking off the names on a sheet of paper clipped to a board. Then the old woman was wheeled out of the lodge, her body wrapped in blankets, her face white, her lips purple from the cold. Katya and Oblinski, moving her gently, moving her as though now she was fragile and precious, lifted her from the wheelchair and carried her onto the bus.

Koprow was the last to board. He took one last look at the lodge, pulled on his fur gloves, adjusted his astrakhan hat, and closed the door of the vehicle.

# 4

It was a motel of sorts set well away from the sea; cheaper streets, meaner houses, where the resort yielded to residences, the transient to the permanent. It would be safe, Rayner thought, for a time. He checked in with Isobel, using a fictitious name—Fox, curiously enough, the first that had popped into his mind: Mr. and Mrs. Fox. The motel clerk gave them a key to Room 20. Here, Rayner thought, was enough sleaze to last one a lifetime. Ants busily went back and forth across the chipped porcelain sink, some of them sticking to a wet bar of soap, struggling and dying; cockroaches, brazen enough not to flee, clung to the walls. A palace, Rayner thought, as he dropped face down on the bed and shut his eyes. Isobel sat in an armchair and watched him.

How can I even think of sleep? Rayner wondered.

He turned over and looked at her. "Okay," he said. "You tell me. What did we run into back there? A young kid's presexual fantasies or what?"

"She's the real thing," Isobel said. "She's been through all the tests they were smart enough to devise and she came out with her colors flying. No fantasies, John."

Rayner sat up. Sleep, he thought. My kingdom for. He rubbed his eyes and realized that what he had been doing was to avoid the recent experience, relegate it into some darker area where even the mysteries had deeper puzzles within them. But there wasn't time, there just wasn't time; even the concept of a few hours of sleep was some extravagant luxury. There were the pieces of the picture to assemble, and ridiculous as they might have seemed, he saw too many correspondences to reject the ideas that, like hornets, kept swarming back to him. Pennsylvania—but where could he find a newspaper from the day before? Where could he check his memory against the facts? That damn soccer team—

He got up from the bed, went to the door, opened it.

It was silent out there; a sense, through all the disintegrating dark, the flying moon, of dawn coming up in tiny bars of light.

"Stepping out?" she asked.

He turned to look at her. "I need a trash can," he said.

"I should have thought of that," she answered. She closed her eyes and sighed with feigned impatience. "I mean, what the hell else could you possibly need at this time of day?"

He went out, crossing the parking lot to where, against a crumbling wall, a bunch of trash cans stood. A young American, a Chinese soldier, an old woman with some force—and now this, scavenging through the detritus of a scuzzy motel for a copy of an old newspaper. The things people threw away. Used sani-

tary napkins, crumpled tissues, dilapidated sneakers—
you could expect such things; you could expect all the
fast-food trash as well, the soggy Big Macs, the lumpy
leftovers of Arthur Treacher's Fish & Chips, the bones
of what had once been poultry covered over with the
Colonel's secret recipe. But how could you expect to
find a set of discarded Polaroid snapshots of a pretty
girl, each ripped meticulously in half, each snapped
in provocative pose—a lovers' tiff in the motel bedroom? Odd what people cast off. He moved from can
to can, picking out pages of a newspaper here, there,
some of them greasy and dripping, some of them
crumpled, others thrown away unread. He assembled
a collection and took it back into the room and
dumped the pages on the floor.

"Sports pages," he said. "Help me find the sports
pages."

"Can I guess? You made a wager on a horse and
you want to find out?" She got down on her knees
on the tatty rug and placed her hand across the backs
of his fingers. "John. It's late. It's been a shitty day,
if you like understatement. I'm tired. Can't it wait?"

"Just the sports pages, nothing else."

She sighed again and began to sift, stopping every
so often to make a noise of disgust when she encountered something unspeakable attached to the newsprint. Inside a folded-up copy of *The Charlotte Observer*
she found a pair of used surgical stockings, shredded,
filled with holes.

"John, for God's sake—"

"Just look for that piece you saw yesterday. The
Soviet soccer thing, that's all." He was folding and un-
folding sheets madly, knowing how it must appear to
her, how it would appear to anybody who might step
inside the room. "I need to see it, that's all."

"Why?"

"I need to see it, then maybe I can explain—"

"I hope it's one of your better explanations," she said.

He found all kinds of newspapers that had been transported across state lines—even, oddly, a copy of *The Toronto Star* which had a January dateline. Then, when he had sifted almost to the bottom, Isobel pushed a crumpled sheet toward him.

"I think that's what you're looking for."

He smoothed the sheet and stared at it. It wasn't the same report as he had read before. This one was printed in *The Roanoke Times* and had come through a wire service. Its headline read: "Will America Be Good Enough?" It was a snide piece of syndicated journalism concerning the Soviet team's dedication, but all that interested Rayner was the fact that the item had been datelined *Lehighton, Pa.* He sat back, the sheet of paper wilting in his hand, and he stared at Isobel.

"Pennsylvania," he said. "That's what the kid said."

"What are you getting at, John?"

He stood up and, still holding the paper, walked around the room. By the window he stopped. It was fully dawn now, the sky a congregation of thick lines of light. Pennsylvania, he thought. Okay, that one adds up. That's another piece of the problem. What's the next step?

"John. What is it?"

He didn't answer her. He looked at the column again, reading and rereading the last paragraph:

Trainer Charek thinks that his team will beat the American National side Saturday in D.C. Stadium. He says this with great confidence, even if he says it through an interpreter. We hope he's wrong, of course—especially if, as expected, the crowd will include Patrick J. Mallory.

Saturday.
D.C. Stadium.
Patrick J. Mallory.
Saturday. The day that had just lit the sky: today.

"Do you believe what the kid said?" he asked.

"I told you—"

"Think again. It's important. *Do you believe in her?*"

"You're hurting my wrist, John—"

"Do you believe in this story of some old woman with this—whatever you call it—power, force? Do you believe in that?"

Isobel took her hand away from him. "I don't know what's gotten into you, but I don't exactly like it, John."

"Answer my question—"

"Okay. If it's so goddam important to you, sure, sure, I believe Fiona wasn't making it up. There. Satisfy you?"

He watched her face. How could you ever know? he thought. They could get carried away; all this psychic stuff was easily digestible, opening up promising vistas that led all the way from mind reading, from telepathy, to possibilities of a nifty afterlife where you sat around in a wonderful spiritual glaze, where—if you wanted to party—you just hopped from cloud to cloud. No, Rayner, come on. You saw it. What if it's true? D.C. Stadium, Saturday, Patrick J. Mallory. *There's going to be more killing.* Hadn't the kid said something like that? More killing?

Turn it around.

Andreyev defects because of this old woman. This—how do you phrase it?—witch. He wants to blow it. Nobody much cares for the notion and so he receives the treatment. Leaving yourself and Dubbs with the knowledge of his identity. Leaving, alas, yourself.

Andreyev—he doesn't want anything to do with it.

It?

No, come on, surely not, surely not something so beyond the realm of the likely. But all that's as thin as a wafer now. That realm has cracks in it.

Andreyev doesn't want any part of it, because *it*— *it* is a plot to kill the President of the United States, using a means that is undetectable, improbable, insubstantial. No weapons, therefore no proof. *She could take somebody's head and wreck it.* Maybe the way Richard—

He turned to see that Isobel, sprawled across the bed now, had fallen asleep. He went and lay down beside her. My own brother. *He wasn't Richard, John. He wasn't anybody we knew.* Was that it? Was that the same *force* that had driven Richard Rayner into the final absurd act of his short life?

And Gull, fucking Gull, must have known all along. The death of Richard: *I'm so sorry, John.* The killing of Andreyev. The man's identity. And poor little Ernest Dubbs. George Gull must know, he thought, a whole lot of things.

And me, he thought, I'm mad and manic-depressive and probably melancholic into the bargain. I am making it all up. I am piling fictions on fictions, improbabilities on improbabilities; I am going, like they say, off the deep end. *Chip, I have to tell you, there's this plot to kill the President. I know it sounds fantastic, but it's true, and it's going to be done by this old woman, a great plot, no guns, no physical contact—just the Old Man's death: a whammy. Isn't that the greatest you've ever heard? And what with Gull being a Soviet agent and everything—*

He closed his eyes. Rest. Think. Run it through again. But don't sleep.

**2.**

Koprow sat at the front of the bus, directly behind the driver, watching the countryside pass. Frame houses set in the kind of green one knew would be rich during summer and fiery when autumn came. He pronounced the unfamiliar names of the towns that lay off the highway. Strange names he had trouble turning over on his tongue. Walnutport. Schnecksville. Catasauqua.

The woman, Katya, came and sat down in the vacant seat beside him. For a time she said nothing. She simply gazed out at the landscape. This one, he thought, has no time for landscapes, for the relationships of nature, for reflection. A world of color blindness. He wondered if she ever thought of Andreyev, if in her private darkness she ever speculated on his disappearance. No, she would seal herself off from the memory, disappear inside whatever protective casket she had devised for herself. Emotions were games played only by fools.

"She has lost a lot of blood," the woman said finally. "Her pulse is weak. Her heartbeat is irregular."

Koprow, who didn't want to know these things, looked briefly at the woman. "What are you trying to tell me?"

"I am trying to tell you that if she lives another

day it will be some kind of miracle, Comrade." The woman's voice was sharp and angular, grating.

Koprow did not like the slight accusatory note in it. "If she dies before our task is completed, my dear woman, you will be held personally responsible. I will see to that."

Katya was silent for a time. "She needs expert medical help. The bleeding, for example—"

Koprow waved his hand. "Keep her happy on her drug. Show her some photographs. Make promises. Sing songs. I don't care what you do. I need one more day of her life. Do you understand me?"

"The bleeding—"

"No more. Please."

Katya stared through the window for a while. "I'm not a doctor, Comrade. If there's internal bleeding, which is obvious from her excrement, then it must be clear to you that there's danger."

"Give her morphine," Koprow said. "Keep her alive. That's all I require of you."

The woman rose from the seat, stared at him, then walked up the aisle to the back seat where Mrs. Blum sat, slumping against the window, her body wrapped in blankets. She had her eyes closed; her head, touching the glass, vibrated slightly. Katya sat down beside her and opened a small dark bag of medical supplies. Epinephrine, amyl nitrate, morphine. She filled a syringe and lifted the old woman's arm, which was slack and lifeless, like formless putty in her hand.

**3.**

There was a weakness she had not felt before, not even in the worst of times. She had not thought before of dying as something that would involve weakness, but rather as an energetic movement, a confrontation, a rush into darkness. I don't want to die, she thought. I don't want—and she remembered, as if it were all a dream, an illusion, the thin voice that had come to her—when? last night? She wasn't sure because time held no meaning; time was like mercury slipping across a surface, shapeless, impossible. The voice had been that of a child. A young girl. Another, she thought, with this wretched ability. Another with this malformation. When she grows—how terrible it will be for her when she grows. She was aware now of movement and she opened her eyes a little way. A road, white houses, trees. Confused again, insensible to place, to surroundings, to why she was moving: was this her Palestine?

No. There wasn't such a place. She had invented it for herself.

You couldn't find it on any map.

She tried to remember, but even memory had slipped. The man had come to her this morning. He had come to her with a name. *Her final task.* And she tried to remember the name, to keep it in front of her mind and out of the dark places. Mallory. Somebody called Mallory.

The final killing.

She tried to imagine praying, praying even silently to herself, but she understood that it would do no good because wherever God might be he had stopped listening to her now.

If there was one worthy act, one last act of value, one thing that might cause God to reconsider, what would it be? What could it possibly be? But she was so tired and thought was so terrible; and sleep—sleep was the only profound thing left.

**4.**

Rayner woke, startled, remembering what he had worked out, recalling his determination not to sleep—yet he had drifted off, and when he opened his eyes he thought of the nonsensical conclusions of his own notions. Weary, he sat up. He got up from the bed and went to the window, which was bright with early sun.

Somebody is going to kill Mallory, he thought.

Suppose it's true. Suppose.

Who do you tell? Where do you go with this brilliant information? Do you call the White House and warn Mallory's people? He laid his hand flat upon the pane of glass.

Saturday in D.C. Stadium.

He heard Isobel move, and when he turned to look he saw she was awake, watching him. "I dreamed I was back in my own house," she said. "Only it was different somehow. There were all these people sitting in my front room and I didn't know any of them. But I did know them *somehow*. When I tried to talk they just ignored me like I wasn't even there."

She sat up, pushing aside her pillow.

"Anyway, it wasn't an accurate dream. I notice I'm still in the same grubby motel room with you. And I haven't changed these clothes in—God, I've even lost track of time."

She rose, went inside the bathroom. He remained by the window, listening to the sound of running water. *This is John Rayner of the United States Embassy in London. I must warn you, Mr. President, sir, that an old woman is about to kill you.* Jesus Christ. He looked out across the parking lot at the trash cans by the wall and he wondered how he could even begin

to explain to Isobel, where it could lead. *I first really
began to doubt the defendant's sanity when he developed this
insatiable obsession with newspapers picked out of trash cans.
I thought it somewhat odd.*

Today. Saturday, Rayner thought.

What did you do? You could buy a shotgun in
Virginia Beach, then rent a car, drive to Washington,
get through the security guards somehow at the stadium, and shoot every old woman in sight. Sure. Sure
you could.

Isobel came out of the bathroom, drying her face
with a towel she dropped on the bed. He thought of
how he had slept beside her, his body twisted away
from her at some prim angle: a degree of morality.

"So," she said. "When do we check out of the
Hotel El Dumpo? And what happens next?"

She stepped across the papers, grimacing at them,
as if she wanted to put that memory from her mind.
He watched her as she approached the window and
stood beside him. She looked out at the flood of sunlight a moment.

"I fell asleep before I heard your explanation,"
she said.

"Explanation?"

"This weird thing you have about the Russian
team." She shrugged, hands in the pockets of her
jeans.

"That kid," he said.

"Fiona?"

He nodded. He thought all at once of Sally. You
can't go through it again with Isobel; you can't drag
her toward the same destiny.

"What about Fiona?" Isobel asked.

"If your little friend is on the level, I think we
have a situation . . ." He paused. What was the point
in saying it out loud? He could already anticipate her

look, the distance in her eyes, her discomfort. The mad brother-in-law.

"A situation like what?" she asked.

"Like the death of Patrick J. Mallory," he answered.

She was quiet for a time. She moved away from him now, circling the room in the manner of someone stalking. "How is he supposed to die, John?"

"By assassination."

"And what has this got to do with a teen-age girl in Virginia Beach?"

What indeed? Rayner clenched his hands together. He watched the expression on her face: dark, opaque, something he couldn't read.

"The connection is that the same power she talked about last night is the one that will be used to kill Mallory."

There. It was out in the cold, shivering.

Isobel sat on the edge of the bed and stared at him. She was running her fingers back and forth through her long hair. "I have this feeling of a gulf, John," she said slowly. "A distance between your world and mine. I have the feeling of—how do I describe it?—the distance growing wider. And I don't much like it. Do I make myself plain? Maybe in your world—all the codes and secrets and locked rooms and whacky little games of power—maybe in your world there are assassination conspiracies and dark plots, but mine isn't like that, John. Mine's different."

"It's the same world," he said.

"It's night and day," she said, rising from the bed. "It's the sun and the moon, John."

"You take the long route to telling me you don't believe me—"

"Did you expect me to believe?"

He shook his head. He watched her come toward

him. She pressed her face against his shoulder, sighing. He could hardly blame her. Maybe on the spiral down, he thought, you were bound to encounter the resistance of cold sanity. For her it was a matter of dabbling in the inexplicable possibilities of the mind—harmless, comforting, puzzling; it was no more than a jigsaw of psychic pieces. For him it had become something different, something threatening.

"John," she said. "John, look, I would like to believe in your . . ."

"Sanity?"

"Something like that," she said. "I *want* to believe in it. You sure as hell make it damn hard."

She was staring at the pages of newspaper now, as if this were further evidence of his disintegration. She moved away from him, bent down, picked up a sheet with a look of distaste.

He had the feeling of a curious solitude, rather like a mist, moving in on him. The kid, he thought. Maybe she was making it all up, dreaming it; maybe it was just a part of her general tease. He watched Isobel crumple a sheet of paper in her hand, making a ball of it, weighing it in her open palm.

He had a sense now of a delicate shift in the nature of things: it was as if his own skepticism had eroded completely and he was defending that which he had scorned before—defending it against one of its own converts.

"Mallory will be at D.C. Stadium this afternoon," he said.

"I read it."

"The game begins at three."

"You think that's where the event will happen?"

"If I'm right, yeah. I think that's where it will happen."

"If you're right," she said, in the manner of

somebody talking to herself. She aimed the ball of paper at the wastebasket, missing her shot.

"And there's only one person who can tell me if I'm right," he said.

She looked at him. "The girl?"

"The girl," he said.

He was quiet for a while, conscious of time passing in the silence. Three o'clock. Only the kid, he thought; who else could lead him to the core of this? If there was a core, a center, a heart he could penetrate. *If.* Who else could take him there?

## 5.

Chip Alexander was wakened by the sound of the telephone in his room at the Holiday Inn. For a moment he had trouble adjusting to his surroundings. It was the sound of the sea that momentarily threw him; then he remembered and reached out for the receiver. When he spoke into it his voice was hoarse.

It was some dummy from the Virginia Beach Police Department. Alexander sat upright and stared at the slit of dawn that hung between the draperies. He scratched his head, then fumbled for a cigarette, knocking over a plastic tumbler filled with stale water. He listened to it drip from the bedside table to the rug.

"Inspector Crabbe?" the voice asked.

"Yeah," Alexander said, "this is Crabbe."

"This is Scully," the guy said. "I just came on duty and I picked up on a complaint that I guess might interest you."

"Yeah," Alexander said. That first cigarette: Christ, it was a killer.

"You asked Captain Ettinger about a character called Rayner, right? John Rayner? Is that right?"

Come to the point, Alexander thought. How did these small-town stiffs contrive to beat around so many bushes? It was one thing to impress them with fake FBI credentials—they looked at you like you were Efrem Zimbalist, Jr., coming down for the big kill—but it was quite another to have to deal with them.

"What's the story?" he asked.

"Some guy called Ferguson Fox called in a complaint at midnight—"

"Midnight?" Alexander picked up his watch. "Well, you guys are really on the ball. I mean, that's only just over seven hours ago. I'm impressed."

There was a heavy silence on the line.

"I don't think your inquiry was circulated, Inspector," the cop said. "It was only when I came on duty and saw the complaint that I put the things together."

Give yourself a medal, Alexander thought. "What did you put together, Scully?"

"Okay. This Fox called in a complaint about your man Rayner. Seems Rayner was at his house with a woman—a friend of this Fox character's. Anyhow, Fox has the feeling that his friend, the woman, is in some kind of trouble with your man. He called in. He was worried about her."

There was a precision here that Alexander loved. It was the geometrical exactitude of a fog. *Some kind of trouble*, he thought. Feelings. Goddam.

"Your people check it out?" Alexander asked.

"Uh-huh. As soon as I looked at it I called the number you left the captain."

"Address?" Chip Alexander found the stub of a pencil and a sheet of Holiday Inn notepaper and wrote the address down.

"Seems Rayner and the woman left some time before the guy decided he was worried enough to call," Scully said.

"Does your Fox know where they went?"

"I guess I don't know for sure," the cop said.

"Thanks for everything." Alexander put the receiver back, crushed out his cigarette, blinked into the bedside lamp. He shoved his sheets aside and, groaning in the fashion of one who would prefer to stay in bed, stepped out; he drew the draperies and looked out across the gray tide. There was the relic of some faint mist along the shoreline.

Sunlight, he thought. The new day begins. He pulled on his clothes and left the room. He knocked on the door of the adjoining room. After a moment his young colleague appeared. Dressed, shaved, keen as mustard, Alexander thought. With that kind of eagerness you had to be convinced that behind everything you did there lay some holy purpose. Maybe he was young enough to learn otherwise.

"News of our friend," Alexander said. "Gimme a minute to grab my shoes."

The young colleague, whose name was Love, followed Alexander back into his room. Like a shadow, Alexander thought. Like some fucking extra extension of yourself, a limb you don't need, an additional orifice somewhere on your body. He sat on the edge of the bed and started to lace his shoes. He watched Love, fretting with impatience, stride to the window, where he tapped upon the glass with his fingertips. Love turned and looked at him, and Alexander wondered if there was a hint of accusation in the expression. Maybe he blames me for failing to give the order in the coffee shop of the Ramada. Maybe that's what's bugging the hell out of him. Gunned-up and nothing to shoot. Why didn't I just give him his damn signal?

He was irritated more than a little by what he thought of as his own softness; it was like finding a shadow on your lung in an X-ray when you had assumed your body was in excellent health. John Rayner, for God's sake. Was he supposed to go through the pantomime that climaxed in Rayner's death? And the appearance of the woman—well, he could always say he'd been knocked off his stride by the way she had steered John out of the coffee shop. When you had a chit for one corpse, you didn't want to bring home two. Nobody liked that very much. Besides, Rayner was to be hospitalized; he was to be killed only in *a situation of extremity.*

One chance, John, he thought. I can't give you another one.

## 6.

Rayner used a credit card to hire a car from a company called Tidewater Rent-a-Car, Inc. It had taken him and Isobel almost an hour to walk from the motel, by way of back streets of quiet houses, alleys, lanes, to the office of the car rental firm, which didn't open its doors for business until eight. They had been obliged to linger in the street for several minutes before the clerk, a young woman with a painted-on face that made her appear years older than she was, unlocked the door. She immediately went into a sales performance as if her voice issued from a looped tape at the back of her throat. Rayner interrupted: it didn't matter whether the car was a subcompact, a compact, whether it was foreign or American. He settled in the end for a Pinto. The young woman walked with them across the parking lot and handed him the keys. He wondered if the car had the exploding-gas-tank option but he didn't ask.

He drove out of the lot, listening to Isobel's directions. The car was sluggish. How could he drive this damn thing to Washington in time? Work it out. From Richmond, on a good day, a day without traffic jams and accidents, it was two hours to Washington; from Virginia Beach to Richmond, if he went through Newport News, it was—what?—a hundred miles at the outside. But then he had to hope for a clear run through the Hampton Roads area; he had to hope there wouldn't be a snarl-up of weekend traffic, of station wagons stuffed with kids, moms and dads transporting their broods to sight-seeing tours of the Pentagon, the Smithsonian, the National Geographic Society, or whatever other treats lay in the capital. He had to hope. And even as he thought about it he was assailed by a sense of having let reason slip, of some mental dislocation: a tightrope snapping in the mind. What I should do, he thought, is get out of this damn car and turn myself over for that period in the West Virginia facility. What I should do is let them take me.

"Turn here," Isobel said.

He went right, remembering now the street where the Foxes lived. It was quiet and hushed and almost indifferent in its silence; gleaming cars sat behind thick trees in a state of camouflage. He stopped the motor and took the ignition key out and looked at Isobel. She was biting a fingernail.

"What now?" she asked.

He stared through the trees, trying to see the house.

Madness, he thought. *Please, Mr. Fox, it's a matter of great national importance that I take your daughter for a car ride. It's a matter, as they say, of life and death.*

"John."

He felt her touch his wrist. He looked at her.

"What are you going to do?" she asked. "That's all I want to know."

He looked along the street. Thick trees—you could hardly see the houses.

"I need the kid," he said. "I need to take her with me." And he was conscious of a vaguely desperate quality in his voice, as if what he was really saying was *Why won't you fucking believe me? Why?*

"It's a kidnap now?" Isobel asked.

"Whatever you want to call it. I ask her to come, I hope she accepts."

Isobel was shaking her head. Suddenly he was angry with her for her incredulity, her lack of faith, the strange distances in her.

"For Christ's sake," he said. "You don't have to come along. I can drop you any goddam place you like—"

"John—"

"Say the word. Get out of the car. I don't give a shit." It sounded, even to him, absurdly petulant, childish. He slammed his hand against the dash. What right do I have to ask her to believe in my deluded suspicions? Maybe they're all correct. Maybe I've just goddam gone and broken down and need to be tucked away in the funny place. Maybe this is what paranoia is like: shadowy hills and murky valleys in your brain, weird convictions, dizzy suspicions. Why should she believe any of it? Maybe she was just like Sally in her way—seeing Rayner as someone to be comforted, someone to be patronized.

He opened his door and stepped out. Time, he thought. There just isn't time for this goddam nonsense now. I need the kid, that's all there is to it. I need the girl. He watched Isobel shove her door open; she slammed it hard and stared at him across the roof of the small car.

"John," she said, "I'll ask her to come. But I doubt if I'll get past her father. I doubt that really."

He saw her move toward the trees and he followed after her into the shadows and over the lawn. The house looked squat, like something crouching, something ready to jump. He caught her up, holding her wrist, making her turn to face him. How do I look to her now? He wondered. Desperate? Deranged? Gone?

"I said I'd ask," she said. "I didn't promise she would come."

"I didn't ask for a promise," he answered. "It's gone past all that. It's beyond that."

"Jesus, John, what do you want me to do? Wrap her up in a goddam bag? *Steal* her? What do you expect of me?" She pulled her arm away and looked at him defiantly. "If you want my private opinion, I think you're living in a dream. If you want my help out of it, fine. Fine. But don't push me, John. Don't push me."

Isobel turned away from him and went toward the house. A door was opened even before she had reached the porch. Fox stood there in shadow. All this sunlight, Rayner thought. How could you subscribe to the belief that all the things that had happened the previous night were true? Sunlight made it ordinary, changed it around, deprived it of its need for darkness. He followed Isobel up onto the porch. Fox was smiling. Why was he looking like that? Rayner wondered. That tight smug little smile—what in the name of God did that mean? Fox stepped out of shadow, his face dappled by patterns of moving leaves. Maybe he expected us, Rayner thought. Maybe the kid told him, through the psychic grapevine, that we were arriving.

"Isobel," Fox was saying, holding her hand in a slack handshake. "And Mr. Rayner. Well, well. An early visit. Come in. Come on in."

Effusive, oleaginous: it was scum floating on water—all the pretty rainbow colors that were pure poison to drink. Rayner entered the gloom of the house. Uneasy, anxious, hearing the girl play her flute in another room. It stopped. He could hear her footsteps now.

Fox was asking about coffee. Did they want coffee? Tea? Jasmine tea? Maybe a glass of ginseng liquid? Why the menu? Rayner asked himself. The good host, the charm; the cold eyes made huge by the glasses. Fox rubbed his hands together and smiled in the manner of someone who has won a lottery with a single ticket he has forgotten buying. It's wrong, Rayner thought. How wrong can it get?

They were in the front room now. The kid's footsteps had stopped someplace in the house. The silences were like drafts of wind. Rayner listened: the staircase creaked. He looked toward a doorway. A shadow moved in the space and Fox turned his head in that direction, as if he expected to see someone appear.

"Where's Fiona?" Isobel asked.

"Upstairs, I think," Fox said. "Do you want to see her?"

"We'd like to take her with us for a time," Isobel said.

"Oh?" Fox didn't seem unduly surprised. Maybe, Rayner thought, he gets requests like that all the time. We need your daughter to do one of her performances, Mr. Fox. May we borrow her?

"Where are you going?" Fox asked.

"A drive." Isobel shrugged casually.

"Where?"

"Oh." Isobel looked uncomfortable; a terrible liar, Rayner thought. "No place in particular, I guess."

"You want her company, is that it?" Fox glanced at Rayner; it was shifty in its way, almost suggestive, as if the man suspected Isobel of procuring the girl for Rayner. Rayner looked at the open doorway again. The shadow was gone.

"We want her company," Isobel said. "That's right."

"I'll call her. See what she feels like." He went to the open door and disappeared inside another room. Rayner could hear him calling the kid's name. "Fiona." It didn't ring true somehow, as if he were calling for somebody he knew to be absent. It was counterfeit, a bad coin. Rayner looked at Isobel a moment. Paranoia: it grows and it grows like some weed of the mind. Finally you get a jungle. A father calls his daughter and you think it sounds off. Control, he thought. Bloody control.

He heard the flute again. A single piercing note. Isobel smiled at him in a thin way; she might have been smiling at a stranger, a new acquaintance. And then there was the sound of footsteps rushing down the stairway, and the girl, flute in hand, appeared in the door. Behind her, looming up, shadowy, was another figure that Rayner assumed mistakenly to be Fox. But it wasn't. It wasn't Fox.

"You're through, John. This time you're washed up."

Rayner saw Chip Alexander in the doorway and, at his back, the young friend, the colleague. The girl ran across the room and stopped, almost skidding to a halt, at Rayner's side. A trap, and you walk straight into it. He closed his eyes a second, wondering about betrayal, treachery, wondering what prompted it or whether it was something that had always been in the scheme of things, wondering even if Isobel had in some way brought this situation about, betrayed him—

"All washed up, John."

Rayner looked at the girl. What was she trying to tell him? Something. Something, for sure. A message he couldn't read. He watched Chip Alexander step inside the room.

"I'll say this, John. It was convenient of you to stop by because I was sure as hell getting fed up with the dance."

Rayner stood motionless. You come this far and it ends like a whisper; but maybe there wasn't anyplace farther to go, maybe it was meant to be as inconclusive as a dream. What was he meant to do? Tell Chip Alexander that the President was going to be killed—*perhaps.* Show me a little hard evidence, John. Show me something I can hold in the palm of my hand. But show me.

There was a sudden fragrance in the air. Jasmine, he thought. The jasmine tea, the charming treacherous host. The girl, still looking up at him, reached out and tugged his sleeve. He gazed at her. He was conscious of Alexander coming across the room, being followed by his young colleague. The kid, he thought. The kid is telling me something. The kid is telling me to *do* something—

"Give us a peaceful time, John. It helps," Alexander said.

Isobel moved, moved very slightly, her arm touching Rayner's side. Then, as in a tableau, as in a badly planned snapshot, there was a stillness in the room, an artificial lack of motion—almost as if something had happened to stop movement. Only the child's eyes shifted, flashing at Rayner the same message as before, the same unintelligible message. What? What is she telling me?

Alexander coughed, raising a hand to his lips in what was almost a gesture of apology. The young man, his hands in the pockets of his coat, glanced briefly at Isobel, then looked once more at Rayner—and the illusion of stillness was gone. The girl opened her mouth, maybe whisper, but there was no sound.

"Ready, John?" Alexander said.

"Chip, listen—"

Alexander waved a hand impatiently. "Don't make it hard this time. Be good to yourself."

"Chip—"

The kid was pulling at Rayner's sleeve again and he looked down at her, down into her eyes, down into some strange cool darkness there—and suddenly he understood what she was suggesting. Suddenly he realized, from the eyes, the tension in her lips, the slight sideways movement of her head, that she was telling him, Use me, use me to get yourself out of this. Just use me.

Quickly, before there was time for anyone in the room to react, he had caught her by the neck and swung her around so that she created a shield for him. He listened to the sound of her gasping, the small soft sobs that came from her open mouth. And he looked directly at Alexander. Go ahead, challenge me, beat me, Chip. Take this one away from me. It would take only a quick hard snap, the fracture of vertebrae, the dislocation of death.

Alexander watched him. "You don't want to do that, John. Come on. You don't want to fuck with the kid."

Rayner looked at Isobel. She was moving away from him now, moving in the direction of the door. The kid was covering both of them.

"You know what I can do, Chip," Rayner said. "You learned the same tricks once."

"John, John." Alexander was shaking his head. "This makes it a whole lot worse for you, man. Can't you see that?"

"Tell your pal there to put his gun on the table."

Alexander sighed. The young guy didn't move until he was nudged; and then he put the pistol on the table with great reluctance. Rayner reached out and, still holding the girl by the neck, lifted the gun.

"Think, John. Use your head. What's the point of this?"

Rayner backed toward the door. There was a symmetry in things at times, he thought. There was an arrangement that astonished you. He had the girl because she wanted to be taken anyway. He had what he had come for.

"Okay. You've got the gun. Let the kid go," Alexander said.

Rayner shook his head. "She comes, Chip."

"Deeper and deeper," Alexander said. "Finally, pal, you reach a place where there's no way out. *No* way."

"I'll look into that some other time, Chip. Not now."

He had reached the entrance to the porch. He held the kid, but there was no force in his grip; if she had wanted to, she could have slipped free at any time. It was, he thought, quite a nice performance, quite a neat little show of pain.

"One last chance, John. I can't tell you the consequences of this."

"I know them already," Rayner said.

Alexander shrugged in a resigned way. At his back, Fox had appeared in the doorway. He started to rush toward Rayner, then stopped when he saw the gun.

"Let her go," Fox said. "Please. Please let her go."

"Later," Rayner said. "I promise you. In one piece."

He was backing down the steps of the porch, aware of Isobel rushing toward the car. Fox came out onto the porch with his arms extended on either side of his body, pleading, begging. As he did so, the kid groaned as if Rayner had tightened his hold on her neck.

"Please," Fox said.

Holding the kid, Rayner went back down through the trees to the car. What did he have—a couple of minutes at most? A couple of minutes to get out of the street before the license-plate number could be read and the bulletins issued and all the wires singing his name and number? Isobel was already in the passenger seat. He opened the other door and the kid slipped into the rear of the car. Then he had the engine going, turning the car in a quick ungainly circle and gunning it out of the street. He saw the girl smile in the rearview mirror.

"It's tough to get through to you," she said. "You know that? It takes you a long time to get the point."

"I'm not on your level, kid," Rayner said.

"Those creeps." She shuddered. "When he saw you guys coming across the lawn it was like his ship had come home. He put the big guys in the back room to wait. How could I hack that? I mean."

Rayner glanced at the girl. She was smiling still,

as if what she enjoyed most in the world was pulling a fast one on her father.

"So where are we going?" she asked.

Isobel turned around in her seat and looked at the kid. "You better ask John that question. The answer is something he shares between himself and his private demons."

Private demons, Rayner thought. He watched for road signs, for Highway 60, Ocean View Avenue, that would take him around Norfolk and toward Newport News. Private demons. In the rearview mirror he noticed the kid was staring at him.

# 5

*1.*

Inland it was raining, a dreary gray rain that began over Williamsburg in dense banks of cloud. The sunlight that had come with the dawn was gone, suggesting ghosts of itself only in watery moments. Around Richmond the traffic became slow: on Interstate 95 a rig had blown a tire and slashed sideways across the shoulder, surrounded now by the flashing lights of the highway patrol. A cop in a raincoat was directing traffic into the fast lane. Impatiently Rayner waited to get through the narrow gap. He was thinking of the pistol, knowing that he couldn't get it past the security guards at D.C. Stadium, understanding that if the game was to be played at all it would have to be by ear or by whatever miraculous means the kid could provide. Miraculous, he thought, beset again by a sense of stupidity; maybe those private demons Isobel had mentioned were going public now. Perhaps, like dark bats driven out of a cave by dynamite, they were about to be set free in some final conflagration of madness.

He drove the Pinto slowly past the accident spot,

but it was miles before the highway was clear again. He wanted to ask Isobel the time but he didn't; slumped in her seat, she was staring bleakly out into the rain. She must be pondering the Rayner family, he thought. The brother who is going crazy, the husband who already went. Quite a tribe, she must be thinking: some weird inbreeding from far back that had elected to appear now in the form of assassination plots and inexplicable suicides. In the back seat the kid was turning this way and that like an excited sightseer. Sightseer, he thought, there had to be double meanings in that one.

WASHINGTON 90.

Ninety miles.

Isobel looked at her watch and said, "It's just past eleven, John."

Four hours, Rayner thought. Four hours to what? The revelation that will tell you how badly mistaken you've been, how far off the mark you've gone? Or something else? He massaged his eyelids with one hand. Tired, weary—it was an ache doing the Boy Scout bit, like rubbing two damp sticks together in the hope of a spark, a flame. It was a pain to be a hero. He looked in the rearview mirror time and again as if what he most expected to see was Chip Alexander immediately behind him—but Alexander didn't even know what kind of car he was driving, or where he had rented it, or even where he was going. One of these problems could be solved simply by calling the car rental companies in the area. *Mr. Rayner, ah, yes. A Ford Pinto. 1978. White. License-plate Number ADO 692. No trouble at all, sir.* And then Alexander would issue a single message, make a single telephone call, and before you could break open a cyanide capsule the heat would be running around like enraged bees. It takes time, Rayner thought. Time for Alexander to make his calls. Time for me to get to Washington. Time time time—

The kid leaned forward and slipped a stick of pink gum into her mouth. The kid, Rayner thought. How could it all boil down to this adolescent, this gum-chewing little number who played the flute and dreamed of boys and went to drive-ins and who, as it just so happened, had some odd gift?

"Washington. Right?" she said.

"Right," Rayner said.

"It's about last night, I guess."

"Something like that."

"I thought so." She sat well back in her seat. She chewed her gum noisily for a time. "It's a funny thing, you know. But when people want to take me places it's always got something to do with all that stuff. It's never for any other reason."

Some little refrain of loneliness in there, he thought. A melancholic strain. We want you for your parlor tricks. Can you read my hand? Can you tell me my future? What lies in store for me, Fiona? Have some more Coke.

"John has the idea, Fiona, that you can help him exorcise his strange notions," Isobel said.

"Exorcise?"

"As in 'drive out.' "

The girl chewed silently for a time. "Like how?"

"The old woman," Rayner said, and looked at her quickly in the mirror. For a moment he had the feeling she was going to say, *Hey, man, that was all a joke, you know? I was putting you on. It was nothing.* But she was frowning now, frowning and sinking deeper into her seat.

"Yeah," she said.

"I want you to find her for me. Can you do that?"

The girl shrugged. "I don't know. It depends."

"Depends on what?"

"I don't know what it depends on," she answered, rather too quickly, too defensively—as if she had quietly pondered the mysteries herself and had been unable to fathom them.

"You're being vague, Fiona," he said. *"Depends on what?"*

"I said I didn't know," she said.

"John," Isobel said. "She doesn't know. Leave it alone. Let it go."

He watched the kid's expression in the mirror. She was serious now, withdrawn, her mouth distended slightly as if she was afraid of the whole prospect. I can't put you through it, Rayner thought, remembering, even when he least needed it, how the girl had acted last night. You ask a great deal, Rayner. You have to, he thought. You can't ask anything less.

"I'll try," the kid said. "That's the best I can do."

## 2.

When she opened her eyes she realized that the pain was gone now from her body; through glass she saw rain sweep across a stretch of concrete and she understood that sometime during her sleep she had been moved from the bus to a plane—a plane coming down now through the sloughing rain. The young men were reaching up into racks for pieces of baggage. She watched them, feeling oddly liberated for a while, as though the end of pain was an exultation, a kind of rejoicing even if she knew it would come back again and bring the weakness with it. So many young men— they had everything to live for. Everything. The bald one, Koprow, was coming up the aisle, pushing through the throng. She felt herself shiver. He sat in the seat next to her and reached out and took her hand gently, holding it between his own. She looked at him, but there was something, an essence to this man, that she didn't comprehend. It wasn't anything she might easily penetrate; he was locked inside himself, tight, like wax that had hardened. An absence of love and loving. Even the way he held her hand suggested cruelty. She removed her fingers slowly, hiding the hand under her travel rug.

"How are you now?" he asked.

She didn't answer. Across the wet, glistening concrete she could see a building, people passing back and forth behind windows. Shadows. Shadows in the rain.

Koprow sighed. "An unpleasant day," he said. "Do you know the name of this city?"

She said nothing.

"Washington," Koprow said. "The capital of the United States."

She remembered, like a flash of light that suggested a candle blown out abruptly, Aaron: *I'd like to go to America one day to live. To emigrate, build a new life. A different life.* But it might have been a voice in a tomb coming to her through damp distances, tunnels.

The capital city of the United States of America.

Koprow took something from his pocket. It was a photograph, a small snapshot he held in the palm of his hand. She looked at it slowly. It was of a young man, a face that was in some fashion familiar to her, as if she might have seen it in a newspaper once. But what was she to know? A peasant—what was she supposed to know?

"This man is Mallory," Koprow said.

She opened her mouth. Young. Dear God, help

me, help me now, for this is the time of my need, this is the time. How can the killing stop? She shut her eyes. A young face, a kind face.

"I show it to you because I don't want you to forget your final task, my dear."

My dear, she thought. At the heart of the phrase there was poison. The final task.

"And then, of course, I will sign your papers." He patted her knee quickly a couple of times. "You will be free, Mrs. Blum. Free. Think about that."

Free—like the Chinese soldier they took to the wire and shot with their rifles, or like the young American who died, or like Andreyev, who had never returned, or Domareski, who was dead. Free—was that what he meant by freedom? The way he patted her, the sense of his touch—she could feel a chill across the surface of her flesh.

"I think we're ready to disembark," Koprow said, rising. The bald head, like some tiny dome, shone in the white overhead lights. "It has been arranged that you will fly directly from Washington to Israel tomorrow. This has all been taken care of."

*Tomorrow!*

She looked up at him, searching his face for a lie, for a sign of a lie she didn't want to find; no, she thought, you want to believe it, you need to believe it, you need to know that tomorrow will come and with it the end of all this nightmare, this long nightmare. He was smiling at her. Mallory. Why was his face so familiar? Why? A young man with a kind look. Was she supposed to destroy that on the basis of a promise she had heard over and over again? Was she supposed to do that? Tomorrow. In Koprow's world it was never tomorrow, was it? Tomorrow didn't come. Tomorrow was never the time.

She watched him turn away and push busily

through the crowd of young men. Then she looked through the window at the rain falling across the airport.

**3.**

Between Stafford and Triangle there was faraway lightning to the east, forking over the mouth of the Potomac. Then thunder he could hear even through the closed windows of the car, through the noise of the wipers slipping back and forth on the glass. In the rearview mirror he saw how quiet the kid had become, sitting now with her eyes shut, her hands clasped in her lap, and he wondered where she was at that moment, where her mind might have wandered. Isobel opened the glove compartment and took out the pistol, turning it over slowly in the palm of her hand.

"Nasty," she said. "Very nasty."

He glanced at it. She put it back, slamming the compartment shut. Up ahead traffic was slowing in a series of bright-red brake lights that flashed as if they were pulses.

"You're determined to go through with this?" she asked, although it wasn't so much a question as a statement of fact, despairing fact.

He nodded. She looked at him briefly. "Maybe the game will be canceled," she said. "Maybe you don't even need to do this."

*This,* he thought. Whatever it is.

"Maybe all this crazy rush through the rain isn't worth the effort, John."

And maybe there isn't a plan to kill Mallory. Maybe, maybe—you could say it often enough and reduce the whole world to a sequence of conditionals. Maybe the earth is flat. Maybe Chip Alexander has the number of this car. Maybe my brother took his own life, after all. Maybe, too, all the dead are brought back to life.

"John, seriously," Isobel said.

"I've been listening."

"Well?"

"Well, what?"

"Maybe this isn't even necessary—"

He looked at her a moment, then back to the road. "Maybe it isn't. You could be right."

"And I could be wrong."

"Yeah. Somewhere between the two there's an absence of hard options, Isobel."

She sat upright, stretching her legs. "The difference between you and Richard is that he wouldn't have dashed through the rain like this. He would have picked up the telephone and called a couple of numbers. That way, at least, he would have stayed dry."

"The difference is that he had the numbers to call. I don't exactly have choices."

She was silent for a time. She rubbed her knees with the open palms of her hands. "Did they train you for this, John? I mean, did they sit you down in a classroom and explain what the procedure is when you stumble onto a plot to kill the President? How To Prevent Assassinations 101? Was is like that?"

He pulled the Pinto out into the fast lane, passing a truck, an ice-cream van, and a bookmobile with a Prince William County sign. That tone in her voice: how quickly incredulity yielded to heavy sarcasm. He couldn't think of what to say; all he wanted now was silence, quiet, an end to her disbelief.

"Maybe they called the class How To Be a Hero and Get a Pretty Medal?" she said.

"For Christ's sake," he said.

"You tell me, then. You tell me what they called it."

It came out before he could stop it. "I often wondered what drove my brother to death. Now I know."

She twisted away from him. There was an odd silence punctured by the noise of the car, the wipers, the rain on glass. It was a goddam stupid thing to say. Cut out your tongue, Rayner. If she doesn't believe, then who are you to force it on her? Take it from her perspective and see how it looks. A gunman tramples through her garden, she has to run, she hasn't stopped running—how could you blame her?

"Look, I'm sorry. I didn't mean that."

Suddenly she was laughing, a muffled sound made against the palm of her hand. It was the kind of laugh that cuts ice, dissolves tensions. She put her hand on his shoulder and said, "I'm sorry too. Really. I was just suddenly . . . bewildered. I mean. My whole life. I was thinking about my life and I was looking out of this window and it occurred to me that I was being hauled through the countryside for God knows what. . . . Shit, I don't think I'm making sense. I still haven't managed to inter the old self, John. Sometimes she comes out with claws on, that's all."

He touched her hand. Tension, a rope stretched between two points and tightened, and you wonder how long it will hold. Her old self. He tried to remember his own old self, as if what he was seeking had been broken apart in a prism. London, reading the telexes, interviewing the hopefuls—an easy, uneventful life, a nice life. And then a man leaps through a window and some part of that old self jumps alongside him: a tiny suicide all your own.

"Forget it," he said. "You're doing okay."

She brushed hair from her forehead. "I wonder."

The kid leaned forward from the back and tapped Rayner lightly on the shoulder and said, "If you two don't quit arguing you won't notice the fuzz directly behind."

Rayner looked in the rearview mirror. There. Immediately behind him—the flashing lights of a car of the Virginia Highway Patrol. Without thinking, he slowed the Pinto to the side of the road.

"At a time like this," Isobel said.

The kid blew an enormous pink bubble that swelled and suddenly popped.

"At a time like this," Rayner said, waiting for the cop to emerge, trying to control his own quick rush of panic.

## 4.

Outside the White House Patrick J. Mallory stood beneath a black umbrella held by an aide. Through the rain flashbulbs popped; the damned photographers getting all this bleakness down forever on celluloid, Mallory thought. He looked up at the grim sky, then turned to Callaway, who stood at his side.

"Is there a hope that the game will be canceled?" he asked.

"I doubt it, sir," Callaway said.

Patrick J. Mallory smiled at the photographers. "What's keeping the damn car, Callaway?"

"It ought to be here," Callaway said.

Dispersed throughout the group of photographers and quite outnumbering them were the anonymous gentlemen of the Secret Service. Mallory understood that he was known as Hopper to these men, although the implications of this name were lost to him. He looked at Callaway and said, "I've heard of men who would give an arm and a leg for this job. You know that?"

Callaway smiled. "I've heard something like it."

"If you could take that figure of speech and turn it into a literal thing, you'd see people running on crutches all over Capitol Hill and trying to eat their lunches with little metal claws."

Callaway, still smiling, stared through the rain. "A city of amputees. It makes you think. A whole town of Long John Silvers."

"The pirate image is appropriate anyway," Mallory said, stamping a foot with impatience. "You know, I should have sent Lindholm to this soccer game. He would have liked it better than me. Is it too late for me to develop flu? Fall over and sprain an ankle?"

"It's never too late, Mr. President," Callaway said. "The Vice President is in Kansas, however."

"Chewing tobacco, I guess. Goddam. He *loves* to shake hands and have his picture taken. We could have let the old fart meet this soccer entourage." Mallory turned his head slightly and saw the thickset man with the black briefcase who was forever close at hand. Mallory stared at him for a moment: the black case, and what it ultimately controlled, had come to him in the worst of his dreams. He said to Callaway, "That guy's like the reaper. Can't we do something about him? Like give him the slip? He leaves me with bad feelings."

The limousine appeared, preceded by a car of the Secret Service and followed by a group of other dark vehicles. Mallory was reminded of a funeral procession. Callaway stepped forward and opened the door and Mallory got in, wearily smiling one last time for the photographers. It was a reward for their diligence in the rain. Callaway got in beside the President.

"I don't think there's anything we can do about the reaper, Mr. President," Callaway said.

"Like Lindholm, he comes with the job."

"He comes with the job, sir."

The door was slammed shut by a large man in a navy-blue raincoat; a grim face, grimmer in the wretched weather. The car moved forward.

Mallory, gazing out at the rain, sighed. "I never asked you if you liked soccer," he said.

"I don't believe I've ever seen a game," Callaway said. "But I'm quite looking forward to it."

"Then I should've sent you, Callaway, and stayed home with some unmentionable ailment—like diarrhea."

Mallory shifted around uncomfortably in his seat. The Secret Service ahead, the Secret Service behind: there was no privacy left, only protection.

## 5.

The cop had a thin, angular face such as might have been carved out of a rutabaga for some old Halloween. Rayner rolled down his window and watched the cop blink against the rain that ran across his eyelids.

"Got your license?"

Rayner thought about Alexander now; he thought about the humming of wires, the bulletins. He reached inside his jacket slowly for the license and said, "What's the problem?"

The cop smiled. "What's the problem? The problem is you seem illiterate, mister. Illiterate—like an inability to read highway signs. Such as speed limits."

Speed limits, Rayner thought. Was that all? A ticket for a moving violation? Was that *all* this was about?

"I clocked you at seventy-three," the cop said, taking the license. "The zone is clearly marked at fifty-five. Not just in the state of Virginia but all across the nation. Step out of the car."

"Is that necessary?" Rayner asked.

"Would I ask?" The cop looked at the license as Rayner opened the door and stood in the miserable rain. "John Douglas Rayner," the cop said. He stared a moment longer, as if he might find some arcane discrepancy, then walked back to his patrol car. Rayner was cold, shivering now, watching the patrolman reach inside his car for his radio. Into the computer, Rayner thought. A matter of moments. He panicked again, wondering if his name had been marked, if an order to detain for questioning had been registered yet. He looked at Isobel, who shrugged, raised her hand with her fingers crossed: a token of luck, of good fortune. We need it about now, Rayner thought. He watched the traffic slide past, the curious faces pressed to windows, the reflections of the red and blue lights. What was keeping the sonofabitch? You put a name and number over the radio, it slides through the banks of the computer, it comes back clean—a simple electronic operation. So what was keeping him? He saw the patrolman put the radio mike back inside his car and walk toward him. The ticket book was out now and Rayner felt a sense of relief. Okay, give me my ticket, let me get on my way. *If I'm clean, if I'm clean and clear and free.*

"Headed for D.C.?" the cop asked.

Rayner nodded. That chill in the rain.

"Take it easy, fella. It isn't going anywhere so far as I know." He began to write the speeding ticket. A joker, Rayner thought. A clown in a patrol car. He took his license back and stuffed the ticket inside his pocket. The cop, as if there remained some slight suspicion still, crouched and looked inside the Pinto.

"Driving too fast in this weather." The cop shook his head. "You ought to have some consideration for your family."

"I appreciate it," Rayner said, opening his door. He had to get away before any kind of lecture started. I've kidnapped a kid, I'm being looked for by a certain Government agency with headquarters in Langley; what do I need with your lectures now?

The cop stepped back from the Pinto. He watched Rayner close his door. "Take it easy," the cop said.

"I promise," Rayner said. He slipped the car back into the stream of traffic, conscious of time again, of his own damp clothing; time and weather, a twin conspiracy. He put his foot hard on the gas and swung out into the fast lane.

The kid sat forward. "Just for a minute I thought that was it," she said. "My father must be climbing walls."

"More than your father who's climbing," Rayner said. He passed a truck filled with damp timber precariously stacked. "More than just your father."

## 6.

She felt sick again on the bus from the airport. Even as she had been wheeled past the men with cameras at the airport she had experienced a dark wave of nausea, of weakness. Strength—it was something that flew out of you, a vulture that came and went. She opened her eyes a little and looked out into the rain. There was a stretch of swollen gray water beneath a bridge. Beside her, Katya rose and went down the aisle of the bus to talk with Koprow. Koprow, who raised one hand dismissively in the air as if whatever the woman was saying to him had no relevance whatever. The woman stood and looked down at him—a picture of tension, of inflexibility, a tightness of face, a hardening in the eyes. They hate each other, she thought. Even from here I can feel it, like a heat. Hatred. She looked down once more at the river and thought: Washington. Pictures from some forgotten picture book, lost frames, flickers. She turned to look back at Katya and wondered where they were going on this bus through the rain—

Suddenly, unexpectedly, she caught it.

*Where are you where are you*

She closed her eyes. It took a strength she didn't have to shut her mind; it was like trying to force some heavy door shut with a palsied hand, knowing it couldn't be done but straining at it anyhow.

*Please*

She opened her eyes and saw Katya sit stiffly in the vacant seat beside her. Katya, she thought. Afraid of me, yes—afraid of what I can do because she has experienced it; but there's a confidence in her fear, a wariness, because she also knows I can't hurt her now. I only hurt myself if

*Tell me where*

The old woman looked from the window. This voice, this thin voice. Why wouldn't it go away from her?

"How are you feeling?" Katya asked.

There was nothing in the tone of voice, an expressionless thing. How are you feeling? As if it mattered to her in any concerned sense, as if it mattered.

She thought of snow, of how the train had gone through the snow, of the blizzard slashing at the windows endlessly white.

"Well? *How are you feeling?*"

Mrs. Blum turned her face, pressing her skin against the glass of the window. She realized the woman wanted to hurt her, wanted her dead; she realized this with a confused mixture of pity and dread, pity for her lack of feeling, dread because she saw her own fate inextricably bound up with that of the woman—a coupling of destiny, something over which there was no control.

*Where are you*

She wouldn't answer this, she wouldn't answer. Tomorrow, she thought. He had promised a plane, he had promised the papers, the freedom. I want to believe. Dear God, let me believe.

*Where*

"I feel fine," she said. "Can't you tell? Can't you tell how I feel?"

Katya said nothing.

"Tomorrow," the old woman said. "He has promised tomorrow."

A look, an expression, something vague and indistinct crossed Katya's face and then was gone. The old woman stared at her, puzzled, disturbed, wondering at the look, wanting to go inside her, to tunnel deep into her for an explanation of that look—but she didn't. There was dread only now; the pity had gone. A lie? Was that it? More lies? Lies heaped on lies, every task the final one? She closed her eyes once more, afraid of her own impulses to hurt this wretched woman, to break her mind as if it were no more than thin ice, to drive her into a madness from which there was no exit. Strength, no strength.

*Please tell me*

"Give me my photographs," she said to the woman. "I want my pictures."

Katya opened a bag, a canvas bag, and took out the snapshots. Painfully, struggling with her own knotted muscles, Mrs. Blum took the pictures and spread them in her lap and thought, as she stared at the colors, the faces, the looks of love: I must think only of these, concentrate only on these, for nothing else matters now. Not when you're damned anyhow. Not when you're already damned. It was not even a delicate balance, an even equation: some brief time of love weighed against the blackness of whatever eternity you were destined to enter.

*Where please*

She spread the photographs with her clumsy hands. She would think of nothing else.

**7.**

In the limousine, as it approached Lincoln Park on East Capitol Street, Mallory said, "I don't think I'd mind this damn game so much if it wasn't for having to sit down and eat food with that little shit Leontov. Something about that guy makes me lose my appetite."

Callaway, who had been peering out across the rainy park, looked at the President. "I know what you mean."

"He gives me what you might call the willies," Mallory said. "There's something about him."

"An oily quality?"

"Oily. Yeah. That's a fair word."

The President looked at the park. The limousine, following some obscure prearranged route created by the tortuous strategies of the Secret Service—by men who would consider a hundred options only to choose the most perplexing, the most difficult—turned onto Kentucky Avenue. There were times when he longed for simplicity in his life, but complexity, like Lindholm, came with the job.

"Maybe you can give me a quick rundown on the rules of this game, Callaway," he said. "I don't want to look like a total ass."

Callaway reached into his coat and produced a small booklet. "You might like to glance at this."

"What is it?"

"The rules of the game, Mr. President."

"You think that little shit Leontov understands them?" He took the book from Callaway and flicked the pages. He shrugged and then shut it. "It looks more complex than our income-tax proposals. Maybe I can pick up on it as the game goes along."

"I would think so," Callaway said.

## 8.

They had to stop in a rest area because the kid was sick. Isobel took her inside the bathroom while Rayner, sheltering beneath a stone arch that housed a detailed map of Washington, watched the traffic heading toward the capital. She had become sick quite suddenly, her face white, her movements limp and uncoordinated. He waited with increasing impatience. He looked along the row of parked campers, trucks, cars with tourists: a whole catalog of out-of-state plates. So far, he thought, so far so good; at least he hadn't run into a roadblock or been hauled over by an unmarked car carrying Alexander and friend.

These were pluses in a situation where any break was a kind of joy. He stared at the illuminated map, raising his finger and pinpointing D.C. Stadium. A short hop, he noticed, from Congressional Cemetery—and a sudden memory of Richard, of coming down to Washington for the first time to visit with Richard when he was, as he phrased it, "a lackey in State," the old days before he met and married Isobel. They had done the tour bit, seen all the monuments and statues and all the places wherein the country's business was conducted, finishing the day at Congressional Cemetery, where Richard had fantasized being buried alongside John Philip Sousa. *Quaint, ain't it?* They had stood in front of the bizarre grave of one Marion Ooletia Kahlert, Washington's first traffic victim, crushed under the wheels of an automobile in 1904 at the age of ten. "Imagine," Richard had said, "imagine being planted here. Your claim to immortality is something so simple as falling under a goddam car, for Christ's sake." Poor Richard—a mixture of the mordant and the morbid. Remembering, Rayner felt extremely cold, damp, unhappy.

Now, as he watched the banality of traffic streaming through the rain, saw tourists flip map pages inside wet cars, watched some nut trying to get a Coleman stove stoked up in the open doorway of his camper, it was hard to think of places beyond the normal, hard to think of the supranormal, call it what you like. You had to keep convincing yourself over and over and over—yeah, it's a possibility. It's a chance. It could be. Too many connections, too many openings, too many of those dots you could join with straight lines.

A cop car came into the rest area just as Isobel, her arm around the kid, ran through the rain to the shelter of the arch. Rayner watched the car slide slowly along the line of parked vehicles.

Isobel shook her wet hair. "She's feeling rough, John. I don't know what it is. I couldn't get her to throw up. She just keeps saying she feels bad."

Rayner looked at the kid, who was staring at him in a way that might have been accusatory: *You kidnap me for this?* He knelt in front of her and took her hands in his own; they were cold.

"Tell me," he said. "Tell me what it is. What you feel."

"Like sick," she said.

"How?"

"Ever had flu? You know how it is before it starts? Well, that's how I feel. Hot and cold. An ucky feeling in my head."

"I don't have much time," Rayner said, trying to sound patient and rational. Isobel started to say something, then stopped. "Fiona, I don't have time. You don't have time either because getting sick now is like some kind of luxury. Do you understand me?"

The kid nodded. She leaned against the stone wall. She stuck her hands in the pockets of her jeans and there was something stubborn in the gesture.

"Please," Rayner said. "If I didn't think it was important, I wouldn't ask."

He glanced at Isobel. He could see it written on her face: give it up, we've humored you long enough, and now all you're doing is making this child sick. How much more destruction are you going to drag us through?

He looked at the kid again. "What's making you sick? Do you know?"

She shrugged. "I guess it's something to do with *her.*"

"The woman?"

"I guess."

"How? Try and explain."

"I've been trying, I've really been trying, and I know she's near, I mean I *feel* that, but it's like she's closing me out, do you know what I mean?"

"No, I don't know exactly. I'm trying like hell to understand it. Is it making you ill? The effort or what? Is that it?"

"I guess. I don't know."

Rayner stood upright. His damp clothes adhered to him uncomfortably; he wanted to sleep. Something—a slight despair, a sense of uselessness—assailed him.

I haven't been schooled in heroics, he thought. I haven't had on-the-job training. Up the Amazon in a canoe, over Niagara Falls in a barrel, planting the U.S. flag on Everest, or even something simple like smuggling a Bulgarian dissident in the trunk of your car across the Greek border. It was a desk job, rummaging through the lives of the helpless and the unhappy, that's all it was. Now you're thinking in terms of saving Patrick J. Mallory from—

"I think the game's over, John," Isobel said all at once.

He followed the line of her eyes to where the Pinto was parked. The cop car had stopped alongside it; the patrolman was getting out, walking around the Pinto, staring at the license-plate number. Fuck, Rayner thought.

"I think we've reached the end of a very odd line," she said.

Was there relief in her voice? Why wouldn't there be? She could go home and put the nightmare away, stick it in the soil with seeds and disperse it and listen to the tide at nights and get her act back together. No, goddammit. I won't come this far for this. I won't let it slip now. The cop was returning to his patrol car now; he got inside, leaving the door open.

He was using his radio. Okay, Rayner thought. Why couldn't the kid do something with the cop's brain? Blow his mind away? Put him into bottom gear—like a temporary state of amnesia? But if she had that talent she hadn't used it when Alexander was on the scene— ergo, she didn't have it. Something else, then. One of your less spiritual techniques.

He looked at the guy in the doorway of the camper who was still intent on the dumb task of lighting a Coleman stove, hands pumping, matches burning, rain running over his baseball cap. Saving the life of the President isn't the job it used to be, he thought. It's irregular hours, discomfort, dampness, and downright inconvenience all along the line.

He took the kid's hand. It was still chilly, fingers of ice. Kidnap, theft of classified documents—what was simple vehicular theft by comparison?

"That camper over there," he said.

"No," Isobel answered quickly. "You can't."

"When you're crazy, kid, you might as well go all out."

"John, no."

He stared at Isobel. What would it be like to leave her beneath this stone arch, this piece of architectural camp, and run with the kid?

"Look. Either you're in this thing or you're not. What the fuck do you think you can do? Go back to your goddam pillows and your plants? No way, love. *No way.* When you've been this long in my company, you're an equal partner—and that makes you a nifty candidate for the headhunters as well."

He moved toward the camper. There was a rush of wind, a squall, through the rain. The child, limp, seemed to have no will left of her own. She didn't resist when he moved. He heard Isobel come up behind.

"Okay," she was saying. "If it's madness you're after then you're going to need some company."

Good girl, he thought, it makes a change from your little crystal dinner parties in Georgetown; and what good is a life without extremes? From hostess to drop-out to fugitive: the needle of some existential compass gone berserk.

He stopped by the camper. The guy—bearded, slight, wearing damp lederhosen—looked as if he had come out of the wilderness.

"Having problems?"

The bearded man groaned. "Damn stove," he said.

"They can be real pains," Rayner said sympathetically.

"I been pumping and pumping—"

"Maybe it's out of fuel?"

"Naw," the guy said, staring at the stove. "I checked that already."

Rayner looked at the license plates. South Carolina. There was a dealer's logo attached to the plate: *Dorfman's Rec Vee, Orangeburg, S.C.*

"I know a thing or two about those stoves," Rayner said. "You want me to take a look-see?"

The bearded man smiled. "I sure as hell wish somebody would. Getting a flame going in that thing's like getting a goddam genie out of a lamp." He laughed at his own simile and looked at Rayner for response. Rayner dutifully laughed. Keys, he was thinking. You better hope this turkey's left his keys in the dash. It was fifty-fifty. You step out of the cab and come around the shell of the camper to the back door—did you pocket your keys for so short a trip? He tried to look through the camper, the interior gloom, to see if the keys were inside, but it wasn't one of those vehicles with a connecting door. Camper and cab were sealed off from each other. Damn. He pretended to examine the Coleman. He made a series of pontifical noises, like an expert, an archaeologist dating a skull fragment, a physician humming over an X-ray.

"Simple," Rayner said. "Goddam thing's wet."

"Wet?"

"Sure. Look." Rayner pointed vaguely. "Stands to reason you won't get it stoked if it's wet. You want to dry it off. Paper towels."

"I guess." The guy scratched his scalp, pushing the baseball cap back. He picked up the stove and closed it so that it looked like a briefcase of green metal.

"Well. Thanks a lot. Mighty nice of you folks to take the time. Trouble nowadays is nobody gives a hoot about others. Makes a real fine change when you run into people that care." He touched the peak of his cap and began to move toward the bathrooms. Go, Rayner thought, grinning foolishly in the rain. Go. Forget your keys, if there are keys. He watched the guy go under the stone arch, where he paused as if he had recollected something. But Rayner was already ushering the kid toward the cab. He opened the door that lay on the guy's blind side and saw—shining, wonderful, attached to a sham turquoise key ring—the keys hanging from the ignition. He stood back and let Isobel climb in after the girl, let them slide across the bench seat, then he got in and started the motor. The owner would raise hell, but even raising hell took a few minutes, and by the time he had noticed the cop in the rest area, by the time he had supplied the data the cop would need, by the time he had finished bitching about the breakdown of American civilization, Rayner would have a five- or six-minute start. Maybe. Just maybe, he thought.

"If you want my advice, John, you ought to get off the highway as soon as you can," Isobel said.

"My very thoughts," Rayner said.

Between them, the girl leaned forward suddenly, clutching her stomach, her body stiff and rigid, her hands twisted, her mouth open and slack—and for a moment Rayner wondered if she was dying.

**9.**

In the executive dining room at D.C. Stadium, which had been sealed off by Secret Service men, Mallory shook hands with Ambassador Leontov. It was an infirm handshake, slack and loose, like a dead fish in your palm. Mallory understood that because of the seating arrangements he was obliged to sit next to Leontov, both during lunch and throughout the game itself. He shook a great many hands in the dining room: representatives of the American Soccer Federation, the Soviet trainer, the trainer's interpreter, executives of the stadium organization, the entire Soviet team, the entire American team—neither of which would be sitting down to lunch; a matter of dietary strategy before a game, he was told—and even the hands of the waiters and waitresses who would be serving the meal.

He sat down with Leontov on his right and a man called MacMillan, the president of the American Soccer Federation, on his left. The doorways were blocked by the Secret Service men. The whole stadium would be policed, crawling with agents, plainclothes cops, security guards. It was, he reflected in a bemused way, a strange feeling to sit down to a meal that had been prepared in such stringent conditions.

He looked across the table at Callaway; on a chair by the door sat the reaper with his black case. One could imagine, Mallory thought, how the Pharaohs must have felt; the problem was that of keeping at bay the insidious intoxication of power.

MacMillan, who spoke in a subdued Scottish accent, was a tidy man with a small white moustache and a layer of white hair neatly combed flat. "I understand, Mr. President, that this will be your first experience of our game?" he asked.

"I'm looking forward to it," Mallory said. A plate of vegetable soup was pushed in front of him. "I expect to have it explained to me."

"It's not difficult, sir," said MacMillan, spooning some soup with a hand that trembled slightly.

The Presidential aura, Mallory thought. It sends out vibrations. He sipped some soup, which was watery, laid his spoon down, and turned to Leontov. "You want to predict the outcome, Mr. Ambassador?" he asked.

"Only a fool would predict," Leontov said. He smiled in a quick way.

"You expect your side to win?"

The Ambassador nodded. "Of course. But I think the game has made such enormous strides here in America that the result will be a close one."

Mallory looked down into his soup, perceiving a piece of floating carrot that had collided with limp parsley. What was it about the little shit? he wondered. What was it? Something more than the usual scumminess of his personality. A nervous quality, perhaps. Maybe he was a soccer nut and the result was of some real—rather than diplomatic—import to him.

"I think it will be very close," Leontov said.

"But fair."

"As you say, Mr. President. One trusts that violence will not be allowed to interfere with the proceedings." Leontov nodded his head slightly.

Poached fish of some kind was brought. Tasteless and flaky. Mallory picked at it in a halfhearted way, wondering if he might ascribe his unease to the hypocrisy of sitting down to lunch with a representative of Maksymovich's regime.

Leontov said, "A moment ago you asked me for a prediction. I've been turning that question over in my mind."

"I thought you said only fools make forecasts," Mallory said.

"On certain occasions, perhaps there's a fine line between recklessness and foolishness. It's only a game, after all. I think the Soviet team will win. But only by a single goal."

Mallory smiled. "Are you a gambling man, Mr. Ambassador?"

Leontov shrugged. He looked faintly uncertain.

"I've got a dollar that says you're on the wrong horse," Mallory said.

"A wager?" The Ambassador, smiling, displayed a flake of fish stuck to his upper dentures. "I accept, Mr. President. Gladly."

## 10.

For the past fifteen minutes or so Isobel had been holding the girl against her body, rocking her slightly, rubbing her forehead with the palm of her hand. "She's like ice, John. I've never felt anybody so cold."

Rayner, whose attention had been divided by watching the rearview mirror and glancing at the kid, pulled the camper over to the side of the street. He looked for a moment at Fiona. The stiffness—there was something quite unnatural about the rigidity of her body, as if it were less human than humanoid, something lifeless pressed out of a mold. He reached over and touched the back of her hand, feeling coldness even before his fingers had made contact. What now? Just what do you do now? He had intended to dump the camper, and with it his sense of vulnerability, but how could you walk through the streets with a kid who looked like she was dead and fail to draw some attention to yourself? He had crossed the Rochambeau Memorial Bridge sometime before; now, after a series of turns out of the mainstream of traffic, he realized he was somewhere in the vicinity of the Fort McNair War College and the Anacostia River just beyond.

He looked morosely through the windshield, tapping his fingers on the rim of the steering wheel. His only certainty now was that the camper had to be abandoned. He wasn't even sure anymore of his assumption that the kid's old woman would be in the stadium; why did she have to be anyhow? He had simply assumed it. But whatever her force was, it surely had the capacity to cross distances. Ah, despair—she could be almost anywhere, the proverbial needle in the psychic haystack. Pennsylvania even—what difference did it make? He watched two naval officers cross the street. Crisp movements: they might have been looking for someone to salute.

Only the kid can tell, he thought. I sit in this hot camper and think: Only the kid can know. He turned to look at Isobel, noticing her weariness in lines around her mouth, in the way her hair hung uncombed.

"You can't put her through any more of this,"

she said. "There's a point, John, where you have to pause and wonder if you're being reasonable—"

"And I passed that point a while back," he said. He looked out at the rain. "All I know is I've got to get this pile of steel off my back before it's too damn late."

Isobel said nothing. She held the girl's face to her breasts, an unexpected little moment of maternalism, touching in its fashion if he had had the time to be touched. The kid moaned and moved her head slightly. Rayner slid across the bench seat and put his hands against her cheeks, trying to turn her face this way and that way as if it were possible to massage this dreadful stiffness out of her. Come on, kid, he thought. Come through for me. He was aware of Isobel's grip on the girl, her defensive hold—another thing he would have to break through.

"Fiona," he said.

Isobel sighed.

"Fiona," he repeated. He rubbed the sides of her face gently, noticing how dirty his hands had become along the way, the darkened fingernails, a film of grease. "Fiona."

The child's lips moved. But there was no sound.

"Fiona, where is this woman? Can you tell me?"

Nothing.

"Can you tell me?"

Again, nothing. He was irritated; despite whatever better feelings might have prevailed—sympathy, a hint of some compassion—he was annoyed by her lack of response. He took his hands away from her and looked once more through the windshield. Christ, what now? What now? And suddenly everything he had pieced together seemed thinly circumstantial, ludicrously fragile, as solid as the filaments of a spider's web. He started up the motor of the camper and pulled away from the sidewalk, looking for M Street, where a right turn would take him in the direction of the stadium—where else? What else did he have left?

"It's all the way then?" Isobel asked. Her voice was flat.

"It has to be," he said. "You've got a better suggestion?"

Her silence was a reply of its own, a suggestion more profound than any words might have been. He looked quickly at the kid. Her lips were moving noiselessly and he was reminded of an autistic child foraging through the mysteries of its own condition for the simpler mystery of speech.

He reached M Street.


# 11.

It was a room of white tiles, cool and dark, filled with smells of wintergreen oil. She could hear the rattle of voices coming from elsewhere, from close by, perhaps even from the adjoining room. There were gray metal cabinets, lockers of some kind, and she thought it funny somehow that she couldn't imagine their purpose, their function. Another door, halfway open, led into a lit room. Through this space she could see more tiles, gleaming from overhead tubes of light. A shadow moved. There was a noise of running water. Now, rumbling slightly, the voice of the man they called Charek. The other voices were stilled.

She looked down at her photographs, which she could barely see in the dimly lit room. She shut out Charek's voice as she had done with that other voice— the sound of the child, the sound that came in a series of plaintive cries. She looked at the snapshots, unable to feel them in her numb hands, yet trying to imagine the contours of flesh from the tips of her fingers. She could hardly hold them, light as they were; she could hardly find the strength to keep them secure in her hands. I mustn't drop them, she thought. I mustn't drop them. I have to think of nothing else.

She closed her eyes.

*Please tell me I need to find*

The persistence of the child. The sheer persistence. She would snap, snap and die, if she went on. She opened her eyes and gazed at the slit of light through the half-open door. That shadow—was it Koprow? The woman? Both of them? She closed her eyes again because even sight was a terrible effort now.

*Help me find you*

God—one of the snapshots, one that depicted her son's wife, Yael, standing in front of a blue swimming pool with the two children splashing in the water behind her—it slid from her fingers to the floor; it just slipped and fell and she watched it flutter across her knees, over her rug, and touch her foot before it finally landed some yards away from the wheelchair. I have to pick it up, I have to pick it up, I can't leave it lying there like that, just like a discarded piece of trash. And she tried to move, pressing her elbows against the sides of the chair. But she forgot about the rest of the snapshots she held, and they fell also. The whole floor covered with bright colors—how could she get up and bend and retrieve them? She slumped back into the wheelchair, panicked by the sight of the photographs strewn across the floor, panicked and upset, sickened by her own loss of strength. If I lean forward, if I lean forward and fall, if I crawl, she thought. I could do it that way. I could do it that way, she thought.

**12.**

Koprow put the bar of white soap back in its little tray, looked at himself in the mirror a moment, seeing not only his own reflection but that of Katya—Katya, standing against the wall with her arms folded—and then turned around. He pulled a length of towel from the wall and began to dry his hands. The damned woman, he thought. What right had she to dictate the terms of the thing?

He looked toward the open door and into the darkened room where the old woman had been placed. Her proximity irritated him. Katya unfolded her arms and pushed herself away from the wall. Bitch, Koprow thought. Skinny, hard-assed bitch.

"Andreyev understood her powers better than anybody," the woman said in a low voice.

"Unfortunately Andreyev chose to take his own route to salvation," Koprow said.

"In this situation, *he* would have insisted that she be kept as close as possible to the subject," Katya said. "I don't believe you grasp the intensity of energy that is expended in an act like this, Comrade Koprow."

"She should be in a hotel somewhere. Miles away," Koprow said. Blue in the face, he thought. One could argue oneself to a standstill against the stubbornness of this woman.

"In her condition, Comrade, her proximity to the subject is essential. The farther away you put her, the less likely are the chances of success. It's as simple as that. She's sick. She's going to die. I don't think we ought to delude ourselves. Put her miles away, as you suggest, and you are guaranteed failure—"

Koprow nodded. He looked at his pink, clean hands. It still galled him to have the old Jewess so close when he had imagined that everything could be accomplished from a far distance—a hotel in the city, a room in the Embassy, another place. Not here, not in the stadium itself. He looked at his own image in the mirror and thought: What difference does it ultimately make? All that the world will know is that the President of the United States died at a soccer match. That's all. It was the end that counted.

He turned around, smoothing one hand over the surface of his bald skull, and looked at the woman. "Very well. After all, *you're* the expert."

Their whispered conversation lapsed into silence. He wondered what he might do to ruin this awful woman when they returned home. Something altogether simple could be arranged, such as the placing of Western propagandist documents in her flat and having them discovered. Then she would see. Then she would truly see.

There was suddenly a faint noise from the other room, the scratch of a wheel on the floor, the sound of someone sighing, he wasn't sure which. He watched Katya move to the door and open it, and he saw a flood of fluorescent light fall on the empty wheelchair.

## 13.

Mallory observed that the seating arrangements isolated the Presidential party from the rest of the crowd. A rope had been placed around a block of seats, perhaps about a hundred in all—many of which were unoccupied—and outside the rope there were as many as twenty Secret Service men. He sat with Leontov on one side, Macmillan on the other, and gazed down toward the field. Fresh white lines, obscuring a baseball diamond, had been drawn on the turf.

Now, as he stared down at the strange markings, rectangles and circles, he barely listened to MacMillan, who seemed intent on explaining the rules of the game to him. He looked at his watch. It was twenty minutes to three. Twenty minutes of watching the field, peering at the rain, listening to MacMillan drone. Strange, incomprehensible terms—offside, throw-in, corner kick, indirect free kick. Old Kimball, he reflected, was much better at this kind of thing—absorbing, listening, nodding his head; at least, he was better at *pretending* to be interested.

He watched rain fall through the goal nets. Twenty minutes of this. Various photographers on the other side of the rope clicked their cameras. Curious onlookers elsewhere strained to get a glimpse of him. The President as object, he thought; would he ever become accustomed to it? Would he ever adjust to the fact that he was as much a part of the Washington sight-seeing tour as the Lincoln Memorial? He looked across the stadium, noticing great spaces of empty seats.

Politely he asked MacMillan the expected size of the crowd.

"On a good day we would have drawn, oh, maybe forty-five thousand," MacMillan said. "In this rain—it's so hard to tell."

MacMillan nervously rubbed his hands together. On Mallory's other side, Leontov was lighting a cigarette: a distant Leontov, preoccupied with something, brooding, pondering. It could be the prospect of losing a dollar, the President thought. It could easily be that.

# 6

Rayner parked the camper in the parking lot at D.C. General Hospital. He sat for a moment and watched an ambulance whine through the rain in the direction of Nineteenth Street—somewhere somebody is dying, he thought. The quick occlusion, the diastolic catastrophe, the avalanche in the heart. He turned to Isobel, who was still holding the kid. Fiona, her eyes open, was gazing toward the hospital—mindless, Rayner thought, mindless and empty; what in the name of God have I done? Isobel sat with her eyes shut, rocking the girl slightly. He looked at her wristwatch; it was ten minutes before three. Ten fucking minutes. What if it had happened already? What if he was altogether wrong? You nurture alternatives like seedlings in a nursery. You erect opaque greenhouses in which to plant possibilities—

It wasn't far to the stadium, a matter of some blocks. Isobel opened her eyes and looked toward the hospital, as if she wanted to say, You've come to the right place, John. You've come at last to the right place—both for the child and for yourself. She licked her lips, which appeared cracked and dry, but she said nothing. It was all in her look, in her eyes. The stadium, he thought. The impossible stadium. He touched the mascot that hung from the rearview mirror of the cab, a dangling plastic spider. Webs, he thought. The struggle of the fly.

He reached out and took the kid's cold hands and rubbed them briskly. I must make her warm, he told himself. I must rub the life back into her. That coldness, that chill—it was like running your hands over the surface of frost. She moved her head slightly to the side, and momentarily it seemed to him that she was about to say something, but she didn't speak. He raised his hands to her face, turning her around to look at him. If the eyes are mirrors, he thought, these eyes have no images to reflect. Please, kid. Is she there in the stadium? Can you take me to her? Can you? *Please.*

He watched her. Slowly, stiffly, she lifted her arm and touched the inner glass of the windshield with her fingertips, and it was clear to him that it took an immense effort of will for her to move even that much; it was almost as if the arm had been cranked up by a taut rope.

"What are you trying to tell me?" he asked. *"What are you trying to say?"*

She didn't move. She blinked her eyes, and the arm that had been raised fell suddenly into her lap. He thought: I need some psychic infusion for myself now; I need something of that gift, that curse, from the gods who dole these things out at random.

"Fiona, what are you trying to tell me? Is it the stadium? Is she in the stadium? Is that it? She's in there somewhere?" The girl's empty eyes looked at him, seeing nothing. In the stadium, *somewhere,* somewhere in the vastness of that bowl, the moving ramps, the crowds, the tunnels, the press box, the parking lots—where, for Christ's sake? Where? He switched the ignition on, looking a moment at Isobel; Isobel, who seemed now no longer a part of this venture but someone simply swept along on a tide over which there was no possible control. Not the Isobel he had felt some desire for, the Isobel who had said it was "too soon," but an absence of that person. Somebody else.

He swung the camper out onto Nineteenth Street, possessed by the feeling that he had nothing left to lose, that whatever had been lost was gone forever, carried away in a crazy rush—and now all that was important was to get to the stadium in time to do something, something he had not recognized yet, a misty act lying in the immediate future like an object obscured by a veil.

## 2.

"Help me," Koprow said. "Help me get her back in the chair."

They lifted Mrs. Blum, who had been trying to gather her photographs together, and lowered her into the wheelchair. She sat with her head slumped back while Katya, bending here and there in the room, picked up the fallen snapshots.

"My pictures," the old woman said.

Koprow knelt in front of her. He put his hand on the side of her wrist, feeling a skin that had the texture of old newspaper; a touch that appalled him somehow. He smiled reassuringly. "You can have your pictures back when your work is done," he said.

"You frighten us, my dear. You know you shouldn't try to get out of the chair like that."

The old woman didn't seem to be listening to him. She was watching the photographs in the other woman's hands. Katya played with them, shuffling them, flicking the edges of them.

"Please," the old woman said. "Please. I want my pictures."

"Later," Koprow said. "If you behave yourself."

There was silence. In the corridor a door was opened and there was the sound of feet moving past outside, the players going toward the tunnel that would take them out onto the field. Koprow listened for a moment. He was thinking of the TV cameras that would be recording the game. How could they fail to capture the sudden death of Patrick J. Mallory? On videotape for all the world to see—and not a single gunshot to be heard, not a wound to be found, nothing that all the autopsies in the world could possibly reveal with any degree of accuracy. A rupture of the brain—and they would have words of explanation for that: a blood clot, a cerebral hemorrhage; they would have forensic explanations—and like all such explanations, they would come after the fact.

He took the little pile of pictures from Katya and glanced at them briefly. These small icons of color— was that all she had to live for? He tried to imagine the emptiness of such a life, that it could be reduced to a series of celluloid fantasies—fantasies that could never be translated into any kind of reality.

"He is here in the stadium, my dear," he said.

The old woman was nervously watching the snapshots. "Please," she said. "I would like my pictures."

"I know you would," Koprow said. "I understand only too well. But the subject—the man we discussed, the picture I showed you—he is here now in the stadium, not far from this very room. Remember? Remember what we talked of? What you've got to do? The last task?''

He stuffed the photographs into the pocket of his coat and smiled at the old woman.

"You see how safe they are, Mrs. Blum? You don't need to worry about them coming to any harm." He stood upright. There was silence now from the corridor. The players would have reached the entrance to the field by this time. He patted his pocket. "I just want you to think about Mallory now. That's all. Just like you thought about the Chinese soldier, remember? The American, remember? I want you to think about Mallory now."

The old woman continued to watch him. What was that expression on her face? Loathing? Of course, he had seen it before in one of its various forms—overt, disguised, he knew it intimately. But there was an intensity to the old woman that frightened him suddenly.

"Tomorrow," he said. "You haven't forgotten tomorrow?"

"I haven't forgotten," she said.

"Then think of Mallory," he said sharply. "That's all you have to do now. Think of Mallory. It will be quick. Easy. A moment of pain for him and it will be finished. All over."

She watched him a moment longer, then closed her eyes.

### 3.

Mallory saw the American team run out into the rain. They wore a rather colorful uniform of red shirt, blue shorts, and white socks. They lined up in the center of the field, where they were joined by the Russians, dressed entirely in white with small hammer-and-sickle insignia woven on their shirts. Both teams shook hands, then dispersed; and there was a general period of what Mallory assumed was practice, several balls being kicked back and forth around the field.

"Warming up," MacMillan explained. "Then the referee will blow his whistle and call the team captains together for the toss."

"The toss?" Mallory asked.

"The coin, Mr. President. The one who chooses correctly can then elect which goal his team will defend in the first half of play."

"There's some advantage in that?"

MacMillan laughed quietly. "At times, Mr. President. A team may choose to play the first half with the wind behind them, for example, then hope that the wind drops before the second half."

Mallory watched the field for a time. "A team should have either a resident meteorologist then or else a witch doctor."

"Certain African teams," said MacMillan, with great seriousness, "make use of witch doctors."

What was the response to that one? Mallory clasped his hands together in his lap and watched the black-clad referee move to the center of the field, where he blew a whistle. After a few confusing moments during which the extra practice balls were removed from the field, the teams lined up—haphazardly, to Mallory's eyes.

"The greatest danger to our side is if Kazemayov, their number nine, is allowed any freedom," said MacMillan. "He'll have to be watched carefully by our defense."

"Mmm," Mallory said, nodding his head. He

watched the Russian defense pass the ball from man to man in a somewhat systematic manner. There were several lunges made by American players, who appeared overanxious in the early stages. But the Soviets moved the ball over the center line, where it was picked up by Kazemayov, who began to twist and turn, leaving a couple of stranded American defenders behind him.

"That's the one," said MacMillan, leaning forward with great interest. "Look at the balance. Look at the control."

Mallory watched the Russian dash toward the American goal seemingly at will. "Why doesn't somebody tackle him?" he asked. It bothered him to see a look of triumph on Leontov's face.

MacMillan shrugged. "A tackle would be appropriate, sir. But you'll notice that our defense is falling back to defend the goal. See that?"

Kazemayov had the ball directly in front of the American goal, where, rather arrogantly, he paused as if he were waiting for somebody to tackle him. Between him and the U.S. goalkeeper there were perhaps four or five defenders. Kazemayov waited, feigned to move in one direction, then shimmied in quite the opposite, leaving the American defense off balance. Mallory heard MacMillan groan as the goalkeeper came rushing out, and Kazemayov, delicately, accurately, and with all the grace of confidence, flicked the ball over the keeper's head and into the net. Scrambling U.S. defenders, trying to prevent the goal, tangled together clumsily between the goalposts.

"Well, well," MacMillan said, and looked at his watch. "I didn't expect a goal in the first minute."

Mallory stared glumly at the American team, some of whose members appeared to be involved in an argument, a series of recriminations with one another.

"Defense's fault," MacMillan said. "They shouldn't have allowed that fellow so much space because he's a tricky devil."

The ball was kicked toward the center of the field for play to be restarted. The scoreboard flashed the goal, the scorer, and the time of the goal: "1 minute."

If it goes on like this, Mallory thought, there will be some kind of massacre.

**4.**

At first she let her mind wander freely as if it were something liberated from a cage; let it roam through a series of pictures of her own making, imagining a sea crashing down on a shore, dreaming of snow, dreaming of peace; but then she began to pick up on the man Koprow had called Mallory, pick up on him with a dreadful ease because he was at the center of some mass of energy and attention: it was the blind instinct of the homing bird, the flight of a random projectile toward the center of gravity. She picked up on it in a sequence of feelings at first, emotions that began in a shadowy way, then became more and more precise until they might have been her own. Boredom, discomfort, a lack of concentration. She might have been eavesdropping outside the open door of a room, hearing everything that went on within—every whisper, every move, from the loudest sound down to the faintest, from the sound of water being poured into a glass to the stirring of a vague breeze through muslin. Fragments, at first indiscernible, became large and clear and unmistakable. But even as she moved toward it she felt a strange hard pain at the center of her chest and, opening her eyes, saw Koprow watching her, Katya standing beyond him—and she had the dislocating experience of being trapped between two worlds, neither of which was remotely real to her.

She shut her eyes again. She heard Koprow say something, a word she didn't catch, a feeling she did—impatience, the edge of anger, a sense of suspense. Mallory again—but it was difficult because there was a stubborn quality surrounding him. And then it seemed to her that she was standing alongside him and could make out the contours of his appearance, that she could have touched him if she had wanted to, could have put out her hand and touched him. The young face that was beginning, in middle age, to sag around the chin. The dark hair that was already faintly streaked with gray. She held back; she checked herself, beset again by a sense of disquieting familiarity. That face.

*Exactly where tell me exactly I must know*

Why was there this interference now? She thought she had silenced the child, she thought she had stopped all that a while ago but now it was coming in on her again, weak, weakening. She didn't want to hurt the child. How could she do that? And then she wondered if it made any difference at all—if, once you had begun to inflict pain and cause death, there was any difference.

*Exactly where*

She opened her eyes again and saw, as if some mist had developed around them, Koprow and the woman, heard them whisper together furtively, the man's head inclined toward the woman. What are they saying? What are they talking about? Mallory. Now there were voices, conversations, fragments of speech in that place where Mallory was situated. *I don't think it's likely at this stage.* What did that mean? What did that mean? *Why wouldn't they substitute at two goals down?* The soccer players, of course. Of course, what else? *It's too soon to bring a new man on, Mr. President.*

Mr. President, she thought.

Mr. President.

The President of the United States.

She had seen that face in a newspaper once, she had seen it somehow, she couldn't remember where or how, where or how in all the months of her isolation with Andreyev, in all the months of her tests, all the time she had been out of touch with the world, she couldn't remember—a glance, something on a TV screen, a newspaper picture, she couldn't recall—Mallory. The President of the United States.

An old woman. A peasant. You know nothing of world affairs. They don't touch you. Why should they touch you?

Koprow was watching her.

*Tell me*

Go away            didn't I stop you            before
    don't make me hurt you

*I must know where*

That knowledge will kill you

Koprow turned to look at Katya and they whispered again. There was no reality now. There was nothing vaguely real. Only those photographs in Koprow's coat. And even they were sad and pathetic.

They whisper, what are they whispering about?

Koprow stepped toward her, placing his hands on her shoulders. "What's happening? You must tell me what's happening."

There was a violence of pain once more in her chest. She lifted a hand to the place and tried to rub it away but it was inside, it was beneath the surface of skin, beneath bone, like a fire around her heart. She closed her eyes. It was a matter of fighting for strength, for life.

"Is it finished?" Koprow asked. "Have you completed it?"

*Beneath the stadium*

She closed her eyes. Tomorrow, she thought. If you can do this today, then there is tomorrow, the tomorrow you have been promised. *They are bringing in a substitute, I see.* She focused her mind, as if the mind were a series of loose strands that might be gathered into a single hard ball, something that might be concentrated, steeled, an object no longer diffuse, no longer loose—and then she had to reach, she had to reach for Mallory through a space that wasn't a space, across a time which no clock could measure. Mallory. Pain. Terrible pain.

*You are beneath the stadium*
I warn you        keep away

## 5.

He stepped out of the camper in the parking lot at the stadium, looking up into the cab where Isobel held the girl. He felt helpless all at once. This vast stadium—where was he supposed to start looking? But time was against his own helplessness; you needed to act, you needed to act fast, you needed to go inside the stadium and look even if that was hopeless. He stared across the rows of cars, across the rain, at the edifice of the stadium, at the U.S. flag that fluttered in a drearily damp way.

Then he gazed back into the cab again. Isobel watched him, and he recognized the wariness in her expression, that guarded look. It was almost like a sense of loss, as if, having come to like him, having come to a point where she thought a relationship inevitable, she had rejected the idea and was left now with only the ruins of possibilities. The kid, turning her head a little, looked at him. She's trying, goddam, he thought. She's trying to tell me. The way she's trying: beyond speech, beyond the communication of eyes, she's trying her damnedest. He felt the rain soak through the fibers of his clothing, the dampness spreading to his skin.

The girl faced the stadium now, moving her head with obvious effort.

"Where, Fiona?" Rayner asked. "Can you tell me where?"

Nothing. Nothing.

"It's a huge fucking place," he said. "Where do I find this woman? Where, for Christ's sake?"

Demented in the rain, he thought. It was fitting.

She looked downward, her eyes moving slowly; it was as if the merest motion caused her pain. Downward, Rayner thought. What was that supposed to mean? Down, down where?

"Under the stadium? Is that it?"

The girl didn't move. That emptiness, that burnt-out look: it was all his own goddam fault. Under the stadium. Where? The locker rooms. He had nowhere else to look, did he?

"I'm taking her back to the hospital," Isobel said.

Rayner looked toward the stadium, shrugged.

"I have to," she said. "If you think your future lies in that place—well, you go ahead and find it. But this kid needs some kind of treatment."

Rayner nodded. He watched Isobel's face. For a moment, for a quick second, he saw her move her face down in his direction as if she intended to kiss him—but she didn't.

"Later," Rayner said.

"Later." And she drew the door of the camper shut.

<br>

**6.**

After the second Russian goal, a simple affair, simply engineered, the Americans had sent out a substitute. Mallory, waiting for some kind of reaction from Mac-Millan, who had become taciturn in his obvious disappointment, felt a slight headache somewhere at the back of his skull which he attributed to the weather, the dampness, the general inconvenience of having to sit through a game in which the home team was being systematically demolished. His interest had been roused a little but more, he suspected, for patriotic reasons than through any fondness for the game itself. He wished he had some aspirin.

He watched an American attack on the Soviet goal come to nothing while he was aware, from the corner of his eye, of Leontov smirking. He raised his hand to his head as though to massage the slight ache away.

MacMillan leaned toward him and asked quietly, "Are you feeling well, Mr. President?"

Mallory looked at the other man. Did it show? "I find myself rooting for the losing team," he said, trying to sound unconcerned. "Apart from that—"

He stopped. The pain was suddenly blinding, like some acute migraine, and he saw across his path of vision a series of jagged colored lines. There was a peripheral dimness too, as if lights had been switched off in far corners. I must be coming down with something, he thought. Flu? Some virus? He was conscious of sweating, a cold sweat.

"Can I fetch you some aspirin or something?" MacMillan asked.

"If it's no trouble," Mallory answered. Goddam—there was a tightness in his throat, a constriction of some kind. He tried to relax, to control himself, to overcome the vague panic he was beginning to experience. He saw MacMillan move along the row of seats, politely excusing himself each time he disturbed somebody. Whatever this is, Mallory thought, aspirin isn't going to do the trick. The pain in his head, growing more intense, had spread across the top of his scalp—a tingling sensation, each small vibration burning like a tiny white-hot needle. President faints, he thought. He could see it in newspapers. They would question his health and by implication his fitness for the job. Jesus Christ, it was burning him now.

He noticed MacMillan returning with a plastic tumbler of water. MacMillan sat down and opened his palm. Three aspirin and water, the panacea. Mallory swallowed the tablets with a single gulp of water.

"I hope it helps," MacMillan said.

"Thanks," Mallory said. "I'll be okay, I'm sure."

Leontov turned to look at the President. "Is something wrong? Is there anything I can do?"

For a moment Mallory felt relief—but then it came back again, a fire, a rage of flame, rushing through his head. You feared the worst: what the hell could it be? Even his eyes were sore now.

"Is something wrong?" Leontov asked again.

"My team is losing," Mallory said.

"I noticed," said the Ambassador.

*7.*

Inside the stadium, Rayner noticed how tight the security was—agents conversing through their walkie-talkies, undercover guys trying to look like casual spectators, cops. He could hear the roar of the crowd drift through the rain, a massive echo. Now his only opportunity to get past the security people and into the locker-room area was to show his Embassy pass and hope—*hope*—that his name hadn't been marked. *U.S. Embassy, London, Special Investigative Section.* Sure, sure, he thought, that's going to take me a long way. Like hell.

He walked quickly along corridors, passing under white lights, glimpsing through openings the crowd, the rows of seats that rose upward. You could lose your way here, he thought. It would be easy to step inside the maze and never get out again. Which way? Which way now? He continued to rush, clutching in his hand the ticket he had bought at the entrance, wishing it were the gun he had been obliged to jettison along with the car. You're on your own, he thought. There's nobody else now—and maybe that was fitting; maybe when you stepped into madness it was a trip you could take only by yourself.

He saw ahead of him a flight of stairs going down. The problem in negotiating it, he thought, lies in the face of the guy in the navy-blue raincoat standing there by the sign that says: No Admittance Except for Authorized Personnel. Flash your nice little plastic card, Rayner. Your official documentation. What was the guy's affiliation anyhow? Langley? The FBI? A D.C. cop? Some private security type? Rayner hesitated. A plastic card in a grubby hand—there was an incongruity here that displeased him. Still, there was no way down those stairs without getting past the raincoat and you did what you had to—though not exactly without question.

He took his card from his wallet and went up to the man. The face, cemented into a kind of middle-aged sourness, as if all of life's ambitions had distilled themselves into the task of guarding—for God's sake—a flight of stairs, was neither friendly nor open. Rayner showed his pass and asked, "Is the Russian locker room down there?"

The man had his hands in the pockets of his raincoat. He gazed at the plastic card. The gaze was one of suspicion, of grim determination that nobody, not even if it were the Second Coming, would get down the stairs.

Rayner waited. "I have to check, see."

Silence.

"We discovered a visa irregularity—"

"Yeah?"

"Therefore I have to talk with the Russians—"

"Therefore nothing," the guy said. "I have instructions."

"Me too," Rayner said. "Looks like a conflict of instructions to me."

"It's your conflict, buddy. It's not mine."

"Well, yeah," Rayner said. He stared along the corridor. There was a man with a walkie-talkie about a hundred yards away. "Who's your superior?"

The man stared at Rayner. "To get down these stairs you'd need written permission from God."

"That tough, huh?"

"That tough."

"And you don't know the name of your superior?" Rayner asked.

"Sure I do," the guy said.

"You don't want to tell me?"

The man smiled. "It wouldn't make a goddam bit of difference, friend. And your little card doesn't altogether impress me. London, huh? You're way off beam."

It was going to resolve itself, Rayner saw, in a sudden rush; even violence—a violence he could hardly afford, a confrontation he didn't relish. You couldn't reason with this guy, for sure. He was big, clumsy somehow, as if the parts of his body didn't match one another. Rayner turned away, looking once more along the corridor. One swing, he thought, one mighty godawful swing. He felt tense, knotted, wondering if he had the capacity for the surprise attack. Do it, he thought. Do it.

"I guess that's it," he said.

And as the man nodded, Rayner brought his knee upward. He drove it sharply into the region of the groin and listened as the man gasped, groaning, slipping back against the handrail, losing his balance and slithering down a couple of the concrete steps. He stared in an astonished way at Rayner, who was already trying to pass him on the steps, but he reacted with an agility that surprised Rayner, reaching out, grasping the ankle, twisting it so that Rayner felt a jarring pain. A desk job, Rayner thought. You're not cut out for this nonsense. He lifted his free foot and swung it and heard it strike the side of the man's head; he saw the head snap back, skull against handrail, bone against metal, a look of anguish on the sour face. The hand dropped away from Rayner's ankle and he was free—free to get to the bottom of the steps, where, as he found himself in still another corridor, he could hear the guy shouting for assistance.

**8.**

Mallory was dizzy. He experienced a blurry double vision that created from the twenty-two players on the field a spectral forty-four. But it was the sense of panic, of dread, that was even worse than the pains, the distorted sight, the buzzing in his ears, the giddiness, the itching of the skin. It was the dread. Hadn't he read somewhere that it was this dread that accompanied dying? Hadn't he read that somewhere?

MacMillan was telling him how pale he looked. Was there something he could do to help?

Mallory gripped the edge of his seat as if it were a final anchor, the last thing he could trust. He listened to the roar of the crowd, which seemed to become one with the merciless buzzing in his ears. He was aware of a film of cold sweat on the surface of his eyelids. He thought: Is this how it ends? In this rainy stadium on a bleak April afternoon? All at once without warning? Something the checkups never revealed? *Is this all?*

He felt the touch of MacMillan's hand on his shoulder. It's almost half time, he was saying. Perhaps I can find you a doctor, sir.

A doctor? Half time? Mallory suddenly realized that he didn't know where he was, or how he had come to this place, or why. Half time? What the hell did that mean? And the roar of the crowd—why couldn't somebody stop it?

He closed his eyes, rubbed his eyelids, and tried as hard as he knew how to keep control of himself. Now the crowd, as if the rain had muffled it, was totally without noise and the only sound he heard was the frenetic buzzing in his head—like the flow of an electric current through a bad connection, and painful, painful in the extreme.

How could it end here? Here in this godawful rain?

# 9.

Corridors, endless white corridors. A moment before, he had heard footsteps coming down stairways after him and he knew they would have their neat little radios out now, talking with one another—*there's some nut running loose*—rushing to seal off his route, swarming everywhere. You run. Out of breath, no matter what, you run. Beneath the whiteness of overhead lights, through the corridors of the labyrinth, you run. Where—where in this whole fucking place did he turn? There were open doors and empty rooms, doors marked PRIVATE, shower rooms, exercise rooms— which room did *he* want? And when he found it, *if* he found it, what then? An old woman—did you just go up to her and beg her to stop doing whatever she was doing? Did you try and choke her to death? Rayner, Rayner—what began as a series of impossible suspicions has become a monster, an obsession, because you don't even know if she exists, if she's a figment, a creature of the kid's making, a fantasy molded out of the Play-Doh of the adolescent mind. You still don't know. And if she doesn't exist then what you've been doing all along is taking a circuitous route to the paranoid parlor, the funny farm—

Now he could hear the echo of voices in the distance and the sound of footsteps other than his own. Just the same he had to stop, he had to catch his breath. Isobel would have taken the kid back to D.C. General by this time. What would she say? *This poor girl's in a . . . trance?* Instant merriment amongst physicians who would automatically suspect your average teenage overdose and break out the stomach pumps. *Poor girl's a psychic, Doctor.* Ah, yes, common enough problem these days. Where's my stethoscope?

Run. Just goddam run. He came to a corner, turning, feeling like the rat caught in some laboratory maze, all impulses controlled by the whiff of some delectable cheese. Running and running, as if he might never reach a finish line.

# 10.

For a time she had to let go, she couldn't continue, there was a stubborn resistance, a willpower, that she hadn't encountered before, and it was draining her. Eyes shut, swollen hands clenched together, she tried to gather her strength—but her breathing was tight and quick and constricted and she felt strangely feeble, beset by a lack of purpose, a feeling like that of trying to breathe life into a body already dead. Slowly she opened her eyes. Mallory is strong, she wanted to say—but she didn't have the strength for speech. He's very strong. Young and firm and controlled—a disciplined man. She struggled for air and thought: I feel what Mallory feels. His pains, his anguish are my own. And if I go to the very edge with him—what then? But I can't go on, not now, not for the moment. She saw Koprow standing over her. She saw a small blue vein beat madly in his scalp. The woman, Katya, was standing by the wall with her arms folded tightly. Exhausted—they don't understand the price, what it costs me, all they want is the result, all they have ever wanted is one thing from me, nobody has wanted me for myself apart from Aaron and Aaron died when he understood me. Is this all I am any good for now, this unending slaughter?

"Is it finished?" Koprow asked. "Is it done?"

She shook her head from side to side and whispered. *No.*

"Why?" he asked. "Why isn't it finished? What's keeping you back?"

He was angry. She understood that he was trying to control his anger but he couldn't because it was natural to him. He couldn't help himself.

The woman, her arms still folded across her thin breasts, approached the wheelchair. "She needs to rest a moment. Isn't that obvious?"

The cold one's concern touches me, the old woman thought. How very touching. Koprow said nothing. He was bending toward the wheelchair, staring, his eyes the color of a cold sea.

"Andreyev—" Katya started to say.

"Andreyev is dead. Andreyev is of no damn concern to me now," Koprow said.

The woman was silent for a moment, hushed, her face pale. Then she said, "Andreyev was always concerned with her strength. He was always careful never to push her too far."

"Andreyev was a traitor," Koprow said. He reached down and put his hand under the old woman's chin, turning her face upward. "Why haven't you done it? Why isn't it finished? Do you imagine we carried you all this way for nothing?"

She shook her head. The room, the reflective tiles, the whiteness that came through the other door—the room was filled with cruelty, with an absence of compassion, of any simple human feeling. And she thought: What right do I have to think these things? I'm as bad as they are. I'm just as bad. There was fear too, currents of fear that she felt moving among all three of them in complex ways. They were afraid of each other. Each is afraid of me. And I, I'm afraid of myself. Now, like a stain spreading, she could feel the rush of tightness across her chest. I can't go on.

"Have you forgotten?" Koprow had taken the pictures from his coat. He selected one, the top one, and put the rest back. He held it in front of her and, panicked, she stared at it a moment. "Mallory. That's all. Do you understand me?"

The photograph magnetized her; she couldn't stop looking at the way he held it. It was as if he held the grandchild depicted in the picture—the boy; it was as if he held the small body and was threatening to drop it from some great height.

"Mallory," Koprow said. "If you want to meet in the flesh all these nice people in the photographs."

She was numb, unable to feel herself. Why did he have her photographs? Why had he taken them from her? She couldn't remember exactly now, but it was all wrong. They belonged to her, they shouldn't have been taken away from her.

She strained to speak. "I want my pictures back," she said.

"When you're through," Koprow said. "Only when you've done what you're here to do."

She closed her eyes and turned her head to one side. She thought of Mallory for a moment—but Mallory didn't have the pictures; why should Mallory concern her now?

"My . . . pictures," she said. Opening her eyes, staring at Koprow, she held out one hand very slowly. He shook his head, dangling the single photograph well out of her reach.

"My . . ." She continued to stare at him, feeling his unease, understanding his fear, realizing that his fear lay concealed beneath a thin layer of bravado and cruelty. He was all at once like glass to her, a thing she could see through. My pictures, she thought. *I want my pictures.* Koprow took a step backward.

She saw him smile, then take the photograph of the boy and bend it between his fingers, making a crease the length of the picture. Then he tore it into two pieces. He let the pieces fall from his fingers to the floor. She followed them in their awful flight downward. One half lay with the colored side up—half of the boy's face, eyes and nose and hair. She pushed herself forward in her chair as if she meant to bend and retrieve the pieces.

Koprow took another photograph from his pocket and held it out toward her. "These are only pictures. Think of your own family, not as photographs, Mrs. Blum, but as real people. Real people. Nobody wants any harm to come to them. Nobody."

She couldn't take her eyes from the two sliced pieces that lay just beneath her feet. Her anger was a slow thing, building slowly, terribly. She raised her face to look at Koprow. His eyes—what lay beyond his eyes? What lay in that glass heart? He stepped farther back. She wanted to hurt him. She wanted his pain. Now, in a distant way, she was conscious of somebody running, somebody running nearby, running hard. And she wondered who it might be, and why he was running. But there was no time for that now, there was only Koprow, the photograph in the man's hand, the two slashed pieces on the floor which lay, sadly, like some ancient love letter ripped in a fit of anger later regretted.

*My papers. My flight. What time tomorrow?*

There was an emptiness in Koprow's mind. She

concentrated, wanting an answer from him that would be positive and truthful—afraid to hear still another lie.

*What time tomorrow?*

Koprow had moved another step away from her. His face was all fear now. She made him drop the picture, watching his hand open and the fingers spread stiffly. Appalled, he looked at the photograph drifting away from him. You're strong, she thought. Strong. *What time tomorrow? Tell me, tell me.*

There was nothing. There was nothing.

"Mallory," he said, his voice weak. "Remember what . . ."

*What time tomorrow?*

She caught the arms of her wheelchair and, fighting, struggling against her own weakness, pushed herself up. Her limbs were painfully weak, her muscles trembling.

"What are you doing?" Katya asked. "Please— what are you doing?"

She thrust herself away from the wheelchair, dragging her blanket behind her, stepping delicately over the destroyed picture; she pushed herself forward and moved, one hand uplifted, toward Koprow. He thinks he can hide, she thought. He thinks he can hide from me. But there's no hiding place. There's nothing.

"Remember what—"

*Tell me. Tell me the truth. Tell me about tomorrow.*

And she saw. It didn't matter to him, there was no tomorrow, there was no flight, there were no papers to be signed, because all she caught was confusion, the confusion of the liar who can no longer separate truth from fiction. *What time?* Nothing. No time. Lies, humiliation, fear—they had forced her through all of this in return for what? She stopped, thinking she was going to lose her balance, feeling a sudden spasm in her legs. I wanted so badly to believe, she thought. I needed to believe. I needed it. Now there's nothing. Nothing but my own pains, my own endless torment. The killing—there had to be a place where the killing would stop. But not yet. Not now.

She watched him back into the open doorway of the lighted room. His shadow fell across the white tiles. You can't hide in there, Koprow. You still don't understand: there's nowhere to hide.

She glanced at Katya, who, her mouth open, her arms hanging loosely at her sides, stood motionless against the opposite wall. Katya knows, she thought. Katya knows there's no refuge. And you are going to know too, Koprow.

Please, Koprow said.

She watched him fall to the floor and turn over on his back. A game, she could make it a game, something like the things she had done as a young girl. A guessing game—you were always able to guess the cards when they were face down. Sometimes you could tell what was on a person's mind. It was mischief. You reached out with your mind, you sent your mind flying out like some discus until it struck its target. Don't you remember how amazed and puzzled you were when you found that nobody else could do it, and then how ashamed you became as you grew older, how you hid it away like a sin?

Sin: they have made me sin. Played on my weaknesses, my fantasies, my losses: my need for loving. They made me sin for all that.

Koprow moaned, his body twisting, his hands going up to his skull.

Pain, she thought. It's only just begun. One by one by one the bones break. The arm the arm first begin with the arm hurt him. Katya moved slightly as if she might make for the door but she knew—she *knew* when it was utterly hopeless. There was the sound of something cracking and Koprow, his body curled in a stiff fetal position, opened his mouth to scream. But she wasn't going to give him that escape.

"Don't," Katya said. "Don't do it. *Think*. Think of what will happen to your family."

"Family?" she answered. *Family?*

"They'll be killed," the woman said.

She hesitated. She looked down at Koprow. Screaming in his profound silence. Family. They will be killed. There was a knotted sensation within her. How could she bear this pain any longer? And she remembered Aaron—*I'm sending the boy away, I'm sending him to our relatives in Palestine. How can you bring him up? How can I expect you to raise him knowing what you are?*—Dear God. Family. Sending the boy away. The boy she never knew. The father of her grandchildren. They don't want me, she thought. What do they *need* with me? I have built love out of nothing, out of nothing at all. A castle in the air. A dream. The letters, the photographs—what did they amount to? Were they real? Was there really any family? Had there ever been one? She shut her eyes. It has to end here. The killing has to end in this place. No matter what, the killing has to end in this place. She moved, shuffling, wracked with pain, toward the figure of Koprow.

# 11.

It was the smell of burning that made Rayner open a particular door. It was the scent of flesh burning. Even then he opened the door hesitantly, letting it swing slowly inward to the room. Half-lighted, white tiles, shadows, fluorescence burning from another door beyond. He stepped inside the room, trying to make out shapes from shadows, conscious at the same time of a soft sighing noise coming from a dark corner. In the doorway that faced him there was somebody—something—lying. At first he couldn't make it out. He thought: You read of strange things in weird books; you read of unexplained phenomena—a woman in Florida disappears in some wildly improbable outrage of spontaneous combustion. You read it, you forget it, then it comes back to you—all the strange things you've read: objects falling out of the sky, blue sunsets, a man in Kansas disappearing from sight in full view of his family. Other dimensions, they say—as if that explained a goddam thing. The mysteries of living and dying. He bent down over the shape. Startled, he backed off. A man. Maybe. Maybe once. You couldn't say for certain that this had been a man—this blackened object that lay in the doorway, this charred form: a Frankenstein gone wrong. Burnt clothing; was that skin that had been scorched? He shut his eyes a second. A trick of the mind, a delusion, another sign of your condition. But it was still there when he looked again. Blackened bone, that was what he could see. Bones broken and protruding through flesh the color of cinders. A man, something that had once been a man. He felt sick as he stood up and stared at the thing. *She could break your mind.* What was more terrible—the ability to reduce a man to this condition or the capacity for taking a mind and driving it toward a total destruction? He didn't want to look—but he couldn't prevent it. And still, from the dark corner of the room, there was the same soft, sighing sound. He stepped over the body and into the inner room, where the lights made him blink. His eyes watered—from what? Fear?

A cubicle door was open. He went toward it. Like a child crouching in the distant corner of a room, like a child fending off the nightmare monsters of the imagination, there was a middle-aged woman covering her head with her hands, her knees bent, her body doubled. She was trembling. He reached out to touch her and wondered: Is this the one? Is this the kid's woman? Did she just get the age wrong? He turned her face toward him and immediately, as if something had stung him, he backed away, sickened, sickened again. The facial skin was scorched, bloodied, the eyelids swollen—the eyes themselves red and blind as if they had been rubbed constantly for years, rubbed and pushed and pressed to the point of sightlessness. He backed out of the cubicle and the woman turned her face away, once again covering it with her hands.

In the doorway he paused. You reach a point, he thought. You think: I can't deal with it anymore. It's beyond what I know. It's beyond simple torture, simple violence—a place where you dare not go. He listened to the same quiet, sighing sound as he had heard before and he stepped over the charred thing in the doorway and back into the other room, his eyesight darkened and dimmed by the fluorescence. He waited, listening, hearing other sounds now from along the corridor. But it was the sighing that drew him to the corner of the room.

He saw the wheelchair first. Then he made out, through the dimness, the shape of the woman—and he realized he had never seen anyone so close to dying, anyone who looked so utterly close to death. An old woman, sparse white hair, body covered over with a blanket. The old woman, he thought. How could you, in all your most disorganized dreams, ascribe terror to this woman who sat, sighing, sifting mindlessly through a little pile of colored snapshots?

How could you do that? He approached her and, kneeling, looked at her. She stared at him and he was momentarily afraid, but the feeling passed: an intuition, a way of knowing, that something had ended here. That she intended no harm to him. He reached out and touched her arthritic hands. Raising her face, she looked toward the doorway, then back at Rayner.

"Mall-ory," she said.

The tone of voice—Mallory, he thought. Mallory is safe. How did he know that? The smell of burnt flesh came to him again. Mall-ory. She watched him a moment in a curious way and he experienced a faint passing headache, as if something had brushed briefly against his brain.

"Rayner," she said.

That tone—what was that one now? Some kind of . . . sadness? Some kind of *apology?* He looked away from her. Richard, she was speaking about Richard, she was trying to explain her sorrow. She held out the snapshots to him and he glanced at them quickly. He saw unrecognizable faces in a sunlit place. What did they mean to her? She smiled at him and he thought: This is the woman who killed my brother. This is her. This is the woman I've been chasing through my own dreams of insanity, pursuing through my obsessions, my fears. But now he felt nothing. No sense of achievement, no desire for vengeance, nothing. You come to a point and after that there's nothing but a dying old woman dreamily sifting through her snapshots. Go to any old house in America where a widow would sit behind her lace curtains, listening to the clocks of her own loneliness, and you would find the same pitiful scene.

He stood upright.

"Rayner," she said again, and her voice was hoarse.

The woman who killed Richard. This is her.

And then there was confusion, the room suddenly filled with men, raincoated men, men who had expected to trap and corner a free-running madman—but not this, nothing like this. The crackle of their little radios, the noise of their feet, the sounds of their voices. There was silence. I mean nothing to them now, Rayner thought. I mean nothing. Nothing compared to what they have found in the doorway.

He looked at the old woman one more time, then slipped out of the room toward the corridor, listening to the babble of voices behind him. Let them find their own explanations, he thought. The way I found mine.

## 12.

The whistle blew for half time. The players ran through the rain toward the locker rooms. The American team had finally managed to score just before the interval, a goal that MacMillan described as spectacular—coming, as it had, from thirty yards out from the Russian goal. "A thunderbolt," MacMillan said.

Mallory sat back in his seat. What had happened to him? He felt weak, but everything else had gone now—the panic, the pains, the sense of dying. He would have to see about a checkup as soon as possible or spend the rest of his life wondering if the lunch had been poisoned.

Leontov turned to him and asked, "How are you feeling now?"

Mallory nodded. "Fine," he said. "Just fine."

MacMillan looked happy. "I don't care what wonder drugs they discover, Mr. President. Common aspirin is a miracle in itself."

"Indeed," Mallory said.

Leontov rose, excused himself, and slipped along the row of seats. Mallory wondered about that dollar. Was the little shit afraid of an American revival in the second half of the game?

"Do we stand a chance, MacMillan?" he asked.

"That goal has put a different perspective on things," said MacMillan.

# 13.

Rayner left the stadium and went across the parking lot in the rain. Overhead, in the dismal sky, there was the white shadow of a watery sun. He looked up a moment and then he thought: I'll walk to D.C. General. Get Isobel and the kid. Make sure they're okay. He felt a strain of some deep fatigue as he passed among the rows of parked cars. Sleep, he thought. And then what? Do you return to London? Pick up the pieces? Look into the situation with Isobel? Or were the ghosts still too strong for that? The cars gleamed in the rain, row after row after row. He paused, shaking his head, trying to get rid of his tiredness—and with it the memory of what he had just seen. Priorities, he thought. You need some semblance of order first of all. Later, you can sit down and try to figure your way through it all. Coffee. Maybe at the hospital. The first thing.

"John?"

It surprised him to hear his name being called in that familiar voice; it was like a voice in some shallow dream. He turned around and saw George Gull standing some yards behind him. George Gull, he thought. You could have picked a better time. He watched

Gull come toward him and all at once he was conscious of the vast emptiness of the parking lot, the silence from the stadium, the soft sound of the rain. Gull was smiling—and for a moment, a fleeting time of small hope, Rayner wondered if he had attributed all the wrong things to Gull, if wires had been crossed somewhere along the way and mistakes made. But Gull had in his hand a silenced pistol, and Rayner thought: You come all this way, cover all this distance, you cross the barricades of your own incredulity—and for what? To die in the fucking rain? He looked at the muzzle of the silencer. To die quietly in the fucking rain.

"Close, John. But no cigar," Gull said.

Rayner said, "I hope they made it worth your while. Or was it a question of ideology, George?"

Gull laughed. "You can't put ideology in a Zurich numbered account, can you now?"

The finances of treachery, Rayner thought. He stared at the gun. To end like this. To find it wasn't worth shit. Immortality in a parking lot. In the rain. Worthless.

"You knew about this nutty plan all along," Rayner said.

Gull was still smiling. "You can't bitch, John. I tried to warn you off. You can't say I didn't try. I warned you off Dubbs. I didn't want you drifting into the Andreyev business."

"It didn't work," Rayner said. "Your little old lady turned around, Gull."

"I can't take the blame for that," Gull said. "It wasn't my scheme. I only pulled a few necessary strings, John. Who do you think arranged their fucking visas, no questions asked? They're not uncharitable. A piece of paper here, a piece of info there—I was an *impeccable* source. Isn't that the phrase?"

"Words to that effect," Rayner said. Fatigue and death. Maybe it's better to take your leave when you're not wide awake; maybe you don't feel it quite as much. "What about my brother? Did you know about him?"

"After the fact, John. It was the big mistake in my book. Working the old woman on your brother when they could have chosen *anybody*, and you'd never have been involved. I'm sorry about that."

"Sorry," Rayner said flatly. He could smell it still in his nostrils: burning meat over cinders. The old woman. The goddam rain. The silence in the rain. "Killing Mallory—did you ever think about the consequences, George?"

"Consequences? Look, I'm eligible for retirement next year. I intend to take it. I've done my time, John. So I retire—then what? A trailer park in New Jersey? Living on a Government pension? A pittance? Maybe a job like a broken-down store detective? Fuck that. I've lived on my nerves long enough. Sure, I thought about consequences—but only in terms of my own well-being." Gull paused. He raised a hand to wipe a slick of rain from his forehead. "Anyway, is there a difference between one man in the White House or another? Is there any goddam difference? Right now, John, I'm only interested in saving my own ass."

Rayner looked once more at the gun. Gull's pathetic little speech—was it some desperate plea for sympathy, for a belated understanding? *Sorry, John, but now you know why I have to kill you.*

"It doesn't hang together, Gull," he said. Useless words now. "You sent Chip Alexander after me— how could you have been so damn sure I wouldn't tell him about Mallory? How did you know he would swallow that shit about me having a breakdown and stealing classified material? It doesn't jell for me, George."

Gull looked pale. "I took a calculated risk. I thought the Soviets would get to you first. Anyway, I wasn't sure then that you had put the Mallory pieces together, John. I just figured you wouldn't, it was too far-out, unlikely. But when I knew you had the pieces, when I knew that for sure, it became a different game. . . . But none of this matters much, does it?"

"How did you know, George? *How did you know for sure?*" Rayner asked. A different game. It didn't work, it didn't have rules, an internal logic.

Gull shook his head. He appeared to be in some pain. "It doesn't matter now."

Rayner looked at the gun. What would it feel like?

Maybe nothing. Maybe nothing at all. He stared across the rain toward the stadium; the Stars and Stripes fluttered in a restless way. Something, he thought. It still doesn't fit. Something he didn't want to think about. He saw George Gull lift the gun.

"How did you know, George? How did you know I had figured out the Mallory thing? How did you know I'd be here?"

George Gull was sweating.

It doesn't add, Rayner thought. It doesn't add and it doesn't matter that it doesn't add, that the equation is screwed up all over again. He wondered desperately about running, just turning and running, taking whatever his chances might be. Where was that goddam instinct for survival you read so much about? Where was it when you needed it?

"How, George? Tell me."

Gull looked as though he was trying to speak. He opened his mouth soundlessly. Rayner stared at the gun. Why was he having so much trouble firing it?

Has some great god of luck jammed the trigger for you? No, you've used up all your luck, Rayner. This is the place where the well of good fortune finally runs dry on you. This is the place. He saw how Gull was straining with the gun, holding it now as though it was an object over which he had no control, straining as his arm rose. There was a look of panic on his face.

*Christ, Christ,* he was saying. Over and over and over.

*Christ, Christ, Christ.*

Rayner didn't move. He saw Gull's arm continue to rise, he saw the nerve moving in the jaw, the streaks of sweat on the forehead, he saw the gun come up.

And Gull's hand turned inward toward himself. Inward. The gun an inch from his own face.

Rayner turned away and waited, waited for what he knew was going to happen, listening for the sound of the gun going off. Again and again and again he heard the silenced violence of the weapon and when it had stopped, when it seemed to him that there was no other sound in the world save that of the rain drumming on the roofs of cars, he turned to look. Gull—what was left of Gull—lay some feet away. Rayner slumped against the hood of the nearest car. He could still hear the echo of Gull's voice, *Christ, Christ,* a useless litany. He felt the rain falling on his face. He couldn't look at Gull again. He couldn't bring himself to look. He thought of the old woman now, wondering what debt she felt she owed him—a death for a death: George Gull for Richard Rayner. A savage repayment. A sequence of events that began with a broken window in Moscow and ended here, here in the goddam rain, outside a sports stadium in Washington.

But it isn't ended, he thought.

*It isn't finished.*

A canceled debt, a check written in too much

blood. My brother's life: my own survival. What was that power? What exactly? He walked away from George Gull, realizing he was back in that territory where nothing had any proper definition, a place beyond language and sense. The old woman. Repaid with interest. Repaid with more blood than he wanted to think about. He turned and looked back at the stadium.

It isn't over, he thought.

You're left with a piece that doesn't fit.

Maybe a piece you can never make fit.

But it isn't over.

### 14.

The cop in the white overcoat said, "I wouldn't want to put any money on what happened in here."

An agent of the FBI, dressed as an anachronistic hippie, beads and leather vest and flowery shirt, stared across the room. "The smell's doing bad things to my stomach," he said.

The cop stood over the body in the doorway. "Poor fucker looks like he stepped into a furnace."

The room was filled with law officers, guardians of an inscrutable peace. Cameras, lights, fingerprint men, agents from various state and federal agencies; confusion and disorder and bewilderment.

A uniformed officer said, "The woman in the bathroom might be able to tell us something."

"Yeah, if we're lucky," said the cop in the white coat. He stopped in front of a wheelchair where a police physician, an open black bag between his legs, was bent over the shape of an old woman. He had his stethoscope out, pressing it here and there against her chest.

"What's the story?" the cop asked.

The physician took the stethoscope from his ears and folded it. He had been holding the old woman's wrist, trying to find a pulse. He rolled up the stethoscope and dropped it into his bag. "We've lost this one," he said.

The cop shrugged. "I didn't think she'd pull it off." He stared at the doctor a moment. "What a hellova thing to happen—especially with Mallory upstairs. What a hellova thing."

He turned to the uniformed cop and said, "Where did that other guy go? The one that slipped down here?"

"Vanished," the uniformed man said. "In all the confusion—"

"Yeah. Confusion is the word. Confusion is the only word." He saw the thin middle-aged woman being laid on a stretcher. She was being carried out. As she was taken past him, he turned his face away. Some things, he thought, you can't look at. He turned once more to the uniformed cop and said, "See if you can put together a description of the guy from the guard he belted. Maybe we can find him."

He walked back toward the wheelchair and bent down and looked at the expressionless face of the old woman. There was a little pile of colored snapshots, like pieces of a puzzle, lying under her feet. He picked them up and sifted slowly through them.

# Epilogue

He waited in the reception area of the hospital, remembering how much he hated these places: that sense of the sick and the dying shut in rooms you couldn't see. Flowers in vases, intravenous drips, people hooked up to machines that kept them barely alive. Tired, he slumped in his chair and watched two nurses—white, even their shoes gleamed like frost— pass the reception desk. Voices over speakers: *Will Dr. Morris report to Emergency? Dr. Sandman is requested in Maternity.*

A place, he thought, where you don't have to think anymore. Where you can let it all wash off. A shower room of the brain. Where the shock of suspicion might be alleviated by lobotomy. He shut his eyes.

*Who told George Gull?* he wondered. A conundrum of an impossible kind. Who killed Cock Robin? Who? He shifted in his chair and, opening his eyes, looked along a corridor at a window at the far end where a white rainy light fell on glass.

Nobody told him. He just knew. Something psychic in the air, after all. Leave it that way. George Gull just *happened* to know.

Come this far, Rayner. Cover the whole distance. You might as well. There's nothing left to hold back. The whole way.

He stared down the corridor. Nurses and orderlies moved back and forth. Physicians with little clipboards. Nobody else knew, he thought. Nobody. Nobody else.

Goddam. He wanted to get up and walk out and stroll through the rain and make believe he was somebody else in another place, that the time was different, that the season was not the same. Another place on a map: Shawnee, Oklahoma. Council Bluffs, Iowa. Names spotted on the great freeways of America. Nothing places where you might contrive to become another person.

He saw her now.

She was standing by the distant window, talking with a nurse. Their heads were close together: collusion, he thought. *She's going to be okay, Mrs. Rayner. The girl's going to be all right.* He felt both angry and weary, a combination he couldn't handle. Sleep would defuse both sensations. A long sleep.

Nobody else knew, he thought.

She was walking toward him. He got up from his chair and waited. What was that expression on her face now? Disbelief? Shock? You weren't exactly expected, he thought. You're the uninvited guest at a private dinner. The one they haven't laid a place for. No knife, no fork, no wineglass, nothing. And then she was smiling. She was smiling and moving more quickly. When she reached him, she put her hand on his arm. The smile. The smile. She was saying something, speaking quickly, speaking with the rapidity of nerves: *Overnight for observation but she's going to be okay she's okay it's a great relief.*

She put her arm through his and they went outside, back into the rain. She was still speaking—a flow of noise, of nonsense. He didn't listen. Nobody else told Gull, he thought. Nobody else could have known.

He waited for her silence.

And then he wondered: What do I say? What is there to say? You open the door to a room, you expect to find everything as you left it, but something is altered, something has been taken away, you just can't think what it is—

She was looking at him, asking him something now. *Well? Well? What happened?*

He could feel his own heart stop. His mouth was dry, unbearably so. It was the rough cutting edge of things, a serrated surface, an uneven slicing. You don't need to say it, he thought. You don't need it. Leave everything as it stands. Put up your hand and bring the whole goddam world to a halt and stop everything exactly now, exactly where it is now, with questions unasked and therefore unanswered.

He heard himself say it. "George Gull is dead."

He had seen masks before, but never one like this. What moved across her face? Of course, she had the sensibilities of an actress, the poise and perfection of someone who has run through a thousand rehearsals of this moment. Playacting: she had to have it down, neat and tidy; she had to have it perfect.

"Who?" she said.

There was a moment here where he wondered if he had made a mistake, a miscalculation, if he had blundered impossibly.

"I wonder when you called him," he said.

She was shaking her head, laughing, a sound of ice in a glass.

"I figure you must have done it twice," he said.

"I don't know what you're talking about, John."

"Maybe the first time was after I arrived back in the States. Maybe even after I'd called you from Kennedy," he said. "Maybe you dropped your dime just as soon as I'd hung up."

She stared at him in a bewildered way. The laugh was gone; she was still shaking her head. *How did you know for sure, George? How?*

"Then when you knew I was going to Washington, that I was going to the stadium, you called him again—maybe when I fell asleep in the motel or even later, when we had to stop because the kid was sick, at the rest area. Only this time good old George was back here in D.C., waiting."

She turned away from him a moment. He was taken by her beauty—flawed as it was in the rain, he was taken by it. The incongruity of desire: even now, even now as he stumbled around the frayed edges of what he was convinced was the truth.

"Only one person," he said. "Only one person could have told Gull."

She looked at him. The eyes—the eyes were cold. Light, warmth, whatever, had gone out of them. "You've fallen out of your tree this time, John. You've really fallen."

He was silent. It was a day for betrayals, the weather for treachery. Fallen out of your tree, he thought. Yeah, a long time ago. You couldn't defy gravity.

"It makes sense," he said. "Think about it. Think about how much sense it makes. You're with me almost constantly. You know what I'm doing, where I'm headed—and it suits George perfectly. For one thing, you can keep him posted on what I'm doing. For another, you're nicely located to help me out of the clutches of Chip Alexander, because suddenly it doesn't quite suit George Gull for the Americans to take me in. It doesn't fit his plans because there's a chance, a slight chance, they might just believe me. So all along it looks like you're with me, it looks like you're on my side—when your only allegiance is to Gull, to protecting George Gull.''

He stopped. Fatigue, a monster, had hooked onto him. He could feel claws, talons, the shuffling of great black wings through the air. Sleeplessness and hallucination: maybe it was all a construct of his own mind now, something reared in delusion, raised in an indeterminate form of craziness. He thought of the little beach cottage, the new life, the whole new world.

"You even string me along with some pointless little sexual promise. 'Too soon, John.' Implying, Maybe later. Maybe never is what you meant to say." He stared at her expressionless face. "You and George. If I had to put cold cash on it, my best bet would be that you were lovers. You and George. It was going to be cozy. Roses all the fucking way. Right down to the little house, the beach, umbrellas on the goddam sand. It was going to be just you and him with the past all squared away behind you."

The mask moved. Slightly, vaguely, it shifted.

"Your only error was Fiona," he said. "Even there you tried to cut your losses, didn't you? You tried and tried to convince me I was off the wall, didn't you? You never believed I'd pay any attention to the kid, did you? Maybe that was your best card—my own goddam skepticism. It turned out to be your weakest."

Rayner shrugged. In the long run, what did any of this matter? George Gull was dead. Too many people had died on account of a monstrous plan that had become a failure. Too many people had to die because of that. He had a feeling now of great solitude: he might have been standing on a vast expanse of empty beach, staring at an empty sea, an empty sky. What did any of this matter?

She had been watching him, but now she looked away. Raindrops coursed from her eyelids, making tracks across her face. Like tears, he thought. How could he tell anymore? He wanted to take her and hold her and look into her eyes and see there the reflection of his own mistake, his own lack of judgment. Prove me wrong, that's all I ask. Prove me wrong. What was that small part of him that still needed to believe in a morality, a sense of rightness? And he wondered how deeply it had been eroded, how far down into the fiber of himself the damage had gone.

But he knew, he knew he wasn't wrong.

She turned to look at him. "Sometimes you don't see the whole picture, John. Sometimes you come in from such a narrow perspective that it eludes you."

"Tell me about it," he said. "Tell me about the whole picture."

She seemed not to have heard him. "After five years, betrayal becomes a part of yourself. You tell so many lies you start to believe them. You don't know what's true, what's not."

He felt uneasy, a curious emptiness. He couldn't look at her anymore. Betrayal: where does it start?

She said, "I'm sorry about George."

And Richard too, he thought. Richard too.

She might, he thought, have been reading his mind. "I wasn't exactly making your brother a happy man. It wasn't his fault. He had his work. I was expected to be the perfect hostess in a world I didn't give a shit about. Parties, receptions, boring dinners. You have to be a zombie to get through them."

Suddenly he didn't want to hear any more. It didn't matter to him. The history of a dead marriage.

She looked down at the wet concrete. In a broken way, she was reflected in a pool of rainwater. "Five years ago I met George Gull in Washington. What can I say?"

Cry, he thought. Show me your tears. Let me see how you feel.

"Now and then, whenever we were in the same town at the same time, Washington, London, Paris— it was classic back-street stuff, John."

Back-street stuff. He couldn't imagine them together, Isobel and Gull, he couldn't imagine them coupling, the impossible conjunction. All the treachery, he thought. Five years. He slammed his hands together, anger, a damp firework burning out.

"Just like you said, John. We were going to have the roses. The beach. The past at our backs. Just as you phrased it. A different kind of life away from a world we were both sick of."

Was he expected to make a noise of sympathy now? A murmur of consolation?

"You must have known," he said. "You must have known he was playing footsie with the other side."

She didn't answer for a moment. Then she said, "Whatever he did, it was for me. One side, the other side—he didn't care. I didn't care. It must be very hard for you to understand that, John. Both sides are the same. There isn't a difference."

"How much more did you know?" he asked.

"You wouldn't believe me if I told you," she said quietly.

"I want to hear it anyhow." Both sides the same, he thought. No differences. A world of perfectly balanced darknesses. How could he accept that?

She broke down, covering her face with her hands, inclining her head slightly, reaching out to support herself against a low stone wall—and in spite of himself he felt pity. He wanted to touch her, even if such a contact would bring her no comfort. He stuck his hands in his pockets and looked away. The afternoon was darkening now. Maybe it was another piece of playacting, this sorrow; another put-on in what was a long and presumably distinguished career for her. He didn't want to know. He felt immensely sad, not for her, not for himself, but for some amorphous thing that defeated definition. Humanity? The abuses that linked people together as much as love did? The small daily assassinations of the heart, he thought. He watched her raise her face and look at him. Her eyes were red, her beauty suddenly a wrecked thing.

"I didn't know anything," she said. "I don't expect you to believe that."

He shrugged. One way or another, it was of no importance.

"So far as I knew, Richard committed suicide," she said. Her voice had become strange, different, as if it came from a source other than herself. "All I ever knew was what George wanted to tell me. I was to stick with you, I was to help you find a safe place to keep you away from your old friends, I was to try and prevent you going to the stadium. That's all I ever knew. The rest—your old woman, the Mallory thing—I never knew any more than you did."

"You didn't stop to ask? You didn't stop to ask yourself what the fuck was going on?"

She shook her head. "Five years is a long time to wait for something you want, John."

"And now you don't have it," he said.

She tried to smile, an odd distorted expression. "You're a pretty determined character. I couldn't keep you away from that stadium. I tried. I *did* try. I even thought of using the gun on you at one point."

"I die laughing," Rayner said. Love, he thought. That blind unquestioning place beyond conflict: was that love? Was that how Richard had loved this woman? There was a loneliness, a sense of some indefinable loss, working through him now. It was finished: it was all over, a body that would have to be interred in the very near future. He gazed across the rain. Then he was aware of lights in all the windows of the hospital, white lights that were like a series of blank, blinded eyes. He thought of the kid now and began to move away from Isobel, back toward the hospital entrance. She called out to him, a phrase he didn't catch, something he didn't want anyhow. She was something to be walked away from, like an unfinished picture that would never be more than hollow and cold and numb.

Inside the hospital he approached a nurse at the reception desk and asked for the kid's room number. The nurse, with her pallid officious face, told him that the child wasn't to be disturbed. *Sedated, needs rest, no visitors.* Rayner reached across the desk and seized the record sheet from the woman's hand, stared at the room number, threw the sheet down, and walked along a corridor. He could hear the woman harping and whining at his back, but what the hell did that matter? Soon enough she would be on the intercom system, bellowing about an unauthorized visitor. You travel through the shit, he thought; what difference does a little more make?

He found the room and paused a moment outside the door, thinking of Isobel in the rain. Dismiss it, let it slide, let her make what she can of her life. He pushed the door open and stepped inside the room. The kid lay propped up against a pile of pillows, her eyes closed, her face tilted to one side. He drew a chair close to the bed and sat down, holding her hand lightly. It was strange how in sleep the plain face had assumed something akin to beauty; one day, after the chrysalis of adolescence, she might be a real heart-breaker. He laid the palm of his hand against her fore-head and she slowly opened her eyes, blank at first as if she were trying to bring him into focus. For a long time there was silence, something awkward, uncom-fortable; and Rayner wondered what he could say, whether he could apologize, make amends, some form of restitution for what he had put her through. Watch-ing her, he said nothing.

When she spoke, her voice was dry and hoarse. "She's dead."

Rayner moved his head slightly. He thought: Be-tween you and me, kid, we've got a story to tell if any-body wants to listen and believe.

The girl turned her face away, gazing at the rainy window. "I knew she was dead," she said.

"Rest," Rayner said. "Rest. Take it easy."

He took his hand from her brow, remembering how cold she had been when he had last touched her. She twisted around to look at him. Her eyes, glazed from whatever medication had been injected into her blood, still seemed capable of penetration.

"Where's Isobel?" she asked.

Rayner watched her eyelids flicker. She was drift-ing away again, floating out on some soporific cloud. He waited until he was certain that she had fallen asleep and then he rose from his chair, looking down at her, watching her, thankful that he hadn't had to answer her last sleepy question.

The door of the room opened and an angry or-derly came in.

"I was just leaving," Rayner said.

He went out into the corridor and walked toward the exit. Outside, a chill wind had begun to blow the rain in a series of whiplike gusts. Isobel had gone. He stared across the parking lot. There would be explanations to be made, reasons to be given, loose ends to be tied together. A whole tidy package to be delivered.

He was tired. It could wait for another day, a better day.

# ▟ HarperPaperbacks *By Mail*

Craig Thomas, internationally celebrated author, has written these four best selling thrillers you're sure to enjoy. Each has all the intricacy and suspense that are the hallmark of a great thriller. Don't miss any of these exciting novels.

**Buy All 4 and $ave.**
When you buy all four the postage and handling is *FREE*. You'll get these novels delivered right to door with absolutely no charge for postage, shipping and handling.

**EMERALD DECISION**
A sizzling serpentine thriller—Thomas at the top of his form.